# A SPOONFUL OF MAGIC

# A SPOONFUL OF MAGIC

IRENE RADFORD

**DAW BOOKS, INC.**
DONALD A. WOLLHEIM, FOUNDER
375 Hudson Street, New York, NY 10014

**ELIZABETH R. WOLLHEIM**
**SHEILA E. GILBERT**
**PUBLISHERS**
www.dawbooks.com

First Printing, November 2017
1  2  3  4  5  6  7  8  9

DAW TRADEMARK REGISTERED
U.S. PAT. AND TM. OFF. AND FOREIGN COUNTRIES
—MARCA REGISTRADA
HECHO EN U.S.A.

PRINTED IN THE U.S.A.

*For Miriam Elizabeth Bentley Radford, my mom who taught me how to cook without burning down the house. (Close call a couple of times.) And Catherine Cassarno who taught me to dance from the heart.*

# One

**"H**APPY ANNIVERSARY, DAFFY. And thanks for the last thirteen years, the most wonderful years of my life." G raised his champagne flute and waited for me to click mine against his.

And waited.

*Oh, tell another whopper, you lying S.O.B.*

Somehow, I cracked something resembling a smile.

"Gabriel Sebastian Deschants, what is my name?" I knew he hated his full name. He'd been G for so long he probably didn't remember how he signed our marriage license application. I'd never seen his birth certificate.

He grimaced, and I almost rejoiced in causing him a small bit of pain. He deserved it.

Still, we'd been married for an unlucky thirteen years, together nine months before that. That should count for something.

But it didn't. Not to him anyway.

"Daffy, what is this about?" He set his flute down carefully and speared me with his fabulous royal blue eyes. He knew what he was doing. Used car salesmen melted under that gaze. Bank loan managers lowered interest rates by three points under the scrutiny of that gaze.

Not me. Not any longer anyway. I fell victim to him the first day we met. After that, I'm not sure if any decision I made was *mine* or his channeled through my mouth.

"You haven't used my real name in so long, I just need to know that you remembered."

"Daphne Rose Wallace." He ground out each word as if dragging them from the back of his memory, a place he didn't go very often.

"Daphne Rose Wallace Deschants now." I lifted my own gaze to him. "Remember the Deschants part?"

"Of course, I remember. This is our wedding anniversary. What's got into you, Daffy?"

Our waiter came over with the bill for our very expensive dinner enclosed in a discreet black folder. He must have sensed the end of our sojourn. "Was the meal prepared satisfactorily, Madame?" he asked hesitantly, staring at the slices of rare prime rib still on my plate, along with half the garlic mashed potatoes and roasted asparagus. And the still full flute of champagne.

"The food was just right." I smiled genuinely at the troubled waiter.

"Daffy?" G slapped his credit card into the black folder and handed it to the waiter.

"Eugene, Oregon may look like a thriving metropolis built around a major university and agricultural crossroads, but it is still very much a small town in attitude," I said almost reluctantly. As much as I had practiced my speech, I still hesitated to say what I needed to say.

Maybe I should just keep quiet.

But I'd never be able to live with myself, live with him, if I didn't get it out there.

"Everyone knows everyone else and they gossip. A lot."

Was that the beginning of a blanch on his face? I wanted to make him squirm, and he'd given me the ammunition.

"Last week when you were supposed to be in Dubai on *business,* Belle tripped over her own shadow and broke her wrist. She got a black eye to go with the blue-and-green cast. You didn't answer your cell. You weren't registered in the hotel where you said you'd be. *And* the emergency number of your employer is disconnected."

He had the grace to look away.

"However, I received an email from one of *your* email accounts with pictures attached."

His blanch took on a green tinge.

I held up my phone with the most incriminating photo showing. A naked G with an equally unclothed blonde sprawled upon a mattress. The white sheets and pillow-cases looked like they were from an anonymous motel or a dorm room. I couldn't see enough of the woman's face to tell if she was jailbait young or old enough to know better. G didn't have his wedding ring on in the photo.

"Daffy, whatever you have heard . . ."

"What I see." I grabbed the phone and flipped to the next photo and the three after that. The time stamp on the pictures, from a high-quality camera showed 02:07 AM. Dated three nights before.

The next morning I'd received a phone call from Flora Chambers, a neighbor who had moved three blocks away to a newer and better house, and fellow officer of the PTA, wondering why G was in old downtown instead of Florida as I'd told her at the last PTA meeting.

"Where? How?" G's throat worked like his fine dinner was about to come up. "You have to know that photos can be altered. *Not everything is at it seems.* You know this town. . . ."

"What about this one? It's a close-up. No distortions from window screens or sheer drapes or glass or anything. She's draped all over you like a tick on a dog's ear!"

He waved the phone away and tried to fix me with that compelling gaze again.

Had he used it on more young women? I focused on the bridge of his nose rather than let his eyes persuade me away from my course of action.

"You didn't deny it, G. You just tried to dismiss the evidence."

"Isn't that the same thing?"

"No." I pushed back my chair and stood. Suddenly, I was more disappointed than angry. Deep inside, I'd truly hoped he had a logical explanation for his actions. Something weird and unbelievable. In this town, not much was too weird and unbelievable to discount. I'd grasp anything he offered at this point.

"This is not what it seems, Daffy." He gulped. "Parlor trick magic is . . . This town embraces the weird. Mundane cameras can't capture magical illusion."

"Spin me another one. If you didn't want to get caught, why did you email me these pictures?"

"I didn't. Someone had to have hacked my account. Which address?"

"Your work account, chiefofficer_GSD@globalwiz ardsoftware.org."

For half an instant, his eyes went wide with . . . fear? What did he have to be afraid of?

"Look, Daffy, there is a dark and ugly world out there that neither you nor the kids are prepared . . ." He trailed off and looked away rather than finish his explanation, which didn't look very logical or believable from where I stood.

The waiter hastened back with the processed credit slip. I waited for G to sign it with his hand-turned wooden fountain pen that always resided in his breast pocket. I watched him add in the tip and sign with upright letters, very unlike his usual florid flourish. I needed to make sure he didn't stiff the kid and force me to pay for the lavish dinner out of my own savings. He'd done that once before. I'd dismissed it then as his being totally distracted about work. Not tonight. If he was distracted, it was because I confronted him with the truth for a change.

I didn't truly know where his money came from. If he was hanging out in sleazy motels with bimbos rather than traveling the world negotiating trade contracts and software installations, then what did he do?

"Don't do this now, Daffy. We've had thirteen wonderful years together." He took my elbow and escorted me out to the parking lot. I shook him off. "I need you now more than ever."

"You need me to babysit your children. Thirteen years when I've raised your son as my own. I adopted him on our wedding day, so he'd never need to ask about the mother who died giving birth to him. I've given you two wonderful daughters, kept house, cooked, and picked up after you."

"And I love you for that. I do truly love you despite the temptations I face every day. I built you a wrought-iron-and-glass greenhouse that fills a quarter of the backyard where the stables used to be. That should prove something of my devotion to you."

"You love me for the services I give you. That I raised your son for you while you traveled the world. Not because you love me. But I do thank you for the greenhouse." I jerked away from him and headed from the parking lot toward the sidewalk.

"Daffy, where are you going?"

"Home."

"The car is this way."

"I'll walk."

"It's over a mile! And it's dark. Anything could be hiding in the bushes."

"Anything like us?" Three young men—barely out of their teens—appeared before me. The center boy, taller than the others by half a head, had a wealth of straight black hair but pale skin and eyes. Three days' worth of beard dirtied his face. He aimed a gun at my head.

His eyes didn't quite focus and looked a bit glassy.

A hasty glance over my shoulder showed us just beyond range of the parking lot lights and security cameras.

What better place to steal drug money than right outside the most expensive restaurant in town! Well, maybe not *the* most expensive, but right up there with the four-star hotels and such.

I froze with fear.

"That's wise, lady. Now give us your purse and no one gets hurt."

I fumbled for the tiny evening purse hanging from my shoulder on a gold chain. It didn't contain much: some small change, house key, credit card, driver's license.

House key! They'd know where I lived and could get in. My kids were home alone. I couldn't do it.

A breath of air stirred behind me.

G leaped forward, pulling his fancy fountain pen from his breast pocket. As he moved, the pen telescoped out into a long wand and shot red laser light at the muggers. He took a classic fencer's pose, right leg forward with his no-longer-pen aimed straight forward, and his left arm up, behind his head for balance.

He wiggled the wand. The red light did not sear a hole into the skull of the boy with the gun. No. Nothing so conventional. Nothing so normal.

The light spread into a complicated web that encased the boy and his gun into a sparkling cage of immobility.

A flick of G's wrist generated two more cages to keep the other two muggers from fleeing.

I couldn't move. Couldn't think. Couldn't understand.

Inside the cages, the three boys blinked in bewilderment; they breathed shallowly. Nothing else moved. Not even an involuntary quirk of the lips or flick of a trigger finger.

"For the crime of frightening my lady, you will leave here with no memory of what you did and no knowledge of what that weapon is. You will feel compelled to complete one thousand hours of public service ... each. Any money you might have used to buy drugs you will donate to charity," he intoned, as if reciting a ritual.

Ritual. That was the key.

He flicked the pen/wand three times, as if tapping each boy on the head. The electrical cages dissolved. The center boy looked at the gun in his hand in horror and dropped it. It clattered noisily on the sidewalk. Then they ran off, each in a different direction, as if they did not know each other.

G pocketed the gun. It hardly distorted the lines of his custom-tailored suit.

"Th ... that's not an ordinary pen." He'd had it as long as I'd known him. He had it tucked into his breast pocket even when wearing G-casual, a polo shirt and khakis.

"Not exactly. No." He stared at it a long moment. Then it collapsed back into its normal shape. I didn't see what he did to make it happen.

"It's not some fancy electronics gadget either." My mind began working again. A few oddities about my husband began to make sense. Like bringing home tree-fresh peaches in January because I had a craving. Or always having the little bit of snow that fell shoveled off our long gravel driveway before dawn, before he got out of bed, or when he was "away" on business.

Or juggling fifteen breakable items as a party trick. Especially if he left them hanging on their own for long breathless moments. Come to think of it, he'd only performed that trick once, at a party of his friends and business associates. Never with my friends.

Oh, yes; he had magic. A lot of people in this town had parlor trick magic.

This was something else entirely. And that pen was ...

"No, it's not ordinary."

"What is it?" A wand if I had a guess.

"For your own safety, you don't want to know." He lifted that fabulous blue gaze to my face and held me captive. "Daphne Rose, you do not remember. ..."

"The hell I don't!" I broke free of his hypnosis—or enthrallment—or whatever it was. I had to turn my face so that I didn't look directly at him, any part of him.

Especially the bulge that began stirring in his crotch. He was turned on by this ... whatever it was.

"You just used ritual magic to subdue three drug addicts and force them to dedicate their lives to service rather than finding their next fix. Did you cure them of their addiction, too?"

"No, I can't do that. I can only redirect their resources and energy until their bodies become clear of the addiction and their brains reset."

"Nice of you. So where did the ritual magic come from?" My anger was stirring again, as much as his lust. "That's a whole lot more than a parlor trick."

"How do you know about ritual magic?"

"This is Eugene, Oregon, G! Home of the Fairy Festival, the center of all things weird in the Willamette Valley. You can't walk two blocks downtown without running into six shops selling some variety of mystical paraphernalia. I'm half owner in a coffee shop that sells incense and crystals and candles and books about magic on the side." I had to stop to draw breath.

"There's something in the water around here that makes this town a vortex of . . . of magic, great and small. Magical ley lines converge here. There are rumors that this was once the home of many fae races who have interbred with humans."

"So how does this explain the woman you took to a motel?" He'd lied to me on so many levels I'd stopped counting. But this magic thing . . . another lie. And it scared me.

It also spiked my curiosity. I needed to know more. Not tonight.

"Don't be like that, Daffy. I'm trying to protect you. And the children. You need protection now, more than ever."

"Don't change the subject, divert my attention, and then seduce me into forgetting while you delete the pictures on my phone. Let me tell you I downloaded those pictures to my computer and uploaded them to . . . gee, I don't know, ten social media sites just waiting for my password to go live. And don't tell me you know my password. You know the one I use for online banking. You've guessed the one I use for my baking blog. You do not know this one."

I marched toward his car, the big, midnight blue town car he bought to impress clients. Clients of what?

When he tried to follow me, I spun around and slapped him. He reeled back three steps. Just far enough for me to get into the car and lock the doors.

As I started the car, I rolled down the window two inches. "You can walk home. I'll leave a packed suitcase and your car keys on the porch. And I'm changing the locks in the morning." Actually, I'd had the locksmith out *this* morning.

So why was I crying all the way home?

Because now I had to tell the children.

# Two

WHEN I CAME IN through the kitchen door beside the driveway, I found three young faces staring at me in bewilderment, eyes wide, and chins trembling.

Without a word, I knew that they knew. I gathered them all into a big hug that lasted far beyond their normal comfort zone.

Finally, I sniffed back my tears and asked, "How did you know?"

"Shara found the pictures," Jason said. He swallowed deeply and straightened his shoulders like the strong young man he was becoming. At nearly fifteen, he was responsible for his two sisters when I was out. And often when his father was in.

I let go of my children and marched toward my office space in the sunroom—previously a screened back porch. My desktop computer sat on an old school desk with the monitor still on and one of the photos of G and the blonde bimbo.

"Shara?" I didn't have enough energy left for anger, but still, I tried to let her know I was not pleased that she'd been mucking about on *my* computer.

"Mom, you know she can't resist a locked door or a puzzle. Computer passwords are games to her," Jason said. Always defending her.

"Yes, I know. But that is no excuse for invading my privacy. Locked doors are one thing. Passwords on private files aren't." But it saved me a lot of explanations and dancing around the issue of their father's infidelity.

"Shara?"

"I know, Mom. I know I shouldn't, but I was doing a search on active volcanoes for an extra credit report I have to make up for my hacking the school computers, and that storage thingy kept blinking at me demanding action. . . ."

*Shit!* I hadn't totally backed out of the program.

Okay, half my fault. But the girl really needed to learn some manners.

"Does this mean that Daddy isn't coming home?" Annabelle asked, bringing me back to where we needed to be.

"Yes." My tongue tied in knots at anything more.

"Ever?" Shara demanded, big tears spilled over her lashes. Her father's big blue eyes that could charm the socks off anyone, or the pins out of any lock.

"Not forever. He'll come visit. He just won't be living here anymore."

"Can I call him for rides and such? We've got auditions coming up for the autumn and holiday programs," Jason asked.

"One way or another, you will all get rides to all of your events. You can call your dad in an emergency. But you know how often he's out of town, out of the *country*, for work." Not that I really knew what he did work at anymore.

"Most likely he's at that motel rather than out of town," Belle said in disgust. Named for G's grandmother, she seemed to know his mind better than I. But that was where the resemblance ended. Heavy glasses and heavier braces had become almost a mask of disinterest when the "cool" kids ignored or bullied her for being a klutz and a geek. She pushed her glasses farther up her nose.

We all turned our backs on the computer screen.

"Chores done?" I asked, trying for blithe and not quite making it.

"Yeah," came the chorus from all three.

I checked the kitchen clock. Not even eight-thirty on a Wednesday evening. The sun sets late around here in June. They should be headed for quiet time before bed, but I wanted them close and thinking about something other than the removal of their father from their lives. "How about a movie, something where there's lots of explosions and guns." I wanted to blow up more than a few things, starting with G.

"You know, Mom," Jason whispered as his sisters ran for the living room. "Dad is really ripped. No wonder that girl fell for him." He looked down at his own skinny abdomen. "I need to start lifting weights."

"Oh, Sweet Pea, you need a big 'ol dose of comfort food!" Gayla Burnett exclaimed, much too loudly, as she wrapped her long arms around me. I found my face buried in her bony shoulder. Try as she might, she couldn't quite shake off all of her Texas drawl despite living in the accent-neutral Pacific Northwest for close to thirty years.

Multiracial with near equal mixes of Anglo, African, Cherokee, and Asian, she'd been my best friend and substitute mother for longer than G and I had been married.

My parents disowned me when I married "That Man," and he took me out of their control.

Well, their judgment of his untrustworthiness was right. But I wouldn't give them the satisfaction of "I told you so."

So I turned to Gayla with my tears.

Tears threatened to flood again as my partner at Magical Brews rubbed and patted my back as a mother would comfort a teething toddler. The other remedy for a teething toddler—scotch rubbed on the gums—wouldn't hurt either. But I wanted more of the cure than just a few drops on the gums. I wanted half the bottle. Make it an Islay single malt while you're at it.

"What did he say?" Gayla asked, pouring us each a tall mug of black coffee from the pot we kept in the kitchen. Then she paused and handed me a mini cinnamon bun on a napkin. She nibbled at hers delicately, savoring every bite. "Magic. I don't know what you do or how you do it, but your baking is pure magic."

There was that word again. I didn't dare utter it lest I spill G's secret. He was a lot more powerful than a party entertainer.

I ate my treat in one gulp, the first solid food I'd had since the disastrous dinner last night.

"He said not enough and too much." I ground the words out through gritted teeth. He'd left me with more questions than answers and new secrets I couldn't unload on my best friend.

I took out some of my anger at G's lies and secrets on the yeasty dough for the next batch of cinnamon buns. I punched it down and slapped it against the marble countertop. I liked my work space for pastry cold. Marble stays cold for nearly forever. Like G's sense of morality.

Not satisfied, or mollified, I pounded the dough with my favorite wooden spoon. That felt better. Without thinking, I tucked my cooking tool into my jeans back pocket, as I often did, and started rolling out the dough into a large square with a marble rolling pin.

Gayla surveyed the rack of finished pastries, cookies, and breads ready for customers when we opened at six. In fifteen minutes.

"You been here all night?" Gayla asked, donning her pale blue apron painted with stars and quarter moons.

"Only since four." Normally, I started at five, left at seven to get the kids off to school, then back again at nine or ten to start the second round of baking. When I left for the day at two, I'd have cleaned the kitchen from top to bottom and set dough to rising for the next day.

Weekends we were closed, so I came in Sunday night to start more dough for Monday morning.

"So what are you going to do, Sweet Pea?"

I shrugged. "I kicked him out, but we didn't talk much. I tried, but he pulled his usual G dance of waltzing away from any answers."

"If you need an advance on last month's profits to make ends meet, we are in the black again. And if you feel guilty about the advance, we could use more help in the afternoon."

"Put it in the reserve fund. If I need it, I'll take it, but I don't need it yet." Then I choked back a laugh. "You forget I have three kids who aren't old enough to drive yet. I live in the minivan from the time school lets out until dinnertime. Sometimes until bedtime. Jason has ballet classes and rehearsal from three to six. Belle has chess club and Math Olympics from three thirty to five. And Shara is only nine, and I don't dare leave her alone for five minutes let alone three hours."

"What's the little imp up to now?" Gayla emptied her coffee with two long swallows, put the mug on its special shelf so I wouldn't wash it, and angled toward the front of the shop to open the coffee/bakery/mystical-doodads-so-popular-these-days shop. I'd already set up the cash register and ground enough roasted beans to last the day.

I didn't want to talk about Shara's little adventure with my computer. "She broke into the principal's locked office just to prove she needed only one of my hairpins to do it." I started to run my hands through my long, ash-blonde hair, currently captured into a ponytail and confined by a hairnet. Then I stopped before I could dirty my hands with hair and my hair with flour.

"Then she hacked his computer and changed some of her teacher's comments from 'lacks focus and has the attention span of a gnat' to 'excels in all subjects and behaves well.'"

We both shook our heads in dismay.

"Um, Sweet Pea, G is waiting at the front door, and

from the way his nose is pressed against the glass, I don't think he's in a patient mood." G never used the alley door because he might run into our latest homeless guests or have to smell the dumpster.

I took three deep breaths for fortification. Still five minutes to official opening. "Let him in. I'll talk to him back here while I finish off these buns."

If my hands were busy shaping and rolling dough around an aromatic filling, maybe I wouldn't slug him.

Maybe.

# Three

"**D**AFFY, WE HAVE TO TALK," he said without preamble.

One glance at his long legs encased in casual slacks and his muscular chest (yeah, he was really ripped) straining at the seams of a knit golf shirt—pen/wand in the breast pocket—and I almost gave in to the tears and flung myself into his arms. Almost.

I bit the inside of my cheek to remind myself of all the lies he'd told me over the years. All the manipulation. The more I thought about it, the more I wondered if he'd ever truly loved me or manipulated me into thinking we were in love so that I'd raise his son while he traveled so extensively for his "work."

"Talk. I'm busy."

"Daffy, I . . . I've taken a suite at the residence hotel by the airport until I can find more permanent lodging. Here's the number in case . . . there's an emergency." He slapped a business card on the counter beside me. "The kids have my cell number, my real number that will find me anywhere. You do, too, if you haven't already deleted it from your contacts list."

I had.

"Thank you." If I didn't care what happened to him, why was I so relieved that he was safe?

"How do you want to do this, Daffy?" His voice turned soft, almost plaintive. "I need to know that you and the kids are comfortable and *safe*. I can't protect you if I'm out of the house. But I need to separate my life from you to keep certain ... people from targeting you to get to me."

I resisted looking into his eyes. But my shoulders relaxed.

"I don't know. I've never filed for divorce before." I'd never been intimately involved with anyone else either. G was my first and—I'd thought—my only, but now I didn't know.

"Divorce. Not just separation?"

"Not unless you stop lying to me and manipulating me. And tell me why and who you went to bed with."

"Daffy, I can't."

"I'll make an appointment with Bret Chambers this afternoon." Flora's husband was a divorce lawyer and a fundamentalist Christian who had no patience with adulterous spouses. He'd get along great with my parents. He might already know them through his church connections.

G winced and pinched his nose as if fighting a headache, just like Jason did during allergy season. "If I give you the kids, child support, alimony, and the house, will you find a different lawyer?"

I was pretty sure I'd get that much at least with Bret at my side. "What's the 'but' after getting all I want?"

"Open visitation rights with the kids, or joint custody."

"Yes. You've never hurt them, and you are their father—of that we can both be certain." Who knew how many other children of his were out there.

"I know, Daffy. I know you've been faithful." A gentleness I hadn't heard in years smoothed his voice. He reached to run his finger down my cheek, then jerked it back as I leaned away from him.

"Did those girls—I presume there was more than just the one I saw—did they *know* what they were doing? Did they go with you of their own accord, or did you use your mind whammy thingy on them?" *Just like you used it on me.*

That was the most important issue for me.

He puffed out his chest in indignation—or was that peacock in full mating display?

"I don't enthrall. There's no satisfaction if my partner doesn't remember." Now he sounded as bitter as I felt. "And those pictures were not what they seem." He didn't elaborate about what they actually were.

"Oh? Care to tell me what they really were?" I asked smugly. I didn't trust him to know the truth if it bit him in his fine ass.

I felt him approach, the heat radiating from his body along my back. A month ago, I would have melted into his touch. I still wanted to.

"Give me your phone and I'll transfer my new contact data," he ground out.

I twisted so he could retrieve it from my apron pocket—a duplicate of Gayla's protection garment, but not so clean—I didn't want to get my hands dirty in the middle of brushing the mixture of cinnamon sugar and melted butter over the dough. My movements brushed my hip against his. A sharp stab of desire swept over me.

I swear I didn't do it on purpose. It's just . . . just that old habits die hard.

He did the automatic transfer thing that I could never figure out, then tucked the phone back where it belonged. His fingers slid up and down my hip and belly.

Old habits die hard.

But I knew what was happening this time and jerked away in a move a belly dancer would admire.

G sighed, as if he dragged the air from his heels all the way to his mouth. "Jason is almost fifteen. He's started shaving and his voice is deepening. If he's inherited any of . . . my talents . . . he'll need my guidance. Any day now. I need to spend time with him. Teach him control. I will not turn an untrained magician loose on the world ever again."

*What?*

"Are those talents age dependent?" A safer topic. I

sensed he would avoid the issue of an untrained magician wandering around.

"Mostly. A few demonstrate signs earlier, Shara's only ten and hasn't shown any signs of anything unusual, so she's safe for now."

He obviously didn't know that our youngest daughter had yet to meet a lock, password, maze, or puzzle she couldn't defeat, mechanical or electronic. Now if she just attacked her schoolwork with the same enthusiasm, she wouldn't be facing summer school. Unless she finished her extra credit report before Friday noon.

"In the general population, only one in ten thousand has a true magical talent—even if only parlor tricks. Most magicians manifest at puberty, and a very, very few blossom in adulthood, usually a very minor talent that doesn't qualify for Guild voting rights." He looked at my wooden spoon stuck in my back pocket, narrowing his eyes. "I expect Jason to start doing weird things any minute now. Annabelle, too, since girls mature earlier than boys. They need me, Daffy. Don't keep me away from them. I need to know if they adopt an implement, something, anything, that might become a wand."

He eyed my wooden spoon. "Your grandmother had the second sight—according to your mother—which is not unusual in the Scots. I'm equally afraid and surprised you haven't shown any signs of even parlor trick magic. You've almost got the wand."

I shrugged that off. I'd heard too many fanatical rants against my beloved Granny from my pastor father. I didn't want any magical talent even if I had any.

Oh, God. Belle had used most of her allowance to purchase a pair of Chinese ivory hair sticks embellished with dangling agates of cream and soft green shaped like a chess queen and bishop. At almost twelve, she'd suddenly developed an interest in fashion and boys that had nothing to do with her next chess tournament. She stuck the sticks into her long dark curls even when she wore them down. All three children had G's dark hair. Only Belle inherited my waves.

"Jason? Other than his ballet slippers, I haven't noticed anything."

"I don't see how ballet slippers can become a wand. Keep your eyes open; he'll find something. He might show some signs of . . . emotional instability coping with his new powers."

"Fifteen-year-old boys are emotionally unstable by definition."

"This will be more than typical. You might think him on the verge of . . . insanity at times."

"Okay. You can see them whenever you like. But you have to let me know if you plan to take them anywhere, especially out of town."

"Agreed. The house is paid for. It's been in my family since it was built over a century ago. You can live there rent free with my children. But if you *ever* remarry, or bring another man home, I expect you to vacate immediately and I will take the children." The last came out on a sneer, as if he still owned me and resented even the thought that our separation left me as free to pursue a new romance as he was to seduce coeds.

"Don't worry. I'm rather soured on romance right now. But there is something I need to know."

"Daffy, please don't."

"I need to know what you are, what you do, where your money comes from. Obviously, you aren't a big-gun negotiator and troubleshooter for a software company. Globalwizardsoftware.com doesn't exist. Where do you go when you are supposed to be in Shanghai or Budapest or Dubai?"

"*Usually* I'm in Shanghai or Budapest or Dubai. My job title is Sheriff to the old-fashioned men who employ me. I work for, and am handsomely paid by, the Guild of Master Wizards, an international collective and judiciary elected by all legally practicing magicians."

"Sheriff?"

"Head of security and law enforcement."

"What are you the sheriff of?"

"My job is to make certain that magic practitioners keep their spells benevolent, useful, and invisible. Emphasis on invisible. Mundanes outnumber us ten thousand to one. Only one in one thousand magicians have the kind of talent to disable a gun, and only one gun at a time. Full wizards with a broad spectrum of talents, like me, are even rarer.

"You can't tell anyone about what you know. If someone like Bret—or your parents—got wind of this, there'd be another witch hunt. Look at how polarized society has become in the last few years, where hate of anything different is the norm and violence the only solution. Racism is now acceptable. Magicians can be classed as a different race. I'm serious. Unless you want to see a bunch of innocent people die horribly at the hands of very fearful fanatics, you won't speak of this to anyone. I need to protect you and our children."

I nodded, gulping back the agony of thinking my children might be caught up in horrors akin to Salem, Massachusetts, in the seventeenth century. I had a History degree and teaching credentials, but I made more money brewing coffee, baking, and catering than I would teaching school. "You must use that mind-erasing trick a lot." I could live with that, as long as he didn't use it on his girlfriends.

"Yes." He looked away, gaze resting on a rack of cooling cookies. "I need one more favor, Daffy."

He'd softened me up with acceptance of anything I might rightfully demand.

"What?"

"I have a safe embedded in the cement foundation of your greenhouse. I built the greenhouse for you and your herb garden. I took advantage of the foundation to encase the safe. No one else even knows it is there. It's protected by multiple locks and magical wards. I've also placed wards all around the property, so you and our children are as safe as I can make it."

"But?" Damn it! He'd built my favorite place in the world: glass windows and gazebo roof supported by a white wrought iron frame enclosing rows and rows of herbs and produce. He'd built it for his safe, *not for me*. More lies and deceit.

"I need to keep some evidence in that safe. At least until I build another, but it takes years to get the wards in place and up to full strength. Please, this is important."

"What kind of evidence?" This was the first time he'd ever been open with me about his *other* life.

"If you don't know, you can't tell. I need to know you and the children are safe."

That was the fourth or fifth time he'd emphasized our safety.

He'd said the word too often this morning and last night for me to dismiss the idea of potential danger spilling out from his job.

"Then why tell me your evidence locker is there?"

"So that you don't accidentally find it when you get mad at me and tear the greenhouse apart." He flashed me his quirky grin. "I half expected to find it in slivers this morning, just because I built it."

Yeah, he sometimes knew I was about to do something before I even thought about it.

He grabbed three oatmeal, raisin, cranberry cookies with ground walnuts and took a large bite of one. "Hmmm, magic. You are the best baker west of the Rockies." He ate the other two before I could slap them out of his hand.

But he'd said the M word. I knew he didn't use it lightly. And that tied my stomach in knots.

"About the safe?"

"You can tie my golf clubs in knots if you want, but you enjoy the greenhouse too much to destroy it just because I . . . I can't tell you."

"You can't tell me about your bimbos." I almost laughed. He made it sound so normal. "Damn, you couldn't even drive the extra mile to East Springfield where no one cares and everyone half expects men to stray. You were *seen* in old downtown." No motels there. Or college dorms. Just tiny apartments above small businesses. Students rented them because they were cheap and within walking distance of the university. I'd lusted after one myself my senior year at the U.

"Try to believe that if I stray, it is nothing more than a triumphant celebration when I put away some bad guys." He shrugged as if none of it mattered.

"You could come home for sex after taking down a bad guy."

He shrugged again and looked elsewhere. "Mostly, I do."

*Mostly!* Not always.

I grabbed my spoon and tried to hit him upside the head with it. He stayed my wrist easily with a firm grip. "Want to finish this back at my suite? I've got handcuffs in the car."

I slugged his jaw with enough force to propel him out the back door.

Now my hand ached and I still had pastry to roll.

●━━━

G waved to the homeless man leaning against the dumpster. "How's it going, Raphe?"

"Same old, same old." He shuffled down the alley, carrying his blanket over his arm. His floppy straw hat could shield a football field with its brim.

"Kind of late for you, Raphe? The sun has been up for over an hour. Closer to two."

"Saw some dogs wandering. Didn't want to move until they took their overly curious noses elsewhere." Raphe draped his blanket over his head, covering any skin that might be exposed as he approached a shaft of sunlight at the end of the shadowy alley.

"Good. I need you to keep Daffy safe." G grinned to

himself and followed the shambling man with a hint of a limp. As he walked, he extended his senses, seeking stray movement within the shadows.

Then Raphe pulled a pair of wraparound prescription dark glasses out of one of his numerous pockets and covered his vulnerable, almost colorless, pale blue eyes.

At the alley entrance, Raphe stopped and turned to face G. "I was surfing the net yesterday and found some interesting vintage Zippos for sale on eBay."

G froze in place. His blood heated just as it did before a chase—or a fight. "Are they selling well?"

"Not as well as expected. No one is bidding on the one with the death's head or the skull and crossbones."

G bent double in relief. He forced himself to breathe deeply, in and out, in and out. By the time he'd straightened, Raphe had disappeared into another alley a block east. Too much evidence contradicting what he knew had to be true.

The alley behind Magical Brews was free of the dangers he expected to pounce any minute. He always expected danger within the shadows. That was why he'd survived as Sheriff for the Guild for twelve years. A deputy for five before that.

He needed his field khakis for his next trip. Daffy hadn't packed the clothes he kept in the office closet. Tonight, he needed to be in El Salvador to take down a village shaman who had begun demanding virginal girls as blood sacrifice in order to protect his village. If G hurried, he could retrieve his work clothes and hug each of his children before Daffy returned to get them going for the day.

A pang of remorse felt like a suffocating drill press around his heart.

He could delegate the arrest to a deputy. But he needed to be out of town as much as possible for now, to draw attention and assassins away from Daffy and the kids.

"This is for the best," he told himself. "They'll be safer

from *her* if I'm not around. She wants revenge on me. If I stay away, maybe the bitch will ignore my family."

●━━━━━

"Cue music," Maestro Bellini commanded, his slight Italian accent filling the auditorium. "And a one, two, three, four." His hand came down in a sharp gesture.

Jason raised his arms and slid up onto the balls of his feet. The commanding beat of *Night on Bare Mountain* by Mussorgsky vibrated through the floorboards of the stage. His feet knew the steps. He didn't have to think about them, just feel the music and let it command every movement.

"This is just audition," he murmured to himself. "Do it right. Save spectacular for performances."

"One and two, three and four!" Bellini shouted.

Jason felt the three other boys on stage with him falter as they forced themselves to catch up to the music. He kept right on going, using the rhythm to anchor him, feeling the composer's fear and anger as he explored demons and dark beings rising from the crevices in the land.

And then ... then the dance, the music, and his body melded into one being as they never had before. He was the demon, he was the dance. He was more.

Step, step, pirouette tall and straight with one arm up, the other on his hip. Tombé into a sweeping preparation and soar into the wings. Back out again on another *grand jeté*, finishing with a blinding series of six chainé turns, pause for double *c*hangement quatre entourant, twice, then another series of chainé.

His blood pounded in his ears and sang through his veins. He'd done it. He'd danced the routine he'd been shown once and did it in tempo. And he wanted to do it again and again.

"Nice, Jason. Stick around for the 'Ritual Fire Dance,'" Bellini called. Then he dismissed the other boys.

"Nice?" Jason asked the milling crowd of dancers

backstage, who were waiting their turn to audition for the autumn program of Halloween-themed dances.

"Silly, boy," Tiffany Tyler laughed. The tall blonde, as tall as he with legs that went on forever, was the most beautiful woman in the world, and prima of the small regional pro/am company. She could have any part she wanted. "Don't you know yet that, from Bellini, 'nice' is the best compliment ever?"

"Yeah, I guess so." This was his first year in the company, his first audition. He had only rumors of the maestro's sour temper to go on. "Yeah, that was nice."

# Four

**"M**OM? Did you know there's a safe hidden in the foundation of the greenhouse?" Shara announced from the kitchen door. Not a question. A statement. I'd named her for my Scottish grandmother—the one with the second sight that my father hated almost as much as he did me.

Inwardly, I groaned as I sorted laundry, my usual Saturday afternoon activity.

My mind veered away from the forbidden topic toward something safe. Jason must be growing again, all his socks had holes in the toes.

"If it's hidden, how did you find it?" I asked, trying desperately to keep panic out of my voice. Shara's curiosity was becoming a problem.

Was already a problem.

"I dunno." She shrugged, just like her father when he lied.

"Not good enough." I beckoned Shara inward to the formal dining room of the century-old, gargantuan, Edwardian-homage-to-Victorian-Gothic house, complete with two towers and a widow's walk. I loved the old place and hated the thought of ever having to move. I wondered if G knew what a favor he'd done for me in letting me stay here with the kids.

We never ate at the long mahogany table where I continued to sort laundry. It had been in G's family since the house was built. Maybe they built the house around the table. We hadn't used the formal dining room for eating except for major holiday meals since long before Shara started school. Homework, yes. Meals, no.

G had been gone the entire summer. An entire season to find my bearings and realize that I did miss him, but not horribly so. Sleeping alone, however. . . .

He'd been gone so much the previous two years that being alone with the kids had become normal.

The impending official divorce date loomed. I felt like we were all living in limbo until then.

My phone screeched an alarm. I grabbed it with one hand while holding up a hand to silence Shara.

One flick of my finger across the screen connected me with the alarm company for Magical Brews.

"Smoke alarm," the tech answered my query. "No emergency vehicles dispatched. Ms. Gayla Burnett canceled the call. She said she has it under control with a portable fire extinguisher."

I thanked him and flicked the screen twice to disconnect with him and reconnect with Gayla.

"Nothing serious, Sweet Pea. Just a bit of a grease fire. More smoke than fire, actually. I handled it. Though we'll have to have the fire extinguisher recharged on Monday."

"Grease fire?" I screeched almost as shrill as the alarm. "Where?"

"Middle of the stove top."

"I cleaned the stove top yesterday. I always thoroughly clean the entire kitchen. There was no grease there. No olive oil, nothing!" I could not work in a messy or dirty kitchen. "And what ignited it? No one is supposed to be in the kitchen on Saturday except you and me."

"Um . . . I'm not sure. But there is a greasy residue on the stove top that was smoking badly with a few bits of flame. It went right out." Gayla sounded as surprised as I was.

"I'll be down there . . ." I paused while I estimated how long before I could leave my chores at home. Such is the life of a small business owner, on call 24/7. "Probably after dinner, but I will clean the entire place again."

"You sure, Sweet Pea? I can handle a little puddle of grease with baking soda and then cleanser."

"If you say so. But I'll make sure it is spotless tomorrow night after I start yeast dough rising." I recited normal signing-off platitudes and returned my attention to Shara.

"Mom, what's in the safe?"

Maybe Shara hadn't breeched G's wards and locks yet. "Now, why did you feel compelled to move heavy planters and search behind stacks of tools and bags of potting soil for something that isn't there?" I wrapped my arm around her thin shoulders and pulled her against my hip.

"But it is there."

Just like G, she'd learned early to divert and distract.

"Answer the question. Why did you go looking?"

"I dunno."

My heart stuttered and then pounded hard enough I could hear it, feel it beating against my rib cage like it was trying to break free.

"Something sent you there and made you disturb my planters. I hope you put them back where they belong. I arranged them carefully for the best light."

I'd rearranged them after *I* found the safe, making sure someone would have to work hard to find it, if they knew it was there.

"I can't explain it. I just *needed* to look there. Like someone was whispering in my ear, demanding that I find whatever is there."

Part of me froze. If G kept magical evidence in that safe, did that magic call to Shara's about-to-bloom talent?

"Are you sure you didn't watch your father rummaging around out there?" I couldn't be sure, but I thought I saw him slip into the backyard three nights ago around four thirty, about the time I got up to go to work.

"I'm sure, Mom. But Daddy called me yesterday and

said he'd pick me up from computer camp and take me out for ice cream. I'd rather go to the antique mall. If he won't take me there, will you? Next week before school starts."

Nice of him to call *me*. I'd thought we'd agreed on that. A good excuse to call him and slip in the information that Shara was "manifesting" well before puberty.

"We'll see if there's anything left in the budget after we buy school clothes."

"We didn't have a budget before Daddy moved out." She pouted.

"You're the one who found the incriminating pictures on my computer," I reminded her.

Actually, I could have kept the photos in my email a secret if Flora Chambers hadn't called and asked why G was skulking around town when he was supposed to be in Dubai. He'd promised to bring me some silk for a new dress. I'd worn the little black thing with a fitted bodice and flared skirt too often. Waltzed with G too often while wearing it. I didn't want to wear it again, but the silk had never appeared.

Gossip in this town spread far and fast. Flora Chambers seemed to be the central clearing house.

"Hey, Mom!" Jason screeched from the back door. He ran through the mudroom and kitchen toward me, letting the screen door slam behind him. I cringed as the bang sliced through my ears to my brain. He must be excited if he forgot my one irrevocable rule of no slammed doors or yelling inside the house.

"Mom! I got the part." He skidded to a halt beside the big mahogany table.

"Which part, Jason?" I offered my cheek for him to kiss. I didn't have to bend at all. At fourteen and five eight he stood an inch taller than me. Next week I expected him to be as tall as his six-two father. "There are cookies cooling in the kitchen. Oatmeal with nuts and dried fruit." With mashed banana as part of the moisture. An easy way to sneak *some* nutrition into treats.

"I'm one of the four ghouls in *Nightmare before Christmas*, that's the show opener. And then I'm a skeleton in *Danse Macabre*, and a demon in *Night on Bare Mountain*, but not a broom imp in *Sorcerer's Apprentice*. Best of all, I'm the understudy to the lead's sidekick in *Tubular Bells*. Matt got the second soloist role, just like everyone expected. He'll be premiere next year when Aaron graduates. We've got a solo and everything. And I may be a spark in the 'Ritual Fire Dance' if Billy flakes out. He's talking about taking up soccer rather than sissy ballet. I just think he's lazy and soccer is less work." He grabbed three cookies and began stuffing them into his mouth.

I knew how many calories he burned dancing. And he was growing again. I didn't have to worry about spoiling his appetite. Belle, on the other hand, was a very picky eater, afraid to get food caught in her braces. She brushed her teeth five times a day. More fastidious than G.

"Um, Jason, is it okay if I come in?" asked an elfin-faced blonde. She stuck just her head around the swinging door to the kitchen.

"Sure, Tiffany. Mom, you remember Tiffany. She's prima in the company and gave me a ride home from the auditions."

"Welcome, Tiffany. Of course, I remember you. I thought your performance in Vivaldi's *Spring* last June was inspired."

She sidled inward, as tall as me, but weighing about half as much, I don't think she could move without fluid grace. A sophomore in the university's performing arts program, rumor had it that she'd forsake our tiny regional semi-pro company for New York before the year was out.

"Thank you for bringing Jason home," I added. "Is there something I can do for you?" Normally, when Jason begged rides, they dumped him at the door and sped off.

"Um . . . Jason said you might have an ointment or something for sore feet. I can pay you."

Immediately, I looked at her raw and swollen toes. She wore flip-flops instead of regular shoes to keep from irritating them more.

"Come with me," I said, placing a gentle and reassuring hand on her back. "Sit." I pointed to the bench seat beneath a bay window in the breakfast nook. I handed her two cookies to keep her there.

"My dad's waiting in the car...."

"Jason, go talk to him. He can come in and watch or come back in an hour. We've got plenty of cookies, and there's milk in the fridge." While I spoke, I dug out a dish basin and started filling it with hot water. While that was happening, I poked around in the back of the pantry, on a shelf that used to be too tall for the kids.

"Mom, this is Mr. Tyler, Tiffany's dad," Jason called.

"Take a seat, Mr. Tyler, I'm Daffy. I'm just giving your daughter a good long soak with Epsom salts with some mint, aloe, arnica, and ginseng mixed in," I said, carrying a sealed plastic container to the sink and the rapidly filling basin. "Oh, and I'll add some alum, that helps toughen the skin against further abrasions." There were a few other secret ingredients in the dry mix to promote healing, but I don't always remember which ones I add, —just what feels right at the moment.

"Are you truly daffy, or is that just a nickname?" asked a forty-something man in a light baritone voice. He stood about six feet tall, maybe a little less, with the same silvery blond hair as his daughter. A rugged face, not handsome like G's, but pleasant enough; a cute little mustache filled the area between nose and upper lip. Briefly, I wondered if it would be soft or bristly.

We'd seen each other off and on over the years, at dance recitals and waiting for children at rehearsals. But I'd never communicated with him more than a neighborly wave. Now I looked at him more closely, and my heart started beating double time.

He didn't wear a wedding ring. But that didn't mean much these days. G only wore his when he was at home.

My hand felt naked and too light now that I'd removed my wedding band and the one-carat diamond engagement ring.

"It's short for Daphne, but I've been Daffy most of my life." I had to smile at his easy banter.

He hitched his jeans and plunked down on the bench on the opposite side of the built-in table from Tiffany. G never succumbed to the casualness of butt hugging jeans.

"I'll gladly pay you whatever you ask if you can keep my daughter dancing," he said. The endearing smile vanished, replaced by a concerned frown. "When her mother died ten years ago, dancing was the only solace she found. It helped us both get through the worst of the grief, but then we discovered what a special gift for dance she has. She needs to keep dancing. I'm Ted, by the way."

So he was single. I put a plate of cookies on the table between them. "Help yourselves; there are plenty more."

Then I gave the herbal mixture a quick stir with the wooden spoon that just seemed to live in my jeans back pocket these days. Something not quite right about the mixture. I stirred it twice more, then added a hint more alum. When it felt ready, I placed the basin on the floor by Tiffany's feet. "It might feel a little hot at first, but it needs to be for all the salts to dissolve and mix together properly."

She touched a toe to the water and jerked it back, then let it sink slowly to the bottom of the basin. Almost immediately, she sighed in relief.

"Ballet is not kind to a dancer's feet," I said. "Even Jason gets blisters and aches, and he doesn't wear toe shoes." I placed a hand on Tiffany's right foot when she tried to jerk it out of the hot water after only a few seconds. Those salts could be a bit abrasive on open sores. "Let it work. It's uncomfortable now, but it will feel so much better in just a few minutes. Now relax and enjoy not having to be on your feet for a little while."

She did so.

"I haven't seen her so relaxed in dog's years. A driven

personality, she's not happy unless she's moving and accomplishing something," Ted said.

"I bet she finishes her homework on time and completely the first time just so she can spend more time dancing," I replied, looking pointedly at Jason.

"Something like that," Ted said.

"Speaking of which— Jason, have you finished mowing the lawn?"

"It's Belle's turn," he argued.

"Belle is at a chess tournament with her father right now." G taking Belle meant one less hour in the minivan for me, which meant I had time to do the laundry so I could send the kids to school on Monday with clean clothes.

"The lawn can wait for her to do it when she gets home. But one or the other of you will do it by tomorrow afternoon," I said. "It's going to rain."

"The weather critters on TV say no chance of rain." Jason rolled his eyes. He loved keeping up with the weather forecasts, hoping to catch me in a wrong prediction. I watched the same forecasts and made my own guess based on the radar and jet stream. I was rarely wrong.

Jason pulled a chair from the dining room to sit and stretch his long legs out in front of him. Yep, those socks beneath leather sandals had holes in the toes, too. Time to hit the bargain store again.

"Trust me, it is going to rain tomorrow afternoon." I didn't add that the first drops would fall at three-o-five. TMI.

Magic? Not really, more like smelling the differences in the air and humidity and long experience watching the volatile weather of the Willamette Valley between the Coast Range and the Cascade Mountains.

Shara seemed to have disappeared. I hoped she hadn't sneaked out to the greenhouse again. Maybe I would have to tear it down and get rid of that evidence locker, despite my promise to G. He'd drag his feet for years if I let him.

"I don't know what Jason did over the summer, but his leaps are amazing now. He has much more power than he used to," Tiffany said. She looked at my son with admiration, but not adoration.

I wondered if he knew the difference.

"If I'm so good, how come I didn't get the second soloist part instead of understudy?" he grumbled. Yeah, he knew that Tiffany used compliments to gain an introduction to me. I kept his feet fit, and he sometimes bragged about it. Foot care was that important to a dancer.

"Maybe because Matt has more experience and more polish to his technique," I suggested.

Back to Tiffany's feet. "Soak for thirty minutes every day, before bed. Do that for two weeks. Expose your feet to the air as much as possible. Sandals that strap on, not flip-flops. Keeping those dang things on will screw with your back. And blowing out of them will cause even more damage to those raw and blistered toes."

"See, I told you so," Ted said. He smiled hugely at his daughter.

I bet he didn't win many arguments with her.

"Okay, Daddy." The love between them flowed in both directions. They had the kind of bond single parents develop with their children. I could tell they spent a lot of time together and he supported her dancing completely.

"Can you stay out of toe shoes for three or four days to let some of the worst lesions heal?" I asked, knowing she'd agree to maybe a day and a half, until Monday. "Do you see where your little toe curls under the next toe?"

She peered at her feet through the water.

"It may be broken. I'm not a doctor, or even a naturopath, just a . . ." I wanted to say "kitchen witch" as part of current slang. But I wasn't one. Not really. And now I knew that real ones existed. "I'm just a baker with an herbal hobby. You need to have that x-rayed and taped by a professional."

"Possibly . . ." she hedged.

I looked to Ted.

"We'll stop at the urgent care clinic on the way home."

"Daddy!" Tiffany sounded more than a little put out. "What if they make me stop dancing for weeks? What if I lose the part in *Tubular Bells*? That's the showpiece in the collage of Halloween numbers. What if it screws up all the auditions I did this summer?"

"I'm outta this argument," Jason said. He scooted his chair away from the center of the action and aimed for the back door. "Lawn. Maybe last time I have to mow it until spring."

"Jason, check on Shara. She may be in the greenhouse." Then I turned back to Tiffany. "I can't keep you from dancing. I can't keep my son from dancing. But at least wrap your toes in some lamb's wool inside your toe shoes. I don't care what your teachers and directors say. It's not being a sissy, it's protective maintenance."

More grumbles.

"About that payment. I meant it," Ted said. He reached behind for his wallet in his back pocket. No, I hadn't really noticed how nicely his jeans fit his tight butt. Really.

Well, maybe.

I was on the rebound; I didn't want to notice men at all.

Yeah, right.

"Actually, if Jason can share rides with Tiffany, that will be more than enough." I raised my eyes to him in hope. I didn't need the money right now. Between G's financial support and my share of the profits at Magical Brews, my checking account was okay if I didn't go overboard on school clothes. What I needed was time, the one thing mothers never had enough of. And, right now, I needed to spend more time with Shara before her natural curiosity got out of hand.

That settled, I went about mixing dry ingredients for Tiffany to take home. Then I put many of those same ingredients in a base of linseed oil and camphorated olive oil. Okay, it started as a commercial moisturizing lotion I bought in bulk at the big box store. "Salve in the morning, soak in the evening. And stay out of toe shoes for a couple of days. A week if you can," I told her, handing the remedies to her father.

"All natural, nothing harmful?" he asked as he stood.

He was very close. Too close for normal comfort. I could smell the lingering remnants of his aftershave and natural male. Damn it. He was attractive, and I hadn't had attentive male company in months.

"All natural doesn't always equate to nothing harmful. But I did not knowingly add anything that would hurt your daughter. I would never willingly deprive the world of the beauty of her dance."

The front door slammed, and I jumped back two steps.

G and Belle stood frozen in place at the swinging door. The three tall, perfectly groomed, fashionably dressed adolescents behind them and looking at Belle with fascination didn't register until later. All I could see in that moment was the scowl on G's face, and hear the animal growls coming from his throat.

# Five

JASON UNWOUND THE THIRD long extension cord for the electric mower. Shara had handed it to him from the depths of the toolshed. He didn't know what fascinated her about the cement block flooring, but she wasn't in the greenhouse like Mom said. So he guessed she was okay.

"I need a riding mower," he grumbled. "I could finish this . . . this meadow in half an hour with a bigger, more powerful mower." Not that Mom would consider anything as noisy and polluting as a gas-powered machine. If she had her way, the whole, bloody acre would go back to wildflowers and grasses.

He flipped the switch, and the machine purred, the blade spinning beneath the housing. At least, the electric mower was easy to start. His friend BJ Chambers complained about the shoulder-wrenching pull start of his gas mower. He only had an oversized corner lot, maybe one hundred by two hundred feet, and a house that filled most of it.

Even klutzy Belle could manage the electric stuff, if she didn't run over the cord. That had happened a couple of times.

A snazzy red sports car drove slowly along the narrow road at the front of the house. Jason turned off the mower and gawked at the dream car. "Mr. Mooney!" he called to the man who climbed out of the sexy vehicle.

Oops. His father's friend wore a tie-dyed caftan and

sandals today instead of his weekday business suit. "Coyote Blood Moon, what brings you to our neck of the woods?"

"Is your dad home?" The slender man of average height stayed by the car, didn't approach him or the house at all. Something about his mystic outfit made his neatly cut and groomed hair look fuzzy. Actually, his whole figure looked fuzzy as if he never worked out or did any exercise at all.

"Yeah, Dad drove in a couple minutes ago. Some kids from the football team followed him home." He jerked his head toward a gleaming, oversized black pickup truck parked across the street and down a ways, closer to BJ's old house than this one.

Jason couldn't decide if he'd rather have the macho truck or the snazzy sports car. He still had a year to wait to get his license. No sense even asking for his own car until then.

"All right. I'll call your father later. It's not terribly urgent. Don't bother mentioning I stopped by. Got to get back to my shop. Oh, I did notice that CD you wanted came in. African drums music is kind of weird for someone as young and white as you."

"African Jazz is the coming thing in innovative dance. You see it all the time on the competition shows on TV. I want to be ahead of the game. Maybe do some of my own choreography."

Coyote Blood Moon nodded and smiled. "I'll keep it under the counter by the cash register. You can pick it up anytime."

"Might be a week or two. Have to wait for my allowance."

"I'll let you have it on account, and you can bring in the money whenever. I know you are good for it." He tucked himself back into his car and drove off slowly, looking carefully from side to side, down each widely separated driveway. In this semirural part of town those driveways could be half a mile apart, leading to ancient farmhouses or old and crumbling mansions. His dad had kept up their house pretty well. But he did wish for a better mower.

Jason shook his head. He often wandered into Coyote Blood Moon's music shop a couple blocks away from Mom's coffee shop in old town. He liked the weird drums and flutes and the books about magic, but sneezed mightily from the incense and candle smoke. Somehow the image of the middle-aged hippy didn't mesh in his mind with the sophisticated real estate developer.

Which man was he in truth? Too fuzzy around the edges to know for sure.

This was the first time he could remember Coyote Blood Moon coming to the house at all. Dad always met him in town alone.

Oh, well. Speculating about his parents' weird friends didn't get the lawn cut.

A whiff of scented candle smoke and heavy incense drifted back to Jason as the sports car turned around in the neighbor's driveway and Coyote Blood Moon drove back past the house.

Jason's nose itched, and burned, and finally exploded. His eyes ran, and his sinuses pounded with building pressure.

No way could he mow the lawn now. He wasn't allergic to grass, but adding that pollen to the incense did him in.

He unplugged the mower and abandoned it. Belle would have to finish the job.

He trudged back to the house in search of meds, almost grateful that he'd taken off his shirt because it was hot out. Maybe Tiffany would be impressed with his newly defined abs and biceps. Summer workouts paid off.

---

"Introduce me to your friends, Belle," Daffy said, not looking at G.

"Who?" Belle looked around, as if amazed. The green

agates on the ends of her hair sticks jiggled, and a long curl of dark hair escaped from the sloppy bun at her nape.

G took note of how the boys' eyes didn't track to anything but the movements of those jade charms dangling from his daughter's hair ornaments. He felt the blood drain from his face. He knew magical enthrallment when he saw it.

Time to have a long talk with Belle about the dangers of uncontrolled magic. And uncontrolled boys. Damn, she was facing her twelfth birthday. Much too young for this.

He wanted to wring all of the boys' necks.

"Oh. Mom, this is Bill and Mike. You know BJ already." She zeroed in on the cookies still on the cooling rack on the kitchen island.

G threw out his arm to keep the boys from following Belle. He'd had enough of their dogged parade behind Belle. BJ, in particular. The boy had been Jason's friend since preschool, and though his parents now lived in a new home closer to town, he was still a fixture in this house. Bret Junior was six months older than Jason and a year ahead in school. He'd been so much a part of the family G hadn't thought about him as a potential "date" for Belle or Shara.

Not that either girl was old enough to even consider dating yet.

"Belle, be polite and offer some refreshment to your guests," Daffy reprimanded her.

"Um, we have an appointment with an X-ray machine at the urgent care clinic," Ted stammered. He stood and offered a towel to Tiffany.

She hastily dried her feet and took her father's hand. "Thanks, Ms. Deschants. My feet feel a lot better, and I promise to use the balm and the salve every day." She ducked her head as they made their escape from a potentially embarrassing situation.

"Do I have to invite the boys in?" Belle asked on a whine. "They followed me home. I didn't ask them."

Daffy looked to G for confirmation. He shrugged, relaxing his stance now that the Tylers had fled.

He'd known Ted for years. An honest man. But not right for his Daffy.

The boys had a glassy-eyed look similar to the muggers after G enthralled them. He'd had to learn that skill. Belle seemed to have it born into her.

Damn. Belle had manifested her talent. Who'd have guessed that the class klutz and geek would become a siren? Come to think of it, she'd only stumbled twice today and dropped her chess set once. He'd wondered at the time if she did it deliberately to manipulate the boys into picking it up for her.

●━━━━━

As I watched the boys standing still and moving only their eyes to follow Belle, I remembered something. I'd been reading in some of the books Gayla and I stocked at Magical Brews. Coyote Blood Moon had written one on using ritual magic as a form of hypnosis. Made sense to me. More sense than magic actually working. A lot of people in town did parlor tricks, though none quite so magnificently as G's juggling. Something in the water. So I stepped between Belle and the boys, breaking their line of sight.

Of course, they didn't shake themselves free of the spell. Of course, they merely looked around me, or over the top of my head. Mike might be only in his mid-teens, but he already topped me by two inches.

G narrowed his eyes and shifted his gaze between the boys and his daughter. The fingers of his left hand twitched, and he started to reach for his pen/wand. Then he looked at me as if trying to read my mind for clues.

La, la, la, la, I sang to myself, not letting thoughts leak. Not going to let that happen. I didn't know if he could read my mind or not. I was not about to let him.

Standoff. No one moved except Belle who munched on a cookie with studied and determined bites and working her tongue to loosen crumbs lodged in her braces. Her glasses slid down her nose as she kept her gaze on the plate of cookies in front of her.

"Belle?"

"Yssmmam," she mumbled around a giant bite of cookie.

"Daffy, what is happening?" G asked. He put his taller and broader body between the boys and Belle.

I knew something he didn't. Our daughter had started her first period a week ago. She'd entered puberty, and I had this awful feeling her magical talent had manifested.

My lungs needed emptying of pent-up air. So I released it, and took a deep breath. Somewhat fortified, I spun and grabbed the hair sticks from Belle's untidy bun.

"Hey!" she slapped her hand where mine had just been. Dark tresses tumbled about her shoulders. I watched the air around her blur, like a magical glamour sliding off.

The boys sighed and blinked, then blinked again. BJ shook his head, his eyes cleared. "Um . . . hey, Ms. Deschants, um, I see Belle got home safe and sound. Tell her if she needs a ride again, I'd be happy to drive her."

G growled something that resembled, "I'll drive my daughter," but included a bunch of other impolite words. Two of them I actually knew.

"Great chess tournament, Belle," Mike said, clearer and brighter than he'd been a moment ago.

"Nice finesse with your bishop at the end of the third match," Bill added.

They turned in sync, as if managed by the same puppet master and marched back the way they'd come.

"What was that about?" Belle asked.

I handed the hair sticks back to her. She wound the mass of her hair into a wad and started to stab the knot with a stick. I held up my hand to halt her actions.

"I believe it is time you and your father had a long talk about your heritage." I sighed. I couldn't deny it any longer, I'd married a warlock, or wizard, or whatever, and he'd passed his talents to our children.

"I know about magic. This is Eugene, after all. Half the people in town have some magic. Dad already told us about it."

I remembered that. Three years ago, when Jason was twelve and beginning to mature. I'd eavesdropped as best I could, but G kept getting up and checking the doors, so I missed big chunks of his lecture about the existence of magic and the need to never admit it to outsiders and to tell him as soon as "things" started happening. He also warned them to watch each other for changes in personality. Insanity was not unusual until they got used to their powers.

Part of what I missed was just how powerful he was and that a Guild of registered magicians existed. But I had seen his hands shaking to the point where he had to stuff them in his pockets. That alarmed me. Fastidious G risked marring the line of his trousers to hide shaking hands.

It happened as he mentioned the personality change.

"We've talked. But only that magic exists. Now it's time to talk about training and control," G replied. He slouched into an uncharacteristic posture reminiscent of the fearful stuffing of his hands in his pockets. He looked almost as if he had to have the first sex talk with his daughter. I'd already done that one; the day after I kicked G out, I had to explain the pictures to the girls. Jason, thankfully, already knew.

Which one of my kids would be next to manifest?

Oh, wait. Shara had already listened to magical evidence that wanted to be found. And she'd found it.

Which left Jason. Three years older than Belle, he should have been first. He should have started three years ago when G had the first talk with the kids. I sighed again.

"G, you'd better stay to dinner and talk to each of them in turn. Or all three together. Then you get to advise me on how to deal with them."

"I always look forward to your dinners, Daffy. What are

you cooking tonight? It smells like Spanish flank steak. Done about six?" He gestured to Belle to follow him.

I hated to tell him that his home office was now my sewing and craft room. The kids had gleefully helped me move every scrap of paper, file cabinet, and desktop computer to the basement. They had prevented me from carrying it all out to the compost pile and setting it afire.

I could still do that.

# Six

"**I** KNEW IT!" Shara exclaimed. She jumped up from her seat on the end of the curved bench around the kitchen table to G's left.

G winced at the steam-whistle pitch of her voice. He shifted uncomfortably in his straight-backed chair. So did Belle on his right.

Belle reached for her hair sticks, fingering the dangling charms rather than the ivory shafts. That told him a lot about her wand of choice.

Jason, across from G, in the middle between his sisters, stared at his bare feet, his hand paused in midair reaching for a bag of chips.

Daffy had gone back to the shop to clean up after the small grease fire. She should be here, listening and learning so she could help the children. But she needed to clean, to control the world around her with a bottle of bleach before and after she turned her own magic loose on baked goods.

He needed to think about that. Would she ever be more than a casual kitchen witch? He knew she had power. A lot of it. He'd sensed it the first time they met. But she'd suppressed it. Her father had instilled a deep fear of magic in her at a very young age.

"I win my chess matches with logic. I don't cheat with magic," Belle insisted.

"Chess and math are a natural part of your mind, Belle. Your magical talent seems to be something along the line of being a pied piper." Better than giving her the real name for her talent, siren. That word had sexual connotations he did not want to explore with her yet.

"Pie piper," Shara giggled. "Mom's teaching you to bake pies and pipe icing. Though all you pipe are strict geometrical designs. No graceful swoops and swirls or even rosebuds."

"Geometric is graceful and elegant." Belle gave her sister a quelling look that in a couple of years would discourage the most ardent of suitors.

A brief shaft of light from the setting sun caught her profile. The stark outline reminded him of a bust of Nefertiti. But with glasses perched on the end of her nose while she looked over the top. An Egyptian goddess in the making. Gorgeous. She wouldn't need magic to attract attention. She had beauty beyond belief. Her thick glasses and braces were but a temporary mask.

The clumsiness, on the other hand, might present problems. She hadn't started walking until well after her first birthday because she kept falling down. She tripped over everything and dropped whatever she carried. With her beauty, she'd have boys picking up after her willingly. As they had this afternoon.

Then the light shifted again, and he saw her real silhouette: too long of a nose, asymmetrical eyes, mouth and teeth too big. She'd grow into most of that but ... that brief moment told him that the magic was the mask, not her impediments.

"Is ... is that why all the cool kids are following me around? Because the hair sticks give me the illusion of something they crave?"

"I'm afraid so." The ache in her voice felt like a knife wound to his heart. He'd do anything to protect his girls; his son, too. Which could be a problem already. He needed a report from Marseilles. His bosses were amazingly reluctant to part with information. He'd deal with them later. When he had more protections in place here.

"What does this mean? What are we to do about

this . . . this magical talent we seem to have inherited from *you*?" Jason asked accusingly, still staring at his feet.

*Not just my talent. You inherited your mother's as well. And that scares me shitless.*

"It means you must learn to control your talents so that they only work when you want them to. In the way that you want them to. Which means you must practice." He called up a document on his laptop that he'd created years ago, hoping to delay this conversation, but knowing it would have to come someday. "Is the printer hooked up to wireless?"

Shara rolled her eyes. "Of course." She jumped up from her place on the bench of the breakfast nook and dashed into Daffy's office on the old sun porch. "Okay, you can hit print now," she called back to them. She flitted around the kitchen and the office, too excited to contain her energy. That was something she'd have to learn to control before her magic worked right.

Seconds later he heard the printer chatter to itself and spit out the first of several sheets. "I've drawn up some basic lessons in general magic, because until today I didn't know how your talents would manifest. You have to understand that these lessons, your talent, *anything* about magic does not leave this house. You speak of it to *no one* except me and maybe your mother. If she has any talent, she has suppressed it, so she won't understand a lot of what you tell her." He speared each of them with the same gaze he used to subdue criminals into obedience.

They each nodded, eyes wide with wonder but not enthrallment. Good. They understood in their hearts and their heads. It wasn't imposed on them.

"You each need to spend some time every day practicing these lessons but also honing your individual talents, understanding your strengths, overcoming your weaknesses. And thinking through magical problems with logic. Otherwise, it will twist your mind inside out and sideways."

"All I can do is leap to the ceiling and land as lightly as a feather, without noise." Jason still hadn't looked his father in the eye.

"Leaping to the ceiling is merely the easiest thing for you to do. What you are actually doing is levitating your entire body. Pushing against the Earth, defying gravity. If you can do it to yourself, you can do it to anything else." G drew a deep breath and concentrated on the open laptop in front of him.

It had been a long time since he'd done this. Though it had been a useful skill to lift jail cell keys and bring them to his hand when that sorcerer in El Salvador had conned the local policia into arresting G for littering.

"I'm a full wizard," he explained. "Which means I have a variety of skills. Three primary, but a number of others I've learned. Most witches or warlocks have only one."

"Like?" Belle prodded him.

"My primaries are Water—I can make it rain, or stop raining, I can melt snow, and I can swim long distances because water gives me strength and won't drown me. Then there is Mind Magic—sort of like hypnosis. I use that a lot in gaining cooperation from rogue magicians and criminals. They want to confess every crime, every lie, every cheat on their spelling tests at the age of eight. Kind of boring, but useful."

"And the third?" Shara asked, handing him the first set of collated sheets of paper.

He passed the pages to Jason. The boy frowned deeply at the first command. "I know how to breathe and to control my breathing. It's basic to any athletic endeavor."

G let that pass.

"What's your third power?" Shara urged, bouncing from foot to foot.

"My third primary power is channeling the flow of electricity. Magic is a lot like electricity in needing a conduit, positive and negative, leaping a gap to mate one spark with receptive fuel. I have to stay away from electrical appliances or I short them out."

"So that's why Mom won't let you in the kitchen," Belle snorted.

"One of many reasons. She does like to control her kitchen and doesn't like any interference. One of the talents I learned, however, is levitation."

What would impress his children? He looked around and spotted the food processor on the counter. He pointed his pen at the wall socket and channeled his thoughts through the receptive wand. First, he had to remove electricity from the equation. The pen telescoped out and bobbled almost of its own volition. It knew what he wanted, sometimes before he knew what he wanted. The unique bond between a wizard and his wand grew over time.

His concentration wavered as he wondered how Jason would find a wand that allowed him to levitate himself. Was it unique to the stage at the theater, or would any wooden floor do?

Back to the food processor. The plug wiggled in the wall socket. With a pop it bounced, severing the electrical connection. Ah, now the appliance was his. Another wiggle of the pen, and the processor slid to the edge of the counter.

"No, Dad. Mom will kill you," Belle cautioned.

He let the side of his mouth quirk toward a smile as he pulled the processor toward him and let it hang in the air a moment before lowering it to the floor.

He released the breath he'd been holding and felt his arms go limp and a headache pound behind his eyes.

Another deep breath in and out, another. Feeling returned to his hands. He had enough strength to retract his wand into a pen again.

Water. He needed water to drown the headache.

As casually as he could, he rose and sauntered over to the food processor, and lifted it back into place, but he didn't plug it in. Not yet. The electrical power was too close in frequency to his own power. If he touched the socket, he'd blow the circuitry in the whole house. He'd only done that once. When he was seventeen and wanted to impress Coyote Blood Moon, his best friend and fellow wizard. His grandfather, Gabe, had laughed (the house had needed bringing up to code for a long time) before taking the cost of rewiring out of his college fund. Money G had to replace by working as a clerk at the grocery store for five summers.

Three glasses of water later, he plugged in the food processor and returned to his chair by the table.

Belle hopped up and began searching for hidden wires and levers.

"Can I do that?" Jason asked, gape-mouthed.

"With practice. It is not my primary talent, so I have to work hard at it. And because I have to work hard, I need to replenish my body afterward. Water is important. Drink lots of it, even when you aren't working. Food is also important. Not just empty calories, though right now about six of your Mom's cookies sound very good. Keep up your protein and fresh vegetables. Fruit is better than candy. But if nothing else is available, a bar of dark chocolate will do."

Shara put a plate full of cookies in front of him. "Sorry—there's only five. That's the last of that batch," she said meekly. "Mom said she'd bake more tomorrow. And I don't like dark chocolate."

"Thank you, sweetie. I'll survive on five cookies." He reached an arm around her and held her close for a few moments. "You'll learn to like dark chocolate better than milk chocolate the first time you desperately need to restore."

"Wouldn't the milk protein in milk chocolate work better?" Jason asked.

"Negligible," G dismissed his argument. "The antioxidants in dark chocolate are better than the minimal amounts of milk in lighter blends."

"What else do we need?" Belle asked. She worked her way down the first page of lessons and flipped to the second. Jason lingered in the middle of his first page, needing to absorb and question each one.

"Sleep." G answered Belle's question. "Make sure you get enough, even if you have to skip a TV program or time with your friends. You'll find your natural life rhythms soon enough."

"As if Mom would let us do anything else," Jason grumbled. "BJ has a later bedtime than I do, and you know how strict his parents are. They don't even have cable or satellite and only watch the news on local TV."

"Your mother is formidable in many ways. Listen to her," G said emphatically. "Shara, please retrieve your pages from the printer. I want to be here while you go over my outline."

Daffy had done such a good job raising these precious children that they obeyed. Why was he surprised?

Because when he was a teen, he'd considered it part of his job to defy, rebel, and do everything his own way. He learned better by making mistakes and having to correct them. Like the rewiring.

Jason stood on his portion of the curved bench and proceeded to leap over their heads, using his arms to propel himself along the ceiling and drop in front of the refrigerator. He landed without a sound or vibration, arms descending in a graceful curve. Everything about him shouted a lithe grace that defied straight lines.

"Show-off," Belle sneered.

"What? I'm hungry, and it was easier than asking everyone to move out of the way."

# Seven

DINNER WAS A SILENT, contemplative affair. I
wondered what the kids would have to say when
they'd digested what their father had told them. Jason, at
least, ate every bite on his plate and half of my serving.
Belle toyed with her food, pushing it into neat geometric
patterns on her plate more than eating. Only Shara acted
normal. She picked the peas out of her mixed vegetables—
from the garden and the greenhouse—scarfed the garlic
mashed potatoes, and cut her meat into tiny bits, chewing
each one carefully eight times before swallowing. She approached her food in much the same way she solved a
puzzle or ferreted out a password, one section of vari-
ables at a time.

G ate. But he spent long moments staring at each of
his children.

Finally, I set them to clearing the table and cleaning
the kitchen. G settled in to the family room, playing with
the TV remote.

"I don't recall inviting you to stay." I grabbed the remote from him and turned off all the electronics. No
games system, no high-tech music, and definitely no TV
or movies.

"An invitation to dinner usually includes . . ."

"An invitation to dinner was just that. I provided fuel
after what must have been a grueling afternoon of heart-
felt discussion. Now you must need rest. I know the children do. They are still children and still growing." A

vision of Jason's socks and how high on his ankles his jeans rode meant a trip to the clothing store sooner rather than later.

"I need to monitor . . ."

"They can call you if they have questions. Or, better yet, you can take them to the mall tomorrow. I'll give you a list of what clothing your children have outgrown. School starts in ten days."

"Ah yes, I remember the mad scurry of every parent in town taking the kids to the mall for complete new wardrobes. I'll leave the girls to you. They both show signs of maturation, and they'll need things that will embarrass them if purchased by their father."

"Jason is the one who worries me. He acts confused. This talent thingy won't interfere with his dancing, will it?"

"It shouldn't. If we monitor him closely and channel his training properly." He paused, frowning and working his throat as if he needed to speak but was afraid to. Then his face cleared, and he looked me in the eye. "Actually, dancing in an international company might be a great cover story for him if he should be able to follow in my footsteps." G puffed out his chest with pride.

"Just go. Go do whatever it is you do on a Saturday night now that you are single again."

"Not totally. The divorce won't be final for another two weeks." He grabbed my hand and pulled me down beside him. One arm draped across my shoulders, the other crossed in front of me. "We can still call it off."

The warmth of his body next to mine felt so very familiar, comfortable. My face grew hot, and tiny shivers shot through me with fire and ice. He lowered his face, inches from mine. There he paused, licking his lips. His eyes half-closed and . . .

He paused a fraction of a second before I lost my will to resist.

"We're good together, Daffy. We belong together. We need each other, now more than ever, dealing with the children."

"The children." I sank away from him, sober and outside his influence. "You have lied to them and to me for a long time. How can I be sure you aren't lying to me now?"

His arms fell away. "I have told you all my secrets. I no longer have a reason to lie to you."

"The evidence safe in the greenhouse."

"What about it?"

"Shara found the safe and wanted to know what is in it."

"She didn't tell me that. How did she find the damn thing? You've got planters and bags of potting soil, pots, and stray tools resting atop it. *I* have a hard time getting into it."

"She said something in the safe called to her. The safe needed her to find it."

He flopped back on the sofa. But one arm rested on the back, within easy dropping distance to my shoulders.

I scooted away.

"Next week, before school starts, I'll take her out for the day, a picnic, shopping, something. I'll talk to her."

"She's been bugging me to go to the antique mall."

His eyes opened wide, and his body grew rigid.

"What?" I asked, a bit confused by the intensity of his reaction.

"Which antique mall?"

"She didn't specify."

He relaxed a little.

"What about the antique mall has set you on edge?"

"Nothing."

"You're lying. I can tell when you lie now."

He heaved a sigh. I watched resolution smooth his face.

"My colleagues and I sometimes find magical artifacts at yard sales or collectible stores. People clean out grandma's attic and find bits of old jade jewelry that are really amulets and talismans. They find planters that are really cauldrons. Sometimes they'll find an old diary that's more a grimoire than memoir."

"Why does that alarm you? Maybe Shara wants an old Rubik's Cube, another puzzle to solve."

"She's seeking a wand."

"I thought she's too young."

"She is."

"Mom, I don't get it," Belle said at five thirty the next morning.

It might be Sunday and my day off, but my body clock didn't know the difference.

"Don't get what?" I gestured toward the bench in the breakfast nook across from me. I had the greenhouse schematics spread out before me, planning the autumnal plantings.

"This whole magic thing. I mean, when school let out in June, all of the cool kids laughed at my clumsiness, they ridiculed my brains, and they made jokes about how ugly I am." She ducked her head and blinked rapidly to hide her tears.

"Were BJ, Mike, and Billy among the cool kids who were afraid that you are smarter than them and that very shortly you are going to be so beautiful you will outshine the most glamorous of the cheerleaders and prom queens?"

"Yeah." She sounded discouraged. Then her head reared up and she stared at me in wonder. "Am I really going to be pretty?"

"You already are. For now, the braces and glasses get in the way. But the braces come off next spring, and your ophthalmologist says your eyes should be mature enough for contacts about the same time. Possibly Lasix surgery when you're eighteen. I'm afraid your clumsiness is not something you'll outgrow. You refused ballet classes that might have helped."

"But Jason fell in love with dance at my first and only class, so not all was lost." She flashed me one of her wily grins that used to melt my heart and manipulate me.

"Yes, your brother does love dancing more than anything else. So what bothers you about going from pariah to the most popular kid in school?"

"It just doesn't seem right that because I hold up my hair with antique sticks, suddenly I'm a people magnet. Those boys only came to the chess tournament in the park because they wanted to cause trouble, break things, prove that they are cooler because they can intimidate other people."

"BJ, too?" I had to wonder at that. The boy had been in and out of my house almost as an extra child since preschool. He and Jason had bonded the first day and never looked back. They shared everything, especially the stuff they wanted to keep secret from their moms. If he was finding new friends among the rougher type of school kids, I'd have to look at him differently. Deal with it differently. I truly wanted this to be a temporary aberration. Not . . . not . . .

"Bullies," Belle confirmed. "He's been different this summer."

"Do I need to talk to his mother?" Gossipy and judgmental Flora Chambers was not my favorite person, but she was an ally in the battle that resembled parenthood these days.

"I dunno." She shrugged just like Shara and her father when they didn't want to say what was really on their minds. "So what about those sticks turned them into sheep, and me the shepherd?"

"I don't know. But I've been reading a lot since I found out that magic is real—real magic, not minor talent and sleight of hand—and your dad is part of it. He says that Coyote Blood Moon is the real thing, not some wannabe like so many in this town."

"I've heard of him. He's local. Do you know the flute and drum shop two blocks east and three north of your shop?" Belle asked, eagerness back in her eyes and in her posture. "It seems really cool."

"I've seen the shop. Never thought to stop in."

"Coyote Blood Moon owns it. If Dad vouches for him, maybe I'll go talk to him."

"Take your father with you. And read the book. I've got a copy up in my bedroom."

"And the hair sticks?"

"From what I've read and what your father has said, I think those sticks are your magic wand. You need to keep them with you at all times. What made you buy them anyway?"

"I was walking through the antique mall with the chess club kids one day. Jimmy thought he might find an old chess set. I saw the sticks and just needed to touch them. Did you notice that the agates are carved like chess pieces? The queen and the bishop—power pieces. They just seemed to say they were mine, and I had to buy them. But I didn't have enough money with me. The clerk said they'd been sitting there for ages and she'd give me a discount. Like seventy-five percent off. Which was precisely the amount of money I had in my wallet. No one does that. So I bought them before she could change her mind. Or the sticks could."

"May I examine the sticks a little closer?"

She looked appalled and started to shake her head.

"I just want to look. I don't have to touch them. Before long, when you've had them longer, no one but you will be able to touch them."

"Okay." She scampered off.

I took a long drink of coffee while I gathered my thoughts. The greenhouse could wait until daylight.

Belle returned a few moments later, hair sticks in hand. She'd taken the time to pull on shorts and a tank top and brush her hair. Carefully, she placed her wands on the table and lined them up, precisely parallel, level with the table edge, the charm end of one beside the pointed end of the other.

She was a mathematics genius after all, taking senior classes in eighth grade. Logical and organized to a fault.

With my hands in my lap, I leaned over to inspect the

ivory. They had the speckled cream color of aged ivory, not plastic, and not harvested recently. The points were a bit blunted but not broken. The rounded and knobbed end had tiny drill holes for a silk thread. Again, the material had the rough texture gained only with years of wear and tear. I saved examination of the charms for last. For weeks, I'd seen them only in passing and from a distance. Belle was most defensive and territorial about her wands. As she should be.

The tiny bits of carved stone, each about an inch high, had a clarity of color in the cream-and-green streaks I didn't expect. Agates should be mottled with irregular veins of different minerals, or shades of the same primary color. And cheap, easily found. These charms, a chess queen and a bishop, had some variation in color but remained a dominant green.

*Precious Jade green was worth much, much more than her allowance. Seventy-five percent off hinted at manipulation. From Belle? Or the shop owner?*

# Eight

TWO GIRLS TURNED LOOSE on the mall on a Sunday afternoon should have been full of energy and excitement. New clothes, new school year, new classes, and classmates. For Belle, this represented an advancement to the top of middle school, from the middle of an arcane hierarchy unique to 'tweens. Next year she'd advance to the bottom of the high school hierarchy, leaving childhood behind. For Shara, this was stepping up from the height of elementary to the bottom of middle school, a year ahead of her age group.

But nothing satisfied my youngest. Clothes and shoes decisions, she left to me. She tossed school supplies into our cart willy-nilly without looking at them. She was restless and cranky with fatigue.

Belle attacked the clothes and shoes with enthusiasm, looking to transform herself into the butterfly waiting within the chrysalis of her braces and thick glasses. Lunch at the food court, however, was a grand experiment in seeing who she could attract simply by wearing the magical hair sticks.

"Mom, do we have to put up with her?" Shara demanded. "She's being obnoxious." She and I sat at a separate table a scant two yards from Belle. In teen parameters, sitting *with* family members, especially a mother and younger sister, was not cool.

I masked my smile by sucking up raspberry iced tea through a straw. I swallowed as much as I could without choking. "Actually, she needs to do this while she has the safety net of family to intervene if she goes too far."

"I call that going too far," Shara sneered.

"I think you're right." I pushed back my chair and stood. Then I noticed G and Jason sitting on the opposite side of Belle. They'd just settled trays of food and drink, Jason's piled considerably higher to fuel his growing body. G stood up again, gesturing Jason to remain seated. He approached Belle's table where two tall, blonde girls with the perky personalities and slim figures of cheer-leaders sat with Belle, and two athletically large, and hulking boys wearing fashionably casual grunge clothes that looked like they hadn't been washed in a month and never pressed, slouched against a support pillar. Those clothes probably cost as much as the six outfits combined I'd bought for Belle.

The cool kids, and upper classmates at that, had suddenly discovered that Belle, a mere middle schooler and a geek, was the center of their universe.

But they'd discovered this through magic; as soon as the magic went away, so would they.

"Belle," G said, looming tall and awesome over the table. His suave sophistication and the silver wings of gray at his temple against his dark hair marked him as the ideal older man personified in romance novels. But he rubbed the wooden fountain pen in his breast pocket. His jaw worked as if he subvocalized something. A spell, I was willing to bet.

"Introduce me to your friends, Belle."

"Not now, Daddy."

"Now, Annabelle."

She blinked rapidly several times. "Dad, this is Jessica and Marilee." She nodded toward the two blondes. They simpered and squirmed as they scanned his left hand for a wedding ring. Then, as I expected, they smiled and extended hands for shaking while thrusting out their bosoms for his inspection.

Much to my surprise, G acknowledged their presence

but shifted his focus immediately to the two boys. He hadn't admired the girls' offering.

The boys cringed back and slumped, to make themselves appear smaller and less important.

Classic beta behavior in the face of an alpha wolf. A very alpha wolf.

"I've met Billy and Mike," G said with careful scrutiny. He did not offer to shake hands. "I hope you have a good football season. Now, Belle, you need to join your mother and get home. I believe you have Math Olympics to study for."

"But, Da . . . ad!"

"Calculus and the mystery of quantum physics," he said as if he savored the finest dark chocolate from Belgium.

Belle's face brightened with enthusiasm. Then she looked at her companions as if seeing them for the first time. "Calculus this year, and tutoring the jocks who have to keep up their grades in algebra to stay on the team." She looked pointedly at her companions. "I don't get to play with quantum physics until next year, and I have to go over to the U to take that class." She scooted her chair back, gathered her packages, dropped one, dropped another trying to pick it up, then stumbled over them on her way over to me. The cool kids ignored her clumsiness, not cracking jokes about it or sneering as they had done last year. Belle paused and looked over her shoulder at her father, then her companions who stared after her as if starving for her friendship. "Bye, guys. You can go now."

When she turned her back on them, they slumped as if a puppet master had just cut the strings holding them upright. Surprised they could still move, they looked at each other, bewildered, then left to go about their day impressing real people with their coolness.

But their spines lacked the starch of youthful confidence and arrogance.

"We will talk later, Belle," G said. Then he approached me.

At the end of the day, with rain drenching us between the mall and our parking space, I ended up with Belle and Jason in the van while G took Shara off to the antique mall. "We'll see if we can find a cure for her restlessness," he said and whisked her away.

Jason shrugged, just like his father, threw his bags and boxes into the back of the van, then immediately claimed the shotgun seat. Belle huffed at her demotion to the backseat.

"Can you drop me at the studio, Mom. I need some practice time," Jason said.

"It's Sunday afternoon. No one will be there."

"That's okay, I know how to jimmy the lock. Shara showed me."

"What is so crucial about dancing now? You have stuff to do at home."

"It's just . . . it's just that I've been walking on those awful tile floors all day. I need to feel wood beneath my toes."

I had to stop and breathe, holding the key halfway to the ignition.

"Wood," I whispered. The rain on the van's roof muffled my voice. Tiffany's words about Jason's power jumps and leaps. Wood. Wooden floors to give him power.

Jason's wand wasn't a stick or something he could hold. His source of power was a wooden floor. Probably any wooden floor. I wondered just how high he could jump and how far he could leap, as long as he had a wooden floor to propel him.

"Compromise," I said, jamming the key into the ignition and setting the wipers to high. "The attic has a wooden floor. It's also full of junk and dust and cobwebs. Clean it up, and you can set it up as your own private studio." Where I could monitor his progress with those power jumps and talk him down if he found himself stuck on the ceiling.

I wasn't very anxious to see what kind of wand Shara had found at the antique mall. Maybe the rain would change her mind.

Not likely. Nothing ever made that child change her mind.

Jason threw his bags and bundles on his bed, not caring that half of them fell to the floor. His athletic shoes bounced against the closet door while his ballet slippers flew neatly to his hand from their place of honor on top of the bookshelf. One deep breath of relief and he was halfway up the enclosed attic stairs. Who cared if the door at the end of the upstairs hallway slammed closed?

His feet were free, and he was headed toward a solid wood floor. The hard work of clearing the attic meant nothing. He'd get that done in a couple of weekends. Then he'd have his own studio. All his own. And he could lock the door to the stairs to keep his sisters out.

That thought sent him spinning on one foot at the landing and moving in the new direction the stairs led.

His gaze went first to the ceiling. A good twelve feet at the center, sloping down to about four feet at the outside walls. The room covered the same area as the central portion of the downstairs: living room, dining room, and kitchen. The original part of the house that dated to long before the addition of the den, downstairs bath, and sun porch/office along with the turrets. Mom's bedroom and bath rested atop the addition. His and his sisters' bedrooms and their shared bath were original.

As soon as he stepped off the last stair, his feet automatically raised him onto the balls of his feet. He stretched up and down several times, letting his toes get used to the idea that this floor belonged to them. He had to let them get used to the uniqueness of the boards. Every floor was different. But this was *his!*

His nose tickled. He scrunched his face to suppress a

sneeze. He had no time to indulge in such mundane itchiness. He had a floor to explore.

Then he did sneeze. Not just a little release of an irritation. This was a full-blown explosion of dust and old perfume lingering on vintage clothing in the trunks. His eyes watered, and his head ached.

Damn. He added a few other words he wasn't supposed to know, but everyone in school said them when adults weren't around.

A quick look at the actual space, not just the height of the ceiling above the exposed rafters, told him exactly what he had to deal with. Boxes. Dozens of cardboard boxes, old trunks, heavy antique furniture, and oddments scattered haphazardly all over. Old sleds, bedding, dolls, clothes. Anything and everything his family had discarded over the last century. Or more.

And all of it covered with dust.

His nose itched again and his eyes watered. Pressure pounded from his sinuses to his temples.

Shit.

No time to deal with it. He had to bring order to the mess. Maybe Belle could help him find the most logical organization of the discards. Little sisters had to be good for something.

———————

"He's almost fifteen. He needs to be a slob for a while," I repeated to myself over and over. "He's fourteen. Almost fifteen. Shouldn't he have outgrown this phase by now?"

I vowed once again that I would not hang up Jason's new clothes, put away the new underwear, or stow the shoeboxes in the closet for him. The packages lay strewn from one end of his room to the next. A part of me craved that the children would keep their space as neat as I demanded of my own kitchen. The mother part of me knew that they needed to learn to pick up after themselves. I would not restore order to Jason's room. Where was he anyway?

A thump and the sound of heavy things being dragged across the wooden floor of the attic answered that question. The promise of his own dancing area was much more important in his mind than any other aspect of normal living.

"Jason! That will wait." I marched upward.

"But, Mom. You promised." His dark head appeared at the top of the stairs overlooking the landing on the staircase. Of course, he'd slammed the door hard enough that it bounced back open, not latching. That left the access to the attic wide open, allowing the hot air stored up there all summer to flow down into the living area.

"Now. You have chores, starting with picking up your room and making your bed. And don't stuff your new clothes under the bed because you are too lazy to find hangers for everything."

Bang, clatter, slam. His noise now drowned out the sound of the diminishing rain. "Can we have a garage sale and get rid of some of the crap up there?" he asked as he stomped into his room and clung to the door in preparation for slamming it in my face as soon as I answered his question. "I could use the money to buy a mirror and compact speakers for the music on my phone."

"Ask your father," I replied. "Most everything up there is from generations of his family. I have no idea what is valuable, or just sentimentally important." Since I'd moved in with G when I started my senior year at the University of Oregon and married him the same week I'd graduated, I hadn't much to bring with me in the way of stuff. Just clothing, books, and a few mementos that had worked themselves into the household décor rather than gone into the attic storage. I think there was one box of college pennants and movie posters in my walk-in closet (originally it had been a large nursery or spare bedroom attached to the master bedroom. We'd made a nice master bath out of part of the space).

Slam.

*Teenagers!*

I now knew that a wand was important to each of my children, and they needed to learn to use them properly. But they also needed to learn how to be ordinary *people*. That was my job.

That was why G had married me in the first place.

Belle, at least, had inherited my craving for neatness and order. Her room was set out like a mathematical equation or a chessboard. She hummed an old movie tune while she reorganized her closet, neatly folding the things she'd outgrown and would either pass down to Shara or donate to charity.

Alakazam. Magic Slam! Followed by a dozen half nonsense words that sort of made sense in context of the movie the music came from. I could see her bouncing from foot to foot and hopping back and forth from her stack of clothes on the bed to the closet.

The first time Jason and I had watched the movie when he was about three and I was heavily pregnant with Belle, I'd found "Alakazam, Magic Slam" cute and endearing. I think I was an emotional mess with pregnancy hormones.

A thousand times later as each of the children watched the DVD over and over and over again, it lost a lot of its charm. I now found it more irritating than fun. Of course, it stuck in their brains as the ultimate song of magic.

Maybe if I made them eat the DVD . . .

G needed to broaden their musical education before they drove me crazy. Crazier?

I shook my head, trying to clear it of Belle's song. A few steps down the hall I peeked into Shara's room.

Shara? Was in transition. I decided to wait until she got home and see how she treated her purchases before helping or leaving her alone.

# Nine

G STUFFED HIS HANDS in his pockets to keep his itching fingers from touching everything in the antique mall. He knew this place. It had been here for at least twenty-five years, maybe longer, under different names and owners, but always specializing in oddities, collectibles, and a few genuine antiques.

He took a deep breath, savoring the familiar scent of dust and old bricks that reminded him of his grandparents, his foster brother, home, and safety. Childhood memories. Adult memories tended to cloud his emotional attachment to the place.

Nothing specific called to him today. He sensed magic wands that had been here. He bought most of them for study and evidence of how they came to be separated from their owners. Most were ordinary household items, favored by minor practitioners. Most of those practitioners did not have enough talent to register with the Guild.

Sort of like Daffy with her wondrous baking and gift for herbal remedies. He'd have sworn when he first met her that she had a talent just waiting to burst forth. Separating her from the soul-shriveling control of her parents should have allowed her to manifest. But in fourteen years of exposure to him, she'd done nothing more interesting than bake and cook exquisitely and know instinctively what herbs worked best in combination for whatever she needed at the moment. Not enough for her to register with the Guild. Or to need a wand.

And, frankly, that satisfied him nicely. He'd grown to love Daffy the way she was, not what she could be. The thought of his first wife's power and the insanity that followed scared him to his bones, shaking every bit of ethics and morality his Nana had pounded into him. She and G-Pop had died too young, from wounds inflicted upon them by his insane wife. His parents had died in South Africa, trying to rescue a tribal shaman from murderous state police when he was an adolescent. In a way, he was thankful they didn't have to experience D'Accore's depravity.

But then, his dad had been savvy enough; he might have recognized the signs of an untrained talent eating away at her brain. She was a siren and had trapped him. She was also a fire wizard. Her wand was a Zippo lighter.

Over a lifetime of use, wands absorbed quite a bit of power that had to be grounded and needed to be destroyed to keep them out of the hands of rogues. Unfortunately, mundane families didn't know that and took a deceased magician's belongings to antique malls or sold them at garage sales.

Something special called to Shara. Was it someone else's discarded wand, or something unique to her and her budding talents? She'd spent approximately ten seconds sniffing right and left, then ran two aisles to the left and down all the way to the back wall of displays. She knew what she wanted and where to find it.

G followed her at a more relaxed pace, knowing that the farther into the mall they traveled, the cheaper the rent and therefore the price of the goods. He removed his hands from his pockets and flexed his fingers, letting the nerve endings on each digit sense anything untoward. He'd been trained for this when he was recruited as a deputy. When the Guild elevated him to Sheriff, he'd undergone a long and grueling process to enhance every nuance of his multiple talents. Except for the judges on the Board, he was now one of the most powerful wizards on the planet.

And his youngest daughter was manifesting her talents long before she should. Girls often matured at ten, but her older sister had waited until she was twelve. He'd have to keep his eyes open to guide both of them, and teach them control. Especially Belle's siren enchantment.

But he also needed to keep some distance from the family before his greatest enemy discovered their presence. Only the knowledge that distance between him and his family would save them kept him from fighting to regain his place in their home.

He found Shara rummaging around in a bowl of oddments; sleeves of hairpins, compacts missing powder and puff, mechanical pencils, and bunches of old keys. Twenty or more of them bundled together with a disintegrating twist tie. She held each one of the keys up to the light, examining them closely, sniffing them, and running her fingers along them.

Then, halfway through the bunch, she paused and went back to the previous key. It looked dull and lifeless to him. She pulled it free of the bunch easily, without damaging or opening the twist tie and laid it flat on her small palm. She'd have long and nimble fingers one day, but for now they were still a bit pudgy and unformed with childhood vagueness. Still growing into herself.

"This one, Dad. This is the one that has been singing to me in my dreams for weeks now."

G's knees felt watery and unstable. He wanted to scream *You're too young for this!* He'd been fourteen when he found his hand-turned wooden fountain pen in this very booth. He suspected that Belle's hair sticks also came from here.

"And look, Dad, the sign says everything in the booth is seventy-five percent off. That means I can afford it. I have two dollars in change left in my purse. I only need a dollar and a quarter. Isn't that great! It's almost like I was meant to have this key. This one and no other."

"May I see it?" he asked, trying to hide his hesitancy.

"O-oo-kay." She handed it over reluctantly.

He'd only be able to touch the thing with bare hands for a little while. Soon it would link to her and her only. Anyone else, even a master wizard, would feel a shock or a burn when touching another's wand. A really powerful magician's wand would repel the touch of another like a force field.

G examined it much as Shara had, holding it up to the light. Her little fingers had already burnished off bits of the tarnish. She'd found silver. He looked for the sterling stamp. Not much of it left, but as he narrowed his focus and touched his pen with his free hand, the tiny, stylized *S* jumped out at him. He handed it back just as his skin began to warm and tingle with warning. The key wanted Shara.

"I think you found the right wand, Little Bit."

"No. It found me." She danced back toward the cashier at the front.

They'd been inside for all of five minutes.

Out back, a car door slammed, followed by little feet pounding on the paving stones between the detached garage and the back porch. G and Shara must be home.

"Mom, Mom, Mom!" Shara called as she ran through the mudroom into the kitchen and stood at the base of the back stairs. "Look what I found!"

She nearly glowed with happiness as I descended toward her. "What did you find that Daddy bought for you?" I asked, warily looking toward G as he emerged from the mudroom.

"Show her, Shara. I had little to do with this other than driving her to and from. She found what she needed inside five minutes and paid for it with her allowance. It was marked down to what she could afford," he replied, bestowing a fond smile on our girl.

"Look, Mom. A key. A real skeleton key. You know— the kind they show in old movies for opening dungeon doors." She held out her hand, palm up. Across it lay a metal key about three inches long. It shone as if just polished inexpertly, bits of tarnish clinging to indents and crevices.

"Um . . . is that silver?" I asked. Iron, the usual material used for keys, had ancient legends that said it was anathema to witches and negated magic.

"Probably," G admitted. "More ornament or jewelry than utilitarian. But she zeroed in on it like a bee to a rose."

"Fitting," I muttered. Each of the children seemed to have adopted something aligned with their interests and personalities for their wands.

"Shara, please go put away your new clothes and wash up for dinner. We're having leftovers in an hour."

She scampered up the stairs, eyes glued to her new purchase.

"G, before you go, we need to talk. About Jason."

His head reared up from his study of his car keys. He'd been stalling, as if waiting for an invitation to stay for dinner again.

I couldn't let that become a habit. The divorce was almost final. I needed space and time alone, without a man making decisions for me or acting as a safety net if I made a mistake.

I'd never had to survive on my own before. The time had come that I needed to find out if I could.

"What's up with Jason?" he asked.

I led him into the dining room, away from the open sound channel provided by the kitchen stairs. "He found his wand."

"Oh?" He cocked one eyebrow in curiosity.

"Any wooden floor, like in the dance studio or a stage, or even here. His feet hurt after walking the linoleum floors of the mall. They hurt every day when he came home from school last year. But the hurt goes away the minute he kicks off his shoes and steps on a wooden floor." I looked at the old hardwood beneath the Oriental carpet beneath the dining table.

A loud bump and drag punctuated my words.

"I guessed something of the sort. Is he practicing leaps in the upstairs hallway? Only an eight-foot ceiling there," G said. He looked like he was trying for amusement but was really appalled.

"No, he's rearranging the attic to turn it into his own studio. He wants to host a garage sale to get rid of a bunch of stuff and use the money for a mirror, barre, and sound system." I pulled out one of the straight-backed chairs and flopped into it, suddenly aching with exhaustion.

"Jason, stop what you are doing," G yelled as he raced through the living room and up the front stairs. "You might damage something valuable."

Valuable as in family heirloom or *valuable* in terms of magic?

For the moment, I was too tired to care. And I still had dough to set to rise at Magical Brews.

Why had Gayla and I ever decided to call our little coffee shop and bakery *Magical*?

By the time I'd set out the leftovers for the kids to reheat in the microwave and put plates, cutlery, and paper napkins for them in the kitchen nook, I'd had enough. I couldn't face their bright eagerness or the way they looked to their father with adoration.

I needed to bake—smell sifted flour, feel dough kneading beneath my fingers, dust something with cinnamon sugar. Beat my frustrations into cake batter with my wooden spoon. For as long as I could remember, I'd turned to baking to sort my thoughts and bring order to my world. My Granny had taught me to bake before Dad sent her to the asylum for electrical shock treatments to cure her of her second sight.

I fled to Magical Brews on foot—it was only three quarters of a mile away, and the evening was warm. The century-old Gothic horror house that G's family had built and added onto with each new generation of extended family sat smack dab in the middle of the Ferry Street Bridge area, at the base of Skinner Butte Park. G didn't talk much about his family. I'd gleaned information over time that he'd lost his parents when he was young, and his grandparents shortly after he married his first wife, D'Accore (I imagined her as an exotic French beauty with an impeccable sense of style and elegance I'd never achieve). He'd never had siblings, other than a foster brother, and only a few cousins who were scattered across the country.

What was so special about Eugene, Oregon, that a family of magical practitioners had settled here? We were a university town with a winning football team and a world-class track program. The town began in the nineteenth century as an agricultural crossroads, important in its own right but not special enough to need magical protection. Or feed magic.

I crossed into the old downtown neighborhood that housed my shop. Each block was lined with long, two- or three-story buildings of side-by-side shops opening onto sidewalks with broad overhangs. Above the small businesses, mostly independently owned, were apartments for the business owners or rented to college students. An alley ran between the two halves of the block for deliveries and dumpsters and an extra fire exit.

Yesterday's tiny fire preyed on my mind. I needed to examine the entire kitchen again for the source of the oily substance I'd cleaned off the stove top. Grease needed heat to ignite. A spark from somewhere. Where did the heat or spark come from?

Where did the grease come from?

Early Sunday evening the sidewalks of this part of town were still filled with people, dressed in tie-dye and exotic beads. Nearly every man wore a beard and a ponytail, and the women wore their hair long with ribbons, beads, feathers, and streaks of color. The aroma of incense wafting out of various and sundry shops couldn't mask the distinctive acrid odor of marijuana. Pot was legal now, both medicinal and recreational, and more prevalent here than elsewhere in town. Flute and drum music completed the background.

My insides vibrated in the rhythm of a small drum echoing a heartbeat with an occasional flutter that sounded like a little bird taking flight.

Flutes and drums. Coyote Blood Moon's shop was right there in front of me. I'd turned right without thinking at the last intersection rather than going straight two more blocks to my shop. Was the universe telling me I needed to talk to this man?

Whatever.

I wandered through the open door, pushing aside long strands of beads that kept the bugs out. They clattered together in a distinctive jangle, announcing my presence.

"Hello," I called into the dim room lit only by fading sunshine through the big display window and a series of votive candles inside multicolored glass bowls. The little flames sent arcing prisms in every direction.

I turned in a full circle, looking at the dancing rainbows in wonder.

"Good evening, Ms. Deschants," a deep and mellow male voice said from the portal to the back room.

"How . . . how did you know my name?" I spun sharply until I found him just emerging from a series of shadows. Then he stepped into a patch of light, and I recognized him as a regular at Magical Brews. "Oh, hi, John. Two shots, caramel mocha, no foam. I didn't realize you owned this shop and wrote those books." I pointed to a shelf that contained six copies each of his six published titles.

"I have many personae, only one of them mystic and magical." He grinned, showing amazingly bright and straight teeth behind his neatly trimmed beard and mustache. His hair, too, looked freshly barbered.

"Is one of your personae a businessman for a Fortune 500 Company?"

He laughed long and loud. "You are as observant as you are expert with an espresso machine." He gestured toward two comfy looking chairs in an alcove between bookshelves, away from the wooden flutes and hand drums. "Actually, I'm a real estate broker and developer and have to wear suits to that job. I own this entire block and other rental properties in town. I bought them to ensure that developers did not try to move in and destroy our unique little neighborhood."

"So this shop is a part-time business for you?"

"Unfortunately, yes. I have hired help during the week and can only immerse myself in the magic of my shop and my music on weekends. And wear comfortable clothes." He opened his arms wide to display his batik caftan. Then he paused, looking ... contemplative but not sad. He'd carved out his place in the universe to his satisfaction. "Enough about me. What brings you to Mystic Music?" He flashed that amazing smile at me, and suddenly he seemed younger and more vibrant than I remembered him at six in the morning when he was in too much of a hurry, ordering coffee and buttermilk biscuits with butter and jam.

"I think I need to know something about the magical properties of jade." That's what Belle needed to know. But as her mother, I did, too.

"Ah, jade. Balance and wisdom, protection from fear. I have just the book, right here." He leaned forward and plucked a book off a shelf, not one of his own, and handed it to me. "Is this for yourself or your daughter, Belle?"

"Both. But how did you know about my daughter?" Maternal protectiveness prickled my back.

"I've seen her around town, and her father has

brought her in once or twice. Everyone in our . . . community knows G and his offspring. This summer, Belle has begun wearing the Chinese hair sticks with the jade charms. I know something about those sticks and the antique mall where she purchased them for the exact price she could afford. I own that building as well, but not the business. That I leave to someone who knows mundane old artifacts better than I do."

"But you know about the magical artifacts and keep track of them."

"I find it useful to poke my nose in there occasionally. G is a frequent browser. We were close in high school, but our lives went in opposite directions soon after. We wave and speak casually now but don't socialize much."

Pieces of the puzzle that were my children began to fall into place.

"I suspect that G has finally had to give you nuggets of information. I'm surprised it took him this long," John said, peering acutely at the space around my head. Looking at my aura?

"I have been willfully blind to him and his work for too long." And his lies and the bimbos he took to no-tell-motels.

"But now you are no longer blind, and you seek information on your own. G rents an apartment from me on the upper floor of this very block. He needs to remain close to the center of our community."

Was that where the incriminating photos were taken? And, if so, who was the photographer?

"Are there many participants in your community?" He'd mentioned it twice.

"Not as many as those who want to have the ability to belong. We find it easier to hide among the many pretenders. Invisible while in plain sight."

G had said that part of his job was keeping magic invisible. Where better to hide than amongst the wannabes holding a street party outside this shop, drinking and smoking and dancing in the street. It happened nearly every summer weekend evening. I'd just never paid it much attention.

"I look forward to you making my coffee tomorrow morning. You combine everything perfectly, just the way I like it. No one else seems to know how to do that. Take the book. It's free to members of the community."

"Am I a member?" That scared me. I had no magic of my own and didn't want the talent. My fundamentalist family had filled me with childhood nightmares about the sins of witchcraft and the necessary punishment of burning at the stake to cleanse the soul of the taint of Satan. They'd separated me from a beloved grandmother when she started predicting the future for our neighbors and her prophecies came true—especially the bad ones. Until recently, the world of magic was a fantasy found only in books. But I'd been a history major, and I knew how real magic had been to older civilizations and cultures. Maybe it had been with us all along, just driven underground by the fearful and paranoid.

My parents would rant long and loud about the evils of magic, at the same time declaring it would not, could not exist. Modern science had proven that.

Yeah, right.

"You are G's partner. That makes you a member of our community, knowingly or not," Coyote Blood Moon said, disrupting my fearful looping thoughts.

G's partner. Not his wife. His partner.

What had he gotten me into?

# Ten

"**A**NOTHER DEAD MAGICIAN?" G asked the familiar voice at the other end of this phone conversation. He flicked several keys on his laptop, zeroing in on a map of Australia. A red star blinked rapidly in Melbourne. He clicked it and brought Zeke into video conference mode.

"What do you mean another?" G's deputy replied, his Aussie accent came through thicker than his usual Oxbridge affectation. "This is the first one I've been called in on."

"First one in your jurisdiction, Zeke. I've investigated five others in the past three months. When did she die?" Not recently, he surmised. "What was the deceased's talent and her wand?" All magicians powerful enough to register with the Guild had an acknowledged wand that needed to be grounded and cleansed upon the death of the practitioner. He pulled up a spreadsheet on another screen.

If this murder followed the same pattern as the other five, D'Accore would have stolen the wand and absorbed most of its stored magic before dumping it on the body. She had to restore the talents stripped from her when the Guild incarcerated her in their inescapable dungeons. How she escaped and who helped her was still a mystery. He knew the killer was D'Accore.

No one else could have cast an illusion to make him think he was meeting Daffy for a quiet romantic interlude without the kids. When he'd seen the photos—the camera couldn't record illusion—he'd seen her for who she was.

She'd tried to drain some of his power. But she needed too much energy to maintain the illusion and didn't get much from him other than fast sex that wasn't as clandestine as he imagined.

He could only guess that his bosses hadn't told him of her escape out of embarrassment, and the long-ingrained habit of secrecy. But he knew now who his enemy was, and why she was gathering wands.

What he didn't know was who helped her. Someone with a lot of money for bribes, fake ID, and travel around the world to steal wands.

Wands only had echoes of their owner's power. D'Accore would need hundreds to bring her up to the levels she'd lost. She lost a lot of borrowed power each time she used it.

That meant she had to keep killing, keep absorbing power from stolen wands and from her victims. Death held its own energy.

But the D'Accore of old knew how to harness the power of death. Dangerous energy that didn't last long, but demanded release. Like to like. *Death causing death.*

G brought up a third screen with his database cataloging the murders, their location and time, wand, and talent.

"Jilly. She tamed fire." Zeke interrupted G's musings, caught in a circle of dread. "Mundane police think she's been dead four months." That sounded about right. "Jilly lived in an isolated rural area. No one thought to check on her until a client needed to take delivery of a metal sculpture. Jilly used the fire of a tamed welding torch to make the most amazing symbolic structures that speak to the heart." He paused and sighed with regret. "I got called because I'm listed as next of kin—a nephew for the record, but no blood relation."

The timeline fit D'Accore's movements. One of

D'Accore's first kills after escaping would be to work with fire again.

"Wait. She *tamed* fire?"

The opposite of D'Accore's original talent. She'd conjured and released fire to work its own will. Taming meant controlling. D'Accore reveled in fire running wild. As wild as she wanted to be. The Guild had stripped her of that ability first when they found her guilty of using black magic.

"This Jilly. Could she start fires as well as containing them?"

G found the name and talent on the registry. Not much info other than name, date of birth—and now death, location, next of kin—no family other than the Guild's local deputy, and two words about talent and level. Fire mage.

He really needed to expand this database.

"Starting fires? Not so much," Zeke said. "We're pretty dry out here and starting a fire can be disastrous. Controlling or stopping a fire is crucial. She needed the aid of an old Zippo lighter to start a fire, but she could put one out or contain it with a flick of her fingers. Sometimes, all she needed was a thought."

"A vintage Zippo?" All the heat drained out of G's face and hands. He had trouble typing the new information into the database with his suddenly numb fingers. "Was the Zippo found with the body?" He had to control the trembling in his gut.

This was getting worse.

He had personally thrown D'Accore's Zippo into a vat of acid.

"No. It looks like Jilly was strangled, then set afire with her own wand. There's a blank spot in the charring over her heart, the same size and shape as her wand. That's where she kept it, in her shirt pocket. The wand had created a small area of protection from fire." Zeke turned his phone so that G could see the grisly remains.

"What kind of decoration did the Zippo have?" G fought to control the shake in his voice.

"It had a skull medallion soldered to the metal case. And it had a bullet hole through it from a Japanese machine gun. Supposedly the lighter had saved the life of Jilly's father during World War II."

G gulped and looked deep within to find calm authority. "Zeke, I can't come to help you right now. I trust you to investigate this. I want a full autopsy and all the crime scene photos on my desk ASAP. Scrutinize every detail. Observe everything. I *really* need to know anything out of the ordinary. Use *all* of your senses on this one."

"Yes, sir. And, um, thank you for your trust. I've never known you to delegate before. I'm proud to be your deputy."

"Just do your job and get back to me. Don't expect to spot the perpetrator or capture her. She's moved on. I'm zeroing in on her location as we speak."

"Yes, sir. I do know that the murderer is a female. Blonde hair. Long legs and a figure to stop traffic. She was seen hanging around Jilly's metal sculpture studio around the time of death."

"That sounds like our perp. But I am surprised she hasn't disguised her true appearance as she murders her way across the world." She'd done it here in Eugene.

"Holding a disguise, either magical or mundane takes a lot of energy. She needed to conserve her power in order to get around Jilly's defenses and get close enough to kill."

"Get me as much information as you can gather. Deputize others if you need to." G thumbed his phone off, severing the connection to the computer. His hands shook so hard he needed three swipes to manage the disconnect. He had to close the laptop to silence it. He couldn't manage to power down or turn it off.

Whatever, D'Accore was up to, he had a bad feeling that he was not her ultimate target—just a nasty piece of revenge along the way. While trying to escape her magically locked straitjacket, she'd burst blood vessels behind her eyes. She could only restore her eyesight by stealing it from a *blood* relative. He now knew that she'd killed her entire family when she manifested her talent at twelve, the only magician in her genealogy. Without training, her talent had driven her insane. Jason, her son, was the only genetic connection she had left.

Would his inheritance from his mother eat his brain as well?

---

I thought about my conversation with John—Coyote Blood Moon—all the way to Magical Brews, only a few blocks away, on the edge of the busier newer section of town. Certainly, I was G's partner in raising our children. But now that they had all manifested—all at once seemingly—they must come under his influence much more than mine.

I realized with mind-numbing shock, they were no longer my babies. They'd grown beyond needing their mother as the center of their universe. Right now, they needed to send out feelers into the big, bad, real world, and G was the one to help them master their talents. They needed to use them for good and be useful. *And* they need to keep their talents hidden for the good of the normal world.

G had probably known this moment would come when he married me, a normal person. I'd fallen madly in love with him the moment I'd met him. But had I truly been in love, or had he manipulated me because he needed someone to raise his toddler son after his first wife died in childbirth?

That day was deeply ingrained in my mind. Toward the end of summer just before my senior year at U of O. I was working as a barista at a coffee shop frequented by students and business people alike. Gayla managed the place but didn't own it. Maybe Coyote Blood Moon had owned that shop, too. He seemed to own most of this neighborhood. But not my building. Gayla and I had purchased our shop—along with a hefty mortgage, which

G helped negotiate. He got the percentage down to affordable levels. When Shara entered first grade and didn't need me home all day, we'd pooled our combined savings. Renting was the usual option, especially for first-time business owners. But since the place had the right feel, and the elderly owner of the building wanted to sell off the entire block piecemeal to make it harder for developers to move in, we purchased one sixth of the building. Gayla lived above the shop.

But before that, while still in school, I'd been working the noon-to-closing shift, trying to make and save as much money as possible for room and board. My parents helped with tuition and books, but they'd only pay for a heavily supervised dorm room, nothing coed, not the tiny space off campus I craved. They expected me to get my teaching certificate and then go home to Seattle to live with them and teach locally. They'd already selected a member of Dad's church as my future husband. As far as they were concerned, I had no choice.

I had news for them. I had no intention of returning to rain-drenched Seattle.

And then that day in late August, I was getting a head start on the final cleanup before I flipped the Open sign to Closed. A man about ten years older than me slid into the shop at almost the last possible moment. He wore a freshly pressed, light gray suit with a discreet blue-and-silver tie. He smelled of soap and aftershave, like he was going out for the evening. I looked up into his fabulous blue eyes and knew that he wanted an extra tall skinny vanilla latte, extra foam. I started fixing it before he asked. Words failed me as I handed him the cup with its cardboard heat sleeve.

"You are the most beautiful woman I've seen all week, and you made the latte perfectly," he said, looking at me and only me rather than his drink.

"Thank you."

"What do I owe you?" He slid one hand into his inside jacket pocket for his wallet.

"N . . . nothing. It's the last of the grounds for the day. I'd just have to throw them out if you hadn't needed them."

"Then I must thank you. I haven't been into this shop before. Do you work every day?" He smiled. After just one smile I knew I'd have come into the shop to work at any time, without pay, to serve him. "I'm G, by the way." He offered to shake my hand.

I took it as I cocked my head in question.

"I have a longer and more pretentious name. Everyone just calls me G."

"I'm Daffy. I, too, have a longer, lyrical name that isn't me."

We laughed at that. Then I rattled off my complicated schedule.

"I'll see you tomorrow at noon, just before you leave for the day. I presume you have appointments to register for classes in the afternoon?"

"Yes."

"Then perhaps you will allow me to escort you to campus, perhaps buy you lunch."

A week later I moved in with him. We celebrated his son's first birthday together. Three weeks after that, he left town for ten days—his first business trip for his new position with his company. The pattern held for the next fourteen years.

# Eleven

**"I** SEE YOU HAVE redecorated again. I like the flour-and-sugar flocking on the wallpaper," G said. He'd come in through the alley door to Magical Brews. Unusual. He normally disdained the alley because of the dumpsters and the haven for the homeless. Only one tattered gentleman, as slow of mind as of limping gait currently claimed our overhang as his camp.

"Oh," I said, awakening from my trance of pounding batters and doughs with my wooden spoon. The much-abused pastry would become offerings for our homeless man—and whoever else stopped by to share with him— Old Raphe had camped out in the alley during the mild weather of summer. Come winter, with the usual onslaught of rain and wind and sometimes snow, we'd have to move him to something better than seeking the relative warmth of the nooks and crannies between the dumpster and the brick walls. The imperfect dough I'd nearly beaten to death would be tasty enough but not the perfect texture for our paying customers who'd come to expect nothing less than perfection from my kitchen.

"I guess I've made more of a mess than usual."

"The kids have eaten and cleaned the kitchen at home. I set them all lessons with their new wands, so they will be happily occupied for a while. You may have trouble getting them into bed they are so happy," G said, inspecting my kitchen. "But not a lot of trouble. Magic drains people of energy. They'll sleep well and long once they do get into bed."

"Thank you. I think I'm done here, so I'll just clean up and go home." I ducked my head to avoid looking at him while I gathered the flattened dough into a giant crockery bowl and covered it with a linen towel. Finding the perfect spot to let the dough rest and rise overnight occupied a few more minutes. My rising oven—a brick cubby kept warm by hot air passing over the building's boiler—was already full.

Why was I so uncomfortable with the man I'd lived with for fourteen years?

Because he was being helpful and nice and represented warmth and safety and our divorce would be final in a matter of weeks. I didn't want him to be nice and helpful when he'd rarely been before. It was like I'd done the job he'd hired me for—raising his children to the point where he could take over their education—and then fired me. Because I was no longer useful. Or sexy. Or arm candy for him to parade before his business associates—were the infrequent cocktail parties really computer business people, or high-powered wizards? And he lied to me. Frequently. And not just about the magic. About where he traveled and when he'd be back and how to get hold of him in an emergency. I could not believe anymore that he truly loved me.

Strengthened by my anger, I finally turned and faced him. "Thank you for dealing with the children and checking in with me. I'll just finish up here and go home."

Clearly dismissed, he turned toward the front of the shop, obviously so he wouldn't have to brave the gauntlet of bad smells and bad-smelling individuals in the alley. He stopped at the swinging door between the kitchen and the front. "Have you eaten anything since your chicken strips and fries at noon?"

I looked up at the clock above the ovens. After eight. Oops.

"How about I get a pizza and bring it back here? I didn't get much of your leftovers. Jason ate almost everything in the refrigerator."

We shared a smile at the boy's appetite and his growth spurt. I hoped G had bought socks for him at the mall. They were on his list.

"That would be okay," I replied. I did need to eat and the kitchen would require more than a few minutes to clean, not at all my usual orderly style of baking. And I wanted to check again for signs of a grease leak beneath the burners.

I set to work. Fortunately, the dry stuff came off the walls and counters quite easily. Then it was a matter of sweeping it up and mopping the floor and the counters and wiping down the walls with a clean sponge on a long handle. The mild bleach solution should take care of any lingering nastiness and break up any remaining grease.

Before I knew it, G had returned with the fragrant decadence of cheese and sauce and pepperoni, with lots of veggies on a thick crust. He'd bought a large pie and a bottle of wine. Looks like Jason would have a substantial bedtime snack with the leftovers and I'd have the soft mellowing effect from the wine.

If G thought he could work his wicked wiles on me, at least the wine and pizza were natural and not magical.

We sat at one of the little round tables by the display window. Before I took my chair, I made sure the front door was locked, the blinds pulled, and the closed sign firmly in place. Many times in the past, I'd had people expecting service if they noticed any lights on or someone moving about inside. Closed signs didn't mean anything to coffee-and-sugar addicts.

Companionable silence enveloped us as I munched through my usual quota of two slices. I was contemplating a third when G spoke.

"I have to go away for a while. A flare-up at work."

"Where to this time?" I asked. My curiosity wanted details. Of his work, not the aftermath. I didn't need to know about the bimbos he found when the work was done.

"I start in Marseilles. I don't know how long I'll be gone."

"A big case, then."

"Unfortunately."

In my imagination, the number of bimbos doubled. I put down that third slice I no longer wanted. "Have fun," I said with more than a bit of contempt.

G didn't need to read my mind to know where my thoughts led me. He reached over and rested his big hand atop mine. I looked small and frail in comparison to his strength.

"It's not always like that, Daffy."

"Like what?" I fixed him with a determined glare.

"Look, I have, upon occasion found release with another woman when I was far away from you and the amount of magic I had to cast in order to close a case was too much to contain. Not often. Not habitually. There is always a woman of age I can pick up in a bar who is very willing to share a one-night stand. And I always use a condom."

He paused long enough to chew a bite of pizza and swallow it. "Normally, I hop the first flight home and return to you, my love."

"But last spring you flaunted your wanderings in front of half the gossips in town. Like you wanted me to find out and force me to divorce you. Well, look. You succeeded." I slammed my chair back and returned to the kitchen, unable to face him anymore.

"And what about the kids? Are they going to be bed-hopping after every practice session? Shara is only *ten!*"

"No. They will be too tired. They won't have the energy to even think about sex until a long time after they gain control of their talents."

Why was I not relieved?

"Will you consider the fact that I need to put distance between us to protect you!" He breathed deeply until he was calm. "Keep a close eye on the kids. They shouldn't be out on their own much this early in their training. New situations and people could trigger impressions and decisions that are out of character and they'll have no control yet. You might think them insane until an expert talks them through the situation. I'll call when I get back. I've left you a satellite phone with my number. It should reach me anywhere, though I may have to call you back if I'm in the middle of something important." The front door slammed with a rattle of glass and shades. He took the remaining pizza and the wine with him.

As I walked home, darkness had fallen, but the road and the streetlights were familiar. We lived in a low-crime neighborhood. I had no fear.

At first.

Two blocks from the shop I heard footsteps behind me. I thought it might be the remnants of the street party breaking up and heading toward their own homes in the neighborhood.

Another three blocks and the footsteps persisted. A shiver of apprehension climbed my spine. I increased my pace.

So did the anonymous footsteps.

At the next streetlight, I looked behind me as I crossed the street. A blur of movement into the shadows. No one visible.

I kept walking, moving a bit faster as I opened my phone. My finger hovered over the emergency icon.

The footsteps continued at the same distance and did not get closer.

As I turned down my driveway, a shadowy figure continued on toward the next-door neighbors' house and beyond.

I breathed a sigh of relief and unlocked the back door.

The smell of smoke greeted me. Faint but distinctive. The fire alarm remained silent. Before I could shout for the kids, the smoke was gone, leaving no trace of its presence. Except in my memory.

# Twelve

"I NEED TO REVIEW the evidence of any previous investigation into this matter," G stated firmly to the seven elderly and crusty men lounging around the club room, deep inside an ancient ruined castle. Of course, it only looked ruined. The illusion of a boring pile of rocks that had nothing left to disclose discouraged even the most ardent historian, archeologist, and paranormal investigator.

The Languedoc region in the foothills of the French Pyrenees was the perfect location for Guild Headquarters. The landscape was littered with ancient fortresses left over from the turbulent Middle Ages when life was uncertain at the best of times and everyone trained for war as a profession.

"Any investigation will be impossible," replied Sergei Bolovnovich. Fifteen years ago the bespectacled Ukrainian wrestler had held G's position as Sheriff for the Guild of Master Wizards. He'd handpicked G as his successor. And trained him meticulously from the first day of recruitment as a deputy.

Everyone agreed this was a natural choice since G's parents had been roving field agents for Bolovnovich. They'd been on assignment in South Africa when they were executed by government forces.

"Why is it impossible?" G demanded, barely in control of his temper. With flight delays and rental car snafus, getting to Marseilles and then here on a barely accessible crag overhanging the Mediterranean, he'd run out of patience hours ago.

"An escape from our dungeon is unprecedented," Bolovnovich replied. He spoke German these days, without a trace of his Slavic origins. He'd never spoken English or French well. The rest of the board spoke whatever language they chose. And they all understood each other. Fluency in multiple languages was a prerequisite for officials of the Guild.

"I know how hard it is to escape our dungeons. I helped design the magical wards as well as the impenetrable locks. That is why I must review the evidence now that I am aware of the criminal's goals and plans. I know the how; she had help. Expensive help. I need to know the why and the who."

The seven men stirred uncomfortably, turning their attention to their cigars and brandies.

"We have erased all record of the prisoner's existence as well as her capture, trial, and incarceration rituals," Bolovnovich muttered, staring into his half-empty snifter. He'd been delegated spokesman even though he disagreed. As a former sheriff, he looked embarrassed. Good law officers never erased evidence files. You never knew when a closed case would come back and bite you in the ass.

"But you did not erase *her*! She's still out there, murdering members of our community. Absorbing power from their wands. She is more dangerous than ever. Deep anger at us now fuels her rampage and her insanity," G protested. "And whoever helped her escape is also running free, planning more murders, more wand stripping. We can't afford to allow this to continue. Our numbers are few enough as it is. And she is coming closer every day to revealing her powers to the entire world. Her sociopathic behavior endangers us all!"

"You don't understand . . ." Pickering, the oldest of the lot, said in his hesitant and rusty English voice. "Our Guild cannot afford the humiliation of this news getting out. It will weaken the structure of the community that has protected our kind for centuries." He sounded as if he'd been part of the first Board over a thousand years ago when the Catholic Church had come down hard on magical practitioners. The Cather heresy had only been one front for the community. Pope Innocent III's Crusaders had thought they wiped them out along with their strongholds. Conveniently, they left a number of ruined castles for the Guild to restore and obscure those restorations.

"And how strong will you be when two rogue magicians have murdered us all in our beds?" G demanded. His voice rose in pitch similar to Shara's steam whistle. He hated when he lost control. But that might be the only thing capable of penetrating his employers' foggy brains.

The seven men squirmed some more. G stomped out of the exclusive room and their rarified presence. Bolovnovich tried to stop him with a hand to his arm.

G shook him off as soon as he felt the tiny weight of a thumb drive drop into his coat pocket.

He stomped down the winding stone staircase, making as much noise as possible so his bosses could follow his path in their minds. Maybe he could get a sense of the sequence of actions lingering in the stones of the dungeon cell and the guardroom. Maybe he should have brought Belle and let her charm cooperation from the Board. Shara could help him figure out who picked the locks and how. Jason could jump up and inspect scenes from above for traces of footprints, or disturbed dirt and stones.

He missed them all terribly.

Daffy's calm good sense most of all.

In the movies, magic spells are accompanied by pretty sparkles and dynamic music.

In reality, magic spells are accompanied by small fires,

overturned furniture, and breaking glass. Lots of breaking glass, especially mirrors.

And constant refrains of "Alakazam, Magic Slam."

I learned to hate that song.

A loud thump. My balance teetered as the floor tilted. I had to grab hold of the kitchen table as I set out sandwich makings. The entire house shook and windows rattled.

"Jason!" I screamed.

"Sorry, Mom," he called down the kitchen stairwell.

I steadied my balance, took a deep breath. And then another. This had been going on for a week. And G was nowhere in sight to help. I had to handle this on my own.

By the time I had enough starch in me to march upstairs, Jason clattered down them. For a ballet dancer dedicated to landing a four-foot-high jump with as little noise as possible, he could certainly make a heck of a lot of it in bare feet when he wasn't on stage. Right. The stairs were carpeted, he wasn't in direct contact with wood when he planted each big foot.

"What fell over?" I asked.

"You know that big, heavy wardrobe thingy that was Dad's grandmother's?" He stopped on the first stair, making him taller than me. A position of power.

I knew the wardrobe well. I'd loved it when I first moved in with G. But it wasn't large enough to hold both my jeans and his suits. So, as soon as we converted the nursery to a bigger closet and a suitable bath (shower stall big enough for two but no tub), the magnificent piece of furniture with inlays of blond wood against the dark cherry, and artistic scrollwork around the edges had been banished to the attic.

We'd added that bathroom about the time I got pregnant with Belle and morning sickness made the trek down the hall to the only other bath on that floor problematic.

"How many pieces is the wardrobe in?" I wanted to

bang my head against the old-fashioned white cupboards with glass fronts. Instead, I grabbed the wooden spoon in my back pocket and thought about the chemistry of baking powder versus baking soda combined with cream of tartar.

G had exacted a promise from Jason that he couldn't sell, donate, or trash anything in the attic until he got home and could make decisions on family treasures. The wardrobe was one of those treasures.

"It's still in one piece. Except . . ."

"Except what?" I demanded, patience exhausted.

"Except maybe the mirror inside the left-hand door." He sounded mighty casual about that.

"Isn't breaking a mirror supposed to be seven years' bad luck?"

"Nah. Dad told Belle not to worry about that when she dropped a magnifying hand mirror. Someone invented that old superstition because wizards frequently break mirrors to close a spell. And being caught being a wizard during the Burning Times was bad luck. So breaking a mirror was a sign of being a wizard and you got hauled off to jail."

That was news to me and omitted from every history book as well as the ones about mythology and superstition. Clearly, I needed to read more on this. Did Coyote Blood Moon have a book in stock?

"Why did you push over the wardrobe? It weighs a ton and took your dad and two other men to move it up into the attic."

"I think I sorta remember that and wondering if it was a portal to another realm like *The Lion, the Witch and the Wardrobe.*"

He would have been two and a half or three at the time. I'd been reading to him since the day I moved in with his father.

"Answer my question." He was getting as good as his father at diverting conversations.

"I needed more room to practice." He turned to bounce up the stairs, probably with as much or more noise as when he descended. "Um . . . I thought real hard about where I wanted it and then I pushed, and I guess I thought a bit too hard 'cause it slid across the floor real fast and hit some trunks and a dressing table, then tumbled forward." He had the grace to redden and look abashed.

Then he brightened and his eyes widened. "Does that mean I'm really telekinetic? Dad said he thought that was the source of my power jumps."

"Wouldn't surprise me." Nothing would surprise me anymore. "Well, get it upright the same way you shoved it. After lunch, we'll see about moving it to my sewing room. I can at least make use of it." I thought about calling Coyote Blood Moon and Ted Tyler. While neither was as big nor as strong as G, with Jason's help they'd probably manage it.

And I'd like to see both men again. But not necessarily at the same time.

"I won't need help," Jason replied blithely. "I'm telekinetic, remember?"

"Don't push it. Remember what your dad said about new power driving people insane. And headaches." Or did the headaches lead to insanity? I couldn't remember. "You already get migraines during allergy season and when you have to study for a math test. We'll get you help, and you will accept that help graciously."

"Sure. Whatever." He caught sight of the plate piled high with sliced ham and cheese. He smiled and moved farther into the kitchen, relinquishing the position of power that was really only an illusion. For about five minutes I still had the authority of *mother*. And he knew who prepared the food in the house.

Training a teenager is a lot like training a dog. Speak their name very clearly to get their attention. Give them one specific chore, and only one at a time. Reward with food.

Belle came in through the mudroom, muttering the

words to that damnable song. She carried two fists full of dry sticks and leaves with bits of torn cloth in the mix. It looked like the makings of a bird nest without the coherence of a bird's instinctive weaving.

"Belle, what is that?"

She placed her treasures neatly into the big porcelain sink. "Dad said that my talent was like attracting a moth to a flame. Dangerous but irresistible, so I need to learn to control both the flame and the dousing of it." She sang two notes and smoke wafted upward.

The fire alarm screeched. Jason grabbed a towel and waved it in front of the device to dissipate the smoke and silence the ear-splitting life-saving noise.

"NO! Not in my sink." I turned the water on, dousing the mess before it scorched anything. Actually, since it was almost a magical fire, I believe "scortched" was the proper spelling.

"But, Mom, it's the only safe place to start a fire, and there's water close by to douse it if I need to."

"There is a perfectly serviceable *brick* barbecue/fireplace in the backyard. The one with the tall chimney, the grill, and the spigot." I think it might have started life as the chimney for a log cabin long before the house was built.

I had to hold on to my wooden spoon so tightly I thought I'd break the handle. But my balance steadied.

"Go find Shara and bring her to the lunch table."

"She's probably in the basement, trying to hack into Dad's old computer," Jason said, aiming for the steps beside the set that led upstairs.

All the heat drained from my face. The spoon wasn't enough to contain my reeling head. I needed the stove, which, thankfully, was cold.

"That's okay, Mom. Dad said she could," Belle reassured me. "He said that if she could get past his passwords and firewall, he'd see about getting her into the computer programming club Mr. Coyote Blood Moon is running for teens after school."

I sat down hard on the floor. My world had spun out of my control.

It was Saturday on a holiday weekend. I had no excuse to run down to Magical Brews—we were closed Saturday and Sunday—and bake up a storm of stress relief.

So I set about making a cake for anyone who stopped by to help move the massive wardrobe.

# Thirteen

"**HOW IN HELL DID** you get this thing up here?"
Ted Tyler asked, standing with hands on hips, after he finished measuring the wardrobe and the stairwell.

Jason had already cleaned up the glass—under my careful scrutiny—and I was still trying to decide if I needed to replace the mirror or not.

"I don't know how it got moved." Back then, I'd been too busy throwing up with morning sickness that lasted all day. "My ex called two friends and they wrestled and wiggled it up here about thirteen years ago and it hasn't moved since," I explained.

"I was one of those two friends," John, or rather Coyote Blood Moon, said. He wore jeans and a pocket T-shirt today, very much the real estate agent on his day off.

"Hey, BJ didn't have anything better to do, so I asked him to help," Jason said, stomping upward. He stretched out his arms within the stairwell to define the width of the space. He nodded as if he'd figured out that the wardrobe would fit.

"It's going to be tight, but . . . Daffy do you have some blankets we can wrap around it just in case we scrape the sides?" Ted asked shifting his dolly along one end of the wardrobe.

"Coming right up," I replied, digging through a cedar dowry chest full of surplus linens I didn't want filling the linen closet. All I could find were some king-sized flannel sheets. I threw them toward John.

"I'll get some twine," Jason said, "To tie around the sheets and keep them from slipping." He and BJ disappeared down the stairs.

I heard them all the way to the kitchen, laughing and clomping, competing to see who could make the most noise. Like two puppies wrestling for domination. Just like old times.

While we waited for them to return, Ted positioned the dolly while John and I shifted the wardrobe just enough to let him slip the device lip under one end. That little bit of movement revealed a band of different colored wood in the floor, inlaid rather than painted on or resting atop the floorboards.

Curious, I traced the stripe away from the wardrobe and lost track of it beneath an old three-mirrored dressing table. On the other side, it veered off at a sharp angle to disappear beneath a bunch of stacked boxes. Neatly stacked with G's kind of precision and order, a block of three across and three up, all the same size, not a millimeter out of alignment. Belle would approve.

John shrugged his shoulders like he didn't know what, if anything, that stripe was.

But he'd been up here years ago. He should have noticed it when he helped move the wardrobe in place. Unless he'd had his back to it until the wardrobe sat atop it.

I wondered in that moment if G had maneuvered the huge piece of furniture into place, at an oblique angle to the stacks of boxes. Obscuring the nature of the inlay.

When the boys returned with twine and we'd draped the sheets to best protect the lovely wood, then tied them in place, the four males positioned themselves to pull, balance, and push. Jason put both hands flat against the piece at the head, while John took up a position behind Ted who managed the dolly. And BJ didn't do much other than hold up a trailing corner of the flannel sheet. A year ago, he'd have been in the thick of the project, directing the adults. He wasn't always right, but he pretended to be in charge, just like his father. For him to stand aside and look bored was new.

Belle said he was hanging around with new friends—bullies. I wondered if I should "chat" with his mother about other personality changes. School health classes drilled this into students, to look for signs of drug use and intervene before it was too late.

I grabbed a broom from the corner where Jason had stashed it during his cleaning blitz.

The attic was not as filthy as I expected. The aftermath of my son's ministrations or something else? He'd had an allergy attack and migraine the first day he was up here, but tried to hide it from me. So the dust had been thick at one point.

I winced with every bump and creak. G would... what would he do? I realized I'd never seen him angry or out of control. In all our years together, the only fight we'd had was the night of our anniversary, the night I asked for a divorce. Any other time we'd disagreed, we'd talked it out logically and calmly. Then fell into bed for truly great make-up sex.

And he always won every argument through logic. Or lies and manipulation. But the sex was still great.

If we damaged a valuable antique from his family, what would he do?

Probably just repair the piece with magic and compel me not to move anything else in the house, ever again.

I spun around and plotted how to get that beautiful dressing table into Belle's room. She was old enough now to appreciate an adult piece of furniture and to use it to apply makeup (only a pale lipstick for now) and dress her hair with her ivory hair sticks. The three mirrors would give her a better view of the sides as well as the front.

Shara had long envied her sister's white painted, small chest of drawers with the purple unicorn and pink flower stickers. Her own small and ordinary unfinished chest of drawers was cheap and had started to fall apart.

Yes, the time had come to shift many things in our lives.

I lowered the broom to remove any lingering dust and stopped short. Moving the wardrobe had revealed a pointed angle that looked tantalizingly familiar. I shoved the dressing table into position to take it downstairs. Another angle. Back into the shadows toward the eaves, a third angle.

My heart thundered in my ears. I reached for the wooden spoon in my back pocket to ground myself. It wasn't there. Panic galloped through my veins. The broom handle had to suit. I clenched it with both hands, closed my eyes, and did my best to control my breathing.

"That's it. Breathe in. Breathe out," John whispered from right beside me. "Let the air fill your being. Draw light in and exhale the darkness of your fears."

I obeyed, as his words compelled me until my body accepted the pentagram on the floor as a natural part of the house.

He handed me the spoon. It had apparently fallen out of my pocket while shifting stuff. "G's great-grandparents included the pentagram as protection in the original design of the much smaller house. This place is a safe haven for all of our kind. But if a mundane sees it and suspects, the hatred and fear of those who do not understand us, those who refuse our help because they cannot conceive of it coming from their God, will bring fire and destruction down upon us all. Fire is the only way to destroy the protective wards."

"Understood. I'll keep Ted and BJ in the kitchen while you and Jason move the dressing table down to Belle's room. I think the mirrors come off for safe transport." Tonight, I'd change the batteries in the smoke alarms, just to be sure.

I headed for the stairs, dropping the broom with a loud clatter. "Join us for cake and coffee in a few moments. Please."

"Certainly. Jason could probably move this himself.

He took most of the weight of the wardrobe with his telekinesis. He didn't need me at all other than to steady and ground him."

"He's that strong?"

"Youthfully so. That will sap some of his strength and befuddle his mind. But he needs to learn better control. In the meantime, I suggest you find some cork as an insole for his shoes."

"Cork?"

"It's made from tree bark."

"Of course. Wood next to his feet instead of rubber and linoleum. I see a trip to the craft store in my very near future."

I walked down the stairs with plans and visions, and a lot less fear. Coyote Blood Moon was good for me.

"You know, the insulation up in the attic is intact. Not as efficient as modern bats or spray foam, but still adequate. Finishing the walls and ceiling and adding a half bath up there wouldn't cost much. Actually, I could easily run the plumbing up for a full bath and the wiring for a kitchenette. Then you'd have an apartment you could rent to college kids. Is there a separate entrance?" Ted asked while toying with the last crumbs of the Boston cream pie I'd made for my work crew. He mashed bits of cake, custard, and dark chocolate frosting together with his fork, making sure he didn't miss a molecule of the desert.

"Um." I looked to John for confirmation that we didn't want anyone outside the community up there. "There used to be an outside staircase from the garage area. But it fell apart about the time I moved in here. G removed it and barricaded the door inside and out with plywood. Last time we painted, the coverings just sort of blended in like a part of the siding."

John gave me a brief nod.

We sat in the breakfast nook while Jason and BJ had taken their cake to his room, as they'd been doing since they were in first and second grade—old enough to hold a plate steady while climbing the stairs. Belle and Shara were in the greenhouse with their desserts, sitting on the little white wrought-iron filigree chairs with a matching table, pretending to take tea in the conservatory.

"I think remodeling anything is a bit outside my budget at the moment," I demurred.

"When you do decide to remodel," John said, "I can recommend Ted and his crew. He's brought a number of properties I've handled up to code and modern concepts."

I gathered that John and G would do *something* to the pentagram to make it invisible. When G got home. If G came home.

I'd had three texts from him in the last week— something unheard of—all cautionary. All warning me to keep the kids close and not let them roam as they were used to. Eugene still had many characteristics of a small town, low crime rate and people watching out for each other and monitoring where and when every child was spotted.

But that changed every time the university football team had a winning season, or the U hosted Olympic trials, and more and more outsiders came to town.

The texts had tracked G from Marseilles to Florence, and yesterday to Bruges.

"We'll see about updating the space later. Right now, I promised Jason the attic as a dance studio. It's not far from the bottom of the stairs to the main bath. He'll make do."

"Okay." Ted smiled at me with enough concentration that I suspected he might be offering to do the job just to spend more time with me.

Warmth invaded my tight and chilling tummy. More time with Ted was something I wouldn't mind. For now, however, I needed to remember that G's job was to keep magic invisible, real magic and not the pagan attempts at parlor tricks by nontalented people.

A horn beeped outside.

"That's Tiffany," Ted said, rising from the bench seat. "My truck had a flat tire this morning, so she dropped me off here before running her own errands. That dang truck is starting to nickel-and-dime me to death. And it's only fifteen years old with two hundred fifty thousand miles on it."

John smiled behind his hand. A vehicle that old and well-used sounded like a candidate for the junkyard to me.

"Please take a piece of cake to Tiffany. There's one left, and if you don't take it, Jason will eat it and not even taste it." I quickly put the little slice on a paper plate and wrapped it in plastic.

"Thanks, anyway, but I doubt she'll eat it. My girl is dedicated to getting maximum nutrition from every low-calorie bite she takes. She's a dancer first and foremost."

"Then you eat it." From the way he'd savored every mouthful of his own portion, I guessed he didn't get desserts at home very often.

"I'll do that. Thank you." He leaned over as if to kiss my cheek.

John cleared his throat, a reminder that we were not alone.

Ted backed off. "Let me know if Jason needs help refinishing the floor. I've got an upright sander and can recommend varnishes." Then he vanished out the back door to the drive that ran alongside the house toward the detached garage.

When I'd heard the car back out and drive off, I lifted the coffeepot toward John. "One last cup?"

"Thanks anyway. I've had my caffeine limit for the day." He stood, but made no move to leave.

"John . . . will you speak to Jason, let him know that outsiders aren't allowed in the attic for a while? He'll probably listen to you in the absence of his father, where I'm just the usual nagging voice reminding him to clean his room."

"Good idea. If you don't mind, I'll go upstairs now and speak to him."

"He's with BJ."

"No, I saw BJ sneak down the front stairs and out that door when I used the restroom."

"Oh. I wonder . . ." BJ always said good-bye when he left. Always.

"He's a teenager. Pushing the limits of bad behavior and defying adult authority is part of his job."

John kissed my cheek and wandered up the kitchen stairs.

Before I could decide what to do about that, my cell phone buzzed an incoming text.

Bruges a dead end. Headed for Tallahassee. If you need anything, ask CBM. Luv you, G

CBM? Coyote Blood Moon. Or John, as I'd come to think of him. I knew that a lot of the pagan shop owners in town legally changed to a craft name, something that reflected their new belief system when they converted to a pagan lifestyle. John, of course, had to have a professional name to go along with his real estate business, so he used both depending upon his associates and the situation.

He'd remain John to me. John what?

Before he returned, I flipped through the phonebook—yes, I still kept a paper one in the drawer beside the landline. John Mooney Real Estate.

Logical.

John Mooney blew me a kiss as he crossed the kitchen to the back door. "See you around."

I captured the kiss with my hand symbolically, then closed my fingers. I did not place it on my lips or even my cheek. I just held it, like a promise of . . . something in the future.

Two seconds later the landline rang. The shrill bells startled me. Not many had that unlisted number.

I didn't have to look at the caller ID to know the call came from BJ's mother, Flora Chambers, or Mrs. Chambers as she preferred, as if her marriage to Bret Chambers the lawyer, was more important than she was as an individual.

"Is BJ over there?" she asked after formally introducing herself.

"Not anymore. He left about half an hour ago. But he was most helpful. I needed some heavy furniture moved."

"Where did he go?" No politeness or formality. Her high-pitched voice (her husband referred to it as whimsical) grew shrill.

"He didn't say." He hadn't even said that he was leaving. Perhaps he felt that if he said nothing he could escape his mother a bit longer.

"Are you lying to me?"

"I resent that, Flora."

"Well, it wouldn't surprise me if you are covering for him, just like you covered for that philandering husband of yours until you couldn't ignore it any longer. And I'll remind you who warned you about him. . . ."

I hung up on her.

The phone rang again. I let it go to voice mail. I had the wardrobe to fill with craft supplies and fabric and such. Much more important than listening to Flora's vitriol.

# Fourteen

G MOPPED SWEAT OFF his forehead and neck with an old-fashioned blue kerchief. His straw Panama hat didn't help much in alleviating the Florida heat. Three weeks from the Equinox and the temperatures were still in the nineties with equal humidity. He'd gotten too used to the moderate climate and four seasons in Eugene.

The climate alone made his hometown the best place in the world to live. The fact that it was a crossroads of magical power, the previous homeland of a couple of fae races, and a magnet for paranormal energies were secondary in his opinion. One of the reasons so many people in his hometown had minor talents was a long-forgotten faery ancestor native to the place.

Tallahassee should be his last stop before heading home. Home to Daffy and his children. When the kids were little, he never quite knew what to do with them, and gladly left their care to Daffy. And he'd enjoyed his adventurous travels, taking down the bad guys. Now his children were older, almost adults. He could talk to them. He missed them. He missed Daffy, too, especially since returning to her was no longer a given. She wouldn't be waiting for him with open arms, a hot meal, and a bed to share.

He sighed and pulled himself out of his reverie. In this heat, all he wanted to do was sleep in an air-conditioned room.

He had a dead body to investigate. D'Accore and her minions—he'd learned that she'd collected several disaffected youths over the past few months—had gotten very good at dumping bodies. No fresh murders and no wands at the crime scene. That forced him to work with mundane authorities and MEs.

And there was the city morgue. A flat-faced building, anonymous stucco with a red roof, windows flush with the exterior flanked by green storm shutters. The entrance was elevated twelve steps from the street, allowing for something resembling a basement with a natural coolness that predated modern AC systems. That was where they stored the unclaimed and open case bodies. According to the police report, Paul Marchand, a young Cajun man who hailed from New Orleans but had recently moved to Tallahassee, had died approximately three weeks before. Not only young, early twenties, but a talented wizard in the making—he had some ancestors among the Merfolk. His talents spread across the board, from protective shields, to love spells, to singing a crowd from chaos to peace. He was on the watch list to recruit as a deputy for the Sheriff's office. A fisherman had discovered his body two days ago, floating in the bay, trapped in an old net.

G had papers identifying him as the man's uncle come to claim the body. Few cared about skin color anymore, especially in Paul's case where his blood had mixed and flowed among several races. He could have uncles from around the world or under the sea.

G stepped up to the uniformed woman at the information desk. "Um . . . I got a call about my nephew. You think maybe he drowned?" Highly unlikely for a man who could hold his breath a full two minutes underwater and had thick webs between his toes.

G had no trouble projecting sadness, grief, and an aching heart as he produced his genuine Oregon driver's license. He really liked Paul, whose bright smile and laughing eyes always found humor in dire circumstances.

He'd made a living as a grief counselor, encouraging people to remember the best about their lost loved ones.

"I am so sorry for your loss, Mr. Deschants. Let me call Detective Billings for you." She sent a text from her computer screen.

He only had to wait long enough to mop more sweat from his face before a tall, bulky man with light chocolate coloring emerged from a door halfway down the long corridor that the reception desk blocked.

"We've identified the body from dental records, sir. You don't have to view it," Billings said as G settled into a comfortable armchair in front of a small black-and-white monitor.

No more did they expect people to walk into a chilly morgue smelling of strange, acidic chemicals that burned the nose but kept the bodies from decaying. No more the shock of watching a tech open a drawer and pulling back the sheet or opening the body bag. Now they sat you in a chair, plied you with bad coffee, and showed you videos of one dead body after another.

"Please, it is important to his family. They practice a religion with roots going back to Africa over one thousand years ago. I wrote my doctoral dissertation in Cultural Anthropology about how ancient customs and rituals still affect our lives based upon this religion. I must see the body and bless it. I must run my hands the full length of the body, not touching it, but drawing out any residual life that may linger before burial. His family believes strongly in ghosts. I must set his ghost free." G gave Billings his best wide-eyed nerd look.

"But you don't believe this...er...religion?" Billings asked. Now he started to sweat, like he'd seen too many weird things in his years on the homicide squad.

"I don't know," G replied. He, too, had seen a lot of things this normal man would call spectral or supernatural. And he knew for certain that ghosts did exist and not all of them were friendly or simply lost souls seeking guidance to the ever after. But ne needed to see the body, touch it, and determine if magic had killed him. A relatively fresh body that hadn't been burned or exposed to hundreds of passersby in a shallow grave.

He needed to find Paul's wand.

Billings shrugged and led G through a twisted corridor and down a flight of steps into the basement. Only one door greeted them at the base of the stairs. MORGUE had been decaled on the pebbly glass upper half of the door.

G braced himself for the shock of the change in temperature and the onslaught of chemicals.

As bad as he expected. Tolerable, or at least it would be shortly when he got used to it. In the meantime, he breathed through his mouth until his nose became desensitized.

He'd done this before. Too many times. And yet it was still always a shock to his body, his mind, and his soul.

They went through another ID check and signatures. Then through more heavy steel doors to the room lined with metal drawers, four up and ten to a side.

G's knees turned to water at the thought of all that death trapped in this room. He wanted to turn and run.

He wanted to vomit.

But he had to see this through.

The tech consulted his tablet screen, double-checked a number, and marched to the proper drawer. He paused a moment, hand on the pull so that G had a moment to settle himself. Then the drawer rolled open a full six feet in length, though Paul didn't need that much space. He'd been short and wiry.

Billings himself pulled open the zipper on the black body bag, revealing the pasty, bloated face. The eyes and nose were gone, sacrificed to some scavenger of the sea. The lips pulled back in rictus revealed stained teeth. That once bright and happy smile turned into this grimace at the moment of death.

"Please, I need to see the entire body," G said, gulping heavily. So young. So happy. Reduced to this.

"It's not pretty, Mr. Deschants. Drowning victims rarely look like the person they were."

"I know." G gulped again. Then he bowed his head and silently mouthed the words of the spell he needed. *A spell is nothing more than a prayer,* he reminded himself, as Billings crossed himself.

By the time he linked his thumbs and placed his hands flat above the face, a scant half inch above the flesh, Billings had pulled the zipper all the way down to the toes, revealing a naked body. The ME had stapled closed the Y-shaped incision for the autopsy. That wouldn't prevent stray magic from returning to the body. Every time he did this, G wondered if the soul escaped during the examination procedure and then returned when the humiliating process of being reduced to a series of numbers was over.

Inch by careful inch, he moved his hands down the body, pausing at each of the chakra points. All the while his fingers tingled and twitched. When he reached the misshapen toes with their vestigial marine adaptation— still bright pink and vibrant—he reversed the process.

"Those webbed toes are unusual," the ME said. "I see them often enough. But most people have the toes separated so the kids can learn to walk normally. Those are much thicker than normal."

"I know." G paused in his spell to breathe and concentrate on a reply. "It runs in his family. Coming from New Orleans, which is below water level, the local joke is that children are born with webbed toes and learn to walk with a flutter kick. Environmental adaptation. They say the same thing about Portland and Seattle."

They all smiled, and G finished his ritual.

"Thank you, gentlemen. I may now make funeral arrangements with the family. I will notify you of the details." G bowed his head to gather himself, clenching his fists so that the information he'd gathered didn't leak out.

Slowly, carefully, he retraced his steps until he emerged from the horrible building into the streets and fresher air.

Not until he'd turned three corners did he hail a cab back to his hotel by the airport.

A quick check of the airlines showed the next flight to Chicago didn't leave until nine that night. He had time. He didn't have Daffy to go home to and needed, oh so badly after that major spell reading a dead man, he needed a woman.

Five o'clock. Happy hour was in full swing in the hotel bar.

Only when he'd sent his companion home with a kiss and no promises and begun packing his few belongings, did he let the knowledge he'd captured from Paul's last memories infiltrate his brain.

And the information Bolovnovich had slipped him on the flash drive. Financial records that showed a key player amassing a great deal of money in shadow accounts. That had been going on for fifteen years, starting the day after G had arrested D'Accore for murdering his grandparents.

D'Accore and her faithful companion had spoken as they stripped a conch shell of Paul's magic. That was the final bit G needed to know, but not concrete evidence to put them both away. They needed to go to Chicago to find a young and pretty virginal witch with a talent for pushing people aside to make her way through a crowd, or to the top of a beauty queen pageant.

Paul's conch shell wand had been left in the warm waters of the bay. It would return to nature on its own, useless to the pair of murdering sorcerers.

The image of D'Accore's companion was burned firmly into G's mind's eye.

Coyote Blood Moon.

# Fifteen

I SENT THE KIDS off to school on Wednesday morning. The beginning of a new school year meant new classes, new challenges, and a whole new schedule for all of us. When the last school bus had roared down the hill, I sat back in my favorite chair in the living room and contemplated what to do next. I still had some time before I needed to return to Magical Brews for the afternoon round of baking and dispensing perfect cups of espresso, lattes, mochas, or just plain coffee to regular customers, like John Mooney aka Coyote Blood Moon. Well, John was a regular when he was in town. I remember lapses in his attendance for about four consecutive days every three weeks or so. Business. He was a power broker in the real estate world.

He stopped in at the shop every day lately. Twice. Once when we first opened, and again after lunch, close to the end of my shift. More often than not, he walked me home. He kept a wary eye on everyone we passed and turned around frequently as if he heard someone following us. But I had no repeat of my one scary experience.

Every day John asked about Jason's progress with his new studio and if I'd heard from G.

Truthfully, I could tell him that G never called when away on business. He had texted me, but that wasn't a call, merely notification of change of location. Actually, the texts were new, and so was his sign-off. "Luv U" had so many meanings I chose not to interpret.

I wasn't sure why I kept his destinations to myself. From Tallahassee, he'd gone to Chicago.

The phone beeped an incoming text as I sat back in the recliner with my feet up.

Home late tonight. Don't wait up. Keep the children close.
Luv U. G

In other words, he didn't need a ride home from the airport and he feared something. Something about the children.

I sent him a text on a whim.

Found 5 points in attic.

The phone rang. An actual call, not another text.

"Yes, G."

"What happened?" he demanded, sounding anxious. "I don't have a lot of time, so just say it."

"Jason moved the wardrobe. It fell and broke one of the mirrors. He wanted it out of the attic for more room to dance. CBM and Ted Tyler helped move it down to my sewing room. I discovered the inlay in the flooring."

"Did anyone else see it?"

"Just CBM and Jason and me. Jason has orders not to let anyone else up there."

"Make him obey. I'll take care of it tomorrow. Gotta go." He hung up. No good-bye, no endearments.

I exhaled so long, my lungs felt like collapsing. For three months, I'd skirted around thinking about the future of my relationship with G. I'd ridden my anger and hurt for so long, it was all I needed to justify the divorce. But the legal end of my marriage was coming up soon. One week before the point of no return.

The landline beside my chair rang before I could

think further. I picked it up expecting a robocall advising me that my credit rating needed attention.

"Daffy, I saw your two girls on the school bus this morning when it passed my house. They looked so cute in their new outfits. Skirts are so much more appropriate for girls than jeans. I know the temptation of going casual . . ."

"Did you have a reason to call, Mrs. Chambers? Because I really don't have time to just chat right now." I should. But I wasn't ready to discuss second-hand gossip about her son.

"Oh, I know, you being sole support of those three precious children and all. I just called to ask if you'd seen the news last night."

"I don't think so. I took the children to a movie."

"Not one of those horrid thrillers with death and sex, and bad language and all."

"No. It was a safe movie." Actually, it was the latest action-filled science fiction flick, and we'd all enjoyed it enormously. But I was pretty sure she'd disapprove of speculative fiction as much as nudity and long strings of four letter words.

"Oh, that's good. Family time and all."

"What was so interesting on the news?"

"Mr. Chambers has decided to run for state representative, on a conservative platform, of course. I presume we can count on your vote in the primary."

"I don't know who else might be running. I need to be fair and evaluate each of them."

"But no one is more qualified than my husband!"

"Probably so. But as a concerned citizen I have to look at every candidate equally."

"Oh, yes. There is that. I'll let you go now. But may we put a campaign sign in your yard? The whole town needs to look unified. Having other campaign signs around will look messy."

"Good-bye, Mrs. Chambers."

"About the sign?"

"Good-bye."

I'd barely hung up when the front door reverberated from the force of someone pounding on it. I sped over to it and yanked it open. I know, I know, I should use the peephole. But this sounded too urgent.

BJ stood in front of me, clutching several rectangles of fiberboard stuck to garden stakes. "Please, Ms. D., can you get rid of these for me?" he asked thrusting the signs at me. "Mother wanted me to put them in the front yards of the entire neighborhood, without asking people. That . . . that's littering or something and I won't do it. Anyway, could you burn them? I'm going to be late for school."

He dashed out the driveway with an easy lope to the sensible compact car his folks had given him for his sixteenth birthday.

I looked at the topmost sign. "Bret Chambers for State Representative. Returning Oregon to a Godly course in politics."

I had just the place for these. I took them out back to the brick grill shaped like an old log cabin chimney, and thrust them into the hearth. A single match set them to burning merrily.

Strange. I thought they would need several matches and maybe some dry grass for kindling.

Whatever. Flames shot high with a whoosh, forcing me to step away. The smoke smelled rancid, like the stray whiffs I'd been catching about town lately.

I shouldn't leave anything that volatile. So I fixed a glass of iced tea, crushing some fresh blackberries from the back fence into the liquid, all the while watching the fire out the kitchen window. Then I settled into a garden chair with the book about the mystical properties of jade while I monitored the fire. "Healing and stability. Lessens anxiety and lightens emotions. . . ."

Ted Tyler took to spending his morning coffee break at Magical Brews. He showed up about ten, when I returned from getting the children off to school.

"You're needed out front," Gayla whispered conspiratorially through the swinging door, just as I donned my apron. For once I had a clean, if faded one. Gayla must have done laundry recently. "He's here."

I didn't need to ask. This made three days in a row that Ted had asked for plain black coffee and a cinnamon bun. I met him with a smile.

"Tiffany's feet are much better," he said by way of opening the conversation. "She wants me to ask you for more of the ointment and the soaking stuff."

"Have her stop in when she brings Jason home from rehearsal. Having her drive saves me a lot of time and hassle. Helping ease her dancer's feet is the least I can do for you two." I wanted to give him his drink and pastry for free, but there were enough regulars hanging around I didn't want to set a precedent. Or start more gossip. I had no idea who reported to Mrs. Chambers.

"That will work. And if Jason needs help with finishing the attic floor . . ."

"Thanks anyway, but he promised his father he'd do the work himself. He's already rented a sander and made great progress. But he wants to move more stuff and define square edges before he varnishes. And with school starting, he's not going to have much time until he settles into a routine and figures out which classes require the most study," I demurred. As much as I was coming to like Ted, I didn't know if I could trust him with all this magic business, or any of it. I needed G to come home and do something to obscure that pentagram.

Having listened to one tirade on the part of Bret and Flora Chambers on the evils of witchcraft and why BJ couldn't go with us to watch any of the Harry Potter movies, in the theater or on DVD at home, I was leery of any exposure. Their fundamentalist church had the largest congregation in town.

And G seemed to think the Burning Times might very well descend upon us soon. Sooner than he wanted to think about.

Bret Chambers running for state office brought the possibility even closer.

"Well, then perhaps I should take you out to dinner on Saturday night so Jason has the freedom to work on his private space without his mom watching over his shoulder."

"That would be nice. Rehearsals are done by five."

"I'll pick you up about six. But I will warn you, anytime I can eat without Tiffany's supervision I go for fat, beer, and sugar."

"Pizza at the brew pub?" I laughed. "I'll make sure there's a dessert at home. Provided Jason doesn't find it and devour it in one gulp. I swear that boy grows an inch a week."

This time Ted laughed. "At fifteen, eating and growing is his job."

Other customers shouldered into our conversation, demanding exotic coffee drinks of their own. For some reason, whenever I worked the front counter, customers wanted *me* to fix their brews. Gayla and I used the same ingredients, the same routine, the same machine. And still they swore my lattes and mochas and espressos were better, perfect to their palate.

"I'll restock the cookie case. I don't know what you did to the coconut-chocolate-chunk but they are disappearing faster than usual," Gayla said on her way back to the kitchen.

"I'll take one to go," Ted said, not moving very far away to make room for the others.

I grabbed one with a square of waxed paper and handed it to him. "Get back to work. You need to make money so you can pay for my pizza and beer."

The rest of the day vanished in a whirl of customers and baking. The whole town seemed to drift in and out of the shop. There was an excitement in the air that always accompanied the end of summer laziness and the first day of school. College classes would start soon, too. Then I'd lose my afternoon employees to the university.

"Can you stay an extra hour this afternoon and help train two new kids?" Gayla asked as she straightened from stacking cookies in their case.

"Half an hour. Shara's in middle school this year and gets out of class a little later than the elementary school."

"That will have to do. The afternoon crew are rearranging their classes to have a couple of afternoons off each week. By bringing in two more part-timers, I think we've got the late shift covered. But *you* need to teach them how to use the roaring beast. I can work it, but only you can make it obey." She gestured toward the espresso machine.

It did indeed roar when steaming. And it could be a cranky beast. But it always worked for me.

"Speaking of Shara, her birthday is next week. I will need this kitchen to make cupcakes. Presuming it doesn't rain, she wants a garden party. Ten-year-olds manage cupcakes easier than slices of cake when running around being obnoxious."

The entire crowd giggled at that. Many of them were parents of Shara's classmates and knew what happened when children of that age were turned loose out of doors while on a sugar high.

"Make red velvet cupcakes with cream cheese frosting and send some home to the parents," a woman called from the back of the room.

"I prefer the chocolate, chocolate chip with dark chocolate icing," another said.

"Cinnamon hearts in pink cake with strawberry frosting."

The list of favorite treats went around and around the room, each one more decadent than the last. The cupcakes we had on hand started disappearing from the counter.

I had my work cut out for me. Work I loved, in a community that made me feel at home and welcome. No way would I return to Seattle and my parents' constant disapproval when I had this every day.

I had two new men in my life to flirt with. I smiled at John when he came in for his own coffee and treat at the end of my normal shift. He didn't even object when I sat him at one of the little round tables while I trained two new college students on the arcane ritual of working the espresso machine.

# Sixteen

"**NO**," Jason said into his phone. After ten. He should be sound asleep by now. He needed his rest to cope with school and rehearsals tomorrow. BJ, on the other hand, didn't seem to need sleep at all. Or if he did, he preferred to nod off during his afternoon classes.

"Look, J, I know it's your house and your rules and all, but I really *need* to see that pentagram in your attic," BJ replied. "It's like it is calling to me. If I could just touch it once...."

Jason ran his hand through his hair, hoping the gesture would banish the yawn tightening his jaw. "I said no. And that's the end of it. I still don't see how you saw enough of the floor to know that anything is there."

His best friend was really getting weird. Hanging out with bullies instead of demeaning them with scathing put-downs, sleeping odd hours. Following Belle around like a lost puppy dog. If he, Jason, didn't know better, he'd think BJ was on drugs. Like all the teachers drilled into the kids to be on the watch for.

He swallowed hard.

His parents had warned him about taking anyone up to the attic and that he had to keep the pentagram a secret. He wished his dad was here to help him.

But Dad couldn't keep his pants zipped. That made him unreliable on so many levels Jason didn't want to think about.

"Mr. Mooney pointed out the blond wood to me. He

said that if it calls to me so strongly I should get an invite to touch it," BJ whined.

That brought Jason awake faster than ice water on his head.

"Mr. Mooney told my mom not to let anyone in the attic but me. Why would he then tell you to try to get up there?"

BJ hung up.

Damn, damn, "Alakazam, Magic Slam."

Now he was awake with no chance of sleep. Maybe he should go up to the attic and do some pliés or something. Maybe take a blanket. With the heat turned down in the house, it would be cold up there. He needed sleep. Sleep within the pentagram to prevent a new headache. BJ was causing headaches now, not helping him forget them.

•————

"What are you doing here, G?" I whispered early Thursday morning. I'd used the front stairs to come down from my bedroom because the backstairs had a creak and I didn't want to wake up the children too early.

Of course, if G was a wizard, he'd know how to open any lock. Shara must have inherited the talent from somewhere.

Unlike any other morning that I could remember, I found G asleep on the sofa, his suit coat over his torso like a blanket. The afghan from my chair lay crumpled over his feet and knees.

Dark shadows made his closed eyes look like ghostly holes. He'd discarded his red-and-navy-striped tie and opened his shirt at the neck. His usually impeccable clothes were rumpled.

In all the years I'd known him and lived with him, I'd never seen him look vulnerable. Even naked and asleep beside me, he retained an aura of power and protectiveness. Now I felt I had the place of protector.

"G," I whispered, gently touching his shoulder.

He mumbled, started to roll over, and awoke. He was

sitting and reaching for his wand/pen before he'd fully opened his eyes. His suit coat flew off to the side and he freed himself from the tangle of the afghan in one smooth movement.

"G!" I stood up and stepped back, hands out, half defensive, half showing myself as unarmed.

"Oh. It's you." He rubbed the sleep off his face. "What time is it?"

"O' dark thirty, the time I usually go to work. What are you doing here?"

"I got in late and didn't want to wake you." He righted his shirt and shifted his trousers as he planted his feet on the floor. Before he stuffed his feet into his loafers, I noticed a hole at the heel of his dress sock.

"You have your own apartment where you don't need to worry about waking someone. Or do you?" I started toward the kitchen, not really wanting to know who shared his bed these days. "I'll make coffee. Then you need to go." Did I smell smoke again? Not in the house. Maybe a neighbor had started a fire to ward off the morning chill. Or the campaign signs still smoldered. Not likely. I'd doused them with water before going back to work.

"Can't," he said around a yawn.

"You don't live here anymore."

"No, I don't. But you and the children are still my family. I need to know you are safe. And . . ." He followed me through the swinging door between the dining room and the kitchen, catching it before it could swing shut between us. His nose worked, he'd smelled the smoke as well. Acrid, not sweet and fresh like a wood fire in a hearth with a chimney.

"And what?" I rounded on him, not knowing if I should be angry or frightened. Or just exasperated.

"I know I can trust you and my children. No one else. I can't trust anyone else. Never again."

"Trust?" I asked, going through the motions of filling the coffee carafe with cold water and setting grounds in a filter. Busywork. I kept my hands busy trying to concentrate on him and not throwing something at him.

"Trust. The Guild has been compromised. My contacts have gone to ground. We are all in terrible danger and I can't trust anyone. No one but you, Daffy."

"You can't hide here. We are divorced."

"Is the pentagram intact?"

"Yes. Jason has only sanded the floor around it. He's been busy with school and rehearsals. But I think he's afraid to work inside the pentagram until you are here to supervise."

"What about the safe in the greenhouse?"

"I haven't checked."

"Shara?"

"Has been busy trying to hack your work computer in the basement. She says she's close and really wants to enroll in the computer programming club, so she hasn't spent any of her unlocking skills on your safe."

"Good. Board up the greenhouse if you have to, but don't let her in there at all." He sat in the breakfast nook, looking as if he expected me to serve him breakfast.

I shoved a coffee cup toward him and poured from the carafe. Black, no sugar, no cream, nothing to come between him and the sharp, dark jolt of awareness. He sipped greedily, like a starving man taking his first nourishment in days.

The dark circles beneath his eyes hadn't lightened any with wakefulness.

I put four slices of bread in the toaster, found jam and peanut butter and put them on the table along with two plates.

"Board up the greenhouse against Shara?" I laughed. "You have got to be kidding me. I don't think there is a lock she can't open. And she's working on hacking into a pretty sophisticated security system on your computer."

"Oh, yeah. My daughter the budding safecracking thief. Or maze runner?" His expression brightened with that thought. "If she can unlock anything, then she can find anything. . . ."

"You can't stay here, G. We aren't married anymore. The divorce decree . . ."

"Damn the decree. I can't protect you by remote control."

"Can't you? What about pentagrams and wards and stuff."

"Illusions at best."

"So you are the all-powerful wizard, the Sheriff. Make the illusions solid." I put two pieces of toast in front of him and prepared my two. He spread his own two slices, meticulously making certain the peanut butter covered the entire surface evenly, all the way to the corners. Then he turned equal attention to the jam. His jaw worked as if talking to himself.

"Make the illusion solid?" He looked up at me, holding his breakfast sandwich in both hands. "The perfect solution." He bent to eating without another word.

"I have to go bake things. I'll be home by seven to fix breakfast for the children. It seems a bit strange that they are all so big now, they don't need me to push them into showers and set out their clothes."

"They are growing up, Daffy." G covered my hand with his own. Just like he used to when I needed reassurance, or strength, or courage. He'd approved and guided me through every step of setting up Magical Brews, like he knew I'd need the independence when he was done with me.

Did he deliberately arrange for the one thing that allowed me to emotionally and financially separate myself from him?

Probably.

"You should be gone by the time their alarms go off. I don't want them getting ideas that I've forgiven you. They haven't."

"Yes. There is that little matter of my . . . indiscretions. Now that I've rested and eaten," he looked dubiously at his toast that had mostly disappeared, "I am in charge of my faculties now, I can defend myself. Thank you for the safe haven, Daffy. I'll be back later to strengthen the protections I have in place. Tell the girls to keep their wands close and touch them frequently, especially if someone makes them feel uncomfortable. I don't know quite what to say to Jason."

"He has cork insoles in his shoes now."

"Cork?"

"It's tree bark. Thin layers of tiny chips pressed together. I found small circles of the stuff at the craft store, designed so people can make their own decorative coasters to protect furniture from sweating glasses. We found a different use for it."

He threw back his head and laughed with joy, as I hadn't heard him laugh since the day I accepted his proposal. "I should have known you'd find a solution. So be it. Off to work with you now, Daffy. I'll do a couple of chores here first, then take myself off to my tiny, dark, and dismal apartment above a shop that plays flutes and drums night and day."

"Your choice to live there."

"Could I come home?"

"No. You can afford a nicer place anywhere else in the city. Shara showed me your bank accounts online. Leave the cheap, dismal, and noisy apartment to the college kids who need cheap and don't care about dismal and noise."

"We'll see. I need to be close."

"Not my problem. I'll be back by seven. Be gone by then."

G's words worried me more than I let on. *The Wizard Guild compromised. Can't trust anyone.* If I hadn't seen G so rattled, vulnerable, and indecisive at the edge of waking up, I'd have dismissed the words.

So I chewed on them all day. When Ted came for his

morning coffee break, I smiled bleakly and sent him on his way without conversation or flirting or anything. John showed up just before two. I signed out of the kitchen and sat with him for a moment, twisting my own cup of latte around and around as I thought of an approach.

"How long have you known G?" I blurted out before I lost my courage.

"Most of our lives. We went all through school together. Speaking of school, don't you have children to transport to various and sundry activities?"

"Not yet. The girls will stay at the middle school for Math Olympics and programming club. I understand you had a part in getting Shara admitted to that activity."

"She is qualified, but a bit too young. Since I sponsor the club, however, I have some say in admitting students outside the normal club rules. Besides, G twisted my arm. Significantly."

I smiled into my cup at that. G could be most persuasive when he needed to be. And right now, Shara needed extracurricular activities to keep her from finding trouble behind locked doors. Or in warded safes.

"If you and G are such longtime friends, how come I didn't meet you until two weeks ago?" I guess I'd met him when he helped move the wardrobe to the attic all those years ago. But other than a brief greeting at the shop, I couldn't remember seeing him since.

"We ... um ..." He looked around to see who might be listening. The shop was quiet for a few minutes in midafternoon, between lunch rush and those with dragging feet requiring caffeine in the afternoon. "We in the community don't socialize much. It draws attention to who is in and who isn't," he whispered.

That almost made sense. All the parties G and I had attended over the years had been held by *my* friends. Only twice had he taken me to cocktail parties with his *business* associates. I now had no idea who they really were.

Didn't the community meet for rituals and such? They

certainly didn't meet at my house with that giant pentagram in the attic. Where else would they go for a private
ceremony?

The top of Skinner Butte? Not during summer when
rattlesnakes made their homes up there. More likely an
isolated copse outside of town. Or maybe someone else's
home or above one of John's shops.

If G ever attended a ritual when he was home, he'd
sneaked out in the middle of the night. A few times over
the years I'd risen at four thirty to find a note and a
flower beside my pillow. He'd been summoned to work
and would call later. He'd traveled so much during the
years of our marriage I couldn't account for his where-
abouts most of the time. Maybe he didn't go out of town
every time he said he did. Maybe he'd kept the apartment above the flute and drum shop all along and merely
hid out there, working remotely with another pentagram.

Or did he hide in our own attic working remotely?

"Well, it's a quarter after. I need to take Jason to
dance class. Tiffany Tyler has classes this afternoon, but
she'll bring him home this evening. From the theater, I
have to run to pick up the girls. They only get an hour
after school for clubs. I hope Shara gets an interesting
assignment to keep her occupied." And out of the greenhouse.

"Let me walk you home." He shoved back his chair.

I gestured him to stay. "That's okay. I drive on school
days."

Now that Jason had been fully admitted into the ballet company, he took his classes at the theater. After
warm-up and floor exercises, they'd set about learning
the pieces in the classroom, or working on trouble spots
or group pieces. Then they adjourned to the stage for
rehearsals. Considering that this was a very small regional pro-am company, he only stayed about two or two
and a half hours. In the past two weeks, they'd put the
dances for all the Halloween numbers together, step by
step, aiming for a mid-October opening. Jason had

assured me that the wicked witch part in *Danse Macabre*, traditionally danced by a man, was worthy of the Halloween season.

I wondered if he had made the connection yet between Halloween witches from ancient morality stories and himself as a magic practitioner.

Now that Tiffany drove him home, my time crunch had eased, and I could spend more time with the girls and keeping the house in order. And cooking. Over the summer I'd spent more time in the kitchen, often teaching the girls some of the basics. Maybe now we'd have time to review the chemistry of baking.

Cooking is an art. Baking is science.

*The combination of art and science equals magic!*

Where had that idea come from? I must have read it somewhere. Otherwise, I'd have to consider that what I did in the kitchen was ... magic. Real magic, like what G did to criminals, Jason did with dance floors, Belle did to attract people, and Shara did with locks and puzzles.

No.

Not possible. G had said that talents emerged at puberty or not at all.

Right?

# Seventeen

I FOUND G WORKING in the backyard.

"Your split personality is showing," I said, aiming for casual. He wore faded blue jeans and a threadbare chambray shirt. Never in the fourteen years I'd known him had he looked so casual. Today was proving a day of firsts with him.

He turned his piercing blue eyes on me, quelling any more words about his wardrobe. I knew from experience I'd get no further explanation.

"Shoring up the fence is hard work. I do have work clothes. Sometimes in the field I have to climb mountains, blaze paths through the forest, and wade through swamps."

*What?!*

"Shoring up the fence? I didn't know it needed fixing."

"It's vulnerable. I haven't tended to it in a long time. Someone has been poking at it from the other side with something sharp, like a tire iron or a pry bar. There are also traces of baby magic in the probes."

"Baby magic?" My mind immediately went to my three children.

"Babies in magic. Those who are about to manifest but don't know they have magic; they attack things with determination as well as tools. That determination has little thorns of magic embedded in it."

"Our kids?" Had any one of the three been out here

alone this summer? I couldn't account for all of their time.

"Doubtful." G stared at the fence, hands on his hips, eyes narrowed but glazing over. "The probes came from the back," he whispered. Then he blinked and shook his head. "Why would one of our kids try to find an opening from the back?"

"Then who?"

"Unknown. But I'll keep my eyes and my tendrils of power open to future intrusion. Sometimes a magician will sprout from a family that has no genetic heritage of magic. We call them 'sports' and they are dangerous, very dangerous indeed, unless a full wizard finds them and teaches them right from wrong." He muttered something under his breath that I couldn't catch.

"While you're at it, you could cut back the blackberry vines." As much as I loved the fruit, mostly gone now for the season, they were an invasive non-native species and a major annoyance. I envisioned Shara's twenty classmates attending her birthday, catching their party clothes in the thorny vines and tearing fine fabric before the near sentient vines let go.

Belle's birthday came later in the month, and she wanted a quieter, smaller gathering of mixed boys and girls (all geeks) for formal tea on the flagstone patio. Dresses or white shirts and ties required.

How did we manage three children with autumn birthdays? Blame it on some pretty wild New Year's Eve parties with a lot of alcohol.

I had to swallow a big lump in my throat. The thought of G and his first wife making merry after a party on New Year's Eve saddened me. She'd died giving birth to Jason.

But Jason's birthday was the last day of September. And at one time G had mentioned that the doctors had performed an emergency C-section on his first wife at seven and a half months, trying to save her life, and Jason's. They failed. But Jason lived. Maybe I didn't have to share the same celebration with her ghost.

"Sometimes a natural barrier entangles intruders better because it isn't expected of me," G replied to my question from many thoughts before. He had his pen/wand in hand as he studied the tall wooden planks that stretched from end to end of our acre.

Then from one eye blink to the next, the wand extruded from the pen carrying blinking spots of sunshine with it.

Before I'd registered the sparkling lights, the worn and weathered boards ceased their sag and stood upright, reinforced by renewed two-by-fours across the top and bottom, and the four-by-four posts every six feet anchored more securely in the summer-hardened ground.

"While you're at it, how about a conversation with the blackberries, something about only snagging people who come over the fence into the yard and not everybody who walks within two feet of them?"

He flipped the pen at the offending vines. They cringed backward, as if slapped into submission.

"That should do it. Magical and mundane menaces repelled." G pocketed his pen, returned to normal size, and dusted his clean hands free of any lingering dirt—or magic. "I checked the safe. It shows signs of Shara's tampering, but will last another day or two."

*Don't bet on that,* I thought as I glimpsed a small face peering out the basement window.

"Dad, I think I got past the last firewall on your computer. Want to come check it for me?" she called up to us.

I knew she'd seen and studied every move her father made. Another puzzle for her to disassemble or reverse engineer.

"Homework first," I called back, loud enough that Belle, too, had to hear me from her own window around the corner on the second floor.

"But, Mom," they both protested.

"I'll come help with your homework. Dining room table in five minutes," G informed them. He must be getting the hang of this parenting thing, knowing his presence was the only way to keep their noses out from where they didn't belong.

———•———

G didn't get back to the greenhouse the next day. He sent me a text that he had to go to Portland on "Business." Back Sunday afternoon.

I breathed a sigh of relief that he wouldn't be hanging around when I went on my Saturday night date with Ted.

How does one prepare for a date with a new man after fourteen years of being committed to another man? As I stared at the clothes hanging in my walk-in closet, I almost wished I had a magical wand. That horrible rapping earworm "Alakazam, Magic Slam" started up in my head.

Like singing could transform my jeans and T-shirts or flannel shirts and sweaters into something that would make me look like a mature and glamorous woman.

Worth a try.

The first notes formed in my throat. My hand beat the rhythm against my thigh.

An idea whopped me upside the head.

I had a little black dress. I wore it rarely, like the abortive anniversary dinner. And before that, two years ago at another New Year's Eve party with a lot of alcohol. For three weeks afterward I bit my fingernails to the quick wondering if I was pregnant again. I wasn't. I still wasn't sure if I was glad or sad.

Anyway, I found that little black dress that flared around my hips and floated in all the right places hanging in the back. Draped over the hangar was a green-and-blue silk scarf to add some life to the black. Maybe too formal for pizza and beer at the brew pub. Ted was not G in his obsession with formality. Ted lived in jeans and work shirts. Surely, he wouldn't wear a GQ custom-made suit for a friendly evening out, away from our children. No black silk jersey for me.

What about the jeans skirt I sometimes wore for business meetings at the bank or with our accountant?

Yes. Denim and lace. A lacy blouse I'd had since college. And flats, no heels. I hated having to watch my balance every step of the way when I wore heels.

I'd dithered so long about clothes, I didn't have time to take a long bubble bath in the kids' bathroom, so I opted for a longer than usual hot shower. A dab of perfume and smudge of lipstick made me presentable.

"Who are you and what have you done with my mother?" Jason chortled as I stepped into the kitchen.

I swallowed my smile. I guess I was presentable for my first date.

And . . . Tiffany grinned back at me from the nook. For once, she didn't have her feet in a basin of hot water with healing salts.

I spun around. For wherever Tiffany was when not on stage, her father couldn't be far away.

"Sorry we came early. I hope it's okay," Ted said from where he propped up the doorjamb into the dining room. "Tiffany needs more of your magical potions, so I thought I should order pizza for the four of them while I take you out."

The first genuine smile in a long, long time creased my face. "Of course, it's okay. Have you been waiting long?" I moved to stand beside him, putting half a room between us and the children.

"A few minutes. The pizza is ordered and Tiffany has money to pay the delivery person. Plus a tip." He waggled a finger at her as if expecting her to hold back a little for her own purposes.

She made a face at him.

I could tell this was a familiar game, all in fun.

"There's soda and iced tea in the fridge. Dessert when we get back," I said, still holding that smile.

We made our escape. I have to admit my heart beat a strange rhythm in trepidation. I'd never left the children alone while I went out with someone not their father. We were long past the days of babysitters, unless I considered Tiffany an overseer of Deschants juvenile activities.

Maybe she'd keep them from trying anything magical. Why did I not believe that?

Ted escorted me to Tiffany's little compact sedan. "Oh, we've graduated to the adult car," I quipped.

Ted laughed. "You wouldn't want to ride in my work pickup. No amount of clearing out and cleaning it up could make it presentable for a lady." He opened the passenger door and handed me in.

"I feel the same way about my van. There are days when we practically live in it. And that means fast food meals, spilled drinks, upset tummies, the works."

"My daughter is a lot more fastidious than I am. Tonight, I'm grateful for that," he said as he got in on the other side and started the engine. It purred softly. We could actually carry on a conversation and not be drowned out by engine noise.

And talk we did, all through dinner and back out into the parking lot. Mostly about our children, about ballet, about his work and mine. And about how much trouble the dancers had dancing *Tubular Bells*, and how the ballets differed from movies and cartoons, and how even modern special effects could not work "Alakazam, Magic Slam" into any of the scores planned for the *This Is Halloween* dance festival.

"Has Jason asked you to remake his costume for *Tubular*?" Ted finally asked as we left the pub.

"What's wrong with the one assigned to him? Mostly he's wearing rags and bones, in the first two numbers," I asked, alarmed.

"For *Tubular*, it's an old, black brocade tunic and made for a larger man. He's very young for the part and doesn't have the shoulders yet."

"That could be why he asked for a set of free weights for his birthday. He wants to do more lift work. Someone named Denise?"

"Denise," he confirmed. "Tiffany's understudy and second lead. Will he get the weights?"

"Probably. Presuming his father remembers and is in town long enough to deliver them."

"Is that why you split up? He's gone all the time? Not a great parent when he is around?"

"Partly. He also manipulates people and has an interesting relationship with the truth."

"Oh."

"He promised he'd be home in time for Shara's birthday party tomorrow afternoon. I'm not holding my breath."

"Do you need another adult at the party?" He held both my hands, and looked down at me with concern.

"Thank you for offering. I appreciate that more than I can say. But I'm used to doing it all on my own, and I will have some other mothers chaperoning. At this point having a man around, even as nice a one as you, will just complicate things."

"You think I'm nice?"

I nodded. He smiled as he lowered his head and kissed me. I rose up on tiptoe to respond. He clasped my waist. I held his shoulders.

And we kissed. Once, a gasp of air, twice, and we sank back into reality. A nice kiss. A comfortable kiss.

No champagne bubbles lit my blood.

After the sizzle I experienced every time G touched me, I was a bit disappointed. But knowing that sizzle was magically induced, another form of manipulation, I'd take nice and honest and appreciate it. Welcome it.

# Eighteen

RETURNING HOME TO MY children from a date felt . . . awkward at best. Ted and I found all four of them, er, five if you counted BJ, in the kitchen. Where else?

That was where the remnants of the pizzas were. And, miracle of miracles, the Black Forest cake I'd made. It still sat in the middle of the round table, on a pedestal, with the cake knife, dessert plates, forks, and paper napkins beside it, and not a single crumb was absent. They all stared longingly at it, even Tiffany who usually disdained sugar.

Except BJ. He stared longingly at Belle. She sat with her back to him, ignoring the invitation in his eyes. But she hadn't removed her hair sticks. Was she playing with him, or just uncertain of what to do and how to do it?

"Okay, math genius Belle, please divide it into seven pieces and start cutting. I'm putting coffee on."

"Decaf, if you please," Ted asked meekly.

"Tea for me," Tiffany added, accepting the first piece of cake on its little plate. She set it down before gathering a fork and placing a napkin on her lap.

"Eight pieces, so Jason can have some more at midnight," Belle said. "Besides, it's easier to divide into eight than seven."

I put the teakettle on and made a small pot of decaf. I didn't need caffeine this late in the day either. "Jason, I need a tall person to get the teapot off the top shelf."

Ted appeared behind me, his body pressed close to mine, suggesting a level of intimacy not there earlier, almost an announcement to our families that we were "together."

"Let me." He reached up over my head for the little porcelain two cupper. I ducked under his enveloping arms to find the assorted teas and bags in a different cupboard. Gahd, I wasn't ready for this.

Would I ever be?

My phone screeched an alarm before I could think harder on that issue.

Gayla wasn't home. Saturday night she played Bunko, some bizarre card game that addicted people, at her church. The alarm company reported that fire trucks had rolled.

"Save us some cake," Ted called as we ran out the back door.

The landline rang. "Jason, deal with that!"

Ted's car was parked behind my van, so we took the little sedan.

We found a single bright red engine just rolling to a stop outside the front of the shop. Smoke crept under the door. The fire crew dropped to the ground from the back and the cab of the truck. I rolled out of the sedan almost before Ted pulled up the parking brake.

I held my keys up to the first responders so they wouldn't have to break down the door. The man in charge—hard to determine age or description behind his face mask—took the keys. First, he held his open bare hand near the doorframe, shrugged, then placed the same hand flat against the door itself. "What the fuck? It's cool." He unlocked it and stepped back as he pushed the door inward, allowing the smoke to exit. Then he and five others barreled inward.

Gayla drove up, looking pale and shaken. "Why us? Why two fires in a week's time?" she kept mumbling to herself.

I hugged her close, too numb to even speak.

Old Raphe lurched around the corner, mouth working as if speaking. But with all the noise of the churning diesel engines and the bangs and thumps from inside, I couldn't hear what he said. He raised his head enough to see me and aimed his halting steps toward where I hugged Gayla and Ted hugged me. "She has smoke for eyes. The smoke sees. Smoke goes everywhere. No barrier to smoke. She has smoke for eyes," he whispered as he drew closer.

"What's he saying?" Ted asked, trying to draw me away from the reeking man.

Gayla and I exchanged a long stare. Neither of us knew for certain that magic was involved. But Raphe was creeping me out. I needed to talk to G.

As usual, G was not here.

"I'm hungry, Mz. Daffy. Got any leftovers?" The vague trance state cleared from Raphe's face. He looked at me with clarity, and an awareness of reality I didn't get to see often.

"We'll see if there's anything edible left. Oh, no! I've got six dozen cupcakes in the walk-in cooler for tomorrow's party!"

"It's okay, Sweet Pea." Gayla rubbed my back. "I'll help you redo them first thing in the morning."

"And if you're tied up here longer than you like, I can hold the fort for you at the house," Ted offered.

Tears burned beneath my eyelids. "Thank you," I sobbed, incapable of saying more.

"She has smoke for eyes." Raphe reverted to vague and mystic. "Mist conceals. Smoke probes."

"This is the weirdest fire I've seen in ages," the fire chief said, scratching his head. He'd shed his face mask, helmet, and gloves as he returned my keys. "Too much smoke for that little bitty fire in the middle of the work counter. Can't even tell what was the fuel and the ignition source."

"I was here this morning baking. I swear I left the

place clean. I always leave the place as if I'm expecting the health inspector," I protested.

"We know you do, Daffy. We know you'd never tempt a single ant to come into your kitchen, let alone a stray spark," Gayla said, still rubbing my back and speaking in soothing tones. Ted began to pace, looking at the ground. Was he searching out clues? Like glowing footprints?

"May I go in?"

The fire chief shrugged. "There's no sign of forced entry. I'll have the electrical inspector out here Monday morning. Maybe some of the wiring in these old shops sent sparks. We've had a few power surges lately."

"We updated the wiring in our section of this building when we bought the place five years ago," Gayla insisted. "Our shop is up to code, top and bottom levels."

"But are the shops on either side of you?" The chief looked skeptical.

"The previous owner sold the shops piecemeal so developers wouldn't come in and level the block in favor of glass-and-steel skyscrapers. Everyone had to update in order to get a mortgage." Gayla took on the look of a Texas Bulldog. Or maybe a Comanche lady warrior.

I slipped inside the shop with Ted in tow. "I've got some heavy-duty fans I can loan you to get rid of some of the smoke smell," Ted said, covering his nose and mouth with his arm.

I had to hold my cotton sweater over my lower face to breathe easily.

Inside, the firemen had opened the back door to help alleviate some of the smoke. Two of them poked at a pile of dry ash on top of my marble pastry board, now cracked from the center out along the wandering mineral veins. That would have to be replaced.

"That fire could not have produced that much smoke!" Ted protested.

"She has smoke for eyes. Needs lots of smoke to probe and poke where no one would let her come.

Smoke sees. Smoke travels where she cannot," Raphe said. He walked right toward the back door and access to his burrow behind the dumpster.

I aimed for the walk-in cooler in the back corner. "Breathe," I reminded myself. The door came open with its usual ease. I had expected resistance, like the rubber seal around the door might have melted. Inside, I was greeted by row after row of rolling racks, six feet tall each, with slots for eight two-by-three–foot trays. During a normal week, we used only two or three racks to restock the front cases. Tonight, I found three trays on one rack filled with cupcakes, each with a towering swirl of frostings. One tray of pink, another of chocolate, and a third of cream cheese with sprinkles. I hoped to please all of the varying tastes of twenty sixth-graders and a bunch of their parents.

Thankfully, the smoke had not penetrated the heavy steel door of the cooler. Just to make sure, I filled a plate with a sampling of each of the three kinds of cupcakes.

The firemen proclaimed them not only safe to eat but worthy of a second helping. Gayla had a pickier palate, and she also decided they'd do for a bunch of middle schoolers who had no appreciation for perfection. Ted took one bite and nearly melted at my feet. "If the Black Forest cake in your kitchen is half this good, I'll kidnap and marry you in a moment."

I hid my blush by closing the cooler and washing the now empty serving plate.

The fire chief came back with paperwork. Gayla promised to handle it and ushered me out the door. "Go home and get some sleep. We'll deal with this in the morning."

"What time do you want the fans?" Ted asked, resting his arm around my waist as he urged me out the front door.

"Is eight too early?" I asked. "That's when I'd planned to load up the cupcakes for the party."

"I've usually been working for two hours at eight," Ted said.

"Oh, good, he's a morning person just like you!" Gayla chortled.

We left.

"Are you certain that Raphe said, 'she has smoke for eyes' and that it was Raphe and not a whisper on the wind?" G asked Daffy at noon the next day.

"I am certain. It creeped me out. He kept repeating it as if it were important," she replied as she set finger sandwiches on a platter for the family and loaded decorative serving trays with cupcakes. The lemonade was chilling, and he'd scattered little bowls of mixed nuts about the main level of the house and on portable tables on the patio, as she directed. He was actually surprised she let him help. Jason and BJ were busy blowing up balloons, while Belle was busy avoiding BJ.

That scene at the mall had bothered Belle more than he thought at first. Instead of preening in her new glory, she shrank within herself, hunched posture, tucked chin, and making sure a full room separated her from her admirer. And she tripped over shadows more frequently.

"This is worse than I thought." G ran his hands through his usually smooth hair. He needed to find "Smoke for eyes" fast, before she did any more damage. And he needed to talk to Belle. He glanced askance at the party decorations and food. "There's no way you can cancel this?" His attention focused on the gray sky that looked too much like smoke.

"Don't even think about it. The clouds are thickening, but we have three hours and forty-three minutes before it starts raining. As long as you don't interfere."

So one or all of the children had told her about his affinity with water.

"I don't weather witch unless abso-friggin-necessary to save the world." He held up both hands in feigned innocence.

"Who is Raphe?" she asked. "We've always had

homeless people around, but he took over the alley last summer and hasn't moved. That's unusual. And he's never around during the day, but always at night. I know he's important to you in some way, or you wouldn't have questioned if he was the one who spoke mystic words as if an oracle in a trance."

G looked everywhere but in her eyes, searching for a plausible lie. He had none. Time for honesty, not only to salvage something from their relationship but for her own protection. "Raphe's my first cousin, his mother and my father were siblings. He's gone, she's still alive. Raphe's a year and a half younger than me. We grew up together."

"If he's family, why is he homeless? We have lots of room here."

"He has an aversion to sunlight. His parents had to home school him because he always, from the day he was born, slept all day and was wide awake all night. Every time he looked out a window during the day, he'd scream and clamp his eyes shut. He lasted half of a half day in kindergarten. I'm sharing the apartment with him, which isn't bad since we mostly keep opposite schedules. I'm paying him to keep watch on the shop and the house. Though he'll never come closer than the driveway."

"What does he do when you don't pay him?"

She had to ask. She'd always probe to the heart of an issue.

"He's the registrar for the Guild. It's up to him to maintain the database of all our members, past and present, most recent contact info, next of kin, talent and wand, etc."

"Why won't he come closer than the drive?" Her eyes glazed, remembering. Remembering something important.

"Because for me the pentagram in the attic is protection, it makes the entire house out to the exterior walls a safe haven from magical attack. Raphe finds it repelling. Not that I'd ever believe him capable of black magic.

He's just different. Almost backward in his life and his magic—dyslexic about reading and magic. But numbers don't bother him, thus the database. For all I know, his warding spells may welcome magic intrusion." G gulped as new thoughts and doubts raced through his mind. "I have to check it out." He pulled his car keys out of his trousers pocket.

"Oh."

"I appreciate that you offer Raphe leftover pastry. He sometimes forgets to eat." G had things to do. Urgent things. So why did he linger, savoring every moment of conversation with Daffy?

"I've always given what I could to the homeless who take up residence in my alley."

"That's one of the reasons I love you. Now I have to go. My present for Shara is on the dining room table, all wrapped nice and neat with a pretty bow and card." He made hesitant steps toward the back door.

"Who wrapped it for you? No, don't tell me. I don't want to know."

He kissed her cheek, leaving a sizzling imprint of his lips behind—old habits die hard. Time to get out of here before he confessed about the three hours he had to kill in Tallahassee before he caught a plane to Chicago.

# Nineteen

I HAD TO PRESS a cold cloth on the tingling patch on my face before I faced the family and guests. The first of which was Gayla, come for lunch and with a bounty of little girl treasures, like a first lipstick in pale pink, pink dye for hair streaks, cute hair doodads, and tiny earrings in gift bags. My present to Shara was the promise of a trip to the doctor to get her ears pierced this week. I'd done the same for Belle two years ago.

I drew a deep breath and prepared to tell Gayla everything G had said. If he was worried about "Smoke for eyes," then I should be, too.

After the party. Could I tell her about the magic? Should I?

G was adamant about keeping magic invisible to all normal people.

Gayla was my best friend. She knew how to keep secrets and often figured them out before anyone confessed to her. And everyone confessed to her, from the college kids we hired to the owners of the shops adjacent to Magical Brews, to the business people who bought our coffee and pastry.

We'd talk after the party.

By midafternoon, the kids had run off a lot of their sugar rush by breaking the piñata and racing around in a weird variation of freeze tag. They kind of made up the rules as they went along. When touching the windows of the greenhouse became a safe zone, I judged the time had come to move indoors to the dining room and open presents. The clouds were thick enough that I expected the first fat plops of rain any moment. Right on time.

G walked in with a shrug and a shake of his head. Whatever he'd set off to do hadn't worked.

"Mom." Belle tugged at my sleeve while I filled the teakettle for the parents.

"What, dear," I replied absentmindedly. I was really contemplating whether the last pitcher of lemonade would last through the final ritual of the day.

"Can you tell BJ that he's not invited to *my* party?"

That shook me out of my reverie. BJ had been a part of our gatherings for as long as I could remember. But he and Jason had been buddies, keeping to themselves, away from the girl cooties. "What did he do?"

"It's just . . . just that he's always right behind me, always intruding on my conversations with other people, always asking questions about the attic."

So he had seen something when we moved the wardrobe.

"I'll ask Jason to talk to him. They are friends. He can soften the blow of being deprived of your presence. Or you could take the hair sticks out of your bun."

"No!" She slapped her hand protectively over the jade charms. "I have to wear them all the time. Dad said so."

"Then talk to your dad about it." I'd reverted to that old ploy too often of late. This magic thing was more than I could handle. I didn't have enough information and experience to deal with it.

Right on cue the doorbell rang. Who could that be? I'd counted noses earlier. The only person missing was Melissa who had to have a gluten-free and vegan diet because of some strange autoimmune disease. I'd offered to bake special treats just for her, but her parents opted to keep her away from temptation.

When Jason opened the heavy front door—wider and taller than most modern homes with stained glass embedded in the top quarter—I gasped at the sight of Bret and Flora Chambers, dressed as if they'd just come from church. He'd shed his tie and she her dainty hat with a veil. Otherwise they looked as if they'd come on a formal call. Or had stepped out of a time warp from the '50s.

Then I spotted the campaign fliers sticking out of Flora's prim pocketbook.

"We wanted to offer the birthday girl our congratulations," Bret Senior said jovially.

BJ disappeared out the back door the moment his parents arrived.

All smiles and proffered hands to shake with the adults, they moved through the living room to the dining room. Flora made polite, but lustful, remarks about the magnificence of the antique table. Nodding as she counted each of the twenty pre-adolescents squeezed in around it, some two to a chair. "Perfect for a campaign fund-raiser," she muttered under her breath, but I heard her. And so did some of the adults as they moved away from the intruders. Bret and Flora stood in the middle of an island of silence.

Then Bret spotted G who was trying to retreat to the kitchen and followed him. I opted to position myself in the doorway. A quick gesture to Gayla, and she organized the present-opening ceremony.

Flora sidled up to me. "You have some influence in the neighborhood around your shop," she said. She lowered her voice, but it still carried. "Isn't there anything you can do about the ugly pagan insignia in all those shops? And the street dancing? Even now those heathens are dancing in the street in the rain, spinning in some kind of devil-worshipping trance. *Tearing off their clothes!*"

"Last I heard, it's a free country. First Amendment gives us the constitutional right to worship as we choose, so long as we harm none," I replied.

Flora bristled. "But all that witchcraft and obscene sacrifices were not the intent of our Founding Fathers. They meant that we could choose a *Christian* denomination."

"Since the Founding Fathers have all been dead for

two hundred years, it's a little hard to know what they intended." My back was starting to itch like it would sprout wings or something. I longed for my wooden spoon to whap her upside the head and knock some civility, if not common sense, into her head. But no, I wore slacks and a sweater set as my nod to less casual than jeans and flannel shirt. So I didn't have a back pocket for the spoon.

"Well," she hmphed. "I can see where *your* sympathies lie. As far as I'm concerned, we should burn the entire neighborhood to the ground and get rid of that bad influence."

I froze in place. Heat drained from my face. I looked into her smoke-colored eyes beneath the dowdy blonde French twist, and knew she believed every word she said.

*Smoke for eyes.* No. I didn't want to believe she would actually start fires in the old neighborhood just to make a point. I'd known her for ten years. Her son practically lived at my house. Actually, more and more he seemed to make excuses *not* to go home. Had she gone off the deep end? Deeper?

"And I presume we can't count on your votes in the primary either since you don't even have the courtesy to display the campaign sign I sent over with BJ."

And then G's roar of outrage drowned out everything else. "I do not appreciate you turning my daughter's *private* birthday party into a photo op for your ill-advised campaign!"

Bret raced out of the kitchen, grabbed Flora's arm, and headed for the front door. He smiled and made nice noises to my guests. He did take pains to close the massive front door quietly and completely. But not before Flora said, "We should bring back burning at the stake."

I sagged against the doorjamb in disbelief. "How to ruin a nice day in two ugly minutes," I whispered.

G placed a hand on my shoulder and squeezed. We tilted toward each other, automatically seeking comfort.

I straightened first. "Shara, have you found all the presents?"

"Just a few more. Did you see what Dad got me? A silver necklace chain so I can wear my key all the time!" At least she didn't call it a wand in public.

A few of the adults made noises about needing to get home. Or flee the embarrassment.

G looked to me like I could pull a rabbit out of the hat. That was his job. Mine was to clean up social messes caused by my bullying acquaintances. It was a wonder BJ had turned out so reasonable. But then he spent as much time here as he did at home. Jason never went to the Chamberses' to play, even when he was five years old.

And BJ was losing some of his normality if I cared to believe the kids when they said he'd added bullies to his group of friends.

"I have a marvelous idea. The last performance of the *This Is Halloween* dance festival is a matinee on Halloween day, a Saturday. Let's have a monster party afterward, invite the whole cast and crew and anyone else we know from work, the neighborhood, or school. Flora wants to burn witches? Let's give her a whole haunted house full. Sound effects, flying blobs of gauze, monster masks, the works."

Come to think of it, BJ had never been allowed to trick-or-treat either. He'd done it secretly with Jason, of course. I figured what Flora didn't know couldn't hurt her.

I wondered briefly where her ultraconservative, puritanical fanaticism came from. For a long time, I had suspected Bret joined the church as a power base for his political aspirations rather than belief.

"I've got sheets of plastic foam I was going to shape and paint into tombstones for the display window," Gayla added. "We could make an unholy cemetery out of your front yard. String fake cobwebs from the trees, too." She found her tablet in her purse and began making notes.

The other mothers came up with more outrageous ideas.

"And we can open the attic," I added.

"Daffy, what about the . . . you know?" G jerked his head toward the upper levels of the house. He sounded outraged. This was his world we were honoring—or mocking, I wasn't sure which.

"It's all part of the décor."

# Twenty

$\bullet$

A NORMAL ROUTINE OF frantic dashing from place to place followed by long waits and hastily grabbed meals before the children settled into homework followed for the next week. G often dropped by to help the kids with their lessons. That was unusual enough to cause a few disruptions, but they soon settled to the routine. Fortunately, Belle needed little help with her math and physics lessons. She grasped them quickly and only worked the assignments by rote. No one else could help her. I had a feeling her teachers were challenged to keep up with her.

We saw little of BJ. Jason reported that he was royally pissed when Belle had banned him from her party. I figured his teenage rebellion hormones had finally kicked in, and he was just being more blatant in expressing his likes and dislikes.

His parents took umbrage at our "rudeness to our guests" at the party and stayed away as well.

I barely noticed their absence until after it was all over and two weeks later G pointed out how well Belle managed her party. She helped me make delicate, crustless cucumber, watercress, and tuna salad sandwiches on white bread, with tea and tiny cakes. I appreciated her help even as I bit down my frustration that I did not totally control my kitchen.

After tea, Belle and her friends indulged in chess games and math problems that left me bewildered.

At the end of the month, Jason and four of his friends went out for pizza with only G hanging around the edges to supervise and drive. BJ met them at the pizza place, driving his own car, but did not come back to the house for video games, even though we had a new one he'd mentioned wanting to play repeatedly over the summer. Still in rebellion or something else?

I'd taken Adolescent Psychology in college to get my unused teaching certificate, so I'd been warned to watch for changes in behavior as a sign of drug use. That really didn't sound like BJ. Besides, his parents kept him on a very tight allowance and a tighter curfew. He shouldn't have enough time or money for drugs.

After the weekend of his birthday celebration, Jason's rehearsals became intense. Not only was the company perfecting several short ballets for Halloween which would debut only two weeks away, they were casting and planning for *The Nutcracker* in December. I made him take his homework with him so he could work on it when he wasn't actively dancing.

And then disaster struck.

"What are we going to do!" Tiffany wailed running out the stage door of the Old Vic Theater when I dropped Jason off. She wore her practice clothes of long-sleeved black leotard, pink tights, pink leg warmers, and pink ballet flats. She'd stuffed her feet into clogs to protect her slippers. Three more ballerinas streamed after her. "Maestro Bellini says we have to cancel *Halloween* and maybe *Nutcracker* as well. It won't be Christmas without *Nutcracker*."

More tears. Jason opened his arms wide and hugged as many of the bevy as he could at once. I wasn't certain if my boy was their confidant and friend or merely the conduit to me and my soaking salts and ointments for abused dancers' feet. Whichever, he seemed to relish having his arms full of beautiful young women.

"What happened?" I asked, stepping out of the van.

More wails and tears.

I ushered them all into the backstage area where it was warm and dry. Maestro Bellini, the ballet master and director of the company, paced the area, from closed curtains to dressing rooms to stage door, pulling at his abundant white hair. It wouldn't be abundant much longer the way he was tearing at clumps of it. He, too, was clad in the male version of practice clothes: black T-shirt and tights, white socks that climbed almost to his knees (leg warmers of a sort), and black ballet slippers.

"What happened?" I demanded in my most authoritative, mother-of-teenagers voice.

Maestro pointed toward a broken door in the far back corner by the corridor that led to dressing rooms and the staircase that led up to the classrooms. In the dim light, I could almost make out the words "Props, no admittance," in decals on the steel fire door. "I smelled smoke when I came down from class and hurried to investigate," he said, sounding as if he'd just left Rome with only rudimentary English lessons. A sure sign he was upset.

The lock looked scorched and melted. Shara would have been neater. Whoever entered without permission or a key was not into finesse. I closed my eyes a moment and took a deep breath before peeking around the door where it sagged on its hinges. The smell of rancid smoke had dissipated but still clung to the wads of cloth inside the room. I'd smelled that kind of smoke before. At home and in my coffee shop.

Instead of orderly racks of brightly colored and sequined costumes hanging neatly on hangers, each covered with old sheeting for protection from dust and accidental soiling by dirty hands, I saw heaps of torn satin and chiffon, tulle and velvet scattered about the room. Thrones and spindly chairs leaned drunkenly on weak or broken legs. Cardboard boxes and their contents of headgear, wigs, fans, and other accessories were scattered about.

"Who would do such a thing?" I asked, bewildered.

"No one sane," Bellini spat, his Italian accent thick with distress.

"Jason," I called to the only nonhysterical person in sight. "Call 911 and ask for the police. Then help me figure out what's missing." As much as my fingers itched to start picking things up and transforming chaos into order, I knew not to touch anything until the police had examined and photographed everything.

Looking at the mangled lock once more, I called G. I didn't think a normal explosive or heat source could cause that much damage without sending the door across the stage into the audience seats.

"Mom?" Jason drew me away from the crowd of dancers, most of them wailing. "I looked real quick and the only thing I didn't see at least pieces of were the three sticks we painted up in jewel tones and covered in glitter with dangling feathers and such that the various sorcerers use as wands."

"What kind of sticks and where did they come from?" Bright paint and glitter would make them visible on stage.

"We'd been using some drumsticks, but they were borrowed from the high school band and we had to return them, so we couldn't paint them. They looked awful, and we could barely see them from the third row."

"The painted sticks?" I had to bring him back to topic or he'd talk for ages about the importance of props being bigger and gaudier than tasteful for stage work.

"Two were polished wood. Maybe turned on a lathe, really smooth with gorgeous grain. The third looked like braided grape vines, really beautiful. It was a shame to cover up the natural woods, but we had to, to make them visible."

"Where did they come from?" I'd seen similar "sticks" in one of the magic shops in the neighborhood of Magical Brews. The owner turned them on his own lathe specifically to bring out the best wood grain. I hadn't seen any braided wood, but the craft store sold wreaths of woven grapevines, so why not a wand? The shop owner sold his work as magic wands for the wannabe witches. And maybe to real ones, too, if that was what they craved as an extension of their magic.

"Shara found them." My son hung his head, unable to look at me. He knew as well as I that if Shara found them, she had to pick a lock to find them.

"Where?"

"Um . . ."

"Where, Jason?"

"Somewhere in the greenhouse."

My knees threatened to collapse. Shara had managed to break the wards on the evidence locker after all.

G caught me as I swayed. He'd responded to my call faster than the police.

———

"What did the smoke smell like?" G asked Maestro Bellini. He kept one eye on Daffy as she roused from a stunned trance. Her whispered words about Shara finding the wands in the greenhouse scared him.

"Smoke is smoke," the ballet master said with a European style shrug of the shoulders that required participation of every body part.

"Was it sweet, like woodsmoke?" G persisted.

"It smelled like it came straight from hell!" Bellini shouted, throwing his arms wide. "This ballet is cursed. We must cancel. It is the *Tubular Bells*! A cursed piece of music. We are cursed for performing it! Cursed, I say."

"Sulfurous smoke," G mumbled to himself. "If not straight from hell, then from someone who's been there recently." He turned to find Daffy peering curiously into the prop room. "Daffy." He spoke in a clearer, decisive voice to penetrate her shock. "I have to go and track down someone who shouldn't be out of prison. Please stay and take care of . . ." he gestured as broadly as Bellini, "of this. I know you can get everything back on track. The show must go on. And there is no such thing as a curse." There was, but not in this instance. He stalked quickly away, wrapping shadows around him as he passed. "And keep a close eye on Jason!"

No one should be able to follow him. He had a wisp of smoke up his nose. Now he just had to follow it.

This was an acquired talent, not one native to him. Still, he'd done it often enough that it shouldn't be a problem. Shara was a maze runner, not a tracker. She'd be of no help.

He stood at the edge of the parking lot, sniffing in all directions. There, north by northeast. toward Skinner Butte.

A whiff of sandalwood incense replaced the acrid smoke. His heart sank. He knew that scent all too well. Long friendship and loyalty warred with his instinctive need to protect his family and the community.

"Why, John? Why'd you do it? I never believed you capable of murder. Cheating on your taxes, yes. But the horrible murder of innocent victims? I don't want to believe this, but I have to follow every clue. And you hold all the cards."

He called Ted's private number. "I need you to stay close to Daffy and the kids for a few hours."

"Um . . . what am I up against?"

G sighed. He didn't have time for complicated explanations. "Can you just absorb any magic thrown in their vicinity?"

"That's my job."

"And clear out any residual at the theater."

"The theater? Is Tiffany okay?" The sound of tools hastily thrown into the back of his pickup accompanied his words.

"She's fine. Everyone's fine for now. But there's loose rogue magic about."

"Understood. And one more thing you should be aware of. There's some mighty funky bookkeeping going on with our oldest friend. Innocent people are getting hurt. I just had to clean up some shoddy renovations by *his* people and reported the contractors to the Better Business Bureau. That corporation doesn't exist anymore. The work would never have passed inspection without a hefty bribe, if they were done at all. And not doing an inspection costs a lot more money. But I know these guys are still around. I see them all the time at contractor supply stores." He hung up as his truck engine roared to life and the sound of gravel flying beneath spinning tires covered any more words.

"The show cannot go on," Bellini insisted. "We have no costumes, and no money to replace them." He sank his face into his palms and shook his head. His usually straight and proud body, superbly fit, sagged. He looked older, flabby, and despondent.

"Maybe, maybe not," I mused. "Jason, when the police have finished photographing and fingerprinting and whatever else they do, you and anyone else calm enough to take action, need to inventory and sort everything in the prop room. Decide what can be salvaged and what can be ripped apart at the seams and the fabric reused to patch something else."

I glanced around at the dancers, a few parents, and stage crew milling around looking hopeless. And Ted. Upright, responsible, and normal Ted. I felt as if the weight of the world lifted from my shoulders. I could do this. Time to put the hangers-on to work. Work, the best therapy for disaster.

"Tiffany, get out the company phone roster and divide it up. Call everyone and anyone. Find the people who know how to sew and recruit them."

"What are you going to do, Mom?" Jason asked. He looked a bit overwhelmed like he did when confronted with one of Belle's math problems, or needing to find where he'd written down a password that Shara would instinctively know.

His sisters had their own talents. They'd be just as

bewildered if faced with learning a complex dance routine and executing it perfectly with only minutes to practice.

"I'm going to do what I do best, organize a bake sale at the Saturday Market. We'll have the money for replacement costumes or at least fabric by Monday."

"Ms. Deschants?" Tiffany asked. "Can we recruit contributions to the bake sale, too?"

"Of course. I may be a professional baker, but I can't do this alone." Recipes for cookies, brownies, and cupcakes spun in my head. I needed flavor combinations that were unique and favorites at the same time, so people would spend money on them.

"My mom has a bunch of old glass-top canning jars she was going to give to the thrift store," a petite dark-haired dancer said. I think her name was Denise—Denise the girl Jason wanted to practice lifts with. "If you could fill them with those healing salts you give Tiffany, we could sell a ton of them. You could reimburse yourself for the ingredients, of course."

"We'll help package everything up. Just tell us where and when," Tiffany added.

I nodded encouragement to each of them as they came up with good ideas.

The chaos receded by increments.

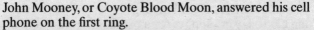

John Mooney, or Coyote Blood Moon, answered his cell phone on the first ring.

"John, you run a booth at the Saturday Market, right?" I jumped right in without explanation.

"Yes. I sell my flutes and drums, some CDs and books. This is the last weekend, though, and there's a good chance we'll also have the last of the bright days now that we're past the Equinox."

"How do I go about renting booth space for just the weekend?"

"How big a space and why?"

I told him.

"Take my space. It's paid for. I got a package deal for the entire season, but I need to show some property out of town and was wondering who I could get to run my booth. You can use my table and awning, too. All I ask is that you also sell my stuff."

"Deal. Your pastry and coffee are free at Magical Brews next week."

"What can I do to help?"

"You've already done it. Unless you feel inclined to pass out flyers to everyone you know. Thank you from the bottom of my heart for the space."

"You draw up the flyers and I'll print a bunch. Can you have it done this evening? I'll stop by the house and pick up a master."

"About eight? I've got a lot to do between now and then."

"See you at eight." He made a kissy smooching sound into his phone.

My stomach turned. I disliked wet kisses. This one sounded very sloppy.

Besides, I wanted to explore a budding relationship with Ted. Nice Ted who didn't challenge me or entice me with magic. Nice. Normal.

I had no time for this.

I left a few more organizational orders with Jason and left to pick up Shara and Belle.

Somewhere in there I managed a call to Gayla, alerting her to lay in supplies for a baking binge. I'd take the costs out of my share of this month's profits.

"You will not!" Gayla protested. "This is a charitable donation. We're in the black again, for the sixth month in a row. We might need to write this one off come tax season. How about I order more applesauce also, so you can present those wonderful vegan bar cookies. And what do you want for gluten-free flour for that segment of the population who are badly treat-deprived? Oh, and I'm adding croissant breakfast sandwiches to our menu. Be prepared. I'll cook the scrambled eggs and bacon. Still thinking about choice of cheeses and where to put a microwave under the serving counter."

"Thank you, Gayla, for being my friend as well as business partner. You're the one who keeps this business running."

"Couldn't do it without your magic in the kitchen, Sweet Pea. Now what do you need from the big box store for those bath salts?"

I gave her a list of the basic ingredients of Epsom salts and alum and a few other things. Some of the herbs I could gather from the greenhouse. In quantity? I wasn't certain. For the more exotic stuff, like jasmine, I'd need to visit an organic garden northeast of town. I'd just get it all there. Denise did suggest I could take reimbursement from the sales. No time like the present to go shopping. As soon as I picked up the girls.

I'd wait to give all three children THE lecture about staying out of their father's safe tonight. Actually, I liked the idea of making him explain it all to them. Magic costs, and magic has consequences.

Hadn't I read that in a novel or six back in the days when I had time to read more than three paragraphs in a sitting?

# Twenty-One

"**W**HAT WERE YOU THINKING, inviting Coyote Blood Moon here!" G yelled about seven thirty that night as I assigned dishes and cleanup to the kids while I generated a flyer advertising the bake sale. My computer blinked at me, waiting for a command. That stupid icon almost accused me of being negligent and stupid for not letting it take care of every detail.

"He offered to help. *And* you said to go to him for help while you were out of town. What happened to 'one of my oldest friends'?" I decided to let the curser blink. I didn't like the picture of toe shoes I'd grabbed off the Internet. I wanted a picture of Tiffany in one of her classic leaps or at the top of a magnificent lift.

And I found one in my stash of photos from Vivaldi's *Spring*. Quickly, I clipped around it and pasted the image into the center of the flyer. Perfect.

"I can't trust anyone in the community right now," G continued. "I told you that. Someone is sheltering the culprit in this case and hiding her with a spell that smells familiar, but I can't locate the source." G started pacing the tight confines of the sunporch turned office.

"*Hiding her*? Does that mean you know who we are chasing?"

"There is no 'we' in this equation." He rounded on me, angrier than I think I'd ever seen him.

Angry at me?

We'd had our disagreements over the years. But no

matter how mad at each other we might be during those disagreements, we always put a good face on it and said "I love you" before we turned out the light. Until I'd discovered his infidelity. Even that night I was more sad and disappointed than truly angry.

Tonight, I knew he was not angry at me. At *her*, perhaps. More likely mad at circumstances.

"Who is she?"

"An old nemesis. Nothing more." He dismissed my question with a casual gesture. G was never casual.

"What happened when you arrested her the first time?"

Silence.

"G?"

"I can't tell you. I am sworn . . ."

"I am beyond the ignorant mundane. I'm the woman who has raised your magically talented children. I will continue to be an important influence in their lives. 'She' just trashed your son's ballet company props and costumes. Your children are involved in this case. I need to know what you know in order to protect them."

He walked out of the room.

I continued playing with graphics for the flyer. G made noises in the kitchen, indicating he got a glass of water, drank it, rinsed the glass, and put it into the dishwasher. Then he tromped back into my office and quietly closed the door.

"Seal of confidentiality. But only because you were my wife for thirteen years and your role in the community is blurred. Blurring."

"Okay." I put the finishing touches on the flyer with a few clicks. Busywork.

"When a magician goes rogue, uses dark magic to do harm, gathers power for power's sake, or breaks the code of invisibility for the wrong reasons, my job is to track them down. I have some authority to scare the crap out of them for minor offenses. For major crimes, I take them to the High Court of the Guild of Wizards."

"And then?"

He drew in a deep breath and let it go, as if preparing for yoga. Or steeling himself for something painful. "If found guilty by a panel of seven master wizards, then they are stripped of their magic using a process that is painful and humiliating. I will spare you the details. Their wands are broken and burned before them. Then they are cast into a dungeon cell for the rest of their lives. They are fed, their medical needs seen to, and granted one hour of sunlight and exercise each day in the company of five guards."

"Five guards each?"

"We have only a few prisoners. Rogue magicians of that caliber are rare. I've observed the process twice, but never been a part of it."

"If this woman is your old nemesis, then I have to presume she was never convicted and incarcerated."

Silence.

"If she had her magic stripped from her and her wand burned, how did she escape and come here? To menace you and my children?"

"I don't know. She had to have had help. In over one thousand years of records, she is the only one to escape her dungeon cell beneath a ruined castle in the foothills of the Pyrenees."

"Castle ruins crumble. Foundations weaken as the elements creep in."

"Not this one. It only looks ruined."

"Protected by magic. And I imagine the spells that make it look ruined also repel tourists."

"Not even avid ghost hunters go there." He cracked a smile.

"What did you find when you examined her cell?" He went to Marseilles recently, the closest big city to those forbidding mountains.

"She had help. Someone in the community went rogue but not overtly. I have theories and ideas but no proof. I suspect her helper must be a full wizard with a wide range of talents. But not one that is registered as a *master* wizard—someone strong enough to overcome wards and guards and physical locks as well as magical ones. Someone who has either manifested new talents later in life or has hidden a major talent all of his—or her—life."

"Either way, that is a problem," I mused. "You will be up against someone of equal skills with no conscience. Who is the escaped prisoner who would attract such a powerful rescuer?"

"You don't want to know."

"I have to know." This was really scary. I wanted to crawl into bed and pull the covers over my head for a long, long, long time. I couldn't. "I have three children to protect."

"That's my job."

"You aren't here twenty-four/seven. You're busy finding this woman and taking her down. I can't be certain that will happen before she endangers me or the kids because we are close to you. I don't have to guess that she came to Eugene to get revenge on you for taking her down. What better way than to hurt your family. Perhaps destroy your home, with its protective pentagram."

"She never would live in this house. I thought she hated the antique décor and the lack of open space in this house, the hidden nooks and crannies. Did you know that, for generations, kids have called this place the 'Witch's Hat House' because of the conical roofs on the towers?"

He paused, drawing in a deep breath and gazing around the rooms he'd grown up in, and I knew he loved this house as much as I did.

"We had a condo overlooking the river, all glass and steel, open concept, every room flowing into all the other rooms, no doors, not even on the bedroom and bathroom. Lots of light. Everything this house is not." He settled his gaze out the window into the far distance, beyond the backyard fence, deep into his past.

"Your lover?"

"My wife."

"D'Accore died giving birth to Jason." But he never talked about her, never reminisced. And he had no pictures of her anywhere in the house, not even in the trunks in the attic filled with family photos and memorabilia.

I searched the computer for other photos I'd taken, and hidden deep behind layers of encryption.

"The D'Accore I loved died long before Jason was born. The laughing, sweet, naïve girl I married in good faith never existed. She cast a spell on me, making me think I was protecting her from reality. All she wanted from me was more power. I was too young and inexperienced in love to realize that at the time. She was a 'sport,' a magician with no genetic links to power."

"A genetic mutant," I muttered. I'd seen enough kids' cartoons and monster movies about mutants.

"Yeah. She grew up with power and thought she was unique, never even looked for a master to train her. That's what eventually drove her insane."

I cringed inside. Had Jason inherited her insanity? Hopefully not. He had a loving father training him, teaching him control, ethics, and morality in magic.

"When I discovered her experimenting with blood magic—my blood by the way—while she was pregnant, I had to do something to protect the baby," Jason continued his confession. "If she'd continued, Jason would have been born blind and crippled, if he survived in the womb."

"So you turned her in." I found a photo of the woman in bed with G, the only one of the batch that showed her face. Blurry, as if the photographer had jarred the camera at just the wrong moment. I pointed to it. I couldn't see more than that she was blonde and had classic, symmetrical features, and a curvy body worthy of a stripper.

G jerked his head downward once in agreement.

"I received a text that I thought was from you. It said, 'Meet R's apartment' and was signed with a heart U and a picture of a daphnia flower. It never occurred to me at the time that you didn't know about Raphe, his apartment, or my connection to him."

"Because you were super horny after a trip out of town."

He gulped and nodded acknowledgment. "I thought you wanted a romantic interlude away from the kids. I admit I was more than ready and thinking with my hormones rather than my head. I wanted you, Daffy, not a one-night stand from a woman I met in a bar. D'Accore wore an illusion of you, in face and form. A perfect match even down to the birthmark under your left breast."

I grabbed at my chest in shock, wondering who could have gotten close enough to me to see that and copy it. No one but G. Well, maybe one high school boyfriend who'd gotten my bra off before I panicked and ran home. Maybe a hidden camera in the shower? "It wasn't me," I gasped.

"I know that now. A mundane camera can't capture an illusion, even one that good. When you showed me those photos, it was the first indication I had that D'Accore had escaped prison. My bosses were too embarrassed to warn me. I think she was trying to steal some of my power. But she couldn't know that I have some psychic implants that prevent that. Imposed by three master wizards who are much more powerful than she is now, or her helper is. You are the only one outside the High Court who knows that, by the way."

"She has no power of her own?"

"Not much. Just what she can strip from wands and the murder of the owners of those wands. Which is why she went after the ones Shara found in my safe and Jason disguised as props. I don't know what kind of talents she could absorb from those pieces of wood. They were pretty much spent, dribbling away power from the time they were separated from their owner. I hadn't had time to truly examine them closely." He pinched the bridge of his nose, much like Jason did when he got an allergy migraine.

Some of me melted inside. G was a victim in this whole mess.

But that didn't make up for his manipulation of me with magic. He seduced me into moving in with him so that I would care for his child, freeing him to travel on magical business.

"I didn't fight the divorce because I thought she wanted to kill me. You and the children would be safer if I was elsewhere."

"What did you do to her fifteen years ago?" Was I asking about her, or about me?

"I built a methodical case against D'Accore and called the then Sheriff to take her away—he has since been promoted to the High Court and I replaced him as Sheriff a year later. I was only a deputy then and assigned to this region, not the world. After the trial and conviction, the Guild kept her in a straitjacket in a secure asylum for four months until . . . until our physicians were forced to take the baby by C-section to save Jason. Then I brought our son home, to this house, with the protective pentagram and family ghosts to care for him while the High Court stripped her of her magic. I had already destroyed her wand."

He'd gone through three nannies and two housekeepers until I moved in with him. None of them satisfactory to guard his precious son.

"What was her wand?"

"A vintage Zippo lighter with a death's head soldered on one side. The names of her victims appeared etched on the back as they died."

"A fire starter with smoke for eyes. Not smoke colored eyes." That left Flora Chambers out of the running. Dang.

"Now her eyes are almost colorless. She went blind trying to free herself from the straitjacket—maybe even gave herself a mild stroke. She tried so hard she burst blood vessels in her eyes, over and over again until she fried nerve endings and brain synapses and lost her eyesight and any possibility of restoration. I have reports that she lights a fire with damp kindling and sends the smoke through keyholes or under doors to 'see' for her. That's what Raphe was trying to tell us after the second fire at Magical Brews."

A foreboding chill coursed through my body, turning my bones to icicles. All those times I'd smelled smoke. The two fires at Magical Brews. "She wants Jason's eyes to replace her own."

"And his power. Blood link. Oh, my God! Where is he?"

"I hope he's in the dining room doing his homework." We both headed for the door. I ran through the kitchen, G right behind me. We skidded to a halt as we passed through the open swinging door.

All three children, plus BJ were sitting at their accustomed places, laptops and tablets open, books piled beside them. Not a word passed among them.

What surprised me was that BJ sat next to Jason without even glancing up at Belle. She secured a sloppy bun at her nape with her hair sticks. Frequently, she turned her head so the jade charms clanked against the ivory. And still BJ did not look at her.

Had she lost her adoration talent?

Or had BJ found a way to circumvent it?

I heard the tinkle of a tiny bell. BJ had left his house key on the table beside his laptop. A silver bell the size of his thumb dangled from the chain. He flicked it twice.

Belle cringed and touched her jade charms.

The chill returned to my body. I'd learned the signs watching my own children. BJ was a late blooming magician—probably a sport—and the bell was his wand.

The doorbell rang, echoing the note from BJ's keychain.

# Twenty-Two

TOO MUCH NON-INFORMATION twisted through my mind as I yanked open the front door. John Mooney, dressed as a real estate agent, rather than wearing his witchy batik caftan stood on the front porch with a bouquet of coral, orange, and apricot roses. In Victorian flower lore, the perfect blossoms symbolized attraction, lust, desire, and enthusiasm.

Or could be just seasonal colors past the Equinox and approaching harvest festivals and Halloween.

G growled deep in his throat as he hovered behind me.

"I've got the flyer ready for you, John. I just have to print it." I stood away from the door and gestured him in.

G moved as if to block him.

"Be nice," I mouthed at him.

He retreated to the dining room and stood at the head of the table where he could see the progress of each of the children. A protective patriarch of the old school.

BJ flicked his bell twice more. Nervous habit? Or a signal.

"Come back to my office," I said to John, uncomfortable with the way the evening was turning out, and led the way past the dining room and through the swinging door, which I closed behind us. In the kitchen, I took the roses from him and laid them on the counter. "I'll deal with these later."

John hesitated within the frame of the glass French

doors. "Your house smells of cinnamon," he said casually.

"I made a batch of snicker doodles." I hit print and watched the paper unfurl from the machine. "Would you like one?"

He took the sheet of paper from my hand. "I didn't know G would be here."

"He often comes over to supervise homework. The kids should be finished soon and clamoring for food. I swear Jason will eat an entire dozen cookies if I turn my back for a moment." When in doubt, talk about the children.

"An active teenage boy in a growth spurt. His job is to eat his way through the grocery store."

We laughed. But it was brittle and false. Uncomfortable.

How would I respond to John if G weren't in the next room?

I remembered the sloppy, smootchy kiss he'd pushed through his phone. Probably the same way.

If John's talent was reading minds, he certainly picked up something from me and returned to neutral business. "I'll run off a hundred of these and have my assistants plaster the town with them. A fund-raiser for our ballet company and the news that Magical Brews will be selling baked goods should guarantee a good turnout. Now if you'll excuse me, I have to run. I need to do the paperwork to put a bid on a house first thing in the morning. For a nice young couple. It's their first purchase, and they require a lot of handholding." His rambling dribbled down to nothing. Was it his manner or his words that sounded false?

"Okay. But take some cookies."

"I'll get a cinnamon bun tomorrow at the coffee shop."

And he was gone, practically running out the front door, which G slammed shut as soon as he'd passed through.

BJ's bell rang three times.

"I thought he was your friend." I admonished my ex. "Even if you don't trust anyone, why not him?"

G retreated to the dining room and guided Shara through the shifting borders of a small Asian country.

*Alakazam!*
*Magic Slam*

I sang as I danced around the shop kitchen, tapping every surface with my wooden spoon, re-creating the catchy rap rhythm.

"Boo!" G whispered in my ear.

Startled, I gasped and spun around, nearly clonking him on the head with my spoon.

He grabbed my wrist, lightly, before I connected.

"What are you doing here?" I asked, still breathless from my celebration of baking and knowing I got all the treats for the bake sale *right*.

"I might ask you the same." His gaze wandered around the kitchen while he still held my wrist.

"I'm waiting for the last batch of cupcakes to cool enough to apply frosting, then I'm going home. Why are *you* here?"

"Checking on you. It's four in the morning."

"What?" I shifted my gaze from his eyes to the surrounds. "Um?"

"Um is right."

All around us flour and sugar and stuff hung suspended in the air, sparkling with my joy.

"It looks like magic," I whispered in awe.

And all around me, in the cooler, on the counters, everywhere I looked were masses and masses of baked goods. Instead of ten dozen cupcakes, I had baked and frosted ten times that many. Gluten-free bar cookies, and vegan sheet cakes as well. Enough to feed my customers for a week, or service the bake sale single-handedly.

"Because it is magic, love." He kissed my nose and released my hand. "I've been waiting for this to happen since the day I met you." He reached to encircle my waist and draw me close. "Hopeful and scared at the same time."

Because D'Accore had magic and she'd scared him badly when he was young, probably only in his mid-twenties when he fell in love with her. I knew that without him having to tell me. I knew that from the way he spoke about her the other night. She scared him to the bones and beyond.

I ducked away from him. "What is that supposed to mean?" I wandered around, mouth agape at the ingredients that looked like stars glinting against a dark sky. Only the room was bright and the overhead lights didn't dim or wash out the glow.

"If you wave your spoon in a big circle once clockwise, you can gather it all together. Then close your fist as if capturing the whole and spin yourself and the spoon counterclockwise. You'll break the spell but not have a huge mess to clean up," he said with a chuckle.

I did so. Strangely enough, the suspended flour and sugar vanished from the air and piled in the prep sink with its garbage disposal. Easy to wash down the drain without extra sweeping.

Then I rounded on him. "What do you mean, you've been waiting for this to happen?" I screamed at him, loud enough to wake Gayla two floors above us.

"I sensed latent magic deep within you that first day in the coffee shop when you knew precisely what I wanted to drink before I knew myself."

"But . . . but I'm an adult. Magic manifests in adolescence."

"Most of the time. But occasionally if the talent is buried deep or repressed—as your parents would have done to you after they locked your beloved grandmother in an insane asylum—it can blossom later. That usually needs exposure to others working magic on a regular basis. Living with me, in my house for fourteen years . . . it had to happen sooner or later. Given the strength of your baking magic, and your weather witching, I'm surprised it took this long." He rocked back on his heels, hands in his pockets, cocky and self-assured. But I'd seen his hands tremble in fear before he stuffed them in his pocket to hide them.

D'Accore had really done a number on him. No wonder he'd used me rather than loving me. He was afraid to love a woman with magical talent.

But he trusted me to raise his children.

"You? You did this to me!"

He nodded. "Afraid so."

"You infected me with this disease! You made me one of you, like D'Accore?"

"Not like her. Never like her." All the color drained from his face. Then he gulped and turned his fabulous blue gaze on me, directly and without a trace of manipulation or lies, or . . . or fear. "You would never hurt anyone for your own gain. That's why I've fallen in love with you. I only lusted after my ex."

"You think you've fallen in love now. What about when we first met? You made me think it was love at first sight."

"Not at first sight. But over the years . . ."

"You *used* me." The old fear grabbed hold of my heart and wouldn't let go. "You manipulated me with magic to make me think I was in love. But all you really wanted, what you needed, was a babysitter so you could travel the world when you got the big promotion from deputy to Sheriff."

"Not entirely." He started backing toward the door while I took a fiercer grip on my spoon.

"You are as big a slimeball as when I thought you slept with every bimbo in town!"

I whacked him across the temple. Once, twice, thrice.

In another brightly colored sparkle of sugar and spice,

he shrank into a black goat and bleated long and loud, tongue hanging out in a wail of bewilderment.

But just like the animal he truly was, he recovered quickly and trotted over to the counter where he pulled a tray of cooling cupcakes to the floor and began eating them.

# Twenty-Three

"**G**AYLA!" I wailed into my phone.

"Wa ... What, Sweet Pea?" she replied sleepily. "Do you know what time it is?"

"Yes, and I need your help. Now."

"Where?"

"In the shop, where else?" G had wandered toward the cooler and found more interesting things to eat. I dashed to bump him in a different direction, and almost lost the phone to his mobile mouth. My hip in his face discouraged him from finding fodder in the cooler. He returned to the crumbling mess on the floor.

"Where the hell did that beast come from?" Gayla screamed. She stood framed in the doorway to the interior stair, still in her oversized T-shirt that hung to her knees and sagged across her shoulders. Her straight black hair stuck out at odd angles, and her eyes were rimmed with red where she'd rubbed the sleep out of them.

"Gayla, this is G."

"Huh?"

"We had a fight. I bopped him upside the head with my spoon which apparently is my magic wand, and he turned into what he truly is: an old goat with an insatiable appetite," I babbled. "I'm a real live witch, and he's a master wizard, and all three of our kids have come up with magical talents." I stumbled over the inadvertent pun of young goats. "And all I did was bop him upside the head." Tears burned behind my eyes and threatened to flood.

Given what had happened, I wondered if once I started crying I'd be able to stop before I flooded the kitchen.

"That's not all you bopped upside the head." She wandered around the perimeter of the room, goggling at the racks and racks and racks of cupcakes. "No wonder I dreamed of that stupid rap magic song all night long."

"Um. That was me. In some kind of trance until G woke me out of it."

"Then you had the fight. Because he woke you, or was it something else?"

"Everything else." This time I sobbed. Gayla produced a paper napkin to mop up my tears before I sank into the oblivion of hysterics.

"Well, it's about time you admitted you're a witch. Everyone in town knows that what you do in the kitchen is genuine magic. More than just talent. Frankly, I'm jealous. I always wanted to be a witch, but I guess you have to be born with it, not learn it in middle age."

I laughed through my tears. Leave it to Gayla to turn my problems upside down, inside out, and backward so that they were really funny, not tragic.

"Now what do we do with him?" She eyed G from every angle, head tilting back and forth, hands on hips. "You know, he does have that certain look about him that could be G. But those bluer-than-blue eyes can only be G."

"You aren't questioning my explanation? You believe all this magic stuff?"

"Of course, I do, Sweet Pea. We live in Eugene. Every other person you meet on the street claims to be a psychic or a witch or descended from faeries, or something weird. What better place for real magicians to hide than in plain sight among the other weirdos? Now can you turn the old boy back?"

"I don't know. I don't know that I want to." Except there was his psycho ex wandering around lighting fires and probably threatening my children. I needed G whole and hale to counter her.

"Well, he can't hang around this kitchen. We'd have a hell of a time explaining him to the health inspector."

"That's for sure. I guess I need to take him home. There's a ton of blackberries along the fence. Goats like blackberries. Don't they?"

"I don't know. But according to the newscasts, farmers are renting out goats to clear property overgrown with blackberries. Let me throw some clothes on, and I'll help you load him into the van. Then he's your problem. I'll set about cleaning the entire place with bleach."

G let loose a mournful bleat that smelled of spun sugar and rotten milk.

Twenty minutes later, we'd finally shoved G's butt into the back of the van. He protested mournfully that we were abusing him, making him go where he didn't want to go. The only thing he could find to eat was an old gym sock of Belle's. I grabbed it away from him. He turned his mouth and his attention to the ribbing along the upholstery seam that separated the back of the driver's seat from the front.

I climbed in and started the engine. Then I batted his nose away. "Five minutes, G. Five minutes and you can work on the backyard. Much better for your tummy."

"Bleahhhhch."

I backed out of the alley while G nibbled at my hair. Over by the dumpster, Raphe threw back his head and laughed. "No cheese rolls or cinnamon buns for you, buddy," I called to him as we passed his favored nook.

G shifted from the loose ends of my ponytail to my ear, sticking his long prehensile tongue deep into that orifice. "I hope you like earwax."

He kept up his attentions, now to my cheek and neck below my ear. The one place G knew drove me wild.

"Stop that!" I slapped his muzzle and pulled his beard down and away from me. "You aren't my husband anymore, in any form. If you keep it up, buddy, I'll turn you into a louse."

Some glimmer of human intelligence must have lingered in his single-minded brain. He closed his bluer-than-blue eyes, fluttered his extra-long lashes, and moaned as if grieving over my grave.

"I'm not dead yet. But our marriage is," I informed him as we climbed the hill toward the house. Two more blocks and I turned into the long driveway, taking it all the way to the back of the house. I stopped in front of the garage beside G's big sedan. The right-side passenger door of my van should open next to the gate in the weathered picket fence. If only I could manage him for six steps. . . .

The lights were on in the kitchen. Not yet five o'clock.

Oh, yeah, we had to be at the Saturday Market by six to set up and open by seven. And Belle had an outdoor chess match that started at eight. This was the last Saturday the chess club could count on good weather in the park where six small square tables invited pickup games among strangers. Club participants welcomed the challenge of playing older, more experienced members of the community. Not all of those adults could beat the club. Few could manage a stalemate with Belle, unless she got hit by a super bad attack of the clumsies and knocked all the pieces off the board. It had happened before.

I jumped out of the van and slammed the door quickly, before G could escape. Then I yelled for Jason to come help.

He opened the kitchen door, sleepily rubbing at his eyes, barefoot and shirtless. "Can't it wait?" he mumbled.

"I need your help *now*!"

He must have heard the panic in my voice for he bounced lightly down the three steps, barely wincing at the chill that assaulted his feet and chest.

When he was through the gate and right beside me, I

finally slid back the passenger door. G didn't hesitate to leap free of his prison. Fortunately, Jason was quicker with his dance-honed reflexes.

"What the hell?" Jason spluttered, instinctively grabbing G by the nape and the beard.

I pushed them both into the backyard, making certain the gate was closed and latched behind them. By this time the girls had appeared in the doorway. They both wore jeans and T-shirts, but hadn't yet thought to don sweaters or shoes.

"Shara, guard the gate so he doesn't get out. Use your powers to secure the latch rather than open anything."

"Yeah, sure." She took up her place and folded her arms across her chest. She mumbled something, fluttered her fingers, and jerked her head downward once. We'd seen that movement performed by a genie on some TV show.

"What's going on, Mom?" Belle asked.

I noted that she wore her hair sticks. Hopefully, her magic worked on animals as well as people.

"Lead him over to the blackberries and let him graze while I think."

"Mom, why did you bring a goat home on a day when we have to be everywhere in a hurry?" Jason asked. Then he stared into the eyes of the beast.

G blinked at Jason, then followed Belle willingly.

"Oh, my God! Is that Dad?" Jason gasped, leaving his jaw hanging open.

"Yes," I whispered.

"What happened, Mom?" Belle abandoned the goat and came to stand beside me. She wrapped her arm around my shoulders. She stood almost as tall as me. When had that happened?

Shara came up on the other side and grabbed my waist to help hold me up. She at least was no taller than I remembered. Still my baby, but acting more like she needed to babysit me.

"He came to check on me. There's four or five van

loads of baked goods at the shop that we need to transport to the market." I trailed off, not sure how to continue.

"What happened?" Jason pressed me.

All three children focused on me.

"We had a fight. I hit him upside the head with my spoon." I fished for the tool in my back pocket and showed it to them.

"Is that your wand?" Belle asked quietly. She peered at the ordinary cooking implement as if it were an alien artifact.

"I . . . I think so."

"Your talent finally manifested," Shara said, sounding not at all surprised.

"Yeah, I guess so."

"So what happened when you knocked him silly?" Jason continued to urge the story from me.

"He became *that* in a blaze of sparkling spun sugar."

Silence. We all turned to watch G strip the blackberry vines from the fence. Only he wasn't there. He wasn't anywhere.

Shara ran around to the back of the greenhouse, to the tiny trapdoor where excess water drained into the creek on the other side of the fence. I followed her, dreading that I would find she had widened the opening for her own secret explorations.

Yep. She had. And G was stuck there, wiggling his butt and pawing at the ground with his back hooves while he happily ripped delicate herbs from their trays. How had they gotten so close to the vent? They should be atop one of the long tables.

I glared at Shara.

She looked back at me blinking innocently. "We will talk later," I promised her.

"Mom, you can't leave him like this," Belle reminded me. "It is kind of funny when you think about what he did to you last spring. But we need him today to drive us around."

"We need both of you, Mom." Shara looked like she

was going to cry, more from the thought of losing her dad than for any punishment she might receive for her exercises in curiosity.

"I don't know how I transformed him in the first place," I wailed.

"Okay," Jason said thoughtfully. "Dad tells us to think it through. Remember every thought, every gesture, down to the deepest motivation in your heart just before you did whatever you did."

"Then back it out. If you circled clockwise with the spoon, you have to go counterclockwise this time. If you thought Alakazam, you have to say Mazakala."

I held my spoon up before my eyes, forcing myself to think it through, every horrible second of my temper out of control.

"Um, Belle and Shara, your father left some of his clothes in the back of my closet." Actually, I'd noticed more and more of his clothes showing up there after every visit, like he was planning on coming home again.

My anger at his audacity welled up.

Jason urged his sisters back into the house while I pulled a reluctant G out of the greenhouse. He blinked at me. Was that truly love I saw in his eyes?

I had been gazing malevolently at those wonderful blue eyes and the thick mane of dark hair just before I struck him with the spoon.

I hadn't been singing when I hit him. I'd been incoherent with anger that he'd infected me with magic and that he'd never truly loved me. He'd only used me.

So I conjured up thoughts of how deeply I'd loved him for many years. Magically induced or not, I did love him, and his children, and the home he'd given me. And the greenhouse he'd built for me.

Finally, I imagined an appreciation for the magic he'd pulled out of the deep recesses of my soul. Magic that my parents had forced me to repress with promises of hellfire and damnation—or imprisonment in an insane asylum with electrical shocks to my brain to cure me.

One strong wallop with the spoon on his butt and the sparkles rose around him like a million fireflies. Black fur gave way to naked skin. His legs twisted away from the backward knees, and his hooves spread into feet and hands, elongating into fingers and toes.

I admired the elegant form of his human body a moment until he straightened up and looked around, blinking in bewilderment. He didn't seem to notice that he was as naked as the day he was born.

# Twenty-Four

**"T**HAT WAS *INTERESTING*," G said over the breakfast table. "I remember everything, but it was like a heavy curtain wrapped around my self-control. I could do anything and everything I wanted without hindrance or rules. Quite liberating. But not something I want to repeat again soon. Or ever." He plucked at the worn chambray shirt Jason had found for him in my closet and looked puzzled. He'd barely touched the scrambled eggs, toast with jam, and coffee I'd thrown together for all of us.

It was going to be a long day.

"I figured casual clothes, for you, are a disguise. No one will recognize you at the Saturday Market," Jason replied to the unasked question. Then he let loose the chuckle he'd been holding in for the last half hour.

"It's a sad thing when a man loses the respect of his children."

Shara snorted her orange juice and spent many long moments mopping up the mess with every paper napkin she could reach.

"I think you did that when you slept with the bimbo. Where was it? At the Jasmine Palms, I bet. That's where all the football players talk about taking their dates," Belle supplied for all of us.

"Work related and not what it looked like," G said, sitting up straighter and looking down at all of us with his best quelling stare.

"Looked like fun to me," Jason said.

G blushed. I'd never seen him so ... uncontrolled before.

"About today. G, I think you and Jason should take the van and load it up with the baked goods. You can monitor the crowd at the market while I take Belle to the chess match. Shara stays with me, and I'll help her with her homework which she has been neglecting this last week in favor of cracking computer codes and drawing mazes."

"How'd you know!" Shara protested.

"I'm your mother. I have eyes in the back of my head."

"In this family, that might be more than just an expression," Belle grumbled. "I found a book that theorizes all the magicians in town have a fae ancestor or two, way back two hundred or more years ago."

"Remember that when you bring home stray boys." G pointed an accusatory finger at her. "But I can't help out today. I have a dead psychic medium in Portland and a dying water witch in Sacramento. I have to secure their wands and investigate. That's why I came to check on you at the shop. I needed to leave to investigate. But I wasn't sure if I should take Jason with me or not. Let him learn the ropes of my job."

I half caught the idea that he wanted to keep Jason close to protect him.

"You have to learn to delegate. That's what you have deputies for," I insisted.

"I followed a trail of dead bodies across Europe and the US hoping to catch D ... er ... our perp before she could harvest power stored in their wands. I'm not giving up on the investigation."

"You aren't giving up. You are saving valuable time by letting your deputies handle it. We know our perp has been around Eugene of late. If anyone at the Saturday Market has crafts and collectibles, some of them may have discarded wands from grandma's attic, not knowing what they are. That's what ends up at the antique mall. Right?"

"Yes. But . . ."

"Oh, Dad, stop being such a control freak and get with Mom's agenda," Belle admonished him. "Haven't you learned yet that no one wins an argument with Mom?"

"Apparently, I'm not going to win this one," he grumbled. "Give me a few minutes of privacy on the phone and then we'll go. I figure I'll need to make three or four trips in the van. Those rolling racks do break up into two parts to fit in the hatch, don't they?"

"Got it covered." Jason held up his own phone. "There will be six dancers with parents and appropriate SUVs and pickups at the shop to help transport in seventeen minutes."

"Make sure you keep the cupcakes in the shade. We don't want the buttercream frosting to melt. It may be cool now, but the sun will break through the clouds around ten. Temps pushing seventy-five by early afternoon."

G looked at me strangely. "Weather witching as well as kitchen witching. And a late bloomer. How will I explain you to the Guild?"

"That's not weather witching. It's just experience and paying attention to weather forecasts," I defended myself, still not comfortable with any of these "witch" labels.

"Yeah, right," Jason said on an eye roll.

"Mom, I want to take my own chessboard today. I think I'm extending my wands into the white pieces. I need to use them as much as possible." Belle rose from the table and cleared her plate and utensils. Automatically, she rinsed them and placed them into the dishwasher.

"Finish your breakfast, G, while I change out of these flour-laden clothes into something presentable." I patted my back pocket to make sure my spoon was in place.

"Find a better holster for that, one that isn't readily

visible," G ordered. "You look kind of strange carrying it in your back pocket in anything dressier than jeans."

"Later." I hoped for five minutes in the shower. My hair felt gritty and greasy. I hadn't indulged in a baking marathon like that since the morning after I threw G out. Actually, this session was more intense, more productive, and longer.

Catharsis. That was the only word that described the experience.

Jason walked down the front stairs, carrying his shoes and fussing with the cork insoles. They helped a lot, but he was still not comfortable in real shoes. He wanted his feet in contact with wood as long as possible before a long day on his feet at the market. At least the market would be on a grass field and not cement or linoleum.

The sound of his father's voice barking into his phone in his old office, now Mom's craft room, brought him up short. "Why is the FBI calling me?"

FBI?

Jason pressed his ear against the door, letting the sound vibrations resonate with the wood and attune to his ear. Dad sounded like he was speaking loudly right next to him. And the other voice ... at the other end of the mobile phone transmission was distant but quite discernable.

"The IRS called, asking us to investigate more than just tax fraud. Maybe international money laundering. Since you know the man in question, we thought this might fall under your jurisdiction."

"I appreciate the interagency cooperation, but I'm not an accountant. I wouldn't know what to look for."

However, Belle was a wiz with numbers, almost magically so. Jason was willing to bet that if his sister got a quick glance at a ledger, she'd pinpoint irregularities without even thinking hard.

He wondered if his dad thought the same thing as he paused before replying. "I may have a file to send you.

But the source is not verifiable. When I have confirmed the accuracy of the information, I will send it to you."

"If the man is using . . . um . . . skills that are your jurisdiction, couldn't you spot them?"

"Maybe. Look, I have a difficult and busy day ahead. I'll keep my eyes and ears open. Then I'll call both you and the IRS to tell you what to look for." Dad sounded exasperated, impatient, and . . . wary. Maybe even afraid.

The man on the other end of the phone line rattled off some names and numbers. Jason heard a stylus tapping a screen making notes. If he listened just a little bit more closely, he might be able to tell what letters and numbers Dad recorded or what file he stored them in.

The sound of a body shifting in a chair signaled the end of the conversation and the eavesdropping.

Jason patted the wooden door and whispered, "Thank you." Then he scooted into the kitchen to receive more instructions from Mom.

The conversation nagged at him like the tricky timing in the "Ritual Fire Dance."

Not the timing. The reference to "interagency cooperation." Who did Dad work for in truth? The Guild, of course. But who gave him the authority to investigate with or for the FBI and the IRS? A black ops US agency?

———————

"G, if D'Accore is stripping old wands to regain her power, does that mean she's absorbing different talents?" I whispered into my phone on the edge of the chess tournament crowd. I tried to keep both Belle and Shara in sight, but milling and growing numbers of onlookers kept getting in the way.

"Possibly. We are in uncharted territory here," he replied. He must have eavesdroppers nearby. Or he'd learned by experience to never discuss his business in a public place.

"If she's stripping the wands, why are you finding her castoffs in antique malls and flea markets?"

"She may have discarded them as unimportant. But there is always some residue. That's why we have to burn the leftovers, to make sure the energy dissipates back into the world." He sounded as if he were walking, moving behind something that acted as a sound barrier.

"Then we don't know what powers she has absorbed and can throw back at us."

"True."

Shara showed signs of restlessness. I needed to get through fifteen people to grab her before she found something more interesting than spelling practice.

Then I spotted BJ. He hadn't been over to the house much since Belle uninvited him to her party. He and four friends made a wedge, pushing through the crowd, oblivious to bruised toes and elbows to ribs. He scowled constantly. The bell on his keychain rang continuously.

All five of them made a beeline for Belle.

"G, get over here fast. I think we have trouble."

"Jason . . . ?"

"Bring him if you have to. Just get here in the next two minutes!"

"Oh, my God! She's here, Daffy. D'Accore is here. I have to stay. Do what you have to do. I'll clean it up later."

As usual, he was elsewhere when I faced trouble with the kids. I had to invent a solution to five bullies out to do mischief to my daughter. I knew of only one thing I could do with my wooden spoon, my *wand*. I shouldn't turn them all into toads in public.

The crowd that had gathered to observe Belle battle it out with a wizened curmudgeon from the university began muttering at the boys' rude intrusion. Murmurs turned into shouts of protest as the boys slapped people aside. One broad gentleman made a point of standing in their way with fists bunched and raised. BJ lifted his keychain and rang the bell three times. The man's face fell slack and he stared, unblinking, into the distance. BJ walked around him, followed by his phalanx of minions.

So not good.

I grabbed Shara, stuffed her tablet in her backpack, and thrust it at her. "Stay with me." I pointed toward Jason's best friend who had suddenly become a menace.

Belle finally noticed the disturbance in the usually silent crowd of watchers. I watched her reach for her hair sticks. BJ's head reared up and he focused on the ornaments.

Uh-oh. He now knew what and where her wand was.

"Shara, do you have your key?"

"Of course! But what can I do against them?" Her pointing finger trembled. She sensed the danger just like I did.

"Can you open the chain that holds BJ's bell in place, make it fall? Maybe trample it in the dirt?"

She snorted. "That's too easy."

"Then do it. Now."

"What about the other guys?"

"They are followers. If they have wands, they are too new and not comfortable yet."

Shara dashed up to BJ and stood in front of him. He was about to knock her aside when she spoke. "What you got there, BJ? A bell. It has a nice tinkle. Doesn't ringing it so much make you want to tinkle?" Audacious. But that's my girl.

BJ looked startled and dropped his gaze from Belle to Shara.

I used his distraction to dash over to stand behind Belle, brandishing my spoon.

Quicker than I could see, Shara pulled her key out from under her T-shirt, got it off the delicate silver chain necklace, and touched the bell with it. BJ's wand fell to the ground with an atonal clank.

BJ's mouth gaped. He dropped to all fours, frantically searching for his wand.

Shara, bless her heart, twisted the toe of her tennis shoe back and forth as if grinding something. Hopefully flattening that annoying trinket as well as burying it.

"What you gonna do with that spoon, Grandma?" one of BJ's thugs asked. "Spank me with it? Ooooh, I'd like that." He spun around and presented his butt to me.

I reached back to gain some momentum and heard a sharp crack. My hand felt suddenly lighter.

Another of the bullies reached over my shoulder from behind and showed me the top half of my wand. He wore heavy gloves to protect him from the magic leaking out of the broken shaft.

"No, no, no, no!" Belle screamed as she grabbed her hair with both hands.

"Young man, take your hands off that girl," the curmudgeon bellowed. "I'll have you up on charges of malicious mischief and molestation." Prudently, he pulled out his cell phone—one of those antique flip phones that didn't do anything but make phone calls—and hit the panic button that automatically dialed 911.

Belle's attacker yanked his hand away from her claws. But he came up with half of one hair stick, the pointed bottom half, devoid of the jade charm.

Belle chanted something, and the sharpened ivory turned on the boy and stabbed his palm. He dropped it and ran with the others away from the sound of police sirens in the distance.

The curmudgeon grabbed his black chess queen and threw it at the boys. The one in the rear stumbled as it thunked him in the middle of his spine.

Belle had better aim. She sent a pawn directly into BJ's exposed neck. He fell face forward into the turf, unconscious and bleeding.

# Twenty-Five

G FOCUSED ON D'ACCORE. Tall and blonde as ever. New streaks of fire-red in her bobbed, bright gold tresses—artificial dye. She wore designer jeans with heels, a white dress shirt, and a leather jacket. She looked like she'd just walked off a fashion runway in Paris. Designer casual. Expensive designer casual.

Who was funding her clothes, her hair treatments, and her travel? The one person he now knew had the money.

And a motive. An old motive that had simmered for a long, long time.

G's gut churned. He frantically sought Jason's lithe figure among the slender dancers behind the table in their booth. At five-ten, headed for six-two, he was only average among his tall athletic friends. Then a dark-haired boy bobbed up. G sighed in partial relief.

D'Accore was three aisles away and examining some handcrafted jewelry. She held up a jade necklace, chunky flat stones in a pavé that would fill the space above a scoop-necked T-shirt. He bet it would cost her benefactor many pretty pennies.

She couldn't see, yet she'd homed in on the most expensive piece of jewelry in the entire market.

He grabbed the opportunity of her distraction to pull Jason out of the booth and around the three-sided tent to the relative obscurity in the alley along the backs of this aisle of vendors.

"Dad!" Jason protested.

"Hush. My perp is here. I need to get you away. Now."

"But ..." Jason tugged his arm out of G's grip and turned back toward his friends.

"No buts. The bake sale is going well. Your friends can handle it. Now come with me." G reestablished his grip on Jason's arm and led him toward the parking lot.

"Dad, we can't take the van. It's still full of cupcakes," Jason reminded him.

"Screw the cupcakes." He took one step closer to the bright red Chevy.

"We need that money. Mom dedicated an entire night to baking for us. I won't desert the cause now."

"Nice pun. But you are right. They probably know the van and that we are here. We need another way out." G searched the periphery for an escape route. He watched Ted Tyler wheel a double rack of cupcakes toward the booth from his battered green pickup. He briefly contemplated hot wiring that vehicle.

"Dad, there." Jason pointed in the opposite direction toward a line of trees on a residential street. The street dead-ended in a heavily treed green space. Behind the mini forest, the land dropped away to a creek coming off one of the buttes. Lots of creeks in the area. Not as much of a fire hazard as he thought.

"She could burn the whole space down with a single flick of her Zippo." Autumnal rains had started, but not enough yet to drench the ground.

"But trees are wood. I can defend myself there. Lots of hiding places and shadows." He added the last at G's attempted protest. "Dad, it's where we need to be. I can feel it."

"When in doubt go with the gut," G said, grabbed his son, and took off at a light jog for the shade of the first Douglas fir.

Instinctively, G let his senses flow outward. Sight, smell, tasting the air, feeling the vibrations of the people moving around him.

A whiff of patchouli perfume overlaying her perpetual smoke touched his nose and his tongue. Of all the things D'Accore might change about her appearance, she couldn't—or wouldn't—change her perfume. It was as important to her identity fifteen years ago as it was now. Behind him. Moving closer.

He gestured silence to Jason. The boy nodded his understanding.

Then G did what he rarely had to do. He mumbled six words in ancient Greek and gestured a circle with his wand that encompassed the two of them.

Instantly, noises and sounds grew muffled as if a wet blanket had fallen over them.

Jason's eyes widened in surprise and . . . awe. He opened his mouth to speak.

G held a finger to his lips to silence him. Again the boy nodded.

They slowed to a rapid walk, conserving energy. They'd both sampled a cupcake or two—well four for Jason and three for G—so they had a short burst of energy for what was to come.

Even through his cone of silence, he smelled a new disturbance in the air. Young male. Three of them. None familiar. Smoke blended with rancid sweat.

At least Jason would not have to face BJ and his buddies in his first fight. Those boys were harassing Daffy and the girls. Damn, he needed to be there. But he had to be here, too.

A fight. G's gut twisted. A fight.

Not all boys indulged in violence at an early age. Jason had never been sent home from school for fighting. Never sported a black eye or the hunched-over posture resulting from a punch to the gut.

Deep down in G's soul, he'd hoped his boy would never know violence, never be placed in a position to be forced to defend himself.

Resolutely, he drew in a deep, fortifying breath. So be it. He'd also hoped that someday Jason would follow in his own footsteps into magical law enforcement. He'd have to learn to fight. Better to start learning now when he had backup rather than later.

They ducked behind the first big tree. One of the ancients, a tall Douglas fir with a trunk as wide as G's shoulders. One hundred to one hundred fifty years old. These guys were like asbestos in fire resistance. D'Accore, before her arrest and conviction, could take one down. She'd had four months to gather a scattering of powers. Only one of her victims controlled fire. He had hope.

They waited on a count of thirty. No sign of pursuit. Yet.

They made a dash four trees closer to the greenspace.

Three boys in their late teens entered the intersection at the back corner of the parking lot. They paused, sniffing.

Bloodhounds. D'Accore, or her rescuer, had recruited boys of minimal talent not likely to bloom into full magic. Useful as minions and bodyguards. The bulk of their muscles extruding from their sleeveless T-shirts suggested how the sorceress planned to use them. She'd probably promised them more power if they did her bidding, then wrapped them in a compulsion spell—standard procedure. She'd been a true siren once, drawing boyfriend after boyfriend into her net. Climbing the ladder of wizardly power until she landed G, as high as she could go without touching the High Court.

These teens would do her bidding doggedly, without fail and without awareness of wounds and pain.

As her current rescuer did.

The power of hypnosis rather than true siren song. She'd stolen that one from victim number three.

The boys headed left, rather than straight ahead. D'Accore strolled after them, a full block behind.

To look at her, he'd not know she was blind. When he pushed his eyesight to examine her more closely, a faint haze circled her head—widdershins. Residual smoke from some fire she'd set. It didn't need to be a big or dangerous one to produce enough smoke to substitute for her eyes. The faintest whiff of wet ashes drifted to him on a seeking breeze.

He dragged Jason closer to the copse. They made it deep into the shadows in two more short sprints. G dropped the cone of invisibility in favor of reigniting his augmented senses.

The first thing that caught his attention was the click, click, click of D'Accore flipping her stolen Zippo open and shut, open and shut. A tiny flame flickered with every flip. Even from two blocks away, he heard it. Even from two blocks away he smelled the rancid smoke of her magic.

"Jason, you'll be safer if you climb a tree. A nice tall one. Stay out of the way and stay quiet," he whispered.

"Who is she?" Jason whispered back. He stepped onto a fallen log, flexing and arching his feet, bending his knees and stretching his arms. It looked like a warm-up.

"My perp. She's dangerous." His boy didn't need to know anything more. For his own safety he shouldn't know anything more.

D'Accore stopped short just as she was about to pass beyond the street G had followed. Her head swiveled right and left, then focused on the copse.

Instinctively, G took one step backward, deeper into the shadows. A part of him remembered her holding a bloody knife and laughing at the corpses of his grandparents in their bed. He quailed in fear and loathing.

Jason bent his knees and leaped to grab a branch that was six feet above the stretch of his arms. Impressive. Satisfactorily out of range of D'Accore and her evil.

D'Accore wiggled the index finger of her left hand, summoning back her three minions. They converged on her corner diagonal from the market parking lot. Like puppets on D'Accore's string, they swiveled and marched directly up the slight rise toward the tree line.

"Up, Jason. Get up higher in that tree. You're still visible." G didn't watch, but he heard rustling branches and felt a shower of dry fir needles. Now he could concentrate. His wand appeared in his hand, almost without thought. One flick and it extended to its full length. It vibrated with his pent-up tension. He broadened his stance for stability.

Lifting their faces as if catching a scent, the minions shifted from their rapid, long-stride walk into a lope and then a run. D'Accore brought up the rear, her high heels and Zippo clicking in rhythm.

G absorbed the rhythm, watching as the boys fell in with D'Accore's steps, matching her movements. Carefully, he wound that rhythm into his spell, using their strength against them. A flick of the wand and . . .

Energy with the force of a loosely mortared stone wall slammed into him, knocking him backward. He stumbled over the fallen log. The backlash energy flew off in every direction like bricks hit by a cannonball.

With the agility of long practice, G propelled himself backward, moving with the fall, arching his back, flipping on his hands and landing on his feet, wand at the ready in a classic fencer's lunge.

"Oh, really, G, don't you think I learned a few things from you all those years I put up with you?" D'Accore taunted him. "Your cute little hypnosis spell won't work on my boys. I got there first. Anything you throw at them will bounce back in your face."

Victim number two's power.

He'd have to enforce the law the old-fashioned way. But he'd have to go through the minions to get to D'Accore, the real criminal in this case.

"The nice thing about borrowing the powers of others," D'Accore continued, "is that there are all kinds of little extras hidden in deep crevices of the mind. They come out with the rest of the owner's magic, and I can weave them into my own spells."

In other words, be very wary when he got to her. The breadth and extent of her powers were unknown territory. Even for her.

G casually stepped up onto the broad fallen tree. An ancient Douglas fir that had come down in a big windstorm a year ago. His soft-soled shoes found purchase in the rough diamond shapes in the bark, worn smooth with time and erosion. Still a lot of life energy trapped in the tree. He soaked it up; used it to focus his senses more sharply.

D'Acorre raised her Zippo.

"Don't even bother, D. Haven't you learned that Oregon rains infuse every cell of our trees with moisture. Takes decades for them to completely dry. This tree won't burn with only your paltry *borrowed* sparking powers."

Before he'd finished speaking, he leaped into a tackle against the middle of the pack of minions. No magic. Just G and his own muscles.

He worked hard to stay fit. In fourteen years of eating Daffy's cooking, he'd only gained five pounds.

As his head butted the foremost minion, he spread his legs and hooked the outside boys' knees with his feet. They all tumbled to the ground, leaf and needle litter flying in all directions.

G recovered enough to send his fist flying, not caring where he connected.

Someone's flailing foot caught his ribs. Adrenaline kept him from hurting. Now. He'd deal with it later.

"That's not fair!" D'Accore screamed. She clicked her Zippo faster. The air warmed around them. But no flames leaped to her command.

G scrambled up, taking a fist to his left eye. Pain exploded around the point of contact. He suppressed it and returned the blow.

"Yiiieeeee!" Jason yelled, swooping down from his perch in the tree. He kicked minion number one in the temple on his way down. That boy's eyes rolled upward, his face grew pallid, and he fell backward. Down for the count.

Minion number two bounded upward, connecting a fist to Jason's jaw and a second jab to the eye before he was fully on his feet. A seasoned fighter.

His third blow slapped Jason with a flat palm against his ear.

Jason shook his head, as if dislodging a bug.

Anger boiled in G's gut. *How dare these upstarts attack his boy!* Before he could react, Jason bent his knees, levitated about two feet up, and flung his feet in number two's gut and head.

That left number three. He hesitated and looked around for support from D'Accore. His eyes widened in hope just as G's fist landed on his nose with a satisfying crunch of crumpled tissue and cartilage. Blood sprayed everywhere.

G wiped his face free of the blinding mess just as another force tackled him from behind. His knee twisted as he fell.

The newcomer squealed as he rolled off of G. His left foot dangled from his ankle at an odd angle.

D'Accore slipped off her shoes and ran back down the street, still clicking her lighter. The height of each new spark diminished with each strike.

"I got you, Dad," Jason said, sliding an arm beneath G's shoulders.

"What?" In a daze of pain and blood spatter, he looked down and saw his jeans stained with dirt, forest debris, and blood. His already swelling knee pushed through the rips in the fabric. "Oh," he said numbly, knowing better than to even try putting weight on it.

He accepted Jason's assistance, noting that the boy pushed some magic into his lift.

"Who?" G asked no one in particular as he settled his weight on his left foot, using his son to balance as the world shifted around him.

At his feet, John Mooney, aka Coyote Blood Moon writhed. "Call an ambulance," he panted through gritted teeth.

His head had connected with G's ribs, worsening the previous damage.

"I think our phones broke in the fight," Jason said.

"Can you drive, Dad? We'll call someone to help Mr. Mooney when we get home."

"Jason, I hope you've been practicing driving on the sly without a permit. I know I did when I was your age. That's my right knee and ..." His mouth grew dry and the world spun.

# Twenty-Six

"YOU HAVE NO RIGHT to hurt my boy!" Flora Chambers screeched at me before I had the front door fully opened.

The sun neared the horizon that Saturday evening. My girls sat huddled together on the sofa, arms draped around each other. Neither tried to watch their favorite trivia TV show, shouting the answers before the host finished reading the question. I'd fed them and soothed them as best I could. I felt as shaky as they from the breaking of my wand.

I hadn't heard from G or Jason.

Denise had called to report glowingly about the money they'd made for the ballet company thanks to my cupcakes and bath salts. They could afford a bunch of new costumes as well as reimburse me.

Good news.

It didn't cheer me because BJ and his friends had broken my wand. I felt helpless, unable to focus. Caught in an endless loop of despair. Empty.

Belle was actually in better shape than me. She still had one intact hair stick—the jade queen glowing lightly in the dim room—and the charm end of the other. The charms held most of her magic, the sticks incidental extensions. She clutched the jade bishop fiercely in her hand.

"What do you have to say for yourself, you witch!" Flora screamed, drawing my attention away from my girls and back to her.

Coming from her, being called a witch was the biggest insult imaginable. A dangerous insult.

I reared back as if she'd slapped me. "Does it bother you at all that BJ and his bullies were arrested for malicious mischief and possible molestation of a minor?"

"False charges, made up by you. You've wronged my boy, and I'll see to it that you pay. He won't be allowed to visit your house of black magic ever again."

"Not such a great loss since he wronged me and hurt Belle." But Shara had hurt him just as badly, mangling his little bell of a wand. I made to close the door.

She stuck her foot in the way.

Oh, how I longed to slam the door and crush her foot. Or make her yank it out of the way.

"Petty adolescent spat," she said and angled her body closer. If I slammed the door, she might get a black eye. Or break her long, gossipy nose. "She disinvited him to her birthday party. BJ has been a part of her celebrations since they were tots! Of course he's angry at her."

Actually, since BJ was four years older than Belle, he'd never been a part of *her* celebrations. He and Jason had been friends, not he and Belle.

Flora was in no mood to view reality, only her twisted version of it.

"And I disinvite you from ever setting foot on my property again. I'm calling my lawyer and suing BJ for malicious mischief and emotional as well as physical damages."

"BJ's father is the best lawyer in town. We're suing you for assault and battery!" She managed to turn around and flee fast enough that the door only spanked her butt. Like I wanted to do with my spoon.

Only I couldn't because BJ and his friends had broken it and stolen the top half.

"Glad I waited in the kitchen until she left," G said as he limped into the living room. Jason held him up by pushing his shoulder under his father's arm. G held his left arm tight across his midriff. His skin was split above his right eyebrow, and that eye was nearly swollen shut, black with bruises. Through the rip in his jeans, his right knee looked swollen and bloodied.

Jason fared better, but he did show signs of bruising on his jaw, around his eye, and on his right knuckles.

"What happened?" I demanded, helping Jason ease G into the recliner. He sighed in relief as he took weight off his knee.

Then he coughed, pain lines radiating around his eyes and along his hollow cheeks.

"Dad was magnificent. If that woman hadn't had four guys with her, he'd have knocked her flat and had her in custody inside of two minutes," Jason said proudly. He brandished his swollen hand. "I helped."

"You held up your share of the fight. I'd like to see how high you can levitate with a real wooden floor beneath you and not just cork in your shoes. And thanks for driving me home. We'll see about getting you a learner's permit next week." G tried to smile at his son and failed. But pride did swell his chest a bit. Until he coughed again.

"Four guys? How could you endanger your son that way?" I screeched, all the while assessing what I needed from the first aid kit. Other than more ice packs than I had in the house and some over-the-counter painkillers, there wasn't much I could do.

"Three minions with more muscle than brains and a protection spell woven around them. And a full-blown wizard. Coyote Blood Moon," G whispered. "I couldn't leave Jason at the market. If they'd separated, one or more could have circled back and taken him."

"John Mooney part of her gang? No. I won't believe that. He's so sweet and has been so helpful," I protested.

"Until you spurned him," G replied, trying to smile again and finding it too painful. "Just like D'Accore spurned him when she started dating me. But she went back to him the moment I realized the extent of her evil and made plans to haul her ass off to jail."

"I didn't spurn him . . . I just delayed responding to his overtures. Delayed until you weren't around growling like an injured mountain lion."

"Y'know, BJ was my best friend until Belle disinvited him to her party," Jason said. I could see the wheels of his mind, seeking patterns in the dance of life as he did the choreography of a ballet.

I hoped he missed the reference to his mother.

"Then he went all distant and started making mean jokes about girls," Jason continued. "I told him to back off, but he got worse. He told me to get lost and took up with some guys that just the day before we'd joked about for being losers and bullies." Jason said. "We heard on the car radio that he and his new friends were arrested at the chess park."

As minors, the police shouldn't have released the boys' names. Belle, however, had informed the press before we left the park.

"They were detained by the police until their parents could claim them," Belle corrected him. She sounded disgusted. "All they got was a lecture and whatever punishment their parents deal out. We couldn't tell the police that breaking our wands was much worse for us than malicious mischief."

"He broke your wands?" G tried to sit up straighter in alarm but fell back against the recliner in pain.

I helped him raise the footrest to ease his knee. Ice packs. I needed to get ice on that knee and his eye. The rest could wait.

"You both are going to the ER," I said firmly. My own troubles faded in importance.

"No. They'll have to call the police with this much evidence of violence," G protested. But he didn't sound very convincing.

"Then tell them you got mugged or carjacked or

something." Shara stood up, hands in fists and with a determined glare in her eye that matched her father's in intensity. "Mom, get the keys. I'll get the ice packs." She marched off to the kitchen. My baby girl had suddenly grown up and taken charge of all of us.

"Not yet," G said, barely above a whisper. "I call a family meeting. There are things we need to discuss."

"I'm still getting the ice packs." Shara marched into the kitchen and reappeared seconds later with two packs, each wrapped in a towel. "Jason, there's one more in the back of the freezer, the segmented kind that wraps. You choose which hurts most, your face or your fist."

G raised his uninjured eyebrow at me. "She sounds a lot like you."

I rolled my eyes. "More like you in a fit of organization."

"What's up?" Jason asked, holding the pack to his jaw with his injured hand. Easing both with limited resources. His eye looked painful but nowhere near as swollen as his father's.

"First off, it's time I told you the truth, Jason. That woman, D'Accore, is not just any rogue magician."

"D'Accore?" Jason mouthed. He knew the name. We'd never hidden from him that I wasn't his birth mother. "That's my dead mother's name."

"She didn't die," I said softly, wrapping my arm around his immature shoulders.

He turned wounded eyes toward me. "But you said . . ."

"I didn't know myself until a few days ago, Jason."

"What happened to her? Why didn't she get custody of me?"

"Jason," G said with enough determination to get his son's attention. "We told you she died because in many ways she did. She turned rogue, using black magic, blood magic to gain more and more power, not so she could use it for anyone's benefit but her own, but because she could. And if someone got hurt or *died* in her quest for power, it didn't matter to her. It was fun because there is power in death."

"Did she kill someone?" Jason asked. His entire body trembled. I held on tighter.

"Five that I know of. Probably more," G replied. "Oh, gods! Her wand. The Zippo lighter with a death's head soldered to one side and the names of her victims magically etched onto the back. The back was so full of names it looked like a mess of scratches, each one so tiny it was illegible. She must have murdered twenty or more. And she was in the process of killing you, before you were born, draining your life energy to fuel her own."

Jason sank to the floor, graceful as ever, legs crossed, elbows on knees, and cradled his face in his hands, ice pack still in place. I dropped down with him, holding him as close as he'd allow. "How could she? How could you have married someone like that!" Jason mumbled.

"I don't know. I thought I married a sweet and funny girl who had a gift for lighting fires but not much else. But her fires got bigger than candles and yard debris. They grew to bonfires at campus celebrations and pagan rites. They got bigger yet and in inappropriate places. She burned down one of the new apartment buildings south of campus. Three people were trapped inside. And she giggled in delight with that news. That's when I knew she was no longer sane. She started scratching me, hard enough to draw blood, then licked the wounds clean. She couldn't conjure fire in this house because of the pentagram. So she took a knife to murder my grandparents."

G swallowed deeply and closed his eyes in both physical and emotional pain. I'd never heard this part.

I wanted to go to him, give him the hug he so clearly needed. Jason needed me hugging him as much or more.

"I threw a stasis spell on her, careless of the niceties. I hurt her. I needed to hurt her as much as she hurt me. While I called for backup, she broke through my flawed spell and fled. She went back to her old boyfriend, John

Mooney. I caught up to her and went with my backup to ... to her permanent dungeon home. She was three months pregnant."

Jason shuddered and the girls hugged each other, then reached out to their dad. He let them linger with their arms around him. "And you lost your grandparents. They'd raised you after your parents died," Belle added, remembering a long-ago story.

"What happened to her?" Shara asked. Her chin trembled in terror. I wondered if she had finally made the connection between her picking locks or hacking computers and consequences.

"When the Guild is presented with a rogue of that magnitude, they use a complicated and dangerous ritual to strip her of her magic. Then they break the wand in front of the prisoner and burn it, or in the case of her wand, a vintage Zippo lighter, I dropped it into a vat of hydrochloric acid. With conventional wands, the ashes are then scattered to the four winds so that they may never reassemble. I dumped the acid into the ocean over one of the deepest trenches in the Atlantic."

Exhausted by his retelling, G laid his head back, exposing his throat. Tears leaked from his right eye. From the damage or his inner pain?

"By that time, D'Accore might as well have been dead. She was locked in a prison cell with magical and mundane locks I doubt even Shara could manipulate. I never saw her again until she returned here last spring."

"How did she escape?" Shara asked, always the one who was curious about locks.

"She had help. I believe Coyote Blood Moon may have orchestrated it. He has the money—he's been accumulating it in offshore accounts since the day after I arrested her—he has the contacts, and the powers to do it. One of D'Accore's victims had an image of him in his dying moment. John was there tonight, at the end of the fight. He caught me by surprise while I was dealing with D'Accore's minions. I couldn't get close enough to her to put a stasis spell on her until I dealt with her boys. Jason launched from the high branches of a tree and felled two boys with his feet."

"Why would John do that?" I demanded, still not accepting that the gentle man who had befriended me was capable of such a thing.

"He knows that D'Accore is the only wizard capable of and willing to get rid of me. I'm the Sheriff, I enforce our laws. John Mooney has been cheating on his real estate deals for decades. He's cheated on his taxes, too."

Jason looked away, showing a trace of guilt. I knew my boy, knew when he tried to keep a secret.

"I just became aware of his cheating recently. My information has not been confirmed. I've never questioned his honesty before. But now he has violated our first and most important commandment: 'Above all, harm none.' Someone who works closely with Mooney got disgusted with the shoddy work he passed off as top of the line repairs on a house he flipped and overcharged for. The homeowners lost thousands in inflated prices and more in unreported foundation and electrical damage that wasn't reported or fixed. The state board for contractors' permits, and the IRS have been called. He's out for revenge." G clamped his mouth shut.

"What about Ted Tyler?" I asked. I had to know if the man I was growing to like was caught in this web of evil. He contracted with Mooney to flip some of those houses.

"Ted Tyler is so honest he nearly squeaks." G tried to laugh but clutched his middle as it turned into a painful cough. "Mooney gives him contracting jobs for clients he doesn't dare offend. And Ted does an excellent job for a fair price. For ordinary people who are beneath Mooney's contempt for being ordinary, he hires an outfit in East Springfield that doesn't bother with permits and codes or even licenses. There'd probably be bribes to inspectors involved, too. There's an ongoing state investigation on the contractors. But they close shop and reopen with a new name as fast as they are caught."

"Then why did you tell me to go to CBM for help when you had to go to Europe in a hurry?"

"Because I didn't know about his schemes to free D'Accore, and I thought he was willing to turn a blind eye on business ethics, but honest in his magic."

"How . . . how could my own mother try to kill me?" Jason asked, raising his bleak and tear-streaked face to his father.

"I don't know."

"Then she isn't my mother. You are." He reached over and gave me a fierce hug. His fingers clutched my back in desperation.

"Thank you, Jason. I love you."

"I know. That's why you are *my* mother and not her."

"Enough. We know the truth. We know who our enemies are. Time to get you two to the ER." Shara took charge once more.

"Call Gayla and ask her to come over and stay with you," I said, bringing Jason up to a stand with me.

"Mom," Belle protested. "We're not little kids anymore."

"No, you aren't. But you are hurt and recovering from the loss of your wand. I want a responsible adult here with you. An ordinary adult who will call 911 at the first sign of trouble and not try to bully through it."

"Both D'Accore and Mooney are hurt, weakened from our physical and magical battle," G said on a wince. "They should be off nursing their wounds and trying to recharge their magic. The minions were hurt and will probably slink away. Typical bullies. I doubt they will return to D'Accore's side, despite her hypnosis spells."

"Dad drained them pretty good before things got nasty. That woman is going to need a bunch more wands to replenish her stolen powers," Jason added. I noted that he didn't refer to her by name or as his mother. "The girls should be safe at home."

"I still want Gayla here. Call her."

It took both Jason and me to get G upright and headed toward his car.

"Don't you need our help?" Belle asked. "We should be together. We are a family."

"Thank you, but not right now. We may be gone all night. You both need your sleep. There are leftovers in the fridge you can microwave." My second night without sleep. Had I eaten since breakfast?

# Twenty-Seven

**"NO I WILL NOT** stay in the hospital overnight!" G shouted for the third time. "Mild pain pills and ice packs will do just fine, now that you've stitched up the worst of it." He'd have a scar bisecting his right eyebrow, though, and two on his knee.

"That broken rib could shift and penetrate your lung," the hapless intern said. He was running out of steam with G's stubborn arguments.

"Then tape it tight so it won't shift. That's all you can do for broken ribs anyway."

"But that has been proven to restrict breathing, and you won't get enough oxygen to heal. Though the pressure does relieve some of the pain. You need to breathe more." The intern looked at me, his brow crinkled with bewilderment.

"I'm only the ex-wife. I can't make him do anything he doesn't want to do." I shrugged.

Why is it that the strongest, most stalwart men are the worst patients? He'd been the same way when he smashed a thumb while building my greenhouse and the time he came home from Kiev with pneumonia. He'd thought he'd heal better at home.

Maybe the pentagram in the attic would help speed his recovery. I didn't plan to stay home and take care of him. I only sat on the rolling stool beside his hospital bed to keep him from wandering around the ER poking his nose where it didn't belong while we waited for X-rays and lab tests and surgical kits for stitches.

I wished now I hadn't left Jason at home so he'd eat and sleep. He could spell me in controlling his father. I'd eaten in the hospital cafeteria—there was a quite good vegetarian menu—but I hadn't slept, and it was way past my bedtime for the second night in a row.

Without my wand to soothe my nerves, the moans and groans, the stench of fear and pain, mixed with disinfectant nearly drove me to dump G here and go home.

"What's the problem here?" An older woman wearing a medical white coat, rumpled slacks, and sensible walking shoes bustled into the cubicle divided by curtains for an illusion of privacy. "I suppose you don't want to stay overnight either?"

"Either?" I asked.

"Bar fights and muggings all over town tonight. Mostly minor wounds and too much alcohol," she said, turning toward me while still perusing G's chart. "He looks as bad as the guy two rooms over. They got the brunt of the bad juju going around town tonight. And he doesn't want to stay two minutes more while we stitch him up and set and cast his broken bones. Real estate agents are as bad as software engineers." She clicked her tongue in dismay.

Then I heard fingers drumming on the metal bars alongside a hospital bed. Impatience gathered around the rhythm of a heartbeat with an occasional flutter that sounded like a small bird taking flight. I'd heard that drumming cadence before. In Coyote Blood Moon's drum and flute shop.

I murmured an excuse and left G's room, following the haunting drumbeat.

"Ah, my beautiful golden daffodil," John Mooney sighed, dreamily—or drugged into submission. "Have you come to whisk me away from this torture chamber?" He rolled his head back and forth, either in agitation or seeking a more comfortable position.

He had a huge bruise on his left temple and a ban-

dage on the back of his head. His perfect haircut had
deteriorated. His hands looked like he'd suffered third-
degree burns, and he had a sling elevating his ankle
where his foot dangled in a loose and awkward position.

As far as compliments go, being likened to a golden
daffodil isn't bad. But I wasn't his in any way, shape, or
form. We hadn't even kissed, let alone slept together.
And after G's revelations, I didn't want to do either.

"No. I heard you drumming your fingers and thought
I'd see if I could hasten your treatment," I demurred.

"Are you here with G?" he asked, more alert, but his
eyes were still glassy and his tongue thick. Concussion if
not drugs slurred his words. "He doesn't deserve you.
You need to leave him. He didn't deserve D'Accore either. She was seduced by his power. You were, too. Leave
him, my daffodil. I will take care of you as you should be
cared for."

I handed him the bottle of water beside his bed with
a straw in it. Stalling. He sipped only a little, then made
a face as if it tasted like garbage and thrust the bottle
back at me.

"G and I are divorced. He lied to me one too many
times." I handed him the explanation I gave everyone as
to why we broke up.

"Good. Don't trust him. He lies to everyone. And
about everyone. Did you know that his first wife didn't
die? He got tired of her and found the most despicable
way to get rid of her without the taint of divorce. She's
blind now, you know. He did that to her. She can't see
anything at all without her smoke. And he took that away
from her again tonight. All G really wanted out of the
marriage was his son. Stupid brat didn't inherit any useful
talents."

How dare he insult my boy!

I forced myself to remember that I was here for information. I had to play nice while the drugs and/or his concussion loosened his tongue.

"Don't trust him," John insisted again. "Not him or

the boy. They are traitors to our kind. Cruel and unjust traitors. He tells more lies than truths."

"You got that part right."

His eyes drifted shut.

I slipped out between the curtains with a sour taste in the back of my throat.

Both he and G told lies wrapped in half truths. One to protect me, the other to delude me. Which was which?

I thought I knew. But that wall of lies still kept rearing up in front of me.

When I returned to G's room, he and the doctor were negotiating what he considered a mild painkiller. She wanted him on morphine. He wanted aspirin.

"Keep him or send him to his apartment in a taxi. I'm going home to take care of our children," I told the doctor, then turned on my heel and fled.

I slept fitfully. Every time I woke and checked the clock to see if it was time to get up or not, I reassured myself that I had left G at the hospital precisely so the medical professionals could monitor him and help him heal. No way could he make it up the stairs to his apartment without aid. He had to stay in the hospital until someone came to get him. Presumably me.

When I was rested enough to think straight, I'd lay down ground rules. If he couldn't climb stairs to his apartment, then he couldn't climb to my bedroom. And he was on his own during the day. I wasn't going to lose work to stay home with him, and the children had school. We could move his old computer up to the dining room table from the basement.

And his clothes that accumulated in my closet must move down to the armoire in my sewing room that used to be his home office. I could move some of my craft supplies from the shelves. The ribbons and laces were much depleted after I'd let the dancers use them to decorate the jars of bath salts.

Did we have a spare bed among all that junk in the attic? If not, I supposed G could rent a hospital bed for a few weeks.

By six, I knew I wasn't going to sleep anymore, so I used up a lot of the hot water in a long shower, bundled myself into my jeans and flannel shirt, then tugged thick socks over my tired feet. Fleece-lined slippers gave me the illusion of warmth. Better. But not whole yet. I still needed a couple of nights of real sleep before I'd manage more than a rough routine, moving more by rote than thinking about it.

I needed my wand.

The exact moment I sat down to eat my strawberry waffles with whipped cream and a side of bacon (comfort food and plenty left over for the kids) my cell phone chimed.

G.

Of course.

I took a big bite of waffle and cream and another long gulp of coffee (my third cup) before answering.

"Can you come get me?" he asked, sounding more like a lost child than the Sheriff for the entire world of the Guild of Master Wizards.

"What do the doctors say about that?" I asked and crunched a bite of bacon in his ear.

"They said if I wear a knee brace 24/7 and stay off it as much as possible, I can come home, providing someone is there to monitor me for concussion until tomorrow. They need the bed for truly sick people. And I shouldn't drive for a week."

"Sounds reasonable. Where are you going to stay?" I almost enjoyed making him grovel. Payback for some of the lies he'd told me over the years.

The more I thought about it, the more I believed that if he'd been up front from the beginning with me about magic, I'd have been okay with it. Unlike Flora Chambers or my father, I wouldn't have run away screaming about the sin of witchcraft. I'd probably have embraced the concept of magic and been a bit jealous that I didn't have any. As Gayla had.

Payback to my parents for their repressive attitudes.

Having acknowledged magic, I might have manifested earlier and been better able to defend myself from BJ and his bullies in the park yesterday.

I was beginning to think that lying was part of the condition of being a human male.

Maybe not Ted. But I didn't know him that well yet. I really liked him, though. His reliability and his devotion to his daughter weighed heavily in his favor.

But he didn't make my blood sing.

I wasn't sure G did either. My reaction to him was part of a spell. If he'd just been honest with me when he first seduced me, he wouldn't have needed a spell to make me fall in love with him.

G gulped loud enough for me to hear him swallow through the phone. "May I stay with you?" Pause. "Please?"

"I suppose so. You can sleep on the sofa, or Jason can move the recliner into the sewing room if you want more privacy. Or you can rent a hospital bed. That might be easier for you to get in and out of."

"Not . . . ?"

"You can't climb stairs. And the answer would be no anyway."

"Okay." He didn't have to say, "For now," out loud. I heard it in his tone.

I had news for him.

Checking out of the hospital took longer than G had spent in the ER. I swear that I had to complete more forms for insurance and stuff than I had the night before. On the line where I had to fill in the name of who would pay the bill if the insurance refused to pay, I really, really wanted to write Guild of Master Wizards. But that wouldn't be fair to the poor clerk who had to process the paperwork. Instead, I put in the shadow corporation that provided the insurance.

Then and only then was I allowed to take a change of clean clothes up to his room. Then I had to wait some more while nurses helped him dress.

Eventually, an aide wheeled G to the front door while I retrieved his car from the parking lot. I figured it would be easier for him to get in and out of that vehicle than the high step to the van. Grudgingly, he accepted the aide's assistance in standing and turning one-footed so that he sat on the passenger seat then swung his long legs in. I'd put the seat back as far as I could make it go. He still had to wiggle ungracefully to get his injured leg in without bending it.

The aide put G's bundle of torn and filthy clothing, a pair of crutches, and the hospital toiletries in the back-seat along with the stack of papers, duplicates of the forms I'd completed along with detailed instructions about his care. The dire warnings about ignoring dizziness and blurred vision, slurred speech, or trembling limbs was almost enough to make me leave him with the professionals another night.

"Don't be a hero now. Use the crutches. Consider it a war wound and not a sign of weakness," the aide said, then he slammed the door shut.

G reclined the seat halfway to horizontal and closed his eyes. His skin looked gray and clammy.

"You okay?" I asked, not putting the car into gear yet.

"I will be as soon as I get home and beneath the pentagram. Pain is exhausting. Painkillers are obnoxious but useful in inducing sleep. I'll grin and bear it." The lines around his eyes and from his mouth to his chin deepened. He looked twenty years older than his forty-five years.

Half a mile later some of the strain in his face and shoulders relaxed. I hoped he'd fallen asleep. Instead he spoke. "What did John Mooney say to you last night?"

"Not much."

"Spill it. You are a terrible liar."

"Unlike you."

"Practice. It becomes a habit. A bad habit I intend to break."

"Do all men lie?"

"Not all of us. Not always. I started lying to you to protect you. And the children. I don't have to anymore. And neither do you. What did Mooney say?"

I noticed that he used John's real name rather than his craft name. Somehow John had lost the right to a craft name in G's mind.

"He warned me not to trust you, because you lie and you framed D'Accore for her crimes and that your malicious treatment of her caused her blindness."

He snorted a laugh, then grabbed his ribs. "Tell that to the three people who died in the apartment fire and my grandparents, and all the others I didn't know about but were engraved on the back of her Zippo. She caused her own blindness trying to break her magically sealed straitjacket. We had to restrain her to keep her from hurting her baby. As it was, the doctors took him two months early by C-section to protect him. If anyone is lying in this case, it's her."

"If John helped her escape last spring, that was long before he met me. He wasn't a spurned lover then."

G paused long enough that I had to glance over to make sure he hadn't fallen asleep.

"No, he wasn't. But he did date her before she met me. I'm the more powerful wizard—my powers were enhanced when I was recruited as a deputy for the Guild. We all have to be able to subdue out-of-control rogues. I now know she wanted my powers. Mooney has never forgotten that she left him for me—although she lied to me in the beginning and said he'd found someone else and threw her out. He's not been overtly hostile until yesterday, but the snide jabs were frequent enough to put distance between us."

Which must be why I didn't meet John until this summer.

"I now believe she cast a spell on John when she ran to him for protection before I restrained her. She planted the seeds then for him to accumulate the several fortunes he'd need to help her escape. I don't think she anticipated that it would take fifteen years."

"Jason complained of a bad headache and blurry vision last night. This morning, before I left to fetch you, I went into his room to tell him where I was going. He wasn't there. He'd moved his bedding to the attic and slept in the center of the pentagram. He said he felt better, but he'd gone up there because he couldn't sleep anywhere else. I almost brought him with me to have him checked out. But he said he just needed more sleep."

"Could be backlash from his first real use of strong magic. I swear he hovered three feet off the ground and kicked the minions in the head and then the nuts. They collapsed and crawled off, leaving behind their half-charged wands."

"What was John doing?"

"He held off until I'd defeated the minions. Then he tackled me from behind, butting his head into my already damaged ribs. I think his wooden flute flew into the woods. I didn't break his wand, just kept him from using it. He'll have a devil of a time finding it again."

"Especially with a broken ankle."

"That was Jason's doing. He telekinetically put something very slippery beneath John's feet. He fell when he leaped. Awkwardly."

I still bristled that G had endangered Jason. But at least the boy had held his own. And I guessed he had to learn to do that in a fight sometime. Just not yet.

"What about D'Accore?"

"She ran at the first sign of confrontation. She's stolen power from a dozen lesser magicians when she killed them and stripped their wands. But borrowed or stolen talents are diminished by the transfer and they dissipate quickly when used. She's not up to full power and hasn't had time to absorb all the nuances layered into magic."

"Then how did she cast an illusion strong enough to trick you into believing she was me?"

"I was not thinking straight, and I wanted to believe it was you. Only you." His smile looked like a grimace. But he really was trying to make amends.

Or get back into my good graces and, therefore, my bed with lies and manipulation.

"Men fight. Men lie. I'm glad I'm single again."

"I'm sorry, Daffy. Maybe I protected you too much."

# Twenty-Eight

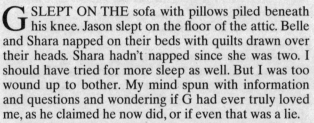

G SLEPT ON THE sofa with pillows piled beneath his knee. Jason slept on the floor of the attic. Belle and Shara napped on their beds with quilts drawn over their heads. Shara hadn't napped since she was two. I should have tried for more sleep as well. But I was too wound up to bother. My mind spun with information and questions and wondering if G had ever truly loved me, as he claimed he now did, or if even that was a lie.

Ted called when I was in the middle of putting together a grocery list and meal plan for the coming week. "I have three dozen cupcakes in a bakery box in the back of my truck," he said after appropriate greetings. "What should I do with them?"

Raphe wasn't really homeless and didn't need my handouts, though he appreciated them. I thought a bit about selling them at the shop as day old ... "Let's take them to the homeless shelter. Meet me at the shop, I've got some day-old bread and cheese rolls that can go, too."

"Deal. When?"

I listened to the house, no one stirred but me. "Ten minutes."

He greeted me with a gentle, reassuring kiss. I leaned against him for a long, restful moment.

"Rough day yesterday?" he murmured into my hair, holding me close.

"Very."

"I saw Jason leave the market with his father. Neither of them looked happy. Then later I heard about the dustup in the chess park. Are you and the girls okay?"

"Yes. The girls are shaken. BJ Chambers has been a near constant companion since he and Jason were in pre-school. His malevolence felt like a betrayal. I should have seen it coming. He's been erratic for a few months. I thought it was hormones."

"That is rough. What about Jason and his father?"

"They got mugged on their way to help me. G is hurt pretty bad. Jason is sleeping off the shock. Can we talk about something else? I need a respite."

"Of course. Do you have an escort to the premiere of *This Is Halloween*?"

"Not yet." I smiled up at him, still clinging.

"May I escort you?" He kissed my nose, and I giggled.

"Yes. Thank you. Now let's get these baked goods over to the shelter, then I need to go to the grocery store."

A gentle, everyday kind of conversation that had nothing to do with magic or evil wizards or pentagrams.

"My offer to help Jason refinish your attic floor still stands. I've got all the equipment. I know how to make that pale inlay really shine," he said when we'd finished our errands together.

My insides froze. This was the third time he'd asked. Was he truly only trying to help, or did he want access to that pentagram.

The one person in all this mess I thought I could trust had crossed the line. I watched him cautiously while he transferred his groceries from my van to his truck. Was that a hint of levitation lifting a heavy bag or just a strong man doing what he had to do?

G opened one eye cautiously the moment he heard Daffy slip quietly out the back door. He had work to do. A quick survey of his injuries and he knew he had to start delegating. He had to trust his deputies to do the jobs he'd trained them to do.

He hated working by remote control.

Fortunately, Daffy had left his phone in his pocket. He fished it out, careful not to twist and irritate his lightly taped ribs. He'd have a devil of a time taking a shower. But if Daffy helped . . .

Not right now. He could barely manage to remember phone numbers—he never left deputy numbers on the memory card and carefully deleted call history every time—let alone seduce his ex-wife.

Dale in Portland and Suzie in Sacramento still had fresh bodies to deal with. He checked in with them and reassured them they were doing a great job; they didn't need him. Las Vegas was always a hotbed of minor magicians trying their "luck," so he shouldn't pull Adam from there. Peter in Seattle was getting ready to retire; he didn't tackle physical problems anymore. His talent was intact, but his knees weren't. G decided to give him one last case so he could leave on a glorious high note.

"I'll take dismissal and a reduced pension before I deal with that broad again," Peter grumbled. "As much as I want her dead, I want to live to enjoy my old age. Go ahead and fire me. I've got a fishing cabin in the San Juan Islands all paid for. No cell phone and no Internet." He hung up.

G couldn't blame the guy.

Melinda in L.A. was new, only on the job eight months. Had she settled into her augmented powers yet? Time to find out.

"I'm prepping to go to trial on a civilian case tomorrow." She had a great day job as a public defense attorney. No better place for her to be for rooting out rogue magicians who used their powers for criminal purposes. "I need this case to establish my reputation in L.A. I can't help you later if I desert clients at the last minute."

Damn it! He needed Paul. But he'd been one of D'Accore's and Mooney's earliest victims.

How had they zeroed in on G's strongest allies?
Raphe. Raphe was the registrar for the Guild. He had
spreadsheets that covered every aspect of life and magic
of every registered magician and wizard. Mooney owned
the building where Raphe and G rented an apartment.
Even with wards and alarms, mundane and magical set
all around the building and inside the apartment,
Mooney, as landlord and a powerful wizard—more powerful than they thought—had access.

Mooney had selected the victims by powers that
D'Accore needed. He'd provided transportation—hadn't
there been an unverified rumor of a private jet owned by
a shadow corporation parked at the local airport? But
she had to murder the victims in order to absorb their
powers and get their wands away from them long enough
to strip them.

They were both guilty, and he didn't have enough
strength or clear-mindedness to track down and arrest
either one.

G's head hurt. He couldn't think beyond the West
Coast to find another deputy capable of helping him. Reluctantly, he put the phone on his chest and rested his
head back on the arm of the sofa. Just a few minutes. He
only needed a few minutes to close his eyes.

He woke two hours later when Daffy let herself in by
the back door, none too quietly.

———◖▬▬———

By sunset, my family began to stir and look to me for
food. Sometimes I thought that's all I was, a giant feeding trough. I had a hearty beef barley stew simmering. It
needed another half hour. Time enough for them all to
wash the sleep out of their eyes and assess the state of
their homework. All three children needed several
hours at the dining room table tonight with supervision
to keep them from wandering off or playing computer
games.

The doorbell rang just as the sun set.

"That will be Raphe," G said on a yawn. He struggled to sit up and get the crutches under him.

I answered the door and left G to manage on his own. He'd have to learn to do that sooner rather than later.

Raphe stood on my doorstep. His khaki sweatshirt hood covered his head, and he wore wraparound sunglasses on a gloomily overcast day.

"Raphe? You look different." He'd cleaned up prettier than I expected, shaved and with trimmed hair. His clothes—khaki slacks and a mint-green shirt beneath the sweatshirt—were also clean and respectable.

"As much fun as I had pretending to be your pet homeless man living behind your dumpster, this is the real me. I've got the rest of G's things in my car." A big boat of a classic red convertible, white soft top up to protect against the rain, sat in my driveway.

"Come in." I opened the door wider and gestured him in.

"Uh. No, thanks. I'll just leave his stuff here on the porch. That pentagram gives me the shivers."

"Won't G be returning to your apartment once he can climb the stairs again?"

G came up behind me, leaning heavily on the crutches and not touching his right foot to the floor. Sweat dotted his brow, and he breathed heavily. I didn't think he could fake the paleness of his skin, so I presumed it wasn't all an act to gain my sympathy.

"Mooney's still in the hospital. His lawyer came by and kicked us out. Said if we weren't gone by sunset, he'd burn our things and make sure the police found evidence of drugs on the premises. I decided not to fight." He wandered back to the car and returned with two large suitcases, three garment bags, and a laptop shoulder bag. He handed me the computer. G couldn't manage it and the crutches. But he breathed a sigh of relief the moment I took possession.

"Thumb drive with the latest register from the Guild is in the side pocket," Raphe said. "I updated it last night and made a list of deputies available for travel on a second spreadsheet."

"Where are you going? Do you have a place to stay?" I asked, concerned that maybe he was truly homeless now. The garage had a loft. Not clean or furnished, but a roof over his head.

"Mom's place is empty." Raphe shrugged. "If Daffy kicks you out again, there's plenty of room for you, G. You can use the guest room on the main floor. Only five steps up to the porch to enter."

"When is Aunt Teresa due back from Spain?" G asked.

"When she decides if she's worn out husband number four, found number five, or just tired of the endless sun and blue seas." He sounded very casual about that.

"And your dad?" G rummaged through the side pocket of the computer bag and came up with a thumb drive, which he secured in the breast pocket of his golf shirt, along with his pen.

"This is the second full week of October? Dad should be in transit from Tierra del Fuego to Helsinki. He doesn't like sunshine much more than I do." He shrugged again and retreated to his car.

"Will you come to our Halloween party?" I called after him.

"Pentagram is still in place. I'll stay in the yard and play ghost to spook trick-or-treaters." And then he was gone.

Leaving me with G neatly entrenched again.

●━━━

"Do you trust him?" I asked G the second the door closed completely. I left his luggage on the porch. Jason could get it if we decided to let my ex stay.

"Of course." He juggled his crutches, trying to turn

around. "Jason," he called. "Come help with my luggage."

I wanted more information, not his usual evasions. "Why do you trust Raphe? You used to trust John Mooney, and now you don't."

"Raphe is family. He knows that if he steps over the line from eccentric to criminal, I will call his mother."

I chuckled in spite of myself. "Never underestimate the wrath of a mother. *Jason, Belle, Shara!*"

Three sets of feet came running.

"I didn't yell loud enough," G mumbled.

"They heard you. They don't dare tune me out. Just like Raphe with your Aunt Theresa."

"Shara, we need to bring up the desktop computer from the basement," G said.

Shara's ears perked up. "Why do you need an internal modem attached to its own landline? That's where the firewall is. That's what blocks an outside hacker." She whispered loud enough for half the neighborhood to hear. Her key shone brightly where it dangled on its silver chain, outside her shirt.

"I'm winging it, Shara. Time we figured out how to find hidden bank accounts and upload them to active IRS files."

"I'll set the table in the kitchen," Belle said on a yawn. She'd affixed the bishop charm to the same ivory stick as the queen. She'd rebounded, mostly, from the shock of losing one half of her wand.

"I need a new wand," I whined, headed for the kitchen with G's laptop case still dangling from my shoulder. As I went to check on the stew and shove the cornbread batter into the oven, I left the bag at the head of the table where G could sit.

"Grab your backup spoon and start using it," G said casually as he stumped over to the big captain's chair at the dining room table. He managed to pull the chair back, stand in front of it, and ease his body down. He still had his crutches on either side to deal with, and no leverage to scoot the chair close to the table.

Jason dashed to his rescue. With his father firmly in place—trapped—Jason yawned and left to retrieve the luggage on the front porch.

Life was on the path to normal. Whatever that was.

# Twenty-Nine

"**Y**OU KNOW, most people don't spend half an hour selecting a wooden spoon to mix batter with," Ted said. He leaned back against the counter that ran the length of the interior wall of the shop's kitchen, broken only by the swinging door into the front.

I needed to set dough to rising for the Monday morning rush. With all that had happened over the weekend, I didn't want to be alone in the shop after dark. I might have questions about Ted's agenda, but of all the other escorts I could call, he was the least objectionable, and the most willing to spend an hour just talking to me.

"I know, but I broke my favorite one," I replied, not looking at him. My hand wanted very much to reach out and grab the utensil that was shaped differently from the others, the bowl was flat and sort of squared off with a half-inch hole in the middle. An odd shape that wasn't suitable for every task, like a traditional spoon. But it worked wonders with sauces, or melting chocolate and butter together. The squared-off corner reached into crevices and scraped off pot sides. And it was stained with the essential oil of chocolate.

And the thing almost sang when my hand hovered near by.

"What about that fanny whacker?" Ted asked, reaching for the tool I considered most likely.

"That's a spoodle. A holy tribute to Saint Custard."

He arched his eyebrows in question as he laughed out

loud. "Holy because it has a hole in it." He spluttered, grabbing it out of the jar.

"Because it makes my liquid custard so smooth it's heavenly." In that moment I knew it was a good candidate, but not the best. Now that it was out of the jar, I knew there was something else in the milk glass stein that called to me more, but there were so many tools jammed in there I couldn't tell which would become my wand.

Ted playfully tapped my bottom with the spoodle. "See? A fanny whacker. Wish I'd had one of these handy when Tiffany was two. She's always had to do things her own way, even if it interfered with everything I was doing."

I breathed a sigh of relief. Ted wasn't into kinky sex, like I feared.

Okay. I'd never chosen a wand before. The previous one had chosen me.

"From what I hear, BJ Chambers and his new friends broke it at the chess match in the park," Ted said casually.

I whirled to face him, the thistle-topped spurtle my Scottish grandmother had given me for my twelfth birthday—the last one before Dad sent her to the asylum—in my hand of its own volition. I guess my new wand had found me. I stared at it a moment. Not the most useful tool in my kitchen, designed primarily to stir thick highland oatmeal that would stick to your ribs all day. But it was a gift of love from a woman I adored. That made it more important than just useful.

"What did you hear?" I asked, satisfied now that I had my spurtle. I wondered briefly if it could be taught to collapse in on itself like G's pen.

"I've heard and extrapolated bits and pieces. But it seems the Chambers boy has new friends of questionable morality. That's not going to help his father's state legislature campaign much. And you and your girls were in some danger, even if the police and the press downplayed it. I wish I could have been there with you, protecting you." He straightened up and approached me cautiously.

I still held my wand upright, defensively. I lowered it and let him put his arms around my waist.

We kissed. Soft. Comforting. I rested my head on his shoulder, drinking in the clean smell of him, ordinary soap and shampoo. Nothing exotic or frightening.

Or exciting.

He offered what I needed at that moment, comfort and security. Nice.

I turned within the circle of his arms and began dumping flour, salt, milk, and eggs and other stuff into the big industrial mixer. "Do you think Bret Sr. has a chance at winning the election?"

"It's early days. The primary isn't until May. But he has the support of his church. That's a large number of people willing to campaign for him and get out the vote. Lazy citizens who don't bother to vote might as well vote for him, since they don't add votes to his opponents. So far, no one has filed to run against him."

"His church. That's what scares me. My parents belonged to a congregation much like theirs. My father was the pastor, no education to be one, just his own fiery speechifying."

"You rebelled." He kept his arms around me.

"As soon as I could. They couldn't afford a church-related school for me, and Mom worked as an accountant to support us, so she couldn't home school me. And Dad refused, seeing that as women's work. I got a taste of reality in public school—which I had to keep carefully hidden. I was never comfortable with my folks' extreme emotional response to religion, reaching for the sky with closed eyes and shouting 'Hallelujah' to every nonsensical pronouncement Dad made. When I was in high school, my parents insisted I go into the most unholy neighborhood, one very much like this one, and 'witness' my faith before the ungodly. I knew kids from school would be there. I couldn't face their ridicule. So I lied, threw my flyers in the trash and kept an innocent face." Like G had done to me so often.

I quashed that thought.

"We have a number of pagans in town. In my experience most of them aren't turning their backs on God, they are running away from the politics of religion, and repressive fanaticism," he said.

"Yeah. My folks wanted me to go to a local Bible College. But when I did a little, and I mean a very little, research, I found that their teaching certificates weren't respected much outside of private Christian schools. I asked my folks what good was it to preach to those who already believed. If they wanted me to be a missionary for them, I needed to go out into the public."

He chuckled at that and tightened his arms.

I needed to move about the kitchen to complete my tasks, so I slipped away from him. Not rejecting him, just keeping busy.

"I was also very uncomfortable with how quickly my parents and their friends condemned anything that was different or exciting. They were more eager to shun outsiders, not eat certain foods, and refrain from anything resembling joy that wasn't based on a hymn. I prefer faiths that embrace outsiders, respect differences, and listen to everyone. That's what I found, mostly, in Eugene. My friends don't care what church I attend, or if I attend, as long as I don't interfere with their beliefs. I'm sure there is a lot of that in Seattle. I just wasn't allowed to find it."

"And that's why Bret and Flora Chambers scare you."

"Yes."

"They scare me, too."

"That's why I'm hosting the Halloween party after the last performance of the ballet. I need to celebrate my difference from their narrow view of life."

"Am I invited?" He stayed on his side of the kitchen this time, letting me clatter about, mixing and prepping.

"Of course, you are. So is Tiffany and the rest of the ballet company, and friends and neighbors, and anyone who enjoys spooky décor and games and laughter."

"Let me know if you need help moving stuff around. That attic would make a perfect party space. But you need to protect that fine hardwood floor from spills and stuff."

There was that request to see the pentagram in the attic again. What was his agenda?

"So are you done here?" he asked, looking around at my controlled chaos.

"I think so. Thanks for staying with me."

"Glad to be of service, ma'am." This time he gathered me into a firm embrace and kissed me long and hard. A faint glimmer of sizzle started in my belly and spread. Not far. Not long. Just the beginnings of a chemical reaction between us.

We came up for air, reluctantly.

"If you have your magic wand, I'll escort you to your car," he said.

"My . . . my . . . what?"

"That wooden thingy. You can't tell me that what you do in the kitchen isn't magic."

That was vague enough to pass as casual conversation. But there was an intensity in his gaze that sent warning chills down to my feet.

"Daffy, this is Eugene. There are a lot of unexplainable things that happen around here we just have to shrug off and accept." He jingled his keys in his pocket.

"Yeah. I guess so." I'd shrugged off a lot of unexplainable things as well, until I became an active participant in them. And then there had been Gayla's response, almost jealous that I manifested a talent and she didn't.

"Now, holster your magic wand in your back pocket where it belongs and let me follow you home."

"I can't ask you in." Did I want to? I was still uncertain.

"I know. You have a houseful of kids and an injured

ex parked in your living room. We'll find privacy another time." He dropped a kiss on top of my head and held the back door open for me. "I'll see you in the morning, right after you open, so that my cinnamon bun is still hot from the oven and my coffee is strong enough to get up and walk off by itself. That's your magic."

———

Jason shifted his feet beneath the dining room table uncomfortably. Then he shook his head, trying to free his mind of the constant buzz left over from the fight yesterday.

"What?" Dad asked, raising his head from studying his computer monitor and making a note on his tablet.

"I . . . I need . . ." What did he need in truth? The dining room floor was wood beneath the old carpet. He could feel it vibrating slightly beneath his bare feet. Soothing in its own way. Not right. No, not *enough*.

"Jason, that's the third time in as many minutes you have shifted your body, transferring your weight, and rubbing your eyes."

"I think I need to take my homework up to the attic." He began gathering books and papers and his own tablet.

"You know the rules, Jason," Belle reprimanded him. "Homework at the table until it's done and Mom or Dad can make sure it gets done."

"Not a problem for you. You love homework," Jason snapped back. His feet shuffled again. The Oriental rug was too thick.

"Jason, your own discomfort is not a reason to snap at your sister." Dad sounded really irritated.

But so was Jason.

"Well, if you all would just think a little quieter, maybe I could focus on my own work." He slammed his chair back, snagging it on the rug.

"Jason!"

Uh-oh, now Dad was mad. He had to get out of here,

to some place quiet. Maybe then the buzz in his head would stop reacting to all this noise.

"Are you becoming telepathic?" Dad asked.

"How the hell am I supposed to know? I'm the stupid one. The oddball one with no specific wand. I need to get away from here. Away from all you!" He grabbed his stuff and bolted up the stairs, knowing his father couldn't follow him on crutches.

Half an hour later he lay flat on his back in the center of the pentagram with an arm flung across his eyes. He listened to the old house, the creaks and groans of settling, the flutter of wind in the tree canopy, the whisper of ghosts that had been so much a part of his life that he didn't notice them until now.

He heard a footstep on the stairs. A real footstep, not his great-grandmother patrolling the house against intruders.

"Go away, Belle." He knew it was her, without knowing how he knew.

"Do you need anything? Food? A soda?"

"No. I just need to be alone. It's the only way to get the buzz out of my head."

"Sounds like maybe you are developing telepathy. Like you can hear people's thoughts, but you can't understand what you are hearing yet, so it's all a confused buzz and it gives you a headache, like when you inhale dust or get too close to the rose gardens on Spencer Butte."

"Or maybe I'm going insane. Like my mother."

Belle shut up and retreated.

If Jason pressed his ear against the floor, he could almost hear his sister—his half-sister—repeating their conversation word for word, sigh for sigh, to their father.

He rolled over and reached for his history text. Maybe he could drown out his own internal looping thoughts by memorizing the insanity of past wars. The Crusades should do it.

# Thirty

FLORA CHAMBERS DIDN'T waste any time gathering her army of protestors. When Gayla unlocked the front door at six on Monday morning, Flora and a dozen others—mostly women and a few older men—piled out of two minivans with placards on wooden stakes. They lined up on the sidewalk and marched back and forth chanting off-key, "A Mighty Fortress is our God."

The signs read "Boycott Witchcraft" or "Black Coffee = Black Magic" and my favorite "Delicious = Sin."

Could she have found phrases that enticed customers more? This was Eugene for heaven's sake. A magnet for the paranormal. I suppose she thought she'd deter a few customers, but only those who attended her church.

When the caffeine addicts pushed their way through the crowd, snarling at the attempted blockade, the two older men—probably retirees who didn't need to be off to work any time soon—threw down their signs and deserted the field of battle.

The women, however, persevered, locking arms and standing in front of the door. Two burly customers, needing their morning fix before running off to complete a road construction project, picked up Flora and her linked companion and moved them out of the way.

The two youngest protestors with infants in front slings dropped their signs and fled rapidly.

"I'm calling the cops," Gayla said. She whipped out her phone and poured coffee at the same time.

"I called the press," Ted called from the back of the line. "Nothing like a little notoriety to bring in more customers."

Bless the man. He set the entire shop full of people to laughing.

I grabbed another tray of pastries and took up my station behind the espresso machine.

Two college students came in the back door and started slicing croissants to turn them into sandwiches, customer's choice of scrambled eggs, ham, bacon, and three kinds of cheese, then a zap in the microwave for thirty seconds to melt the cheese and warm it through.

A siren erupted down the street. Someone propped the front door open so we could all hear the shouted arguments between the blue-clad officers and Flora. Her troops remained silent. A few more drifted away.

"This is a public sidewalk. We have freedom of speech!" Flora's shrill scream sounded like fingernails on a blackboard.

"You are blocking the entrance to a legitimate place of business," the officer countered, quite calmly. He glanced longingly at the coffee and sniffed the enticing aroma of cinnamon and sugar.

"When this is all over," I whispered to Gayla, "give that man whatever he wants in food and drink. I'll put together an extra tray of cookies to take down to the station house."

The inside crowd cheered. Ted stuffed a ten into the tip jar. "To defray the expense of goodies for the police officers who risk their lives, and their sanity, every day for our protection." Others followed his lead with fives and even a twenty.

I turned the espresso machine over to a college kid who'd finished making sandwiches. Then I retreated to the relative quiet in the back for more of everything.

Caught in a baking trance, trying to infuse as much magic as possible into my new wand, I missed the arrival of a newspaper reporter and three TV satellite trucks with their attached talking heads with microphones.

"These people are peddling sin and death by black magic!" Flora screamed.

I doubled the batch of cheese Danish.

Then I heard a more chilling announcement from Mrs. Morality. "She'll corrupt your children with homosexuality and encourage mixed-race marriages."

Almost laughable in this day and age—except since the election, prejudice had become valid again. I added more coconut-chocolate-chunk cookies to the mix. Nothing like decadent dark chocolate and shredded coconut to sidetrack a worried mind.

Flora and her cohort seemed bound and determined to make the fear of the "other" a just form of faith. Along with a lot of politicians in the national campaigns.

A microphone appeared under my nose as I exited the back door into the alley at two that afternoon. I had children to ferry about and errands to run. I tried to elbow away the intrusive reporter at the other end of the mic.

"Ms. Deschants, this is the second time in three days that the police have been called to break up disturbances involving you. And I understand that your husband and son were mugged on their way to one of those disturbances, requiring emergency treatment and an overnight stay in hospital." A perky blonde, not much older than Jason spilled her statement in a rush. Any faster and I'd swear it was all one word.

"Slow news day, sweetie pie?" I borrowed a phrase from Gayla laced with all the sarcasm of her Texas upbringing. I hoped my casual smile, didn't reveal me gritting my teeth to the camera I spied on the shoulder of another perky girl. This one was brunette, though. Network TV producers, and right-wing politicians loved blondes wearing red dresses.

"Aren't you angry that muggers are running loose and your husband and son had to be rescued by real estate mogul John Mooney?" Implying that John was big and strong and G was a weakling. "Mr. Mooney seems to think the incident newsworthy."

"You'll have to talk to Mr. Mooney about that." I shouldered my way past her. I pulled my car key out of my pocket, ready to scratch her with it if she tried to get between me and my van.

"And then this disruption of your business this morning, fueled by angry Christians. Are you a trouble magnet as Mrs. Chambers implies?"

I wanted my wand in my hand so that I could bop this child upside the head.

The wand was in my back pocket. Reaching for it would be too obvious. It would also give fuel to Flora.

Instead, I tried a trick my self-defense instructor freshman year at the U had drilled into the entire class. *If a man exposes himself in public, laugh rather than panic. It takes away his motivation. He wants to provoke anger, fear, humiliation.*

"Sweetie Pie, if you believe everything you are told by protestors who have nothing to protest, then I think you need to go back to school." I made sure the microphone caught my chuckles.

The woman behind the camera gave me a thumbs-up that Miss Perky Blonde couldn't see.

I'd just turned on the ignition when my phone buzzed with an incoming text.

—•—

G stuffed one more pillow under his injured knee, then sat back in the recliner. "Ahh," he sighed, relishing a moment of almost no pain. Then his throat grew dry. He'd already drunk the carafe of coffee Daffy had left him. And the glass of water he'd had at the kitchen sink after his lunch. But now his mouth wanted nothing less than an ice-cold cola over ice.

He swallowed, trying to banish his thirst. Maybe the television would distract him. He flicked on the remote. The first scene up was a refreshing waterfall advertising beer. That only reminded him that he hadn't used the restroom in over an hour....

Nothing for it; he had to lower the footrest of the recliner, groaning with the effort of shifting the lever. Then he wrestled his crutches off the floor and heaved himself upward.

"Someone in heaven is laughing at me right now," he muttered. "Payback for all my sins." And they were numerous, he admitted to himself. But he'd also done a lot of good in this world. He still had a lot of good to do.

He finished his business and found a small bottle of cola in the fridge. Now how did he get it back to the recliner?

The back door slammed open.

G grabbed his pen and pointed it toward the mudroom. Jason emerged, face caught in a deep frown, the bruises on his jaw and around his eyes looked new and bright red, not twenty-four hours into the healing processes. Twelve of those hours under the power of the pentagram.

"You're home early, Jason," G said, replacing his pen in his pocket.

"Yeah." He didn't look up.

"What's wrong, Jason?"

"Nothing." He slung his backpack off his shoulder and dumped it on the counter by the stairs.

"Jason?" G stuck out one crutch to block his path. "Talk to me."

"Not now."

"Now. Before you have time to embellish it, or forget it."

"Dad . . . it's . . . it's just too humiliating."

"High school is designed to be humiliating. It hones our survival instincts."

If Jason said anything in his low mumble, G couldn't discern it.

"What is wrong?" This time G put some compelling magic into his question.

Jason reared up his head, and finally fixed his gaze on

his father. "Don't do that. Don't ever do that to me!" he wailed.

G retracted the small spell. A habit. He'd spent more time interrogating reluctant suspects than talking to his son, earning his trust. "I'm sorry I underestimated you, Jason. Please talk to me. Whatever is wrong won't go away by itself."

"I know. I know." Jason held up his hands in mock surrender. "BJ and his bully friends called me a fag, 'cause I'm a dancer. Stupid perpetuation of a tired myth. I tried to walk away, it's not a big deal anymore even though I like girls a whole lot more than boys. But they followed me, just kept picking at me until I was so angry I took a swing at BJ. He ducked and his new best friends struck back. I think they planned it 'cause they made sure they hit me where I already had bruises. Now I'm going to have a devil of a time covering it all up with makeup for opening night—that's only ten days away." His head drooped and he tried to turn toward the stairs again. "Though they'll fit right in with the ghoul role. And as a skeleton, I have a mask . . ."

"I thought your school had a no tolerance policy for bullying."

"They're supposed to. But it comes down to my word against theirs. I already had bruises. Who's to say these are new ones. Or that the constant buzzing in my head is worse now after they hit me." His voice dropped in despair. "The nurse sent me home before the vice principal could. She believes me. She says she knows those boys and their handiwork. But BJ's dad is on the school board, and running for office. They don't dare reprimand him."

"In your confrontation, did BJ say anything about who is prompting him to this sudden drastic change in behavior?"

Jason's mouth gaped at the last three words, then lifted his face, eyes brightening with new understanding. "Do you think he's into drugs? That's what they tell us to look for in health class."

"Possibly. More likely his drug of choice is a budding magical talent. An uncontrolled sport." He looked at Jason to make sure he understood the use of the term, borrowed from animal breeders when presented with a new puppy, or kitten, or foal who didn't look like either parent.

Jason nodded. He knew the term. He knew his biological mother had been the same.

"BJ seems to have adopted a small silver bell as his wand. Ringing the bell helps him withstand the charm of Belle's wand."

Jason nodded. "Maybe." His gaze went distant as he mulled through the implications. "I'm thinking that's more than likely. And he had a new bell on his key chain today. Bright and shiny and new. And he was ringing it all the time. No rhythm. Kind of off-key and jarring on my nerves. In direct counterpoint and clash to the buzzing in my head. I thought Shara squashed the original one."

"She did. His mentor helped him find a new one. Did he mention a name or any kind of description of who might be guiding his abnormal behavior?"

Jason shook his head. Then he slapped his left ear like he wanted to banish trapped water after swimming.

G's gut churned and his knee hurt and his balance was off.

Jason stopped shaking his head in mid-swing.

"What?"

"Tom told Adam that the bitch wouldn't like it if he damaged my eyes when he hit me."

G froze. Icicles in his gut seemed to stab his heart.

"Can I go now? I need to clean up before rehearsal. Do you think Mom will kill me if I use some of her makeup to cover the worst of the damage? It's not like she ever uses it."

"Go clean up. But you're going to be late to rehearsal. You are going to take the test for your learner's permit. I need you to drive for me on errands and work stuff, so you have to be legal behind the wheel." And to keep him close so that D'Accore couldn't hurt him again and couldn't steal his eyes.

Taking J for permit test. Pls take care of girls. Luv U. G

That would work. Maybe while the girls were at their clubs, I could sneak away to the grocery store. Or sit at a picnic bench in the park and stare at nothing for a few minutes. Or nap in the car.

I acknowledged receipt of the text and headed toward the middle school. Neither of my girls waited for me under the outside awning. A light drizzle and chill wind had probably kept them indoors until they spotted the van. Three long minutes later when they hadn't appeared, I turned off the engine, gathered my purse, and stepped out of the vehicle. Two steps toward the office door, and both girls came running out to me, tears streaking their faces. The urgency of their pelting progress sent me reaching for my new wand.

Both girls wrapped their arms around me sobbing incoherently.

"What?"

"Excuse me, Ms. Deschants, may I have a word?" Mr. Andrews, the principal, asked. He followed the girls more sedately.

"Of course." I gave the keys to Belle and told the girls to wait for me.

"No," Shara insisted. "We have to stay with you."

"Daddy said," Belle added on a whisper.

I looked toward the principal. He nodded acceptance that the girls could stay while we talked.

"What have they done this time?" I asked the minute the office door closed behind us. Shara continued to cling to me. She hadn't done that since she was five.

"It's not Shara. Or Belle for that matter. Both girls are innocent in this matter." He assumed a professional bland face as he folded his hands together on top of his desk.

Belle faced him, a newly adult fierceness on her face. Shara buried her face against my side.

"Shara will have to drop out of the computer programming club at the high school," Andrews said. "We made an exception for her because she is very talented. And Mr. Mooney who sponsors the club recommended her. But now he threatens to withdraw his sponsorship if we continue to allow underage students into the high school clubs. Quite frankly, without Mr. Mooney's support we cannot operate the computer club. And if we remove Shara from participation because of her age, then we have to extend the same policy to all middle schoolers who belong to high school activities."

"That means Belle must drop out of Math Olympics, too," I finished for him. "Even though she is taking Advanced Placement high school classes and is captain of the team."

"Yes, I am afraid so." Andrews had the grace to look abashed.

"Does this affect anyone but my family?" Anger began to boil in my mid-region. I had to rub my wand in my back pocket to contain my emotions.

"Very few families have a genius of the caliber of your girls. Fewer still produce two so close together in age. . . ."

"Anyone else have middle schoolers participating in high school academic extracurricular activities?"

"No."

"Thank you for your time, Mr. Andrews."

I gathered both of my girls and took them home. None of us spoke during the ten-minute drive. But my mind spun right, left, and sideways. As I pulled into the driveway, I asked, "What do you need to host your clubs here at the house?"

"Computers networked to a couple of national sites," Belle said.

"Computers with ten terabytes of hard drive and a couple of external hard drives with as many more terabytes as we can afford." Shara sighed wistfully, as if those requirements were a million miles away because we didn't have them. Yet.

"Flash drives would be better because they have no moving parts to wear down. But ten teras or more will push toward a thousand dollars each. Externals are better," Belle told me.

"If we get those external hard drives, will laptops and tablets with the house Wi-Fi suffice?"

"I guess," they both replied on a shrug.

"Get on the phone. Our living and dining room just became math and computer central."

"And I have a project that will take the wind out of Mr. Mooney's sails," Shara said smugly.

"Nothing illegal!"

"Of course not."

I didn't like the conspiratorial look the girls exchanged just before they ran into the house.

# Thirty-One

**G**'S CAR WAS GONE, so I presumed he was with Jason. I called him anyway. He'd had his own agenda for so long I often wondered if he ever listened to what I needed, or needed him to do.

"He passed the test. Only missed one question," G said by way of introduction.

"Where are you now?" Ten days from opening night, Jason needed to be at rehearsal. I feared that he'd get so caught up in practicing driving that he'd let his obligations slide.

"At the theater, of course. Even an opportunity to practice driving in the parking lot of the abandoned warehouses northwest of town couldn't keep our boy away from dancing. Actually, he's having a final fitting of his costume. You did a good job sewing it. The seamstress just wants to add more trim." He sounded bright and affable, as if we had no worries about magical practitioners ready to pounce on us at any minute.

"More sparkling trim and all the audience will see is trim and not his dancing," I grumbled.

If G heard me, he ignored me with silence.

"I'll be in the greenhouse if you need me. The girls are in the house, making phone calls to avert the latest disaster."

"What's wrong?" G went from hearty to alarmed in one heartbeat.

I told him.

"I'll kill that man," he said, seething danger.

Suddenly I was reminded of his true profession, law enforcement. How many magicians had he killed in the line of duty over the last fifteen years? I didn't want to know the number, but I knew him capable.

A thrill of excitement bubbled up from my tummy, warring with the chill of fear running up and down my spine. I'd married—and divorced—the ultimate "bad boy." A very dangerous man, both to my well-being and my heart.

With my magic wand firmly in my jeans pocket, I entered the greenhouse and let my hands hover over the long beds of herbs and vegetables. The familiar ritual soothed me.

I had enough late lettuce and tomatoes for a salad to go with dinner. A few stubborn radishes, green onions, and the last stunted cucumber came to hand and went into my gathering basket. What else?

Nothing called to me overtly demanding to be picked. The beauty of a greenhouse was that weeds were kept to a minimum. I'd already composted a number of plants that had withered with the changing light of autumn.

But I wasn't ready to go back into the house and face the latest crisis. So I tried something different. I held the wand over the herb beds with my left hand, leaving my dominant right to pinch off a leaf of this, a branch of that.

Nothing.

I switched hands. The wand began to vibrate on its own, moving from plant to plant. I obeyed. This spurtle, oatmeal stirrer, knew what I wanted better than I did. Mostly, it wanted peppers. Cayenne and chili. A little horseradish and some lemongrass.

What was I building?

When the spurtle settled down and let me look at my gathered treasures, I gasped.

Dried and ground together, I had the makings of a caustic powder. If it touched a person's eyes, it would ... burn like hellfire and temporarily blind.

I might be only a kitchen witch, but I had my own weapons. Time to dig out the old cast iron cookware. Heavy and unwieldy, but magnificent bludgeons.

I patted the wand to thank it. It quivered and shrank a bit, as if learning to look unobtrusive when not in use. I think Granny's love helped it bond to me. Raising my face toward the sky, I whispered "Thank you," to her as well.

A comfortable warmth settled around my shoulders. Maybe she'd joined the ghosts of G's grandparents in the house. Or maybe just the greenhouse.

With new confidence I returned to the house and my girls. If I wanted club teachers to attend the new meetings at my house, I presumed I had to convince them they were only coming over for coffee and coffee cake. That I could do in my sleep.

◆━━━━━

Opening night, and you'd think Jason had the lead role instead of understudy to the second lead. He also had all those character roles with the corps de ballet. Still, it was his first year as a full member of the company and not just a group dance with other students. He *had* to get a haircut that day. He spent an hour trimming, filing, and buffing his fingernails. When he wasn't doing anything else that Friday afternoon, he climbed the stairs to the attic and practiced.

I was afraid he'd wear himself out and not be able to perform up to snuff. By the time G ushered him into the car to go to the theater, I was more than ready to have him out of the house. G was getting around more easily, having ditched the crutches in favor of a cane and the knee brace. But he shouldn't drive yet and couldn't climb stairs.

As he adjusted his blue-and-silver tie, my heart flipped over for a moment. I had to admit that he was a most handsome man. A man whom many women would go out of their way to attract his attention.

A niggle of jealousy set my stomach to fluttering.

I squashed it fiercely. He'd tarnished his handsomeness with lies, manipulation, and cheating. The minute he could manage stairs, he was outta here.

Gayla came over to escort the girls to the ballet. They had to be there for their brother. Besides, G wasn't about to leave them alone without at least one magician in attendance while D'Accore and Mooney still hovered about town. And Gayla insisted I needed to go on my big date with Ted alone. No adolescent girls in attendance.

"He is one of the most eligible bachelors in town," she insisted.

"I don't know that much about him," I said shyly. I did know that he made me laugh and we had a lot in common, both of us having children in the ballet. He liked to garden and admired my greenhouse. He was handy with minor repairs. And he was nice. Not sizzling hot like G. Just easy on the eyes and nice. Comfortable.

I could trust that any feelings between us were natural, not magic manipulation.

"He hasn't dated much since he lost his wife ten years ago," Gayla said. "I guess he's been so wrapped up in taking care of Tiffany that he hasn't made the time to meet single women. Until you came along."

Yeah, there was that.

"Now is the time for the little black dress, Sweet Pea," Gayla said emphatically, grabbing a pair of black dressy slacks out of my hand.

"You're wearing slacks with a sequined top and look very nice," I protested.

"But my date is two little girls who are easily impressed. Yours is one hot man. You've got competition you need to beat aside."

"But . . . I've worn that dress before." Like on my wedding anniversary when I kicked G out of my house and my life. But he was still there. "And my glittery top is new."

"Never mind that. Lacking a shopping trip to Nordstrom's in the mall, that's the only dress you have that is appropriate," she insisted, replacing the slacks in the closet. She came back out with the LBD. "And that ruby pendant your grandmother left you."

"You're right, of course." The few jewels G had given me over the years were *his* family heirlooms. Now that the divorce was final, I felt like I should give them back or put them in the safety deposit box for the girls when they grew up.

"The black, slingback heels, if you please," Gayla insisted when I reached for some plain black flats.

"You want me to trip and fall on my nose in front of my date?" I wasn't up to calling him a boyfriend yet.

"A great excuse to cling to his arm for support. But you are not going to take that ugly wooden spurtle with you! It may be your magic wand, but it destroys the look of that dress."

I wondered where I'd stash it. It had learned to shrink a little bit, not enough. The LBD didn't have pockets and my evening purse was about six inches long on a slender golden chain. I wouldn't go without my wand. One day without a wand had taught me how incomplete, how vulnerable, I felt without it.

"Garter!" Gayla proclaimed.

"Huh?"

She dashed down the stairs and came back with a swath of elastic and ribbons and wide insertion lace. Heaven only knows why I bought that spool of lace. I'd never used it. But it came in a grab bag with a bunch of other, more useful, brocade trims that were now on Jason's costume tunic.

In about five minutes we'd cobbled together a decorative garter of white lace, red ribbon, and elastic loose enough to let my blood circulate, but tight enough to keep the spurtle on my thigh. The flared skirt of the dress floated over it nicely, obscuring it from notice.

Wardrobe complete, I descended by the back stairs into the kitchen. A few words sent Gayla to help the girls collect coats, tidy their hair, and give their party dresses one last fluff. I used those two minutes of solitude to place a vial of pepper powder in my purse. Just a little one. Not enough to do any real damage. But it would slow down anyone who approached me with menace.

Cinderella was going to the ball prepared for the wicked witch. And all the ghosties and ghoulies and things that go bump in the night.

Ted cleaned up very nicely. His dark charcoal suit looked off the rack. G would never succumb to such a thing. He went custom made all the way. But Ted looked good, if a little uncomfortable in a dress shirt and an orange-and-black tie with jack-o'-lanterns and ghosts decorating it. He could pull off the hint of seasonal costuming. G couldn't. And wouldn't.

A smile lit Ted's face when he caught sight of me. I preened, just a little, and let him help me into my good wool coat. I felt like I was back in high school going to the prom.

"Tiffany got a call this afternoon from the ballet company in St. Louis," he said as he drove Tiffany's little sedan toward the old theater just west of campus. Excitement tinged his voice. But there was also a hesitation.

I wondered if this was his way of telling me that our relationship had no future because he was moving out of town.

"Is that phone call from St. Louis a good thing?"

"Could be. Based on her résumé and outstanding audition last August, they offered her a position as a demi-soloist."

"That's kind of a step down from prima in her home-town," I replied, thinking through the layers of seniority in a company.

"Yeah, but she's only eligible to dance with this company while she's still in school. Halfway through her junior year, time is limited in Eugene. She's had offers from some really big companies in New York, Atlanta, and Houston. All they can offer is a one-year slot as an apprentice. She'd have to fight and claw for every role along with dozens of other equally competent and experienced dancers. Then, at the end of the year, they have the option of not renewing the contract. No guarantees. St. Louis is offering a three-year contract two steps above apprentice, and the option for promotion to full soloist after only one year."

"Sounds like a decent offer. Will . . . will you go with her?" I felt like I needed to hear the "yeah, but" right off rather than get my hopes up with him.

"No. My business is here. My home is here."

He looked over at me, implying but not saying that I was here. I warmed all over.

"But I will probably be racking up a big bunch of frequent flyer miles. Letting her go off on her own is hard. We've been very close for ten years."

"If she accepts, when would she leave?"

"First of the year, but we'll probably fly out for a week or so next month to line up living space, check out public transportation, that sort of thing."

"I've never been to St. Louis, so I can't offer any helpful hints. I wish you both luck."

"Her in her career and me adjusting to life alone." He sounded sad. "I guess this is something every parent has to endure, wanting our children to grow up as responsible adults, and make lives of their own. And yet dreading the moment when they find their wings and don't need us anymore. Realizing we can't always protect them."

Shock knotted in my belly for a moment. That's what my parents had gone through. They fought for tight control of my life not to hurt me, but to protect me from a big bad world they neither understood nor trusted.

Then the tension eased. Maybe I'd actually call them this year and not just send them a holiday card and commercial shortbread—which they loved but wasn't up to my standard. It shipped better, too.

"So when will Jason start auditioning for New York?" Ted's voice sounded lighter.

"He's only fifteen, and just breaking into the company."

"The perfect time for him to start getting his face and form recognized by the big companies. Now is the time for him to transition. By the time he graduates high school, he'll have worked through the apprentice and corps stages and be ready to launch into soloist positions. He'll be two years ahead of Tiffany rather than five years behind."

"I'm not sure he's ready for that. I'm not sure I'm ready for that."

There was also the whole magic thing. He needed a lot more training at home from G before we let him out in the world.

"Tell Tiffany for me that I'll pack up several pounds of ointment and soaking salts for her to take with her."

"She'll appreciate that. Did you know that most of the jars of the salts you packaged for the bake sale went to other dancers? You could market that worldwide to dance companies just to keep expensive dancers on their feet."

"But . . . every package is unique. I have to talk to the dancer and see their feet to know what to put in each batch."

"You could be a very rich woman if you moved to New York," he replied hesitantly.

"Not likely. My home and business and family are here." I left unsaid, but implied, that he was here, too.

He hadn't mentioned refinishing the attic floor and the pentagram all night.

# Thirty-Two

FORTY-FIVE MINUTES BEFORE CURTAIN, the parking lot at the theater was full and street parking limited. Ted and I decided to walk two blocks, holding hands with shoulders brushing. We fell into a comfortable matching stride without thought.

"Back when Tiffany was about eight, very early in her years of ballet classes, the teacher brought in a live pianist for the first time. Up until then she'd used CDs designed for a classical lesson plan. The young man was a music major at the college and probably needed the pittance the teacher paid him."

"Tall, skinny guy with bad skin and glasses that slid down his nose? Spoke with a stutter? Maybe seventeen?" Ted nodded at my description. "I think Jason had him for classes when he first started. He was amazingly talented and showed signs of growing out of his acne and into his glasses."

"That's him. Anyway, he was a prodigy and hadn't quite grasped the concept of maintaining a steady rhythm throughout the entire exercise. He wanted to 'point' the music with odd emphasis. I'm sure it sounded wonderful. But Tiffany knew better. She still knows better and reminds me anytime I use a juice glass for my toothbrush."

"Of course. She's right," I commented with a smile. I'd heard this story before. It had become legend among ballet students. But I needed to let him tell it.

"Tiffany was executing piqué turns, perfectly of course, when he changed something in the music. She marched over to the upright piano and rapped his knuckles with the teacher's baton. He turned on her, expecting the tall and statuesque teacher, ready to rip her up one side and down the other. Instead he confronted a four-foot-tall blonde demon. She told him that if he disrupted her performance again, she'd fire him. Then she marched back to her starting position and waited for him to recover enough to play the music on a strict 4/4 tempo, so she could turn fifteen times in a row, ending with a perfect double and a curtsy."

"I can just picture her. Nothing comes between Tiffany and her performance." We laughed together.

A high-pitched cackling laugh joined us. I stopped in place, hand reaching for my wand as chills invaded my entire body.

"That does not sound normal," Ted whispered, also alert. Then he pointed toward the theater back door, across a full square block of parking lot.

"Hurry," a woman said, not caring about quiet. "We have to do this while all the dancers are still backstage. I will send smoke from our fire to trigger the alarms. The dancers will evacuate through this door. In the confusion you will grab the boy. But do not damage him, especially around his eyes. I need his eyes intact."

A whiff of sour smoke followed her words.

D'Accore. And she was after my boy.

Jason! I needed to warn him.

I needed to stop this wicked witch.

Sparks rose into the night sky a few feet away from the building. By their flickering illumination I caught the outline of one figure standing and three more crouched close to the building. A woman and three males.

No sign of John Mooney who still had his ankle encased in an air cast.

I fished for my phone in my tiny evening purse.

Ted's hand on my arm stilled my action. "No time.

Got your wand?" he whispered. "G's in no shape to tackle her. And Mooney may be in the far shadows, directing by remote control."

I nodded, as alarmed by his blurted words as the figures and the smell of smoke. I froze in place, then inched forward, my hands held away from my body, forcing myself not to twitch with any indication of where on my body I'd hidden the wand.

My left hand clutched the vial of caustic powder. I thumbed it open.

"Please, Daffy. I'm one of the good guys. G is my boss."

I raised my eyebrows in question, still not indicating where my wand was or that I trusted him.

"What is your talent and why haven't you revealed yourself before?"

"I'm impervious to magic. It bounces off me or passes through me without effect. I have no talent to cast outward. But my neutrality is now a recognized talent of sorts. So I'm the one G calls when he needs a crime scene cleaned. Any residual magic has no effect on me and I'm good at fixing and rebuilding quickly. I'm his janitor! And I know what you did to G. You're a transformer."

My wand began vibrating against my thigh. It telegraphed a sense of trust. And urgency.

Smoke thickened around me. If D'Accore did indeed use her smoke in place of her eyes, then she had spotted us. The malodorous haze did not move on. Instead, it concentrated on us, twisting and twirling in two separate spirals, moving closer. Choking the breath out of me.

"Quickly, use your wand. Transform it into something else!" Ted exclaimed.

Without thinking, I pulled up my skirt, exposing a lot more leg than necessary, and retrieved my wooden spurtle. Ted glanced appreciatively but didn't allow the sight of my stockinged flesh and my garter to distract him for long. He moved between me and the source of the smoke.

Sure enough the cloud hit his chest and returned to its originator.

What could I do? Give me flour and sugar, butter and eggs, and I'd give you cookies.

Give me the chaos of emotions after the Chamberses invaded Shara's birthday, and I came up with party plans. I took the chaos of vandalized costumes and props and I threw a successful bake sale.

Smoke was dirty air. I twisted the spoon in a counter-clockwise circle around the edges of the cloud trying to invade me. Like the flour and sugar that had sparkled in the air of my kitchen when my talent first manifested, I gathered the particulates into a solid clump. Then I closed my fist symbolically and hurled the metaphoric lump of ash like a softball, westward, toward the river.

Distantly, I heard a splash.

The woman in the back-door tableau screamed and clapped her hands over her eyes.

The three crouched figures fell back on their butts, staring at the teepee of kindling and split log campfire.

Sparks were transforming the pile into flames and ash. Not good.

Ted moved forward. I followed, keeping him in front of me like a fire-resistant wall. "I'm making this up as I go along," I whispered to him.

"Most magicians do," he chuckled. "You've blinded her. If you can neutralize the fire, I'll . . . I don't know. Do something to make the boys run."

He sounded as bewildered as I was. I handed him the vial of caustic powder. One sniff and he knew what it was.

Fire. The fire was my responsibility. Transform it. Into what? It had to remain essentially fire, or its component parts. Fire was heat, and light. It had its own internal chemical reaction, just as baking did. Fire wanted to transform fuel into heat, light, smoke, and ash.

Why not more light than anything else?

A flick of my wand while I concentrated on light,

lightning, blinding flashes. "Close your eyes!" I commanded in my most authoritative mother-knows-best voice. And I followed my own orders.

Red-and-yellow bolts of lightning showed behind my closed eyelids.

Male voices screeched followed by pounding footsteps. "My eyes! She's burning out my eyes. Get me some fucking water!" One of the males wailed.

When the flashes of lightning ceased, I cautiously opened my eyes. Three hunched-over figures darted into the shadows across the street. One of them was dragging the other two who were trying to claw out their own eyes.

Ted had better aim with the powder than I did.

"Come back here!" the woman yelled. Then she turned on her high heels and followed the sounds of the retreating boys, stumbling and flailing until some residual smoke found and guided her. A pale hand reached out from behind a tree and grabbed her wrist. She stabilized and let the hand guide her deeper into the shadows. No words. Blind trust.

Mooney?

"We have to go after them!" I started forward, ready to kick off my shoes and run.

"Not this time." Ted caught my hand. "We aren't enforcers, or even deputies. That's G's job, and he's in no shape to apprehend and arrest them." Gently, he smoothed my hair and brushed a layer of ash from my coat sleeves. "We have children performing in just a few minutes. We need to be inside for them. That's the most important job in the world."

---

G settled into his theater seat three rows back from the orchestra. He remembered coming here to Saturday matinees of horrible B-grade monster movies as a child. The place had closed about the time he entered high school, then reopened a few years later as a favored venue for vintage rock bands on reunion tours. Restoration had cleaned up the old place quite nicely.

He grimaced when he read the back of his program to find that bands he'd listened to as a teen were now vintage and on the gray-hair circuit.

Now community theater companies performed plays here, too. And the pro/am ballet company. They had priority on their lease. The other events might make more money, but the prestige of the ballet company elevated the status of the other groups.

He'd gone to all of Jason's recitals—or at least as many as he could when in town—wincing in sympathy at every missed step, or forgotten sequence. School Christmas pageants with off-key voices; he'd endured those, too. The girls didn't seem interested in anything artsy. All the artistic talent in the family had landed inside his boy. A young man now.

Pride filled G's chest when he read *Jason Deschants* in the program. Daffy should be here to share this special moment.

Where was she? Five minutes to curtain. The seats at the center of the first row—reserved for the families of the two principal dancers and people who knew which strings to pull—remained empty. The rest of the theater was full to overflowing. Like any wizard worth his salt, he extended his senses in search of Daffy's emotional frequency. It hummed in the back of his throat, like a welcome taste of dark chocolate laced with cherry liqueur.

Panic. Fear. Shock.

He grabbed his cane and cursed as he tried to leverage himself upright. The docs said he required another ten days of the damned knee brace. Daffy needed him now.

A new emotion telegraphed along his open senses. Bewilderment followed by accomplishment. He relaxed in his seat a bit. Just a bit as he opened the text function on his phone. The blasted thing vibrated and buzzed with an incoming text before he could type the first letter.

Smoke got in our eyes
fire turned to lightning
perps fled. TT

"What the hell does that mean?" G gasped, not caring if the audience around him heard.

A disturbance ahead and to his left. Daffy and Ted Tyler scuttled past the orchestra pit. They excused themselves to the rest of the row and settled into the two remaining seats in that row. Ted glanced his way and flashed a thumbs-up before turning his full attention to the printed program book.

Daffy enthusiastically pointed to the lists of performers and leaned her head close to Tyler's, never acknowledging G's presence. She looked happy, if a bit windblown.

G's heart wrenched. She should be sitting beside him, joyfully sharing Jason's success with him. He couldn't remember seeing her this happy since. . . .

She hadn't been this happy in a long, long time. Not with him anyway.

Their divorce was final. Perhaps . . . perhaps it was time to let her go.

And if he had to let her go, he couldn't think of a more honorable man for her to go to than Ted Tyler.

But it burned in his gut like battery acid.

# Thirty-Three

T HE LIGHTS DIMMED. The conductor emerged from behind the curtains and bowed to the audience. He acknowledged their applause and tripped lightly down the stage stairs to the pit. Another bow and he turned to face his orchestra.

I took a deep breath, anticipating the first strain of the jerky music "This Is Halloween" from *Nightmare Before Christmas*. My fingers drummed familiar themes melded together into an overture, and I closed my eyes to appreciate the fun tunes before the dancers commanded all of my attention.

At last the curtain rose on a misty cemetery. One by one, the ghostly dancers in wispy tatters of gray chiffon rose from trapdoors in the stage floor. And so the spooky tale proceeded. Jason excelled as I expected. He soared into ghostly attacks on a young couple—Tiffany and Aaron—as they attempted a lover's tryst where they shouldn't be. Tiffany commanded every eye to follow her through her performance. In the way of all good characterizations, her portrayal grew from shy and innocent to fiercely defensive to collapsing into death and rising again in elegant but ghostly white for one last embrace.

The other dances proceeded with similar perfection. I didn't think I'd see any flaws, even if I looked for them. This was my boy's night to shine. And Tiffany's to glow.

Then the scene transitioned into a blank open space. The lights hinted at sunset, a ritual bonfire—the fire was all lights and crackling tin foil—for the "Ritual Fire Dance"—I think the music actually started as a sword dance with a driving rhythm by a Russian composer. Matt and Denise performed a stylized contemporary piece with lots of sparks, danced by the corps de ballet. Different dance style, different body types from Aaron and Tiffany, but worthy successors.

During the intermission, I checked on Belle and Shara with Gayla sitting between them. Wise move. My girls might love each other, but they were sisters and bickering was a new hobby. But tonight they were as awestruck by Jason as they were by Tiffany.

"I'm still glad I gave up dance lessons before the first one was over, but she does make it all look easy," Belle confessed.

"Jason is doing okay," Shara admitted.

I sank into my seat with appreciation. Ted returned from the lobby with glasses of champagne. I accepted one with a smile and a new warmth for my companion. This was his night to celebrate the success of his child more than mine. The champagne was excellent. Something G might choose.

Banish that thought.

The ballet continued for the dramatic second act. I heard more than a few gasps at the special effects through *Night on Bare Mountain*, followed by *Tubular Bells*. And then we ended with *The Sorcerer's Apprentice*. Aaron looked nothing like Mickey Mouse in his oversized robe and pointy hat. Tiffany danced as his broom in a parody of a ballroom number. I think the corps de ballet had fun splitting into more and more brooms, getting more and more out of hand.

At the end of the evening's performance, the audience stood and applauded until our hands hurt and our arms ached with fatigue. And still we clapped. Ushers presented bouquet after bouquet to Tiffany and all of the soloists, including a huge one of at least two dozen roses of mixed hues.

"That one's from me," Ted whispered, clapping as loudly and enthusiastically as everyone else.

Tiffany and her company took one final deep bow and tiptoed off stage. The curtain came down and stayed down.

"Want to go backstage?" Ted asked as the audience began gathering belongings and preparing to leave.

"Try to keep me away." I couldn't help smiling.

And then I noticed G at the end of the aisle, his right leg stretched out straight into the passageway beside him and his cane propped up against his theater chair. He smiled and applauded like everyone else. But something around his eyes looked shadowed, dark, and painful.

My heart twisted for him. On this night of celebration he sat alone.

Two gunshots blasted through the near perfect acoustics of the place. People screamed and hastened for the exits, clogging at the doorways and leading to more screams.

My heart leaped to my throat. Fear paralyzed me until I picked out one particular screech amongst all the others. Belle and Shara crowded close to me. I pushed them down, out of the line of fire.

"Get G on his feet," Ted called as he vaulted over the seat in front of him, and dashed onto the stage.

━━━●━━━

"I'm up. I'm moving," G said to Daffy as she shoved people aside in the clogged aisle to get to him. Six people had bumped his knee and sent lances of fiery pain to his heel and all the way up to his shoulder. One man, the last to leave, had paused to offer him a hand up. G had dismissed him. All the others were caught up in the wild panic of a shooting in a crowded venue. Too often in recent years, large numbers of people had died or been maimed in just this kind of scenario.

"Stay with the girls!" he ordered Daffy. Not that he expected her to obey. At least he tried.

With his cane in one hand and his wand in the other

he limped down toward the stage. By the time he reached the short flight of steps in the corner, his knee had eased. The small brace beneath his trousers allowed him a little movement, but it still kept his leg straight, making stairs a slow process. No one was watching him, except maybe Daffy. So he tried a little of Jason's self-levitation.

For once it worked. His adrenaline levels must be higher than he thought. Fear for the lives of one's children will do that.

Then Daffy was behind him, her own wand, that ridiculous spurtle in her hand. At least the thing looked something like a wand and had undertones of her Scottish heritage. Psychics hid behind every rock and tuft of heather in the highlands.

"I thought I told you . . ."

"Forget that. He's my boy, too. And I have a vested interest in all of those dancers." She pushed the small of his back forward to make room for herself. A marauding mother hen—descended from a T. rex—with chicks in danger.

Backstage, he picked out the forms of dozens of costumed dancers cowering in corners and alcoves, behind sets and curtains.

"Jason?" he called in a stage whisper that would reach every corner of the area without sounding loud and alarming.

"Up here, Dad," Jason panted. "I can't hold him much longer."

G looked up, and up, and up, to the top of the flies where a slim young man in silver tights with a brocade tunic clung to the catwalk. His legs held a squirming BJ in a scissor lock around his neck. BJ gibbered in panic, eyes huge, a pistol dangling from one finger as he flailed his arms.

"Stay still," G ordered in the tones of a drill sergeant.

Instantly, BJ stopped. He turned those wide, desperate eyes toward him with the tiniest glimmer of hope that he might get out of this alive.

Behind him, G sensed Daffy gathering up the dancers and herding them into dressing rooms and prop rooms. No sign of Ted and his blonde daughter.

"Okay, Jason, let go of the catwalk when you are ready. Do not, I repeat, do not drop BJ. I'll guide you down. Just like in dance class, land slowly, gently, light as a feather. No noise." He extended his wand and thought a cushioning bubble into place around the boys.

Jason took a deep breath and released his hands. They dropped abruptly about three feet. BJ screamed and dropped the pistol. A revolver. It landed with a thud and the explosion of a single bullet.

No time to mark the trajectory.

No one screamed. A blessing that he'd claimed no victims with that careless action.

Jason made an alliance with gravity. He'd succumb to the elemental pull, but on his terms and schedule.

G breathed a bit lighter as they descended as if supported by special effects harness and wires.

BJ was a gibbering mess, knees collapsing upon contact. Jason released his stranglehold on his former friend's neck and came down beside him, a little jerky and uncontrolled but safe.

Daffy dashed out from her hiding place and enveloped the boy in a motherly hug. Holding him close and admonishing him for endangering himself at the same time. Her fingers arched in a desperate clutch on his back.

G left his son's welfare to her as he banished the protective cushion. Three steps and he pressed his cane against BJ's throat to keep him in place while he sent a stasis spell through the wand into the boy's mind. BJ collapsed against the boards.

"Now what?" Ted asked emerging from the shadows. Tiffany tiptoed behind him as if she disobeyed his orders to remain concealed, but couldn't keep herself from watching.

G tilted his head in the girl's direction with an unspoken question.

Ted frowned, staring at his daughter, hand on hips, anger in his eyes. She returned his glare with one of her own.

"Wipe her memories," Ted replied and pulled out a length of rope from his suit pocket and began binding BJ's hands. His pockets were notoriously like Mary Poppins' carpetbag. And he said he had no magic.

G breathed a little easier. If BJ had had help, they'd fled the scene right after he started shooting. Just like D'Accore to send a boy to do a man's job. Or maybe BJ had rushed in to finish what she started earlier, just to please her.

He wondered what sort of thrall she held over her minions. Sex? Money? Magical power? A release from social constraints to give in to their baser instincts? Or, in BJ's case, freedom from his parents?

A siren's talents, but she didn't need magic for them. Plenty of mundane women could do that.

"Is anyone hurt?" he called to the far reaches of the theater.

"Both shots went wild," Jason said, still clinging to his mother. Daffy. His real mom, not the woman who had given birth to him. "I got to him just before he fired the second time. I think the bullet may have taken out a light on the catwalk."

"Mundane weapon. Mundane authorities," G pronounced and dialed 911. "I'd like to see your father get you out of this one, BJ."

# Thirty-Four

"**W**ALK ME THROUGH THIS one more time, every detail, every sensory perception, and your thoughts, no matter how random," G said. He limped painfully around the living room. Ted and I sat on the sofa, shoulders touching.

I repeated everything I'd seen, heard, smelled, and thought when D'Accore and her anonymous minions tried to smoke the dancers out of the theater before the performance. I contemplated the texture and taste of the air. And when I got to the part about seeing a ghostly pale hand reach out from behind a tree to steady D'Accore's blind retreat, he asked me to repeat it again and again. How had I known it was Mooney? The off-center balance of the silhouette suggested a man walking with a cast. No, I didn't see a face or what kind of clothing he wore. It was dark. He wore dark.

Then G zeroed in on Ted with the same interrogation. This is what television portrayed as standard police procedure.

I was exhausted. Both men had discarded jackets and ties. And still G persisted.

"That's enough, G," Gayla finally announced from the kitchen doorway. "You aren't going to squeeze any more information from them tonight. Let them sleep on it. Maybe their dreams will conjure something new or different."

"Gayla, this is not your business," G said sternly, in what I'd come to describe as his "sheriff's" voice.

"Yes, it is. Daffy's my best friend and my business partner. What affects her, affects me. Besides, your eyes are little more than dark hollows in your skull-like face. You're limping badly, and your speech is becoming slurred. You need to go to bed, and I need to get home. I've put your children to bed, except Jason, and he's too wound up to settle anywhere. At least he's not bouncing off the ceiling anymore."

"Thank you, Gayla," I said, truly grateful for the way she had tended to my family when I couldn't.

"You're welcome." She retreated toward the back door.

"I should be going, too," Ted said. "I want to make sure Tiffany made it home okay after her date. I'm afraid there will be tears. She was going to break up with her current boyfriend before she heads to St. Louis."

"She's wise to do it now. She'll have time to get over her guilt before she leaves and not take that kind of baggage with her," I replied.

"Sleep well, and call if you need anything." He looked at G, then bent to kiss my cheek.

"I'll walk you out," I insisted. I wanted more than that quick peck. G's frown and low throat grumble was enough to put off the most ardent of suitors.

We did kiss in the semiprivacy of the mudroom. But the best part was the tight embrace, the hands clutching desperately to each other for reassurance, and the long moment of stillness with our foreheads pressed together. We'd been through a lot this evening. And it was only going to get worse.

"I'll call you in the morning," he whispered.

"Anytime. I'm up early."

Another quick kiss and he left me alone.

"Tomorrow, I'm going to seek help, the kind I usually resist," G said when I returned to the living room. At least he hadn't followed us through the kitchen.

I heard Jason rummaging around the kitchen for a bedtime snack, his third.

"What kind of help?" I asked.

"Healing hands."

"As in?"

"A massage therapist across town. She's licensed by the state and the Guild. Works miracles on torn muscles and knotted tendons. She uses mundane methods as well as magical, depending on who her client is and what they truly need." G eased himself into the recliner and lifted the footrest. His body looked more comfortable, but his face remained contorted with pain.

"Physical therapy isn't enough?"

"Too slow."

"I've heard of that lady. She's in one of the high-rise bank buildings downtown," Jason said around a corned beef sandwich that leaked sauerkraut and mustard.

I dashed to thrust a paper napkin under his hands and caught a blob.

"Anyway, Aaron and Matt, our two lead male dancers, go to her after intense rehearsals. Is her name Judy? No, Judi with an i. Say, if Tiffany is leaving first of the year, do you think Denise will be promoted to prima? I've been practicing with her on some lifts, and she's got really great balance. She might ask for me as her new partner." He took another bite, almost dislocating his jaw to get around the bulk of the sandwich.

"I think there will be intense auditions for the spring program. And Denise dances with Matt as if they were made for each other. Now off to bed with you. You have both a matinee and an evening performance tomorrow," I ushered him toward the stairs.

"Will the police close the theater?" Jason asked.

Good question.

"Doubtful. No one was hurt and they found all three slugs. They have the perp in custody," G said, more familiar with police procedure than I was.

That hit me like a blow to the gut. G a policeman.

Different title and jurisdiction. But now that I'd seen him dealing with the aftermath of a crime just like an authorized detective, I knew for certain that he really and truly was a law enforcement officer and not just playing at it with magic.

I had to sit down on the bottom step.

"Mom!" Jason leaped to my side, landing with precision and lightness. Oh, yes, he had magic in those feet and legs of his.

"Probably shock," G said, still in the recliner. "Get her up to bed. I'll make her a cup of chamomile tea if you'll carry it up to her." He braced his arms on the chair in preparation of getting up.

"Stay put, G. I'm still the mom in this household. I'll get my own tea. Both of you go to bed and stay there until breakfast. That's an order." I hated chamomile, therapeutic as it was. Peppermint for me, with a double shot of scotch. Maybe a triple.

───────

Ted called at six and asked me to turn on the local news. It was less than inspirational. Bret Chambers Sr. faced the camera with Flora standing stalwart at his side. Not a stumble or emotion got in the way of the "Candidate's" prepared speech.

"The lengths some of our neighbors will go to in order to sabotage my campaign by luring my son into committing an act of irrational passion saddens me. It is not my son's actions that should be on trial here, but the enticement to violence perpetrated by the heathen members of our community who should be held accountable."

He went on for some time. I tuned him out. "Does he honestly believe he can get BJ off with that kind of defense?" I asked Ted bleakly over the phone.

"I don't know. His pastor has made a statement that BJ was weak and needs therapy to strengthen his character while several parishioners say his parents are not to blame," Ted replied. "I'm getting implications that they want to name Jason as a drug dealer so the blame will fall back on your 'broken home.'"

I wanted Ted here, his solid common sense to lean on. Instead, he was on the other end of the phone line.

"What's going to happen now?" I asked, bewildered.

"State mandated competency consultation, probably later today," Ted replied.

"And that means . . . ?"

"State psychiatrist will interview BJ and evaluate his competency to stand trial. Does he know why he's in jail? Does he remember shooting at people? That sort of thing. Since he's sixteen, it's iffy if the parents will be present or not."

"Flora will demand she be present at least. I can't see Bret Sr. staying out of it either." I wondered if G could use his contacts to observe the evaluation through one of those windows that looks like a mirror from the inside. The kind they showed on TV all the time. I'd ask.

"Competent or not, he's going to be locked up for a while. Doubtful any judge will grant bail on criminal charges. Psych charges means the State Hospital for a long time, with supervision, therapy, and drugs."

"Bret Sr. will probably push for the State Hospital. He can spin that to a positive in his campaign."

"If BJ starts spouting phrases like magical coercion and destruction of wands and such, you can almost bet he'll get the State Hospital for a good long time."

That would satisfy me. BJ had been a good kid until all this magic stuff descended upon us. I could well imagine his unacknowledged talents chewing on his mind, driving him insane.

The same thing had happened to D'Accore.

It might happen to me. . . .

No. I had accepted magic before I manifested. I had help, training, and people to talk with about it rather than keeping it all in and hidden from those closest to me.

"Want to come over and help Jason refinish the attic floor before the party?" I had to change the subject before I fell into a deep depression about what magic was doing to us—ripping my family to emotional shreds.

"Love to, but I've got a ballerina in the throes of being delicate until showtime."

"Let me know if I can do anything to help."

"You've already done so much. She's soaking her feet in your special solution and burning up the phone lines with her friends. I'll call you later, even if it's just to chat. Bye."

I felt like I was in high school with the first blush of a crush on the captain of the football team. Only this time he liked me back.

"Mom, when did Dad learn to speak German?" Jason asked, stumbling down the stairs and rubbing the sleep out of his eyes.

"What?"

"He was on the phone all night. Sometimes German. Sometimes French. Once it sounded like Chinese. Cantonese, I think. Not Mandarin. And a really weird dialect that might have been some Indian tribe." Still rubbing his eyes and shuffling his feet, he opened the fridge and hauled out milk and OJ. "Oh, and he made an early appointment with Judi. Nine, I think. He gets the priority treatment for Guild members."

"Use a glass, don't drink from the carton. And how do you know the difference between Cantonese and the other hundred or so dialects of Chinese?" I didn't care about the massage therapy as long as it didn't disrupt Jason's—or my—schedule.

"I dunno." The universal answer of a teenager.

"Wake up and start talking." Before I slammed into G's old office that had become his bedroom to ask what was going on. No more recliner or hospital bed for him. Last week he'd directed Jason, Aaron, and Matt to drag an antique double headboard and bedframe out of the attic. I'm not certain where he found a mattress and bedding. Maybe he and Jason had bought them on one of their driving lesson excursions. Or Jason had dug them out of one of the dowry chests in the attic.

He was taking over my life. Again.

"He was up all night, I think, talking on the phone. His room is right below mine, so I heard it all. Understood some of it. The French part anyway. Maybe he was dragging my dream self into the conversation so I *would* understand." He stared longingly at the pancake batter I'd mixed up earlier. And the eggs. And the sausage.

"I'll fix you breakfast, but you have to let me know what your father was doing on the phone all night."

"I don't think I'm supposed to tell. It sounded like Guild business."

That would explain the multiple languages.

"And I think he might be calling some deputies."

"Good. He's getting better, but he's still not up to snuff. He needs help, and he needs to learn to delegate." I plopped batter onto the griddle and listened to it sizzle. Then I started a half pound of bacon and four eggs in other fry pans. "You need some fruit with this. There should be a melon mix in the covered red bowl."

Jason sat in the nook and stared at the refrigerator door as if it were a mile away.

He got silence from me. Finally, he dragged himself upright and stumbled the ten steps to his goal and rummaged around until he found the bowl right in front of him. He flipped the lid into the sink and began pulling chunks of cantaloupe and watermelon out with his fingers, stuffing them into his mouth almost as fast as he could grab the next piece. I knew he'd at least leave the pineapple and grapes for the girls.

"Get a fork. And save some for your sisters."

"And me," G said, emerging from his room. He limped. Badly. His cane thunked heavily on the floor with each step. He'd been considerably better yesterday. He was dressed, casually for him, in pressed khakis and a polo shirt, also neatly pressed.

I hadn't done his laundry, so I wondered who had ironed his clothes. Or did he use a magic spell to "refresh" them?

"When are you moving in with Raphe?" I asked, trying for casual, but even to my own ears I sounded annoyed. "You can manage stairs again, and you've been here for two weeks." I didn't add that he was keeping Jason up all night with his phone calls.

"Can't. I've got three deputies flying in this afternoon and I need the extra rooms at Raphe's to house them until we settle things with D'Accore and Mooney." He flopped onto the bench seat in the nook, rubbing his injured knee and looking pitiful. Or as pitiful as he could manage in order to get on my good side.

"They can drive you around, so Jason has time to do his homework for a change and rest between performances." I added more batter to the griddle for him. No sounds from above, so I guessed the girls would sleep awhile longer. Jason could use up the batter that should have fed the entire family. He was growing again. Or was that still?

"I need to be with Jason at the theater, so I'll need you to meet my people at the airport . . ."

"I can protect our son if I have to. But I think he can probably do a better job himself. And you need to watch the morning news. Bret and Flora are blaming us for encouraging violent tendencies in their precious little boy. They are hinting that if drugs are involved, they came from 'that fag, Jason.' "

G covered his face with both hands and rubbed circulation into his head.

"That accusation is hardly anything to be ashamed of now, but Chambers still considers 'fag' the ultimate insult. In the current political climate, more and more people are giving in to previously hidden prejudice. Not much I can do about that," he countered. "I can try to observe the competency test, so I know what kind of cleanup I need to do in the aftermath. But I doubt that even my credentials will get me into the interrogation room. That sort of thing is usually kept very private."

"The best we can hope for is that BJ tells the truth and no one believes him," Jason said.

"There is a particularly cute and perky blonde reporter hanging around town looking for her first story. She seems to have zeroed in on the unusual happenings in town. I ran into her after the protests at the shop. Please be charming when she rams her microphone into your teeth," I said. "You might suggest to her your concern that BJ is schizophrenic. Let the press jump on that and thus make it true before the psych eval."

"I'll just say I sympathize with Mr. Chambers trying to defend his son even if he is grasping at straws." He flashed his most winning smile.

This time I detected the sizzle of magic emanating from him. Mentally, I sidestepped his charm.

Jason was hovering at my shoulder with an empty plate. I stacked four pancakes onto it. He used a spatula to gather his eggs and a long-handled fork for the bacon. That should keep him busy for about thirty seconds.

"Can I have Dad's room when he moves out again?" he asked around a wad of pancakes dripping in syrup.

"Don't talk with your mouth full," G admonished, before I could.

I just said, "No."

"But it's quieter than my room right across from the girls and I'd have my own bathroom that I wouldn't have to share with my sisters!"

He had a point.

I saw Gayla drive up along the side of the house and park by the back gate. Her little station wagon looked stuffed to the gills with odd shapes in black and gray. Oh, yeah. We'd planned to start decorating for Halloween.

"New plan. G, you will fetch your deputies from the airport. You are driving again whether you like it or not. I'm taking Jason to the theater and dropping him off. Ted will be there with Tiffany. Gayla and I will be busy with the girls here."

"But ..."

"Mom ...!"

"Are there any pancakes left for us?" Belle asked with Shara right behind her.

And the muted TV in the corner showed fire trucks rolling toward a massive blob of red flames at the heart of roiling black smoke in the center of old town on the block where John Mooney had his shop. The flames threatened to jump streets headed toward Magical Brews.

# Thirty-Five

"**D**AFFY, a little rain right now would help a lot," G demanded as he leveraged himself upright. Damn that knee. He had a major situation to control and an appointment with the healing hands lady in ninety minutes.

"I can't produce rain," Daffy replied. She let Gayla in, and they immediately began discussing what they needed to do to protect their coffee shop.

"You can predict the weather to the minute. Controlling it is only one step above that," G said. He grabbed her arm to pull her out of her discussion.

She stared at his hand as if it were a snake about to bite her. His palm grew hot, her skin burned him. Damn she was developing yet another aspect of her talents.

"Think about it, Daffy. Think hard. Don't just know when the clouds are moving in from the west. Concentrate on how they move and how much water they want to dump." Her eyes grew wide in wonder. "Don't let them drop any water on the coast range. Make them come farther inland."

"It was starting to drizzle when I drove in," Gayla said, probably oblivious to the storm fury going on in Daffy's mind.

Shara bounced to the window. "The sky's getting dark and the wind is picking up," she reported.

"Wind won't help the fire much," Gayla snorted. "It will carry the sparks farther afield."

"Not if we make it circle," Belle added. "Dad, I need to be on the roof. I think I can attract the wind, make it split and crash together, and then let the clouds dump rain to lighten their load while the two halves fight it out."

"That should keep it from spreading too fast and give the firefighters a chance to contain it," Jason said. He stood up, flexing his knees, preparing for whatever he could do to help. But his movements were slow, almost labored. He wasn't as rested as he pretended.

"I need to be outside," Daffy muttered, eyes glazed. She stumbled toward the front door.

"We have to make sure the rain concentrates on the center of the fire," G said, guiding Daffy onto the front porch.

"I'll carry Belle up to the tower roof," Jason almost chortled. "I know I can jump that high."

"Start at the top of the tower and use the door to the widow's walk," G thundered at him. "Do an occasional hover high enough to see over the trees into old town. But don't invite observation, don't stay in the air long enough to be spotted."

"What can I do?" Shara asked, staring at the muted television screen.

"You're the maze runner, kid," G said. "Find the core of the fire."

Shara scrunched her eyes almost closed in concentration as she followed them onto the porch.

"Wind your way down through the flames," G instructed her.

She winced and cringed backward. He steadied her with both hands on her shoulders. "I know it's hot in there, but the flames can't touch you. The flames are an artificial construct. You need to find the fire imp at the core. It's fanning the flames. You find it. I'll flatten it."

"What about D'Accore and Mooney?" Daffy gasped. She'd done her job, bringing the rain and clouds in. Now she had time to think. She wrapped her arms around herself to ward off the morning chill. Then she shook her head and ushered everyone back inside.

Gayla handed Daffy the fruit bowl and started feeding her. Good. The woman didn't have a magical talent, but she knew what magical people needed and when they needed it.

"This feels more like a temper tantrum than planned destruction. We thwarted her twice last night. Now she's taking it out on whoever is closest. Mooney, I guess, since he owns that building." G tasted the essence of the fire through Shara and the televised images.

"Dad, I need line of sight. Up high." Shara slumped against him. Gayla handed her one of Daffy's wonderfully nutritious cookies.

"Balcony off my bedroom," Daffy said. She grabbed their daughter's hand and dragged her upstairs.

G had to follow. Shara would need a few minutes to find the imp while he limped up the stairs.

Gayla handed him his cane. "Need a shoulder to lean on?"

"If you don't mind." He accepted her assistance, too grateful for the help to bother with pride.

●━━━━

Now I knew why so many marginal magic practitioners fell into the wannabe category. Magic took a *lot* of work and energy. My knees wobbled, and my head threatened to dislodge itself from reality.

There was too much to do and no me left to do it.

Oh, yeah. I was the only one who hadn't eaten a substantial breakfast. I'd been cooking while the family scarfed down every calorie I put in front of them. I'd had a few bites of fruit. Not enough.

Gayla ran down the stairs and back up again in less time than I required to think where I could find food. My best friend and savior! She handed me a pancake drizzled with a little syrup and wrapped around three slices of bacon.

"Bless you!" I cried as I inhaled the improvised snack.

"I'll go start cooking more of everything. You finish off the last of the fruit." And she disappeared again.

The tang of the pineapple blended with the salt in the bacon and the thick gooeyness of the pancake. A new breakfast treat I could make for the shop!

Then I heard doors opening and feet clomping all around me. I spotted the cookie jar on the lamp table beside the door to my bedroom. Gayla must have left it there. I grabbed three cookies, took one bite and grabbed three more. Somehow, they were all gone by the time I reached the balcony and felt the cold wind blasting through the French doors.

G and I used to sit out there in the evenings, watching the sunset, sipping beer or wine. Just sitting and unwinding, often not even talking. Not needing to talk. Since G moved out, it was a barren place where I never had time to tend to potted plants or clean outdoor chairs. Or use. Now it housed only dead leaves. I may have swept it clear at the end of summer.

G stood out there with his hands on Shara's shoulders. He spoke softly, following her mind into the heart of the maze that was the fire.

Another story up, on the widow's walk on the main roof between the two towers, Belle coaxed the wind to follow her direction as if it were a puppy. "Come on, baby. This way. Just a little bit farther. Come meet your brother. You can do it. You can touch noses with your brother. Just a touch. That's all I ask. Just a little touch. Then you can join forces again."

Did the wind know its own chemistry? Right and left. Positive and negative. Base and acid. Would the wind willingly meet its other half if it knew the explosion to come?

I wanted my kids back inside before it did.

"Almost there, Shara. Almost to the center. One more twist, another turn, around and there! To the left. Get us around the pile of debris, and . . . Gotcha! You little devil." He released Shara and stepped to the side. "Now Belle, dump the rain now."

"To the right two degrees of arc," Jason guided her. A light thump told me he'd landed beside her. How long had he been in the air spotting for her?

My knees threatened to collapse again. Shara and G showed signs of flagging. The tension in his back told me he needed to hang on a few more moments. Belle and Jason would need an extra boost about now, too.

My job, as mom, to keep them working together until the job was done.

> *Alakazam*
> *Magic Slam*

I whispered against the wind, slapping a rhythm against my thigh.

> *What's you gonna do*
> *When life gets too much*
> *When the world is in a jam*
> *Alakazam*
> *Magic Slam!*

Shara picked up the next line in her childish soprano. Then Belle followed in her maturing alto.

Jason added his lighter baritone,

> *Slay the monsters*
> *Give them a wham*
> *Alakazam*

We all joined together in a rousing finish

> *Magic Slam!*

We sang the song all the way through twice, as a family, working together to get the job done.

And the rain dumped, not just on top of the fire, but all over downtown Eugene, soaking the roofs, muddying the ground, replenishing the creeks that hadn't fully recovered from the dry summer.

G raised his hands over his head and clapped three times. Lightning sparked from his fingers. Or was that the fire imp he'd banished to another realm?

Thunder followed right on top of his lightning. The entire world shuddered and trembled in fear of the mighty clash of competing air masses. Twice more, lightning filled the skies with an eerie bluish-yellow light, followed immediately by lessening booms of thunder.

Abruptly, the rain faded to a soft drizzle.

Sagging and flagging, we trooped downstairs for a second breakfast, just as hearty and filling as the first one. This time Gayla made sure I ate the first portion, standing up while the rest of them found places in the nook.

Jason pressed two fingers against each temple, as if trying to hold his brains in. I detoured to the bathroom medicine cabinet for over-the-counter pain pills and a big glass of water for him.

I wondered if he'd be able to dance tonight with one of his migraines.

On the television, the camera caught Bret Chambers clasping his hands in prayer and rolling his eyes heavenward, saying, "Thank God for his miracles!" as the camera panned the dying fire and the destruction left behind.

Of course, he took credit for it.

A satellite truck pulled to a stop on the street across our driveway, blocking it. Camera operators, sound engineers, and the blonde hopped out.

I foresaw a long day ahead of us.

# Thirty-Six

I KEPT A CONCERNED eye on Jason until the tight lines around his eyes relaxed and he stopped squinting against the light. "The good thing about this is that Mooney and D'Accore can't know that we stopped the fire, using natural forces. They don't know our combined strengths," G said, ignoring the doorbell for the third time.

A single press truck had been camped out front for an hour while we replenished our bodies. Why was the perky blonde here and not at the fire scene? That was the big news of the day.

Unless Bret Chambers had accused us of starting the fire. I flicked the TV back on. Sure enough there was BJ's father accusing us, not only of inciting his precious son to violence, but of starting the fire as part of our diabolical plan to take over the world. But he and his church had countered us with their prayers. He and his people had brought about the miracle that contained the fire.

Give me a break!

G showed definite signs of itchy restlessness.

"Do all fires have imps at the core?" Shara asked. She didn't look happy. In her world imps were cute little beings with smiles and manners and love in their hearts, just like the cartoon shows.

"No," G replied. The sound of the doorbell had reached a higher level of annoying. He winced and his eyes flicked from his daughter's face to the front door and back. "One of the magical talents D'Accore has acquired is from an elderly Welsh woman who communicated with and commanded imps—*dyflyn* in her language. A fire dyflyn will start a fire for her, even with wet kindling and allow her to leave the scene of the crime. The fire will continue to burn without human direction or control until all of the fuel is eaten. *All of it.* The entire city if left alone."

G looked exhausted but exuberant at the same time. And he needed . . . a woman. I wasn't about to provide the necessary service. Though a little . . . maybe just a quickie up against the wall . . . would certainly set me to rights again.

Nope. Not going to go there or do that. That was G's thing. Not mine. I had better ways to use my aftermath energy. Like get this family moving again.

"G, run the gauntlet and get to your appointment," I ordered.

He looked up at me in surprise. "Gayla's car is in the way. And so is the satellite truck."

"I have to get back home and survey everything, air things out to banish the smoke smell, that kind of thing." Gayla fished her car keys out of her pocket, looking at the wreckage of my kitchen, then turned her back on the piles of dirty dishes. "If we drive out together and pretend we'll run down anyone who stays in our way . . ."

"I have a better idea," G said. He walked over to the landline telephone and dialed three numbers.

Then he counted to sixty. A siren erupted from mere blocks away. Even though every law enforcement officer, EMT, and firefighter within twenty miles should be at the fire scene, at least one patrol car responded to G's alarm.

"What just happened?"

"A little alarm system I installed after Chambers tried to usurp Shara's birthday party." He limped toward the coat hooks along the wall of the mudroom.

Jason wearily heaved himself upright; his headache might be better, but he needed rest. By the time he got his feet on the ground, we heard the police siren *whoop* very close to the house. This was immediately followed by the slam of car doors and engines revving as the press sped away.

Oh, boy. I could just see tomorrow's headlines asking what was so special about our house and my family that the police responded in moments to G's alarm when they should be at the more important scene downtown.

"Jason, stay." I said. He sank back down again gratefully. "Your father has to start driving himself now." And answering questions. "You can go back to bed until eleven. Then it's lunch, and I'll drive you to the theater after we're done."

"If I'm not back by then, take the girls with you. I don't want them left alone," G ordered.

"Aye, aye, sir!" I saluted him backward. "How in the hell did you con the police into obeying your whims?"

"Interagency cooperation. I had a chat with the commissioner when I first took over this job, and they bow and scrape to do my bidding now."

"*Interagency?*" I gulped. "Which agency?" I couldn't imagine a normal law enforcement group working with the Guild of Wizards. Unless . . . "As in *Interpol?*"

All I heard in response was the slamming of the back door.

———•———

"Daddy?" Shara's voice came through G's cell phone, meek and hesitant. Not what he expected from his youngest. Ever.

"What, sweetheart?" He sat in the front seat of his car with his legs out the open door. Damn, that knee hurt. But Judi had worked her magic and tweaked and twisted it back into its normal position. She'd also instinctively known his other burning itch and helped him out, now that he was single again. He didn't like having sex with people he knew. It complicated things afterward. Especially with Daffy so close but unavailable.

What had Daffy done to take care of her own problem? She'd pushed as much magic through her body as he had. He didn't dare growl at the thought of Ted Tyler coming by the house to "help," not with his daughters listening anyway.

When they finished, Judi had said he needed a few hours for everything to settle. But it still hurt like hell. And he was supposed to keep moving so it wouldn't stiffen up again.

"I found it," Shara whispered.

He stilled, thinking hard. "Did you get in?"

"Yes. Belle helped me once I figured out that the password was an algorithmic progression."

Leave it to Belle to see the pattern and follow it through to its logical conclusion. Something D'Accore was never good at. Lately, she was even worse at completing a job, probably because she had only absorbed about half of each talent she stole. Did she use it all up with each spell she cast?

Doubtful. His luck didn't run that way. He needed something more to bring her down.

He suspected that Mooney anchored her and coaxed her to complete as much as she did. That fire this morning was pretty thorough, even without the imp at the core.

What did she do with the wands she stole?

He thought she stripped them of any residual, but maybe she could absorb more if she used them a few more times.

"It looks like he's funding domestic terrorists with that offshore account," Belle interrupted his thoughts. They must have Shara's phone on speaker. "But a lot of it is channeling back into a New York bank to fund travel and clothes and jewels. What do we do with it now?"

Domestic terrorists? A good way to describe his bribes and building an army of minions for D'Accore. But what did Mooney have to gain from that?

D'Accore. She'd push him to the illogical activity to gain chaos. She thrived on chaos, the euphoria of gathering the random energy. Mooney would then be able to con his real estate clients into installing "Safe Rooms" with either legit or scam artist contractors. He'd make a big profit on each deal regardless.

And he had D'Accore, his first love. She'd dumped him the moment she met G. But she'd returned to him for help just before her arrest. Could she have cast a slow-working spell on him that led to his amassing money any way he could and using it to gain her escape from magical imprisonment?

He wouldn't put anything past her.

"Um . . ." G looked at his watch. His men should be landing any minute. George Red Hawk, the bird whisperer, Wu Sing Chen, the trap maker, and his foster brother Zebediah Macumbo, on loan from Interpol, totally mundane, sharp as a whip and a brick wall of muscle and quick fists. G had used them before, but rarely. Their oddball combination of talents often caught the guilty off guard.

He waited for them in the cell phone parking area. He needed to get off the line so the men could call him to fetch them from baggage claim.

And what were the girls doing home? Shouldn't they be with Daffy about now delivering Jason to the theater?

"Mr. Tyler is with us until Mom gets back," Belle answered his question before he asked. "He's okay, Dad, just sort of boring. All he wants to do is sand and varnish the attic floor like it's sacred ground or something."

"It is sacred ground to us. Belle, do you have something to write with?"

"My tablet."

"No. Paper. Then burn it when you're done. Don't let anyone see it, even your mom or Mr. Tyler."

"Paranoid, much?"

"Yes." And damn, he hated sharing that information, even with his brilliant and brilliantly talented daughters. But he had to. Tonight, he'd make sure he changed some of the protocols at that special website.

"Shara, while she's looking for paper and pen, are you on my desktop computer with the secure modem?"

"Well, duh. How do you think I busted through six layers of firewall? My laptop doesn't have enough juice to do that, even with the ten-terabyte external hard drive."

"Okay, okay. I need you to go to the secondary browser labeled GoW. It's in a subdirectory of my work notes."

"Wow, you really don't want anyone finding that," she said, almost immediately. He had no doubt she'd located it in seconds. Belle would need a minute or two. Jason and Daffy half an hour.

"Back, Dad. What am I supposed to write down?" Belle asked.

He spelled out a long train of foreign words and symbols. "That's the URL. The password to get beyond their firewall is G@Interpol.eu.it.gov."

"Huh?" Belle came back. "I never knew . . ."

"Very few do. Now forget you ever knew it, or I'll make you forget." He couldn't erase one specific memory and leave the rest intact remotely, only face-to-face, fingers of one hand on her temple, fingers of his other hand on his own temple as he erased the memory out of her mind and absorbed it into his own. But she didn't know that yet.

"Okay, once you are in and you see the welcome-what-can-we-do-for-you page, click on the security badge." He led her through a complex procedure. "Then type in the bank name, the account number, and his password as quickly as you can. It will blank your typing as you go, so you have to be quick and accurate the first time. Then back out the same way you got in and log off at the welcome page. By Monday morning, Mr. Mooney should have an IRS auditor on his doorstep with a dozen federal warrants."

"Is that all?" Belle asked, sounding disgusted. "What can they do to him?"

"Strip him of all assets and slap him in prison. Then I

swoop in and make certain he can't get out by magical or mundane means. I'll make certain there is no bail." His phone clicked and beeped. "Now burn that address and password. I've got to go. Tell your mom we'll have three extra for dinner."

"She's not going to like that."

G sighed. "Tell her to get used to it. She wanted all of us to work together as a family. Now she has to live with the consequences, like I do every day of our lives." Every damn day.

---

I had enough stew and fresh-baked bread to feed the family for three days—even with Jason's enormous appetite. Would that be enough for one night with the addition of Ted and G's three mysterious friends?

And how was I supposed to deal with setting up the house for the Halloween Party of the decade when I had to cook for all these people? I'd made it as far as placing foam headstones around the front yard and draping them with fake cobwebs.

Ted had joined me after making sure Jason was prepared to defend himself at the theater. He knew what to look for and what to sense with magic. Neither Ted nor I wanted to face my jealous ex. I'd been trying to think of an excuse to get him into my bedroom since he drove up to the back door. So far, no luck. G's ghost kept getting between me and follow through.

Inviting Ted to dinner was a risk. Maybe I could use the confrontation to push G out again.

I'd found Raphe's house on the eastern edge of town, almost into Springfield. It was old and dumpy, a Craftsman bungalow. It was also huge, as if built for a large extended family. If Raphe slept during the day in the basement, that would still leave four or five bedrooms divided between the first and second floors.

"I got three strings of pumpkin lights draped around the front porch as well as finishing the attic floor. The pentagram is intact and glowing. How about I take some of that stew to Jason for him to eat between matinee and evening performances. That way he doesn't have to break his concentration by coming home, and I can check on him and on Tiffany at the same time?" Ted asked coming up behind me where I chopped cucumber and tomato to add to the salad.

"If you take enough for yourself and Tiffany." I agreed with him.

"She won't eat much until she's done for the evening. But she's acting a little fragile—more from the breakup with her boyfriend than BJ taking aim at Jason while she was standing next to him. A bit of your cooking should restore her." He wrapped his arms around me from behind.

I remembered my junior year at the U, before I met G, and understood. A protest turned riot didn't bother me as much as worrying about my relationship with the boyfriend of the month.

"Since BJ didn't aim the gun at anyone but Jason, Tiffany didn't feel threatened, just exasperated with adolescent hormones getting in the way of logic. Dumping the boyfriend before the performance kinda fell into the same category. A long-distance romance at their ages doesn't compute for her. He saw it differently and promised to wait for her to come to her senses. He's called six times in less than twenty-four hours. That's more than when they were dating hot and heavy."

"Sounds like she'll recover." I reached into the spice cabinet and started adding a few dried and bottled herbs from my greenhouse. Fresh would have been better, but not enough sunlight this time of year to keep the plants vibrant. A little of this, a lot of that. I let my fingers make the decision while I kept both Jason and Tiffany in mind. "Make sure she eats some of the stew. The bread is organic whole grain and the butter is also organic. No GMOs anywhere in my kitchen. They'll both feel better after only a few bites. I promise."

"Enough said. We know your talents." He turned me around and kissed me.

I let my hands encircle his neck, careful not to dirty his work shirt with the residue of an afternoon in the kitchen. His lips were firm and dry and wonderfully reassuring and safe. No manipulation. A tiny tingle crept outward from my core. I could get used to this.

"Don't let anyone walk on the attic floor for twenty-four hours to give the varnish time to set," he said after several delightful moments. Then he dropped a light kiss on my nose. "I should go."

"I'll pack a picnic basket for you and the kids."

"Sounds good. I'll put my tools in the back of the truck."

The crunch of gravel in the driveway sent both of us jumping apart, as if we were teens caught necking on the front porch by an overprotective dad.

# Thirty-Seven

**J**ASON STRIPPED OFF HIS black-and-silver tunic from *Tubular Bells* and hung it on its rack in the dressing room. All around him, the other boys in the company did the same. A few changed into broom costumes for the final number. Most just chattered and drifted out to watch the finale and catch some extra curtain calls. He could do without them both.

A chill invaded his bare skin. Wrapping his arms around himself didn't stop the goosebumps. But the cool air eased the headache behind his eyes. A T-shirt and hooded sweatshirt took care of the ice in the air.

Ice? This was October, not deep January when they normally got freezing temperatures and occasionally snow. Last summer he'd have passed this all off as his overactive imagination.

Now he knew better.

He sat on the closest backless bench, elbows on knees, fingers pressing tight against his temples. If he could just get rid of the buzz in the back of his head, he could think things through.

He'd had headaches all his life. Allergies mostly. This was autumn not spring. He didn't react to mold the same way he did to flower pollen. Something was out of place.

*Come.*

Was that a whisper from a healer promising relief?

Or just a breeze coming up and rattling through the rafters of the old theater.

He listened more acutely, with all his senses, not just his ears, like Dad had told him.

*Come.*

A little clearer, more insistent. A real voice, or rather a magical voice.

He knew he should resist, listen to some music through the earbuds on his phone. He didn't think music would block out the compulsion to rise and walk out the back door.

*Come.*

His feet found their way to the back door on their own.

*Come!* This time a triumphant laugh accompanied the words. It sounded sort of like Mom when she beat a blackberry vine into submission.

But this wasn't Mom. The laugh was deeper, throatier, then shrill. Like someone on the edge of insanity.

D'Accore. He'd only encountered the woman once, on the day of the Saturday Market when he and Dad had to fight her and her minions.

He told his feet to stop moving. Go back to the dressing room. Put his costume back on and take that final curtain call with the assembled company.

The voice kept him moving. He tried sinking back onto his heels, taking any weight at all from his toes.

And still he kept walking.

His mind swirled and raged in fear and blind panic.

He reached to push open the back door. His hand shook with his effort to control it.

And then light and fresh air burst around him.

Mr. Tyler stood in front of him with Mom's picnic basket and the homely smells of stew and bread wafting around him, filling his senses and pushing away the compulsion. It was like the man put a wall between him and the magician outside.

Gratefully, Jason pushed the door closed, quietly, behind Tiffany's father and banished the voice.

No need to mention this to Mom and Dad. They had enough to worry about.

"My lady." The big black man, Zebediah Macumbo kissed the knuckles of my right hand as if I were royalty. His deep voice rumbled through him and down my spine. No magic in that sizzle, just a beautiful man with a lot of charisma.

"Welcome, all of you." I opened my arms and waved in the three strangers and my ex.

Wu Sing Chen bowed low and proceeded inward with only a glance at me. All his focus seemed to be upward. The pentagram.

"You are moving to Raphe's house tonight. Jason packed your bags," I whispered to G as he passed.

"Not Ted?" He raised an eyebrow at me, not as angry or defensive as I expected. And he didn't limp nearly as much as he had that morning. Though I noticed George Red Hawk had driven G's car.

"Speaking of Ted, he refinished the floor in the attic. No one is to walk up there for twenty-four hours until the varnish dries," I said, making sure all of them heard me.

"Not going to happen," G growled. Back to his beastly jealousy. "We need to tweak the spells for our final confrontation."

"You have a week before the party." We'd talked about this. After the party, close to midnight on All Hallows Eve when the wide-open portals between dimensions start to close. I understood the spiritual symbolism. My family had celebrated All Saints Day on November first. My parents considered Halloween as a night of prayer and fasting, spiritual cleansing to keep the demons at bay. I'd just never realized that the religious overtones had meaning in reality, or metaphysical reality.

"It's going to take every minute of this week to get the spells right, to make it look like the pentagram is not working because of the nature of Halloween but, in reality, is only masked and ready to spring a trap."

"So Mooney and D'Accore and their minions can get in but not back out?"

G jerked his head down once in agreement and proceeded to the dining room—our ad hoc conference room. I had plans for luring those minions in and trapping them in the pantry, the only place they could hide on the ground floor.

Tonight, I'd set the table with a green tablecloth and golden linen napkins along with the good china and silverware. We had guests. We'd eat first and confer later, probably in the living room where G could get his knee up. I had ice packs prepared, just in case.

"Ted promised to bring Jason home before ten, and that's way past his bedtime and mine," I continued. Both Ted and Jason needed to be involved in the conference. And Gayla. We'd need mundane help at ground level and for mop-up.

"Full conference over brunch at nine tomorrow, Sunday morning," I affirmed to all present.

G just shrugged and frowned. He glanced longingly at the recliner in the living room, then limped into the dining room, taking his place in the captain's chair at the head of the table. He barely grunted when Gayla shoved a footstool under his feet. But Zebediah noticed her trim backside when she bent over.

Interesting. They were of similar age, and he was indeed one of the few men taller than she. I could almost feel the attraction blooming. No magic needed.

Then the girls bounced into the room, smiling their not-so-secret secretive smiles at their father. They knew something I didn't know.

But I would know. And soon. I'd make certain of it.

◆━━━

Despite the October drizzle that made the oak and alder leaves in my front yard a soggy mess, Zebediah raked them diligently. By eleven o'clock Sunday morning, only an hour and a half after the conference where G assigned tasks and set up a timeline, then dismissed us all, he'd filled two orange lawn bags with black jack-o'-lantern faces and was working on his third. "Where do you want these?" he asked in his British accent with just a hint of South Africa.

"On the porch, away from the door, a little less spooky than the cemetery for little trick-or-treaters," I answered handing him a travel mug full of café au lait.

"A barricade on two sides of the wraparound porch will slow down trespassers sneaking in from the back. G and Sing are adding a little extra *something* to the back gate and fence that will help, too," he said with a smile as he retrieved a vial of powder from his flannel shirt front pocket and held it up to the misty light.

"What's that?" I asked, suddenly suspicious.

"Just a little sneezing powder. And some itching powder in another bottle. Sprinkle a little on the back side of these oversized pumpkins, and any intruders will have other things to worry about than breaking into your house." He chuckled. "Not all defense has to be magic."

"You've done a marvelous job of cleaning up my yard," I said, not retreating to the warmth of the house as quickly as I should.

"Always finish what you start, my mother used to say." He took a long swig of the hot coffee and returned to his raking.

"Well, I appreciate the help." At this rate, I'd have my house ready for the party long before I was.

"We've got to look busy or the boss will tan our hides. He's not happy that he can't get at the attic."

"He's rarely happy these days. And won't be until D'Accore is back in prison."

"Don't we all know it. He pulled in every favor owed to him to get this team together. Not like him to ask for help. Except now his family is involved, and he's desperate."

"He's also hurt and suddenly aware that he isn't invulnerable or immortal."

Zebediah tilted back his head and roared with laughter. "A nice comeuppance for his lordship." His deep voice rumbled like an earthquake and may have distressed some people in the neighborhood. Thankfully, I'd watched Bret and Flora Chambers drive by very slowly, assessing us, on their way to church an hour ago. They'd be gone all day.

"How long have you known G?" I asked.

"Since we were kids. After his folks died defending my father, my village sent me here, to live with G's family. Grandpa had magic, my dad had magic, but they didn't pass on the gene to me. I fell in love with this town and went to the U with G. I competed in decathlon, he captained the gymnastics and fencing teams. We lived in the same dorm for a year before his family demanded him home and he commuted to classes. I guess every guy needs to live away from home for a while. Don't know what went down to drag him out of the dorms. He liked it there, made friends."

"I've met precious few of his friends outside our immediate neighborhood. I wonder if that's why his family brought him home. Friends outside the community."

"He doesn't like to draw attention to the community. He only calls me when he needs mundane muscle."

And he had lots of those, nice long lean muscles. I was surprised Gayla wasn't here yet to admire how they stretched and flexed while he worked.

My next stop was the bottom of the attic stair where Wu Sing Chen strung wires and fixed hooks for the flowing gauze I'd shaped into a ghost. He accepted his mug of tea with a bow, his long black braid so immovable it seemed glued to his collarless black cotton shirt, and returned to his work.

I watched his slender fingers adjust things with minute care for a few heartbeats.

Then he touched something, and the ghost swooped down on me, tangling my hair and screeching like a banshee.

I screeched, too, and scrabbled at my face and hair to

dislodge clinging bits of the fake cobwebs. I hadn't added those to the special effects, nor the bass voice laughing evilly backed up by "The Ride of the Valkyries" over the improvised sound system in Jason's room.

As I backed away, still swatting at the lingering sensation of ghostly fingers touching me, Wu Sing Chen smiled and bowed. The first expression I'd seen on his face. I had yet to hear a word out of his mouth.

From the attic staircase, I sought the reading nook in my bedroom with the almost hidden door leading to the tower staircase. The open-air belfry had access to the widow's walk. The smell of sodden smoke from downtown penetrated my senses. Already, construction crews were clearing away charred debris. I wondered if Mooney would rebuild in the same style or modernize. He had an entire block to work with.

George Red Hawk sat cross-legged on the bare walkway. The top of his head barely reached the railing. Not a big man like Zebediah, nor small and secretive like Wu Sing Chen. A little taller than me, but short-legged and long-waisted. He'd braided feathers and beads into his two gray plaits and wore a soft gray felt hat. His jeans and chambray shirt with a polar vest and western boots wouldn't stand out in a crowd of Anglos. In Eugene, with a lot of the mystic community affecting tribal connections, the braids and beads didn't set him apart. It was the stillness surrounding him like an inviting aura that made him unique. This was the kind of man who measured time in seasons and generations instead of digital seconds.

I handed him a travel mug of plain black coffee, three sugars.

He took a sip and nodded. All the while his gaze wandered the horizon and the gray skies above.

"Find anything interesting?"

G had called him a bird whisperer. I couldn't see any birds out this morning. Those that had not flown south should be tucked up in their nests, fluffed and enduring the cool autumn weather. Temps were in the fifties and likely to stay there. I couldn't see or smell any clearing to the west.

In reply, I heard a screech from a bird of prey. Instantly, my senses came alert, and I scanned the sky for a rare glimpse of a magnificent creature. A big red-tailed hawk swooped down, barely clearing the conical peak of the western tower. Then it flapped its powerful wings and climbed back into the obscuring clouds.

"Keeli says 'hello,'" George said.

"Hello, Keeli," I called upward.

"She likes you. She doesn't usually speak to strangers."

"Thank you, Keeli. Does she travel with you often?"

He nodded. "She is my familiar. We work together like you and your wand do." He nodded toward the spurtle sticking out of my back pocket. It had shrunk a bit more but was still long and obvious. "She does not like the crate modern airlines require. I had to let her out to hunt before G met us at the airport yesterday. She followed us closely to this house and then to Raphe's."

"I wish you good hunting, Keeli."

George chuckled. "She ate well this morning. You no longer have mice trying to burrow under the greenhouse. So now she spies for me. For a time. Until she grows bored. But I doubt that will be soon. This new territory is an adventure for her."

"What does she find so interesting?" I asked and settled down beside him with my own travel mug of strong black coffee with just a touch of cream and sugar.

"A gathering of angry people. There is a community here that spends a lot of time shouting and little time doing. Today they are finally angry enough to begin planning something. She-who-must-not-be-named by me and her lover are feeding their anger, and ideas. G has warned the police to keep an eye on them, though they can't do much but watch until this group moves out of their church and takes action."

My heart sank. "My parents view life a lot like they

do. In trying to understand Flora Chambers and her husband, I've learned some truths about my past. I'm not quite ready to forgive, but I understand them better."

"And what have you learned, young wise one?"

"We all want to protect our children as much as possible. But there comes a time when we have to allow them to grow up and send them out into the big, wide world around us. It's very scary as well as awesome out here. If we haven't allowed our children to develop life skills, explore, and make a few mistakes, then they will fail miserably. They will make more mistakes, but if they haven't learned how to correct their own errors, or tolerate misjudgment in others, then they will either come running home and hide in the basement forever, or make even bigger mistakes, like drugs and crime, or attaching themselves to evil people. I believe that BJ Chambers did the latter. The boy I've known since he was four isn't evil. He never would have thought to steal a gun and start shooting, no matter how mad he was. Someone had to coax him into that. I believe time in the state mental hospital with therapy and a complete separation from magic and our enemies will be the best thing for him."

"Separation from someone like she-who-must-not-be-named and her lover."

"Yes." I knew a moment of sadness that John Mooney had fallen into D'Accore's traps. For a brief time I had genuinely liked him and appreciated his gentle teaching. The hard-nosed, corrupt businessman that G knew didn't jibe with the man I had met. We all had our Jekyll-and-Hyde moments, I guessed.

"And how did you escape the traps to grow into a wisewoman at such a young age?"

"I met Gayla." I nodded toward the front door where she'd stopped her car at the bottom of the drive and had gotten out to talk to Zeb. I could almost see the sparkle between them, reaching but not quite touching each other. No magic, just natural chemistry.

"She taught me a lot. She supervised my first marijuana cigarette. Without peer pressure to proclaim the miracle of the drug, I found I didn't like the taste or the side effects."

"That was wise of her. She is a good friend to you."

"Yes. She also encouraged me to continue attending church services until I knew that I was running away from my parents and not my faith. I still believe. But I've found that every organized church has its own politics. I'd rather spend my Sunday mornings honoring the God I believe in by sitting still and watching the sunrise, working in the garden, and creating new recipes."

"Did I smell cinnamon, cloves, and nutmeg wafting from your kitchen earlier?" he asked with a boyish grin.

"Pumpkin bread and cookies with lunch at noon. I'm trying some new combinations on tried-and-true recipes," I replied and levered myself upward by holding on to the railing with one hand while balancing my coffee mug in the other.

George Red Hawk steadied me with a hand on my back. Suddenly, I was engulfed in fire, I saw the menacing flames leaping all around me, felt the heat, though it did not burn me. And I gagged on the smoke.

"That is what Keeli saw in the minds and the words of those she watched," George whispered.

"They will come for us with torches and blind fear. Their fear guides them, not D'Accore."

"To them, burning you out on Halloween night will be a holy act."

# Thirty-Eight

MONDAY MORNING AT SEVEN, G and his three companions sat in a rental van parked opposite the glass-and-steel skyscraper where John Mooney kept his official brokerage offices on the ground floor. No advertisements of available property in the windows. No sign on the door. He'd come a long way from the cozy and inviting house with real estate offices in front and living space behind and a big flashy sign announcing to the world that he'd find your dream home for you.

Now, if you needed John Mooney to find property for you, you knew where to find him or had him recommended by someone. He'd cut down on buying and selling homes to average families. The profit margins weren't high enough. Especially since the state and county had begun investigating the contractors who flipped houses for him. Of the dozen or so Mooney used, eleven were out of business for code violations, lack of permits, revoked licenses, and inspections. Only Ted Tyler Construction had survived the scrutiny.

"Keeli does not like this building and wants to fly free," George announced from the backseat of the van.

"Not long now. That's Mooney's car driving into the underground parking lot. We need him to see Keeli," G responded.

George stuck his head out the window and made some reassuring, nonsensical noises high in his throat.

"Almost got my gear patched in," Zeb added from

beside G. He fussed with a laptop and a bunch of wires to an array of gadgets spread on the armrest and dashboard, and two on G's lap.

"If Mooney sees Keeli, he'll look for magical traps," G said, more to himself than the others.

"Traps set," Sing said, then lapsed into his habitual silence beside George.

G smiled. He knew the kinds of traps that Sing set. The kind that dazzled the mind and paralyzed the feet. He and Zeb had had a devil of a time convincing Sing to make the triggers more obvious than usual. They wanted Mooney paranoid about a *magical* attack.

"If he suspects magic, he won't look for *my* traps," Zeb said. He flicked one more switch, and the screen on his laptop blossomed into life with multiple views of the approach to, and the interior of, Mooney's office. Zeb put on his headphones and played with the keyboard. He nodded that full sound was active and recording, as well as the cameras.

"You got the warrant for that stuff?" G asked. He needed to make sure this was all legal.

Zeb touched the inside pocket of his down vest, then pointed to the glass door on the ground level of the highrise.

John Mooney approached with his key ready. He still favored his left foot and leaned heavily on his cane.

George spit some muffled sounds. On the roof, a redtailed hawk ruffled her feathers, spread her wings wide, and swooped down. She leveled out and sped even with the ground, about six feet up. Her talons tangled Mooney's perfect hair as she pulled up and soared toward the nearest tree, across the street and down a block. Then she headed northeast into the hills.

"Hey!" Mooney shouted, looking around with suspicion and alarm. He spotted the van, glanced away, then back again.

G had chosen the neutral white service van because it looked like a stakeout vehicle. He could have borrowed

one from the local police, but that would have been too
easy. He wanted this to look more official than it was.
The IRS had their own stakeout with similar equipment
at the back of the building. If they knew about G and
Zeb's presence with their high-powered credentials that
demanded interagency cooperation, he didn't care.

Mooney shook his fist at G and then spent five minutes examining the door for magical traps. Eventually, he
unlocked the door and spent more time disabling the
first of Sing's obvious traps, the one that activated a Gol-
lum programmed to chant a stasis spell. A flick of the
wrist and the wooden man—that looked a lot like Sing—
burst into flame and collapsed into a pile of ash.

Zeb giggled as he watched it all on his laptop. G relied
on the enspelled plastic eyeball—a cheap Halloween
prop—on the bookcase to feed the video to him. The
eyeball saw but did not hear. For that he had a rubber
ear planted in a flower pot.

Eventually, Mooney disabled all of Sing's spells: the
light display to dazzle the mind and the ensnaring cobwebs. Sing was really fond of the sticky mesh sold in the
higher-end specialty Halloween stores.

"He's spent a lot of magic getting rid of tricks,"
George commented.

"Not a lot of energy left to notice mundane bugs and
cameras. Think he'll notice the slight delay before connections when he uses his landline?"

"Too obvious. He'll use his cell and hope no one has
the sophisticated listening devices in the IRS van," G
mused. He'd done this before. Both with and without the
cooperation of the mundane authorities.

"Right on time." Zeb gestured with his chin at the
three men in black suits, with black briefcases. They only
needed dark glasses on this gloomy October day to
make the parody a complete cliché. The three county
sheriff's deputies with their stiff posture, Mountie hats,
and bristling weapons made the scenario all too real.

Zeb took off his headphones. "We're on speaker."

They listened for an hour, while officers of the court searched Mooney's office. Mooney upheld absolute silence except to call his lawyer in a sprawling office on the top floor of his building. The three senior partners must have had a private elevator at their command in order to walk out of the main building doors and in Mooney's office door less than three minutes later.

And for all of this posturing and display, the IRS got five boxes of files, mostly questionable but probably nothing illegal.

The real treasure was being gathered at Mooney's home up in the Coburg Hills. The sprawling mock Tudor mansion set in the middle of five acres had lots of hiding places. Another team of officials invaded that place. This morning's display at the office was mere show. And Keeli watched it all from her new perch in the upper branches of an oak beside a mole hole. Who would notice a wild bird keeping an eye on a possible breakfast of the mole?

"They found it!" George chortled with glee. "The old stables that he converted into entertainment space and home office. He's just too obvious to be real."

G pulled up his contacts list on his phone and found the head of the local IRS. "Tell your team to keep looking," he spat. "If he hid his files as well as he did his offshore accounts, then you can bet the home office is a decoy. Try underneath the koi pond."

The deputies and the auditors left Mooney's office. The lawyers followed a few minutes later. "Now the fun begins. Let's see who he calls first," G muttered.

Within seconds, Zeb's laptop lit up with a flurry of text calls from Mooney. All said the same thing. *Get out of town.*

But no one arrested Mooney. He was still free to work mischief with D'Accore. *Damn!* G thought, slamming his fist against the steering wheel. "I thought they'd find *something.*"

"You made him jittery," George said. "Jitters burn

energy. Energy lost to nerves cannot be put into magic."
He whistled for Keeli to fly home.

"What am I looking for, Daddy?" Shara asked. She
peered around the clump of scrub oak across the road
from Mooney's driveway. Well away from any security
cameras.

Daffy would kill him if she thought he was endangering their daughter rather than taking her out for an ice
cream treat. As long as she stayed with him, she'd be
okay. He hoped he'd put enough fear into her to keep
her from running off on her own.

"Mr. Mooney has records of his illegal financial deal-
ings. More than just the record of deposits and withdraw-
als in the offshore accounts," G replied succinctly. He
didn't smell any magical traps this far away from the
house. They'd be safe. For now. He was careful. *He could
not, would not put his little girl in jeopardy*.

"He'd be stupid not to. The point of illegal money is
to make it grow, properly invested. What good is money
if you can't keep track of it and use it?"

G did a mental slap of his head with his palm. Of
course, Mooney was laundering the money in the Cay-
man Islands and using it to buy real estate and stocks.
He'd also see that his "brokerage" fees for those real estate deals showed up as legitimate earning in his business accounts; he was just buying property under
assumed names, then selling to shadow corporations that
he already owned.

"Where would you keep those files?" Ask a crook at
heart to think like a real crook. He just hoped he and
Daffy could instill some sense of morality into her before she started mimicking Mooney.

Mooney had probably sponsored the computer club
at school trying to buy the loyalty of the next generation
of computer hackers to work for him.

"On a flash drive. Maybe a dozen of them with

sixty-four gigs or even two terabytes of memory. Say, can I have one of those for Christmas? I know the two Ts are expensive, but I can back up a lot of schoolwork on one."

"What about the external hard drive with ten terabytes of space you already asked for?" Belle had confiscated the one he'd already bought.

"The ten T NAS would be my big present. The flash drives are stocking stuffers." She shrugged off her expensive requests.

"Okay, what do you need to sense where Mooney would stash a flash drive?"

"Probably line of sight, like when we searched for the core of the fire. This will be different. though. There's no maze structure to wind through. It's just looking for the most likely place out in the open."

"Okay, I know a place." G started his car and put it into gear. "Line of sight, hmm, how about those hills ahead and to the left. I know a spot that overlooks his hilltop compound."

"It might work. But isn't that BLM forest land? Could you talk me through the breathing exercises, so I'm ready the moment you stop the car and I can find it right away, so we won't be there long enough to attract attention?"

Spoken like a true outlaw in the making.

G shuddered but obeyed, talking her through the familiar procedure by rote. He needed the front of his consciousness to navigate the twisted logging road up into the hills. He should have borrowed Ted's 4X4 pickup for this trip.

His powerful car hugged the curves well, but slowly. The tires spattered mud all over the sides and the back windshield. He shuddered with every thud, wondering when an axle would break. He'd have to run through the car wash before returning home, or Daffy would ask probing questions. And he'd have a really good mechanic check the undercarriage.

A half hour later he found a turn out at the crest of

the road, overlooking Mooney's home. He pulled over and set the parking brake. "Will this do?"

Shara squinted at the blurry roofline below them, about a mile away as the crow flies. Then she rolled down her window and leaned out.

A hawk cried above them.

"Hello, Keeli," G called up through his own open window. "Will you please assist us?" George insisted on politeness with his bird. He said she did what she wanted, when she wanted, and would only help when asked nicely and it fit into her agenda.

Another screech and she swooped low, nearly scratching the roof of the car with her powerful talons.

Shara jerked and closed her eyes. "This is really weird," she breathed. Then she opened her eyes again and smiled. "Thank you, Keeli." Her head swayed right and left as she followed the bird's flight across the rolling hills northeast of town. She opened her seat belt and leaned farther and farther out the window until she was nearly hanging over the frame at waist level.

Instinctively, G grabbed her ankles with both hands to keep her inside. The car was parked too close to the steep slope broken by jagged volcanic outcroppings and tall trees. If Shara got out of the car, she could easily misstep and roll to her death. He breathed a little easier when she made no move to climb farther out. But he kept his hands on her ankles.

He watched the silhouette of the hawk circle the house and outbuildings again and again. Then one more cry and the bird flew off in another direction. Back toward the city and her magical companion.

Shara slumped the moment Keeli's tether to her mind snapped. She sagged, curling her knees up to her chin and resting her forehead on them.

"You okay?" G asked, rubbing her curved back. "Need some ice cream to restore you?"

"A pumpkin spice milkshake," she mumbled. "I don't

think the flash drive or anything else is there. He's too smart for us, Daddy."

"He's smart. But not too smart for us. We'll get him. Just not today. Do you want to get in the backseat and take a nap on the way back to Dairy Jim's?" The old-fashioned ice cream parlor, family owned for four generations, made the best frozen treats using extra rich milk from grass-fed local cows.

"Yeah." She just sat there.

Reluctantly, G got out of the car, went around to her side, and carried her from the front seat to the back. Her thin arms crept around his neck, trusting him to take care of her.

If only he could do that forever. He'd blown this trust thing with Daffy. He needed to earn it back and make sure he never did anything to lose the trust of any of his children. Ever.

"Ice cream. The best cure for a magic-depleted body."

# Thirty-Nine

**M**ONDAY AND TUESDAY, I found myself making more pancakes and croissants than cinnamon buns at the shop for the morning rush. Our customers liked the addition of "real" food to our menu and spread the word. Many, like Ted, stuck to their cinnamon rolls. I made up gallons of pancake batter with autumnal spices in the mix in the morning and then anyone on staff could cook them as needed. The croissants were labor intensive to start with, though once baked, my part of the job was done. I made sure we had an extra two dozen for the afternoon shift.

I continued to worry about Jason. He was taking pain pills every day to ease his headache. He'd also taken to wearing sunglasses out of doors, even on gloomy and rainy days.

Something was drastically wrong. More than tension headaches from the increased pressure of weekend performances and midterm exams.

After a week of doing nothing more creative than run the espresso machine, I brought in one of our college students and left the shop at eleven instead of two on Tuesday.

As I parked my van beside the back gate, an overwhelming urge to be in the attic swept over me like a sneaker wave. I couldn't breathe and felt like I had to swim against the currents of air between me and the house.

Gasping and panicky, I barely took the time to set my purse on the counter before running full out up the stairs to the second floor and then up again to the attic until I emerged from the "well" of the enclosed staircase into the open space. The all-out sprint left me gasping for air and weak-kneed. I braced my hands on the floor while still two steps down and bent nearly double.

"What's wrong?" I panted. "Who's hurt?"

"No one, my dear. But I'm glad you're here. We are about to set up some spell work. We need a fifth element to complete the symmetry," G said, all calm and neutral.

But I recognized the cat-who-ate-the-canary smile. He didn't need a feather sticking out of his mouth to betray him. I knew him too well.

"You manipulated me," I snarled.

"Did I?"

"Yes. Here I was afraid one of you was bleeding to death and the other three unconscious when all you had to do was pick up the damn phone and call me." I turned around on the stair, careful to keep my balance though my head spun, still recovering from my run and my panic.

"Daffy, please. I'm sorry. My impatience made me put a little too much force into my magical call."

Or perhaps some of Ted's nontalent was helping me recognize magic, and once acknowledged, remain impervious to it.

I continued walking down the stairs.

"Daffy?" This time G sounded a bit panicked.

"I'll be back when I've had a chance to set the kitchen," *and myself,* "to rights and start lunch. The soup needs to simmer a bit longer and I need to put the bread into the oven."

I also needed to close and lock the back door, put my purse in my office, and use the restroom (panic does that to a person). I began to wonder if G had done something to lighten my chores at Magical Brews so I would come home when *he* needed me to, not when *I* needed to. It would be just like him.

I seethed while I made a pot of coffee and another of tea, and—of course—a plate of cookies to take up to the attic, a full half hour after I'd left it.

The full magnificence of the pentagram hit me as I set down my tray and took in the awesome glow of the pale oak inlaid into the dark red mahogany. Whoever had set this up had spared no expense or loving craftsmanship. Not only did the lighter wood shimmer in the dim light, it pulsed. I stared gape-jawed for several long moments until I recognized the beat of the glow matched G's heartbeat, so familiar from many years of falling asleep with my ear pressed to his naked chest.

We were safe here. Protected and cherished.

G might be a manipulative bastard, but everything he did, he did out of love of family and community. He was indeed the ideal candidate to reign as Sheriff of the Guild of Master Wizards, protecting all those with magical talent, worldwide.

"Okay, I'm glad you thought of fortification. We're likely to need it," G said, rubbing his hands together with glee. "Let's get started. I will take east, the director's place." He walked to the point straight ahead of me, at the far end of the large room—as big as the original portion of the house, the living room, dining room, and kitchen combined. "Daffy, if you will, please sit to my right, where you have always been, and always should be." He gave me one of his endearing smiles, the smile I fell in love with oh those many years ago. This time I sensed no magic, no manipulation behind it. Just appreciation and partnership.

And love.

Oh, boy I was in trouble. There is no aphrodisiac like being loved.

We each took places on a point of the pentagram, within the wooden lines but as close to the junction as possible.

"Um . . ."

"What, Daffy? Now is not the time for hesitation," G sounded impatient again, not angry, just anxious to get on with a complex working.

"It won't work."

"Of course it will. I've taken a week to design the spell."

"G, will you hear me out?" I made sure my feet stayed outside the pentagram, even though part of me *needed* to be inside it.

"Daffy . . ."

"Listen to me for once rather than proclaim your superiority." I sounded like a bitchy ex-wife. Maybe that's what he needed to hear in order to penetrate his hard head. "G, this is the *Deschants* family home and it has been for four generations. At least. *Your family.* All that accumulated cast-off furniture and boxes piled up against the far wall belonged to your ancestors and relatives. Your family crafted this pentagram and built up generations of wards and other protective spells. You need your family to work this spell."

"Raphe can't come inside the house until I sink the pentagram and the wards so deep they won't repel him. We need to get this done so that it is fully settled before the party Saturday evening."

"You have three talented children who will be home and without after-school activities by three, and your ex-wife. As much as I respect Zebediah, George, and Sing, they are not related by blood. And Zeb isn't even talented. You said yourself, he's mundane muscle, aware of reality, and backup protection. You need me and the children to work this spell and reinforce whatever other wards you've set."

Silence reverberated around the room. The thunder on G's brow deepened to a grimace, then gradually eased.

Sing bowed to me. "She is right, young master." He spoke for the first time since I'd met him.

"Let's eat lunch," Zeb said, pointedly stepping outside the pentagram.

"Sing and I will provide drum and flute to keep your mutterings on time and in tune," George said. "While we wait for the next generation of Deschants, I believe there is chicken and brown rice soup and fresh bread. I'll encourage Keeli to rest a bit, too. She can aid Zeb in keeping watch while we all work."

Three o'clock, and the girls tumbled out of the school bus in front of the house. They raced each other to the back gate, neatly avoiding the faux cemetery on the front lawn. Laughing and poking each other in some sisterly competition, they flung their backpacks on the kitchen table and grabbed cookies while they raided the fridge for milk.

"It's getting cold out, Mom. Can we have hot chocolate?" Belle called to me.

I was lurking in the dining room. G had returned to the attic after lunch and continued working there. His guests had retreated to Raphe's house for some time away from their brooding boss.

"Yes, you may have hot chocolate if you fix it."

"But, Mom," they protested in chorus.

"Make enough for everyone, including your father's guests. Though I doubt Mr. Wu will drink it. He prefers tea. Jason will probably gulp down the extra portion."

"Are you okay, Mom?" Belle asked, coming to stand in front of me, making sure the swinging door to the kitchen closed.

"Yes, dear. Why do you ask?" I remained in my chair with my elbows on the table.

"You aren't doing anything and you aren't rushing to make sure Shara and I clean up the kitchen after we make the chocolate."

"This has been a disconcerting day. But my doughs

are rising at the shop and dinner is in the oven, so as soon as Jason gets here, we'll all go to the attic and consult with your father." I shooed her back into the kitchen.

Twenty minutes later Jason clomped into the kitchen through the back door. His backpack landed on the dining table right in front of me. "Belle says I need to talk to you," he said abruptly. "She says you look scared. And I agree. Pale and shaky. Talk to me, Mom." He knelt in front of me. "Let me help."

As if he could help anyone, with a headache pounding behind his eyes. I could see it in the texture of his skin and the squint above his nose.

I drew in a deep breath. "We are skipping a few magic lessons and diving right into ceremonial spell work headfirst without knowing how deep the waters are. Get something to eat, take some pain pills, and meet us in the attic."

"Will this help my headache?"

"I don't know. It might make it worse, or it could banish it altogether. I just don't know, and it worries me. You've never had an allergy or a stress headache last this long."

———

G added the last piece of kindling to the five-sided teepee of twigs and grasses on a flame retardant sheet in the middle of the pentagram. He lit it with a snap of his fingers. Then he drew in a deep breath, allowing the cleansing sage, the actinic scent of copper shavings melting into the mix, and other minerals and herbs blended with it, including blackberry leaves, to invade every crevice of his body.

Entangling blackberry canes and desiccated leaves comprised much of the combustibles. This trap required deviousness. Most people underestimated the near sentient lethalness of the native blackberry. Not the big juicy Himalayan berries. They were invasive and non-native. But the little mountain blackberry, with its smaller and sweeter berries with tiny thorns growing backward, were the devil to get out once entangled in the skin. A lot like magic spells.

George began chanting in the most ancient form of his native language. He beat steadily on a small leather drum, alternating the flat of his palm with his staccato fingers.

"I, Zebediah, guardian to this conclave, enclose you. None shall enter or disturb you except upon my death or your direct, uncoerced invitation." His pronunciation carried the weight of formal ritual. He'd done this before. G's grandfather had taught him these duties within a week of Zeb arriving in the household. The door at the bottom of the stairs clicked shut, and the latch engaged.

Sing picked up his reed flute and played an Asian counterpoint to George's rhythms.

G joined in with his bass voice, intoning an obscure dialect of Old French from the Languedoc that was no longer legally spoken in France. The French had a governmental bureau to keep the language pure. Outlawing regional dialects with different roots—especially in areas with a volatile and rebellious history—was their chief hobby. G's family had brought this language with them when they emigrated centuries ago.

When he'd sung all the necessary words, as intended, he translated for the family, though he suspected Jason had absorbed much of the meaning. "We gather in all humbleness to mask the nature of our previous workings. Highest spirits of power guide us in drawing mists and misdirection to our enemies. Help us trap the perverters of truth and justice so that they may no more use their God-given powers for the sake of more power and harm to others. Protect us as we protect others. So mote it be!"

He clapped his hands above his head once and stepped into the pentagram, sinking to the floor and crossing his legs. He placed his extended wand on his thigh, then signaled each member of his family to copy his movements exactly. As they took up the points of the glyph inlaid into the wooden floor, Jason kicked off his shoes and socks so that his bare feet had contact with the floor within the pentagram, his wand. Immediately, the strain across his brow eased, and he drew a deep breath. The girls' eyes grew wide and wondrous as a frisson of power greeted each wand in turn. This was their first major working. They had to be nervous. G nodded to each of them with pride that they remained calm.

He stretched out his hands, as if to clasp hands with Daffy and Jason on either side of him. They likewise reached toward the girls. The points of the pentagram were too far apart to allow them to actually hold hands. The symbolism of the gesture was more important than physical touch.

A tingle began in G's fingertips and traveled to his toes and up to lift the top of his head from his consciousness. That same energy spread out from his hands to Daffy and Jason and continued on to the girls, connecting them all in a circle with a visible braid of golden light.

The flute and drum intensified.

The energy thickened and rose to form a dome over them, shielding those within the pentagram from outside influences and interruptions. The air within the dome grew denser. The smoke from the ritual fire thickened, invading every opening, including the pores of their skin.

G fought back a deep racking cough and noticed the others also working their throats, seeking control. He found himself floating above his seated body, still crosslegged, still reaching outward as if holding hands with his closest relatives, but connected only by that pulsing braid of bright light. The others, too, floated above their bodies, eyes closed, mouths moving with their wordless chants. His own ancient syllables poured forth.

Somehow, the music grew to a rousing crescendo. With a crack as loud as a rifle shot, the dome, the light, the smoke, and the pulsing pentagram all sank beneath them, embedded into the floor, a faint echo of its previous dominance.

They all collapsed sideways, panting and exhausted. All he could do was make sure he fell toward Daffy and clasp her hand.

# Forty

I WOKE UP KNOWING exactly what drove G to find sex with other women. Once I'd replenished my reserves with food and good coffee, I was ready to grab any male in my vicinity for a quick, hot, and satisfying tryst.

*I am better than this!* I insisted over and over as all the adult males at the dining table flicked wistful glances in my direction. G's gaze bored deeply into my soul.

*I will not reduce something beautiful, meaningful, and filled with love to mere lust.* Instead, I took a cold shower, gave the kids permission to skip school tomorrow—they were all hollow-eyed with exhaustion—and went to bed, alone, with a book.

Surprisingly, I slept like a rock. But I awoke with the alarm from an amazingly detailed sex dream with a faceless partner. I needed another cold shower before daring to go to work. Small business owners don't get to take sick leave just because they worked deep ceremonial magic the day before.

I managed work with no problems, too busy to even think about magic and the consequences.

Then Ted walked in for his usual coffee and cinnamon bun and I was back to square one. Without thinking twice, I dragged him behind the counter and into my kitchen. In the dark corner by the cooler I pushed him up against the wall, wrapped my arms around his neck and kissed him soundly, deeper and hotter than ever before in our tentative relationship. He returned my caresses and held me tight. He didn't accept my invitation to explore even when I had his shirt half unbuttoned and contemplated his belt buckle.

"You worked magic yesterday," he said when we came up for air.

I felt like he'd opened the shower valves on me at full frigid.

"As much as I want to make love to you, Daffy, this is not the time or place. Or the reason," he said gently, disengaging his hands to redo his shirt.

"You've seen this before." I backed away from him, aghast at my wanton behavior.

"A time or two. I catch the aftermath of strong magic in my duties. I see what real magicians go through. I'm sorry, but—like I said—not now. Not until we both have full control of our senses and go into it with eyes wide open to the commitment and the consequences."

I took a deep breath, and then another until my head stopped spinning.

He ran his hands through his hair, also taking deep cleansing breaths.

"Rumor has it that G tinkered with the pentagram and collapsed it," Ted said, taking our conversation away from the immediacy of my need. But back to the cause of it.

"That's what it's supposed to look like." I tried to smile but couldn't look him in the eye. "We'll know for certain how complete the working is tonight when Raphe tests it."

"What do you need me to do Saturday night?"

"Aside from be my date to the party?"

"Aside from that."

"Zeb and Gayla are running interference at ground level, to keep mundane witch hunts under control. You should coordinate with them once the party guests leave."

"I'll make sure Tiffany and her friends don't stay to help wash the dishes." He grinned.

"We'd like the house cleared by eleven, definitely before midnight."

"Gotcha." He grabbed me around the waist and kissed me again.

"Ahem," Gayla cleared her throat. "The Beast is acting up again. We need you to tame it into making espresso rather than merely making growling noises."

"Later, love." Ted kissed my nose and made to leave.

"The water line is probably clogged again. Let me get my wrench."

"I'll take care of it. You go back to making the best cinnamon buns in town." He ducked out of the kitchen without a backward glance.

Gayla raised her eyebrows. "This getting as serious as it looks?"

"Maybe. What about you and Zeb?"

She had the grace to blush. "Can't be serious. After Halloween, he has to go back to his day job in Brussels."

"Until then?" I teased.

"Until then, you don't need to know. And I don't need to know about you and Ted. Though I really, really want to know all the gritty details."

"Same here. I'll let you know if there ever are any gritty details that aren't the aftermath of magic."

And then there was nothing to do but wait. And repair and clean costumes. And bake. I couldn't put on a party without presenting something spectacular. I do not carve and decorate cakes into masterworks of art. That requires an entirely different skill set from what I do.

The Christmas decorating magazines hit the grocery store that week. Three of the six I bought featured gingerbread houses. I hadn't done one of these since the kids were little. They had thoroughly enjoyed applying gumdrops and mints to the exterior, and eating more than they used for decorating. One look at the recipes for gingerbread and I knew I had some tinkering to do to the rather bland, beginner ingredients and plans.

By Thursday afternoon, when Jason insisted on going back to dance class and rehearsal, despite his continuing headache, and the math club and computer hackers convened in my dining room, I had the blueprints laid out, with a few corrections on ratios from the math club.

G and his three friends had seemingly disappeared. I had no idea what they were up to, but I did hear a word or three about warrants and observation equipment. The big computer on the dining table bristled with gadgets while satellite laptops hummed merrily. I ignored the high tech and concentrated on my party.

Friday evening, Gayla helped assemble a replica of my twin tower Edwardian home that really was an homage to Victorian Gothic. By that night it stood tall and proud, but not yet solid. We had to let all that frosting mortar set. At midnight, unable to sleep, I sent an email to Belle's ophthalmologist requesting an appointment for Jason ASAP.

Then I began applying icing roof tiles, cobwebs, bats, and ghostly eyes peeking out of the windows to the gingerbread house.

On Saturday morning the girls made fondant trees, also dripping with cobwebs and other decorations. Royal icing became a backyard pond with more otherworldly beings wafting toward the surface. I had other baking to do if I hoped to catch the final ballet performance Saturday afternoon. Red velvet cupcakes with buttercream and fondant ghosts, witches, bats, and pumpkins. Shara wanted Dracula, complete with bloody fangs, but I drew the line at that. Beyond my artistic ability and my motherly sensibilities.

But through it all, we tiptoed through the house to avoid making Jason's migraine worse. The only place he could avoid feeling as if someone dug at his eyes with a spoon was lying flat on the floor at the center of the pentagram with an icepack over his face. Either G or one of his companions sat with him. Sometimes quietly reading his homework to him. Sometimes chanting healing spells.

In those days of waiting, he visibly lost weight, his once lustrous dark hair—so like his dad's—grew lank. His eyes looked like black holes in his skeletal face. Dancing revived him some. But on Friday evening for the next to last performance, his exuberance flagged. He jumped and leaped only as high as the other boys. He barely needed makeup to create the image of a ghoul, or a skeleton. In the "Ritual Fire Dance," he played a spark and nearly glowed on stage, dancing as he usually did.

"This is more than eyestrain," I whispered to G Saturday morning while Jason rested in the attic and George chanted something soothing to him.

"I know." He clamped his mouth shut, unwilling to say more.

I was tired of his secretiveness, his need to protect us by keeping silent. "It's D'Accore, isn't it?" I wanted to sound angry, but the words came out deflated, resigned.

G reared his head up in alarm. In that moment I caught a glimpse of a proud stallion, wary and ready to fight to protect his family. I also saw the determination of a ram or billy goat as he lowered his head, jutting it forward, ready to butt anyone in his way with his solid horns.

"You shouldn't jump to conclusions," he finally said.

"Oh, come off your pedestal, G. I know that D'Accore wants her son's eyes to replace her own. I know that Fire is her element, so he revives a little when dancing that role."

"When did she get her hooks into him?" he asked. "We've been so careful to keep him separated from her."

I shook my head in bewilderment. "Wait a minute." My brain fought through the murk of worry. "The day of the bake sale, you and Jason had to fight off D'Accore's minions. Did any of them touch Jason? Could she have sent some kind of binding or compulsion spell through one of her boys? And there was the night BJ shot at him backstage...."

"What about it? The boy's aim was erratic. He didn't hit anyone." He avoided speaking about the first encounter. That might very well be the source of the problem.

"But when Jason tackled BJ, and trapped him around the neck with his crossed legs, did BJ touch him in any way?" I decided to humor him while clinging to my first suspicion.

"There were a couple of seconds when they landed that they were all tangled together." G's eyes brightened and his frown deepened. "I'll be damned. BJ wasn't supposed to actually shoot anyone, only cause chaos so he could plant a magical worm on Jason."

I shuddered at the thought of magical energy wriggling and squirming under my skin, finding my bloodstream and attacking. . . . The same scenario fit the first encounter. I'd seen glimmers of the headache before the night of the shooting. "What can we do?"

"That's an Italian gardener's spell." He dashed for his super computer and pulled up a database. He scrolled down and down the entries.

"Is that the list of D'Accore's victims?" It was more extensive than I thought possible.

"No, the full registry. Ah, here's the Italian entries. And . . . and . . . There's an early victim of D'Accore's. An old winemaker in Tuscany, retired twenty years ago, but still on the rolls. He died of a heart attack the week after D'Accore escaped from the dungeon. Tuscany is an easy hop from the Languedoc. He had a talent matching bees to pollen. He created some marvelous wines from hybrid grapes by cross-pollinating. He coaxed bees to the flowers he wanted them to gather pollen from and deposit it elsewhere. But he also had a spell for a magic worm to seek out disease and rot in vulnerable roots. I hate to think of the damage it could do if unleashed on a human mind." He shuddered and gulped.

"The bees-to-pollen spell is how D'Accore is snaring young men, including BJ, into following her," I mused.

"Maybe Giuseppe didn't have a heart attack after all."

"Did he have a wand?" I asked. Something . . . something eluded me.

"A shaft of entwined grapevines."

"Like the wand Shara stole from the greenhouse safe and then D'Accore stole from the ballet prop room. She's still got it. But how did it get from Tuscany to Eugene?"

"Giuseppe gave it to me a week before he died. He wanted me to keep it so no one in his family could mistreat it and that I'd know who to give it to when I met him. He was not well. I kept it as a remembrance of our friendship. He was a grand old man and gave me a bottle of wine at the same time. I should have ceremonially burned it and scattered the ashes on his grave. But something about his last request compelled me to bring the wand here. Some budding magician is out there seeking a wand, and now I'll never be able to pass it on." Sadness made his shoulders slump. He buried his face in his hands. "I didn't, couldn't strip it. I thought that keeping it in the safe would be all I had to do."

"Except your daughter found it and felt compelled to bring it out into the light of day. She said one or all of the wands called to her requesting release." I let silence grow between us almost to the breaking point. "Then how do we get it back?" Regret began to engulf me. If only I'd known! If only he'd told me the truth. If only . . .

No time for regrets. We needed to figure this out before tonight.

Suddenly, my brain kicked in, and I began plotting my revenge. I just hoped I'd have time.

# Forty-One

I KNEW HOW TO make an astringent patch that would draw out a tick embedded in the ear, or a bee stinger from anywhere, or even hair-fine barbed blackberry thorns. But a magical worm? I let my wand help me. Without thought, both the wand and I knew I needed to start with baking soda and some herbs I'd gathered blindly while browsing the greenhouse. Stripping a blackberry cane for the thorns took some ingenuity. Finally, I resorted to Belle coaxing them to release their hold on the vine and drop into my collection dish. They burrowed invisibly into the baking soda, almost gleeful at the trickery I planned.

"G," I called up the stairs as soon as I returned to the kitchen. The acoustics in the house guaranteed my voice would find him.

"What now? I'm busy?" He appeared in the doorway to the basement. He and Zeb had taken the monster computer down there for some Guild-related purpose and to keep it away from party guests.

"Get your healing hands person over here, ASAP. I'm going to draw that worm out of Jason's head before he has to dance again. Before the pain drives him blind."

He pulled out his phone and speed dialed without question. "She is very professional and abides by her oaths of confidentiality." His eyes avoided me and I knew, just knew, he'd had sex with her at some point. Strictly professional on her part, I was sure. Still . . .

I swallowed the creeping ick of emotions at having to meet one of his women.

*"Drive him blind?"* G's eyes brightened and lifted to meet my own. "D'Accore drove herself blind with her attempts to release herself from a straitjacket. She didn't damage her eyes by clawing at them, as Jason is about to do. She'd fried her nerve endings and brain synapses, not her eyes."

The one time I'd seen her, her eyes appeared normal, except her gaze was fixed.

"G?" He looked up from his phone, gaze centered on me as if seeking answers to all his problems. "Even if D'Accore could rob Jason of his eyes, would she be able to see? I mean if it's not her eyes that are the problem, but her brain?"

"Good point. I'll work on that. Once in a while logic does penetrate her obsessiveness. What else do you need from me?"

"Not you, George. I need to know if Keeli will eat worms, now that she's eaten every rodent within half a mile."

"Maybe not eat that particular worm, but probably carry it to the river and drop it in the swiftest part of the current." He disappeared again.

Moments later, I heard ghostly moans and witch cackles coming from hidden speakers all over the house.

Judi the massage therapist arrived ten minutes later. A tall woman with a no-nonsense bob of brown hair, devoid of makeup, and wearing a T-shirt that proclaimed to the world "Physical Terrorist." Her long-fingered hands looked strong and capable. She shook my hand with forthright neutrality. Strictly professional.

"G said I wouldn't need my table. It's in the van if we do need it. I've got aromatic oils in here." She patted a square black box with shoulder straps.

"We're working outside today," I told her.

"It's raining."

"It's October. The air will be refreshing after the

stuffiness of the house. And we are between squalls. Nothing more potent than drizzle for the next hour and half. Besides, we'll be beneath the awning on the flagstone patio."

She nodded abruptly. "Heard about your affinity with weather."

The Community might not socialize much, but their gossip network seemed as finely tuned as Flora's.

Then Judi marched through the house and out the back door. G and George helped Jason walk out there, supporting him, guiding him so he didn't have to open his eyes, and steadying his balance.

Jason sat on one of the little white wrought-iron chairs, long legs sprawled in front of him, back slumped. I'd nursed him through childhood fevers, strained muscles, and bewilderment after being bullied. But I'd never seen my boy so helpless, so depressed. So vulnerable.

I was convinced the worm thrived on that vulnerability.

Sing joined us with one of his wooden flutes. This one was longer, carved from some dark exotic wood. Its tones came out deeper, feathery soft, and timed to coax an erratic heartbeat back to normal.

I breathed deeply, relaxed by the music and the fresh, moist air.

Judi took up a place directly behind Jason, fingers gently massaging his neck and shoulders.

Jason tensed, as if her very touch inflamed every nerve ending in his body. The toes of his bare feet curled against the cold flagstone, preparing to endure.

Before I lost my courage, I slapped some of my astringent paste onto each temple, rubbing it in as deeply as I dared.

"Now we wait," I said.

Judi continued her massage, moving her fingers up to the white patches, working the skin around them, touching the center occasionally. Sing continued his flute work. George gently drummed the picnic table with his fingertips.

Shara grabbed her father's hand. "I'll take you through the maze of blood vessels to the worm's head," she whispered.

Then Belle appeared and took her hair stick out of her bun and waved the jade charms across each of her brother's temples.

Magical energy tingled against my skin, just a small amount. It rose in a dome around us, all of us working to help Jason. I heard a sizzle when a stray raindrop touched it near the edge of the patio. Bright blue lightning arced outward, nearly blinding me.

G continued chanting. Judi continued rubbing. And the music deepened. Not so much louder, as touching more than ears, binding souls with a mission to rid my boy of the dreadful worm.

"Found it," Shara whispered.

"Got it by the tail and pulling," G added in the same tone.

"Come on, you little bugger, let go. Release your hold," Judi said. The whiteness around her knuckles told me she pressed harder.

"Follow me," Belle sang. "I am your love, your life. You need to come to me, follow my trail. Come to me." She waved and shook her jade charms in time with George's drumbeat.

And then I saw it. An angry red tendril of magical energy. Darker than fire. More like old blood, knotted and clotted. Two of them. One on each astringent patch. They wiggled as if looking around and started to withdraw.

"No, you don't," Judi pressed her fingers harder around the patches, as if squeezing a giant abscess.

"Don't be afraid. Come to me." Belle separated the charms from the hair stick and dangled one on either side of her brother's face.

Jason gritted his teeth. His features contorted into a grimace of pain.

"Keep coming. Don't break apart, keep sliding out, slide smoothly," G chanted.

Amazingly, the worm obeyed the enticement and the commands. I held the bowl with the extra astringent beneath it. First on the left, the larger and fatter knotted strand dropped into the bowl and writhed. Then the skinnier but darker worm slithered out of the right side of Jason's face. It tried to ooze onto his cheek and down to his chin. I scootched the lip of the dish beneath the pulsing strand of ugly energy and forced it to join its brother. They writhed and twisted away from each other. Two negatives repelling rather than opposite poles attracting.

G slowly dropped the dome of energy. The flute music faded, the drumming eased away, still echoing the rhythm of a heart.

Judi kept massaging Jason's temples, gradually working her way down to his neck and out across his shoulders. With each pass she flung her hands outward, shaking away the negative energy.

Keeli screeched above us, her voice clear and excited now that it wasn't muffled by the dome. I held the bowl up. But George elbowed me aside and held up his gauntleted arm for her to perch. She swooped in on silent wings and dug in her claws through the thick leather encompassing George's wrist and forearm. She took a moment to rub her head against his face in a loving caress. Her eyes zeroed in on the writhing mass of magical energy in my bowl. Delicately, she plucked both worms out with her curved beak, winked at me and flew off.

And Jason opened his eyes. "Mom, what's for lunch?"

I had never before heard more beautiful words.

# Forty-Two

**A**T THE END OF OCTOBER, sunset falls early this close to the forty-fifth parallel, even before going off Daylight Savings Time. The first mob of small children dressed in costumes from the latest Disney movie rang the doorbell at five minutes after five. Twilight, not full dark yet.

I'd just walked in the back door with an armload of Jason's gear from his last performance. He'd shone and leaped and smiled just like his old self. Belle, dressed as the pied piper, opened the door to a hail of "Trick-or-Treat!"

A steady stream of children followed, getting taller as the night wore on. Raphe seemed to be having a good time. In his homeless rags and ghoulish makeup, he rose from behind a fake tombstone, moaning at the older children. Zeb dressed as a Western sheriff, complete with white Stetson and a real revolver on his hip, patrolled the grounds front and back. Gayla, dressed in glow-in-the-dark white draperies over white thermal underwear, drifted around the fake cemetery keeping a wary eye out for stragglers and interlopers.

G had copied Zeb's costume but wore a black Stetson and had heels on his western boots. Heels that hid tiny blades that sprang out when he stomped. I didn't ask what he'd dipped those blades in.

Hopefully, they were left over from some previous job, and he wouldn't need those blades tonight.

George wore fringed buckskin and a fully feathered warbonnet—some of the feathers looked like Keeli's. He still carried his little hand drum and a rattle that he shook at some of the better costumed adolescents. Sing had changed into flowing black pants and a red silk shirt with a standup collar and matching skullcap. Both were resplendent with embroidered golden dragons. I was pretty sure that thread shimmered with more than just high-quality manufacture. The primary dragon on his back had red jeweled eyes that blinked at me.

Shara was still only ten and clung to her fluffy pink princess dress and plastic tiara, probably for the last time. The dress was approaching miniskirt rather than ball-gown length.

When Ted showed up, he looked like he always did: worn jeans, plaid flannel work shirt, and tool belt. He'd added a hard hat. I guess you could call it a costume, as in a uniform of any kind can be a costume.

And me? I decided that if I was fully fledged witch now, I might as well dress the part. Flowing black draperies, green skin, green-and-white-striped leggings with black boots, a tall black hat, and—of course—a prosthetic nose complete with wart. I didn't have enough hands to carry a broom. But I had one, in a corner of the attic. My wand was tucked into the back waistband of my skirt, small enough to be unobtrusive, ready to telescope out. By next week, I expected I'd be able to pocket it like G's pen.

And through it all, the hidden speakers, inside and out, played sound effects and many, many, many repeats of the "Monster Mash." But not a note of "Alakazam, Magic Slam." I think my house was the most popular haunting in town that Halloween night.

By eight, the trick-or-treaters had dwindled, and the dancers, their parents, my friends, the kids' friends, and schoolmates had arrived for the party.

No sign of BJ or his parents. Yet. BJ was still in psych lockup. I'd heard from some of my customers who were deserting the Chambers' election campaign that BJ's parents would try to use that as a justification for burning us out. A conservative Christian movement against immorality was one thing. Burning houses and people were too much for my informants. According to Bret Sr., they bailed to the dark side, engulfed by evil. In my mind, the dark side had begun to look like the bright side of the Force. Or the Farce. I wasn't sure which.

I added a bottle of vodka to one bowl of punch and made sure no one discovered the "special cookies" I'd created for D'Accore's unwanted minions. Those I hid in the back of the walk-in pantry just inside the mudroom door. And I showed them to Jason so he'd keep everyone else out.

I noticed that many of the dancers still wore costumes from the ballet. Lots of ghouls and demons in wispy rags. Jason wore his spark costume from the "Ritual Fire Dance," a black unitard with red flames spiraling around his lithe body. He left off the wire headdress with sparkling red-and-gold wisps of chiffon. On stage, they mimicked more sparks, floating with every move that made the dance so effective.

After his ordeal with the headache worm, I wanted to keep stuffing high-protein food into my son. He did a pretty good job of demolishing an entire loaf of pumpkin bread and most of a platter of crackers, cheese, and salami. All this after an enormous dinner of spaghetti and meatballs. Heavy exercise on a full stomach didn't bother him like some of the dancers.

The sound effects switched to the music from the ballet. *Night on Bare Mountain* and *Danse Macabre* competed with joyous laughter in the attic.

But I heard other voices. Ominous voices outside.

And real flames flickered outside the windows.

Growling, angry voices and flickering torches turned to shouts and a steadier blaze in the backyard.

*My greenhouse!*

I ran for the staircase, not sure what I could do, but anxious to be there.

G stopped me with a firm hand on my arm. "Mundanes. Mundane distractions only. Let Zeb and the local authorities handle it. They haven't and won't breach the fence. Our presence is not required as long as they stay in the alley. Zeb and Gayla will handle it." He looked and sounded calm.

Sure enough, sirens whoop-whooped close by, soon followed by the sound of gravel crunching beneath tires in the narrow passage behind the back fence.

"But . . ."

"Let them handle it. It's a distraction designed to get us outside and vulnerable. Concentrate on keeping the party happy." He moved away to refill someone's punch cup with the spiked mixture. So far, he was doing a good job keeping the underage guests from dipping their cups into the wrong bowl.

I scanned the crowd and found Ted and Tiffany in a heated discussion. He made motions to gather several of the dancers and retreat with them. Tiffany's eyes looked bright. She still wanted to party. She had a lot to celebrate. Some of the dancers were attempting to tango in the middle of the pentagram to the exotic music. George and Ted had both confirmed that since the spell only the family could actually see the paler wooden inlay in the floor. The clock edged toward eleven. Time to close this all down.

Jason and Belle helped me carry the trays full of crumbs and the empty punch bowls back to the kitchen. The gingerbread house was reduced to the puddle of royal icing. Not even a single pastillage bat remained. Shara had crawled into the maze of boxes and discards at the far end of the room and curled up for a well-deserved nap. I decided to leave her there until we needed her to anchor one point of the pentagram. She could probably do that still asleep. For the spell G had designed, her body coursing with Deschants blood was more necessary than her mind.

With the absence of food and drink, the guests drifted downward toward coats and hats and car keys. Any younger guests without a ride ended up in my van with Raphe at the wheel. Tiffany stifled a yawn behind her still angry confrontation with her father. He laughed and gathered her into a hug, easing her toward the stairs.

I pitied schoolteachers on Monday morning who had to deal with still exhausted children with a sugar rush hangover.

One last look around the now empty attic room. What had I missed?

"Mom, why is the junk stacked into a maze?" Shara asked, crawling out from under a Chesterfield chair with mouseholes in the velvet upholstery and a listing leg.

"Because, sweetie, it leads to the back exit," G replied, picking her up and letting her head loll on his shoulder.

I knew there had been a door there. "The outside staircase has been gone since before I moved into the house. You boarded up the door on both sides." My maze-runner daughter should have found it. A testament to G's ingenuity.

I captured my broom before George could put it with the other discarded decorations and began cleaning up crumbs and other detritus. Sing and George dismantled the folding tables.

"I rebuilt the stairs last week. But they and the door are hidden behind an illusion so that we don't have uninvited guests using it," G said, turning his back on the old furniture. "Shara, that's an emergency exit. You only have to navigate the maze and open that door if I tell you to run. You are to take Belle and Jason with you. But opening the door will shatter the illusion, and we don't want that to happen unless we absolutely have to." He carried our sleepy daughter back to the tilting chair and set her down.

She curled into a ball, with her head on the armrest

and closed her eyes. I half expected her thumb to creep toward her mouth as if she were still four.

I returned to my sweeping, concentrating on the center of the pentagram. I felt more than saw the pale glimmer of the outline beneath my feet. My point, on the north side, right of G's east-pointing anchor point beckoned to me with the allure of safety.

Jason and Belle returned to the attic with the tray of the special cookies—much depleted. Belle waved her jade charms over them, enticing unsuspecting visitors to finish them off.

It doesn't take much marijuana to dull responses. Smoke is faster. Ingestion is trickier and slower. Especially since I hadn't added any magic to the blend. Our enemies would be able to smell that and be wary. No one expected a strictly mundane remedy stashed in the most likely hiding place in the pantry.

As always, I counted the cookies. As expected, at least a dozen of them were missing. I raised my eyebrows at Jason. He shrugged in response. He knew what they contained and what they were for. I trusted him to not have touched them, or led his friends to them.

Someone else had crept into the house and hidden. Probably in the midst of a big crowd of friends.

Shadows moved in the corners.

# Forty-Three

I TOOK A DEEP breath and turned to face John Mooney and D'Accore. The five minions behind them were all nibbling absently on the special cookies.

G smiled at the newcomers and took his place at the head of the pentagram. "I presume you crept in and hid in the pantry while we were busy with other guests arriving and leaving," he said as he pulled his wand from one of the bullet holsters on his gun belt.

"You really should be more careful, G. Now that you've overloaded and destroyed the pentagram, just anyone can walk in," Mooney sneered. He still limped but had lost the cast.

The smoke that always clung to D'Accore began swirling and reaching out tendrils as if seeking someone.

Jason took up his place on G's left, bending his knees and flexing his feet.

Belle returned her hair stick to the bun below her cocked hat. "Come here, boys," she purred in a very adult and sultry voice. "Come and have some more cookies."

Then she sidestepped away from the treats and into her place in the family pentagram.

That left only Shara. She still slept in the big Chesterfield. I looked anxiously toward G.

He shook his head slightly, pursing his lips into a silent whistle.

Slowly, she stretched and yawned. The only thing that

gave away her true readiness was her fierce grip on the silver key dangling from her necklace.

D'Accore bent to lift my little girl into her arms.

"Do not touch my daughter," G and I yelled at the same time.

D'Accore whirled to face us, flicking her old Zippo lighter rapidly. It sparked, but no flame leaped from the wick.

Shara used the distraction to scoot out from under the woman's arms and into her place between Belle and me.

The minions kept eating, oblivious to the rest of us. I hoped they didn't throw up and negate the effectiveness of the drug.

Mooney surveyed the room, checking our positions. He frowned and narrowed his eyes.

Zeb's deep voice echoed up the staircase. "I enclose you and guard the entrance!" The door boomed shut and the latch clicked.

Mooney looked about in alarm.

Outside, Sing's flute and George's drum accented their chants as they marched around and around the house, widdershins, reversing the spell that hid the pentagram and allowed outsiders in.

"Come into my parlor, said the spider to the fly," Belle chanted. She moved her head about, making the jade charms rattle together; one more instrument in the magic we wove.

Mooney struggled against the compulsion to move into the center of the pentagram. He knew the danger that lurked there.

D'Accore flicked her Zippo again and again, bracing her feet. "All I want is my son's eyes. I need his eyes to restore my sight. Give them to me, and I'll let the rest of you go!"

She lied, of course.

"*My* son's eyes won't help you!" I screamed, afraid she might convince someone with her pitiful demands.

She even leaked a tear that dripped mournfully down her cheek without smudging her exotic makeup. "You fried your brain when you lost your sight. Your eyes would work if your mind was intact."

"Give me your eyes, little boy. I'll take your headache away. You'll be free of pain. Just Give. Me. Your. Eyes."

"My mom already rid me of the headache. We killed your worm, lady." Jason leaned forward and nearly spat at D'Accore.

The blonde whipped her head around and speared me with her sightless gaze. Her smoke tendrils reached toward me.

I raised my fully extended spurtle, and the smoke retreated.

D'Accore hissed.

"Come, come to me," Belle whispered. She sounded desperate and scared.

The minions had no problem picking up the tray of cookies and bringing it with them. The lead boy held out a partially eaten one toward Mooney. "I'll share, but you'd better come quick 'cause they're almost gone."

"Stupid fool. I knew you recruited idiots when you should have taken more time to find the right boys," he snarled at his partner. He, too, had braced his feet while he rubbed a gold coin where it lay in the palm of his hand.

So that was how he'd replaced his wand/flute when G broke it during their fight.

Mooney still held his weight off balance, favoring the ankle he'd broken. I didn't think he'd taken advantage of Judi's healing hands, and he'd discarded the cast too soon.

I smiled at the thought that his impatience would make him limp for life.

Jason noticed it at the same moment. He nodded to me.

"Oh, just get on with it!" Raphe called. He ran forward from the maze of discards and shoved Mooney until he stumbled into the pentagram. He wasn't so gentle with D'Accore as he planted his foot in the middle of her shapely butt.

In the heartbeat they crossed the line, the protection spells snapped shut, capturing them within a wall of energy controlled by G's wand.

Raphe threw his arms over his face with a gasp of pain. He fled back through the maze, thrashing obstacles out of his way to the hidden exit. With a crack and a crash of magic shattering, the illusion dropped away.

My heart stuttered in fear. G bit his lip in concern.

The sound system quit. Silence filled the attic . . . except for a hint of a heartbeat accented by the distant flute and drum outside. The rhythm of the house fell into alignment with G's familiar and beloved heartbeat.

Jason shouted a triumphant war cry, ululating a primitive call to action. Then he launched himself into flight. Two steps and he leaped at the minions. Right foot to a gut, left foot to a temple. Two down. He landed lightly in front of G, spun around bending his knees, and rose in a whirlwind of fists and feet. He landed back where he'd begun, blowing on his knuckles as if clearing smoke from a gun barrel. "They have hard heads, typical of bullies with more testosterone than brains."

G raised his wand. Mooney rushed him, holding his arm up and away from the center.

D'Accore stumbled toward Jason, still flicking her wand. Not even sparks responded to her magic in the Deschants pentagram. "I am one of you! My magic has to work here."

"Not anymore," G replied. He whipped out his foot and caught Mooney behind his weakened knee. As he stumbled, G lowered and circled his wand, catching the minions in his stasis spell.

Shara jumped forward with a fistful of plastic zip ties from Ted's tool box. She barely had to touch her key to lock the restraints around minion wrists behind their backs.

D'Accore screeched and shoved her Zippo toward Jason's face. "Give me your eyes," she demanded.

"Not this time!" I jumped toward her, wand extended, and slapped her across her temple with it. She collapsed into a snarling, scratching, and biting Tasmanian devil.

Oops. That might be her true form, but too dangerous for the moment. Another rap with my spurtle and she shrank further into a black cat, also snarling and spitting. Shara snapped a zip tie around her neck and yanked until the cat could barely breathe. She clawed at the plastic, loosening it slightly but exposing her paws and gaining another restraint around them. She writhed and bit at this new enemy, rolling around the floor.

Mooney stared at his partner aghast. "You can't do that! You're only a kitchen witch." He lifted his gaze toward me. Something akin to admiration crossed his face. "With you at my side, we could conquer the world."

"Not likely," Belle said. She pulled the hair stick from her bun, releasing her mane of flowing hair, no longer frizzy but as wavy and silky as her father's. From its depths tumbled a flash drive. She tossed it to G. "Shara and I found this in the bottom of Mom's flour canister. He must have hidden it there the night he came for the bake sale flyer. The IRS and Interpol should find it very interesting."

"No!" Mooney tried to pluck the device out of the air. His not-quite-healed ankle gave way as he reached out and grasped the drive. He tucked it beneath his body as he stumbled to the floor.

"I've had enough of you!" I said and stalked toward his shivering body. "What are you really? A snake?" Visions of a rattler crossed my inner vision. "No, too dangerous. We've defanged you. Now you're just an ugly little horny toad." One rap with my wand and he disappeared.

"Ribbit," a frog croaked, bulging neck covering the flash drive.

G snapped a stasis spell around him and grabbed the flash drive before the frog could swallow it and hop away.

"Never underestimate the power of a mere kitchen witch," I said. "Especially when you involve her family."

# Epilogue

G'S HEART BEAT STRONG and solid beneath my ear. Post-coital languor turned my muscles to liquid. But my brain still spun in the aftermath of using magic to foil the woman bent on stealing my son's eyes.

My son, like his sisters, slept soundly and deeply, all of them restoring their bodies after using a lot of magic. They'd not stir until late morning.

I shivered involuntarily.

G stretched and draped his arm across my shoulders. His warmth instantly settled my twitches. With his other hand he pulled up the tangled blankets to cover us.

I was too comfortable. This was too familiar.

G sighed deeply and heaved himself onto his side. He ran his hands up and down my naked back. "This proves that we belong together." He nuzzled my ear.

"Um . . . It's been fun."

"Why does that not sound like an invitation for a repeat performance?" His hands stilled. He opened his eyes. For once, he didn't use his powers to subdue my objections.

I saw love, honest love in his gaze. "Does this mean I can move back home, be a part of this family again?"

This time I sighed, only partly from regret. I rolled over and slid off the bed, grabbing for my robe. "You will always be part of this family. But this, all this," I gestured to the same tangled bedding and our naked bodies, "means you need to be gone before the children wake up. I don't want to instill false hope in them."

"But we just had the best sex ever, and we're ready for more." The look of surprise on his face was priceless. So he had been trying to manipulate me.

"We just had fabulous sex because we cast a whole lot of magic saving our family. I needed to burn off surging hormones and so did you. I'm going to take a shower before I start cleaning up and returning this house to normal. Ted will be by later to clear off any residual magic."

"Daffy? What is behind all this?" He looked thoughtful and vulnerable.

"I was very young when I first met you. You were my first true love. You rescued me from emotionally abusive parents. You protected me. You sheltered and supported me. I've never been on my own, learned from my mistakes, or known if you are my one true love because I've never known anyone else. G, I need time to grow up inside of me and not just pretend to be a grown-up because I am an instinctive organizer."

I shrugged into my long flannel robe and sat on the bed beside him.

He drew in a deep breath and captured my hand, drawing it to his lips. "When I first met you, I'd barely healed from D'Accore's betrayal. Her power and her insanity scared me to my bones. When I sensed your latent power, I almost walked out of that coffee shop before you finished making my drink. You frightened me. I was afraid to fully love you. And though I needed you to manifest, I think I couldn't let you. Because then we ran the danger of you becoming another D'Accore."

I think that might have been the first truly honest thing he'd ever said to me.

"I'm surprised you fell for her in the first place."

"I was young, too, when I first met her. Twenty-six. She fascinated me. And with the naiveté of youth and youthful hormones, and the triumphant alpha male instincts of having stolen her from my best friend, I let her manipulate me into believing in love." He kissed my fingertips again.

"I was so afraid of love that I couldn't face it when I found it, Daffy. I have loved you for a very long time, even if it wasn't love at first sight."

"Thank you for that, G. But I still think we both need time alone, time to grow. Time to learn to talk to each other honestly, and love each other for real this time."

"What happens until then?"

"You continue to live elsewhere. But you can see the children any time you like or they want or need you. I will date Ted to see if he can offer what I really need in a man. You are free to date as well."

"Will that be enough?"

I had to smile. "Probably not. We'll talk once we learn how. We might even date, like we should have the first time around. And we'll find each other when magic stirs our hormones." I kissed his cheek and went in search of a shower.

# Acknowledgments

Thanks much to Joyce Reynolds-Ward and Lou Ward for showing me the real Eugene, Oregon. To Jim Radford, an awesome big brother who took photos of ruined castles on the Rhine. And to Joyce, Sara, Lizzy, and Lea, my bestest friends forever and wonderful beta readers, for finding many of the problems in the book before I submitted it.

No book would be complete without thanking my agent Michael Kabongo and editor Sheila Gilbert, who made this happen.